But Ada wasn't looking at Mary's dress.

She was looking at PAN.

Because PAN had stood up. And she hadn't commanded him to stand up. And he was turning his head to look at her. Which she hadn't programmed him to do, either. And there was a strange light in his silver eyes.

"Hello," he said.

Ada—perhaps a bit hysterically—began to laugh. "He's alive! He's aliiiiive!"

"Oops," said Mary. "I did it again."

MY

CYNTHIA HAND

IMAGINARY

BRODI ASHTON

MARY

JODI MEADOWS

An Imprint of HarperCollinsPublishers

HarperTeen is an imprint of HarperCollins Publishers.

Library of Congress Control Number: 2022931766
ISBN 978-0-06-293008-8

Typography by Jenna Stempel-Lobell
23 24 25 26 27 LBC 5 4 3 2 1

First paperback edition, 2023

To those who love science! And—*whispers*—
poetry.

And, once again, sorry, England. We really
messed with it this time.

Those who have learned to walk on the threshold of unknown worlds, by means of what are commonly termed par excellence the exact sciences, *may then with the fair white wings of Imagination hope to soar further into the unexplored amidst which we live.*
—Ada Lovelace

Invention, it must be humbly admitted, does not consist in creating out of void, but out of chaos.
—Mary Shelley

Prologue

This story should be impossible. It's about a girl named Mary, her best friend, Ada, and a boy who doesn't exist.

You've probably heard of Mary, aka Mary Shelley, aka the author of one of the most famous novels of all time. It's about a monster. (We'll leave it up to you to decide which one was the actual monster: Dr. Frankenstein or his creation. We have our own opinion.)

And then there's Ada, aka Augusta Ada King, countess of Lovelace, aka Ada Lovelace. She was the world's first computer programmer . . . more than a hundred years before there were computers. (She was definitely an overachiever.)

Both women were the daughters of celebrities. Mary's mother was Mary Wollstonecraft, a writer, philosopher, and staunch advocate for women's rights in a time when women didn't have very many. Ada was the daughter of the poet Lord Byron, who was like the nineteenth-century equivalent of a rock star, if rock had been invented yet. So yeah, Mary and Ada had a lot to live up to.

According to "history," these two young women never met, which is probably where things went wrong. Mary Shelley risked everything for love, but her life was marked by tragedy and plagued by scandal. Ada Lovelace, on the other hand, died young, without ever getting credit for her work. But we've never been fans of "history," per se. Too sad. Not enough happy endings.

We have a different tale to tell. This one involves romance, intrigue, a spine-tingling, harrowing adventure, and also (dare we say it?), a little bit of magic.

Let's set the scene: London, in the year 18—mumble mumble (sorry, the exact date is a bit smudged). Napoleon (the short French dude) had just been defeated at the Battle of Waterloo, which was making England feel really good about itself. Mount Tambora, a volcano in the East Indies, had recently blasted ten billion tons of ash into the stratosphere, which was making England feel cold and rainy (colder and rainier than usual, that is). And the Industrial Revolution was going full steam. This was a time of great invention, of science, of philosophy, which was making England feel like anything a person could imagine was possible.

Right smack in the middle of this particular England were our heroines, Mary and Ada, who both had much bigger imaginations than the average person. And at the moment that our story begins, both girls were about to arrive . . . at the very same party.

PART ONE

(in which the frog croaks)

Mary

ONE

It was a dark and stormy night. Again.

Mary peered out the carriage window at the black clouds gathering in the sky. Most nights had been dark and stormy lately, but Mary didn't mind the rain. Storms always made her want to write . . . *something*. Something epic. Something terrible and wonderful and spine-tingling. But she didn't know what. Currently she was amusing herself by imagining the clouds as a herd of wild horses galloping through the sky, streaming lightning behind them. (As we've mentioned, Mary had quite the imagination. You'll see.)

"Hmph, what dreadful weather," remarked Mary's stepmother, leaning to look out the window, too. "Really, William, must we be going out in this? You know I hate getting wet."

Mary sighed. Her wicked stepmother obviously didn't

1

understand anything about finding the beauty in nature.

"It doesn't look too bad," her father responded cheerfully.

At that moment, the thunder boomed so loudly it caused the walls of their shabby carriage to shudder. Then the sky opened and poured down rain.

Mary's father was undeterred. "We can't miss this party, my dears," he said, raising his voice to be heard over the deluge. "It's such an honor to be invited."

There was no arguing with that. They all knew that to be invited to a party at the house of Mr. Charles Babbage was no small thing. Mr. Babbage, a brilliant scientist and inventor, was very selective about who attended his soirees. Over the years his guest lists had included all the best minds in England. That Mary's father was receiving invitations to Babbage's parties again was a relief. It meant that the family hadn't fallen *too* far in the world's esteem, in spite of their recent money troubles. Perhaps it even meant—as her father hoped—that they were on the rise.

"Of course I know that, my darling," Mary's stepmother said with an elaborate sniff. "But I don't care for Mr. Babbage. He's appallingly plainspoken. He says what he thinks, without a care for how it might be received."

Mary, who had never before met Mr. Babbage, thought this would be a refreshing quality for a person to have. But her step-mother obviously didn't understand anything about people and their complexities.

"I quite like Mr. Babbage," said Mary's father. "And there's always at least one reading from a famous author at these parties, and multiple scientific demonstrations. Mr. Babbage himself might reveal one of his latest inventions. This evening is sure to be exciting."

BOOM! went the sky, followed by a stab of lightning that briefly illuminated the carriage.

"I don't care for exciting, either." Mary's stepmother drew the curtains across the windows.

Mary resisted the urge to roll her eyes. Of course her stepmother didn't understand anything about adventure.

"I'm keen to see all of the newest fashions," piped up Jane, Mary's (only a tiny bit wicked) stepsister, from beside her mother. "I'll be content to simply go about looking at everyone, like they're an assortment of brightly colored birds, and I, the happy ornithologist." She fiddled with one of the glossy curls that framed her face. "I'm especially interested in specimens of the male variety."

"Hmph," said Mrs. Godwin. "I do hope there will be a few *appropriate* young men for you to associate with at this party." She eyed her three woefully unmarried charges critically. "Otherwise, what's the point?"

"Now, now, dear, this isn't that type of party," admonished Mary's father. "This is not some ball for the ton. The point is to enlighten our minds, not to trot out our girls like prized ponies."

Mary rather loved him for saying that. William Godwin was a forward-thinking man. But then, he had the luxury of being forward-thinking. Because he was a man.

CRASH! BOOM! went the sky.

The carriage lurched to a stop.

"Oh, good," said Mary's father. "We're here."

"Mr. Babbage!" Her father rushed forward to shake hands with the host the moment they arrived in the parlor where Mr. Babbage was greeting his guests. "So good to see you again."

"Ah, Mr. Godwin," replied Mr. Babbage. "So good of you to come."

Mary's father stepped aside to reveal his slightly damp family. "You already know Mrs. Godwin, but may I present my daughters, Fanny, Mary, and Jane."

Fanny, the oldest sister, performed a small curtsy but said nothing. Fanny almost never said anything. (In fact, if we hadn't mentioned her, you would never have known she was there.)

"Good evening," said Mary, also curtsying.

"You have a splendid house!" exclaimed Jane.

"Thank you," Mr. Babbage replied. He was older than Mary would have guessed, a bit stooped but still stately, with lively green eyes under bushy gray brows. His gaze wandered between Jane, Mary, and Fanny. "You say *all three* of these are your daughters, Godwin?"

Color rose in the face of Mary's father. "In spirit, sir, if not in blood. Jane is my wife's daughter from a previous marriage. Fanny is the daughter of the novelist Gilbert Imlay and my late wife. And Mary is my own daughter, with my late wife."

Mary felt that jolt of yearning inside her that happened whenever someone mentioned her mother. Mary Wollstonecraft had died of a fever when our Mary was just eleven days old, but Mary somehow still managed to miss her.

"Charming woman, that last wife of yours," Mr. Babbage said gruffly, "and an undeniable genius." His eyes skimmed over the current Mrs. Godwin and landed on Fanny. "Are you a writer as well?"

Fanny shook her head. Her passion was needlepoint. (It was a quiet passion.)

"And you?" Mr. Babbage's focus shifted to Mary, which was unfortunate, because she didn't have the faintest idea how to answer his question. Everyone expected her to become a writer, as both her parents were famous writers. There were times she quite enjoyed building her "castles in the air," as she called them, writing about far-off people and places and things. But there were other times that she doubted she had any talent at all. Certainly nothing she had written up to now was good enough to be (gulp) published.

"I would like to be a writer," she said after an awkward pause. "Someday." But deep down, she wasn't sure that this was ever going to happen.

"She's constantly scribbling," reported Mary's father. "I am quite certain that she will be as brilliant a writer as her mother ever was."

"Is that so?" said Mr. Babbage appraisingly. "What do you write?"

That was the question, wasn't it? Her stories were just imaginary incidents for people who lived only in her mind. They weren't fit to be seen by anyone but herself.

"I'm only seventeen, sir," said Mary. "I've had little opportunity to experience anything extraordinary in life. But once I do, I'm sure I will write . . . something . . ."

Something, well, extraordinary. Something marvelous.

She hoped.

"I've never been very good at writing, myself. It was always my poorest subject in school," said Mr. Babbage. "I'm a numbers man at heart, but I can appreciate the talents of others. I look forward to seeing all that you have to offer the world, Miss Godwin." He glanced off toward the ballroom. "And now, if you'll excuse me, I have some more important matters to attend to."

Then he walked briskly away.

"Well, that was brief," said Mrs. Godwin.

"I thought he was nice," said Jane. "Not at all as unpleasant as you made him out to be, Mother. Oh, look, there's cake! I adore cake!"

Having now performed the necessary introductions with the host, the family set out to enjoy the party. It was even more lavish than Mary had expected. Mr. Babbage's house was blazing with noise and color and light, so much so that the outside storm was drowned out, as if the weather itself was too impressed by the gleaming parquet floors and plentiful velvet drapes to make a scene. As Mary's father had promised, there were numerous groups of seasoned intellectuals standing about, earnestly discussing issues of philosophy and politics and so forth, with the aforementioned readings of poetry being held in the smaller side rooms, along with a number of scientific displays.

But there was also music. And dancing. And (as Jane had so enthusiastically pointed out) cake.

"Oh my goodness," exclaimed Mary's father. "Is that the Duke of Wellington?"

They all turned to look.

"He's a fine figure, isn't he?" said Jane. "Not young but definitely handsome."

"Although something about him says 'nefarious villain' to me," mused Mary.

"Villain?" Mr. Godwin huffed. "He's our country's finest war hero!"

Mary shook her head. She was fairly certain, for some reason she couldn't quite put her finger on, that the Duke of Wellington was a villain. (But that's literally a different story.)

"It doesn't matter. He's married." Mrs. Godwin sighed. The majority of the guests were older, distinguished men—scientists and artists—and their wives.

There were only a few *young* men.

"Dibs on that one," Jane said around a mouthful of cake, nodding her head to indicate one of the more finely dressed boys who seemed to be approximately their age. She pinched her cheeks to pinken them and brushed crumbs from her dress. "Watch me go, then."

Mary observed in a kind of awe as her stepsister swept off

toward the unsuspecting young man. She was familiar with all of Jane's moves—the casual, seemingly accidental bump, which Jane referred to as the "meet-cute." The charming introduction, followed by the demure-but-flirtatious smile. The gaze from under Jane's thick lashes. The way she moved her body slightly in time to the lively jig that was being played in the next room, to suggest that she herself might wish to—ah yes, the young man had asked her to dance. And off they went.

"Good on Jane," said Mary's stepmother. "I believe that one is in line to be an earl someday. Lord King something-or-other. He'd be an excellent catch, wouldn't he, dear?" She looked to Mr. Godwin for a confirmation, but Mary's father had gone to introduce himself to the Duke of Wellington.

Mrs. Godwin sighed again.

"He's not exactly handsome, is he?" remarked Mary, meaning the boy and not the Duke of Wellington. This future earl was neither handsome nor homely; indeed, there was nothing striking at all about his appearance. Lord. King. Earl. That guy was a confusing combination of titles.

"But he's rich," said Mrs. Godwin. "That's all that matters, in the end."

"You don't think that's somewhat vulgar?" Mary suggested lightly. "Treating it like some sport, I mean? The hunting and trapping of rich young men?"

"That's life in the real world," snapped Mrs. Godwin. "At least *my* daughter is showing some initiative. Unlike you two lumps."

Mary wanted to fire back a sharp retort in defense of herself and Fanny, fellow lumps, but by the time she thought of something clever and cutting enough, Jane had returned from the ballroom.

"Lord, he was a bore, that one. I take it back, about the dibs." Jane's dark eyes trolled around the room. "If only there was someone else who—" She gasped. "Look, there's Shelley!"

They all swiveled around again.

The young man in question was standing near the door, having just come in from the rain. Mary's breath hitched at the sight of him. He was undeniably handsome, neither too tall nor too short, slender of build, topped by a mass of fluffy brown hair that he could not seem to help but constantly run his fingers through. He had bright blue, inquisitive eyes that seemed to drink in his surroundings, and an impish, yet not quite rakish, smile.

BOOM went the thunder. Or was it Mary's heart? (Reader, it was thunder. But he did have one of those heart-boom-inducing smiles, so we can hardly blame her for the confusion.)

"Shelley!" called Jane so loudly it caused Mrs. Godwin to flinch. "Shelley, over here!"

The bright blue eyes swung in their direction.

Mary resisted the urge to pinch her own cheeks as he strode across the room.

"Hello, Godwins! I did not expect to find you here!" he exclaimed. "What a delightful surprise." Then he seemed to remember the formality of the situation. "Mrs. Godwin," he said with a slight bow.

"Mr. Shelley," Mary's stepmother returned stiffly, but even she was inclined to smile at him.

"Miss Imlay," he said to Fanny. She said nothing, as usual, but as her gaze fell to his intricately embroidered waistcoat, she began to fan herself as if she was suddenly too warm.

He turned to Jane. "Miss Clairmont."

"You're a sight for sore eyes, Shelley," Jane declared.

"Your sore eyes beheld me only this afternoon," he reminded her playfully.

Mr. Shelley was a writer—having recently published his first book of poetry to modest success. Almost a month ago he had turned up at the Godwins' bookshop at 92 High Street and requested an apprenticeship, of sorts, with Mr. Godwin. He claimed that Mr. Godwin was his favorite author (even though Mary's father hadn't been able to sell any of his own novels in years) and had declared that Mr. Godwin's ideas—especially the bits about how society must overthrow its outdated and oppressive institutions, like marriage for instance—had been transformative in Shelley's life. And that was that. Shelley was in. But instead of being paid by Mr. Godwin for his work, Shelley had agreed to pay Mr. Godwin for the honor of being mentored by such an esteemed and influential author. So it worked out well for everyone.

"Dance with me, Shelley," cried Jane.

"Oh," Shelley said awkwardly. This was forward of Jane. Inappropriate, even. He glanced at the floor, then up briefly, covertly, at Mary.

She gave a slight, almost imperceptible nod.

"I'd be delighted," said Shelley, extending his arm to Jane. And off they went.

"See?" crowed Mrs. Godwin. "Initiative."

It was true. Jane had game.

"They make a fine pair, don't they?" said Mrs. Godwin as they moved to the doorway of the ballroom to watch Shelley and Jane dancing. "He's undoubtedly handsome."

Undoubtedly.

"And intelligent. He gets on so well with your father that he feels like family already," remarked Mrs. Godwin.

Indeed.

"And his father is a baronet. So he's rich."

"But not as rich as an earl," Mary pointed out.

Mrs. Godwin waved her off. "Rich is rich. Mr. Shelley is perfect for Jane."

Mary smiled a secret smile and then quickly suppressed it. Shelley *was* perfect. He was clever and sensitive and forward-thinking. If one believed in marriage, he'd be the ideal husband.

But not for Jane.

"You're Mary" is what he'd said when they'd met that first day in the bookshop.

She'd blinked up at him, startled and embarrassed because she'd been so focused on the book she was reading that she hadn't noticed him approach. "Yes," she'd said, blushing at the intimate way he'd addressed her. "And you're—"

"Percy. But everyone calls me Shelley. What is it you're reading that has captured you so?"

She'd glanced down at the slim volume of poetry in her hands. "Tennyson. He's—"

"Beautiful," Shelley'd murmured, and then from memory he'd recited: *"For ere she reach'd upon the tide / The first house by the water-side / Singing in her song she died / The Lady of Shalott.* I love how he wrote it—*singing in her song.* The way it sounds. The way it makes me feel."

And, with those words, Mary had known a simple truth. She and Percy Shelley were the same. They understood each other.

Mary had also known very well that her stepmother would never approve of Mary becoming romantically involved with Shelley (rich boys only belonged with her own daughter), so Mary had made an arrangement with Jane, who'd been all too happy to cover for them in the name of love. And now Jane was the one who got to dance with Shelley, to be held in his arms, to smile up at him. But that was just how it had to be.

The song finished, but instead of lining up for the next dance, the couples began to exit the ballroom in a flood.

"Back so soon?" Mrs. Godwin said as Jane and Shelley rejoined them.

"They're setting up some sort of presentation now," Jane reported.

As if on cue, Mr. Babbage appeared again. "May I have your attention?" he asked, not so much a question as a demand. "Please join me in the ballroom for a demonstration of the most thrilling nature, given to us by one of the world's most cutting-edge scientists in the field of electricity."

"Electricity? How shocking!" Jane cried, and then giggled at her own joke.

They shuffled toward the ballroom. It had been set up in rows of chairs facing a long metal table, upon which there were two mysterious objects shrouded by white linen.

In front of the table stood an even more mysterious man.

The scientist. Mary felt an inexplicable chill shoot up her spine at the sight of him.

"Who is he?" Mrs. Godwin asked, squinting. "Is he wearing a wedding ring?"

Ew. This man was at least fifty. His hair was a dull yellow in color, brushed purposefully forward to lie across his brow. He had impressive sideburns and a long, sharp nose—indeed, his entire face was pointed, except for his chin, which seemed to be trying to burrow inside his cravat to hide.

"That's Mr. Aldini," said Shelley. "The famous galvanist."

At the same moment Mary's father appeared beside them, eyes alight with excitement. "Ah, hello, Shelley," he said, clapping Shelley on the shoulder. "I wondered if I would see you here tonight." He gestured toward the front of the ballroom. "How fortunate we are, to be able to see Signore Aldini in person. Hurry; let's get a seat near the front."

They were able to procure seats in the third row, Mary silently negotiating with her sisters for a place between Fanny and Shelley.

After the guests were seated, the lights in the room were extinguished save for a tall candelabra flickering beside the table. The room quieted, and Mary could once again hear the steady patter of the rain and howls of the wind. Her heart, she found, was pounding. Her skin felt tingly. It was as though some part of Mary could sense that something in her life—something big and powerful and as unstoppable as the storm that raged outside—was about to change. And so it was.

But Mary could never have imagined what.

Mr. Aldini held up his hand. "What is life?" he asked.

TWO
Ada

Here's how the evening had been going for Ada so far:

It was shaping up to be the best night of her life. Or, at least, the best night in a very long time. When Mr. Babbage's invitation had arrived, Ada had assumed her mother would RSVP "not attending" on Ada's behalf, as she always did, insisting that Ada needed more time to recover before she could be seen in public. Instead, Lady Byron had said yes, and so a seamstress had been called to make a dress for Ada, new shoes had been ordered, and they'd even had a fancier cane commissioned—one made of rosewood and (impractically) tipped with gold. By the night of the party, Ada could hardly contain her excitement. All this science under one roof!

Everything was bright with glittering lights. Musicians played a fast waltz. People in the next room laughed and ate cake. And though Ada had come mostly to expand her knowledge, she found a warm pleasure in watching the orderly rows of dancers, the way they bounced and stepped and spun as they worked their way up and down the lines.

"Fix your face, dear," Lady Byron scolded. "People can see you grinning like a hyena."

At once, Ada schooled her expression into something more neutral. But even with her mother's snapping, tonight was still the best.

First, she'd seen Charles Darwin's presentation on evolution, which had involved quite a lot of plants. From there, Ada had made her way to the telescope exhibit, where Caroline Herschel and her nephew John Herschel had spoken about their discoveries (Caroline alone had discovered eight new comets, fourteen new nebulae, and a small galaxy to round things out), and then showed everyone the miniature version of their Forty-Foot Telescope. The actual Forty-Foot was, ah, forty feet long, and it wasn't the type of thing people brought to parties.

Though it was still storming outside, Ada had taken the opportunity to peer through the eyepiece. She'd seen clouds. Lots of clouds. And some rain. But she could imagine the stars and planets that hung in the sky on the other side.

"Stand up straight, my darling," Lady Byron said. "Your spine looks like a question mark."

Ada stood up straight. Posture had always been important to Lady Byron. When Ada had been small and her mother had caught her slouching, she'd had a wooden board strapped from Ada's head to her hips, keeping her back in line and her shoulders square and drawn back. For a month, Ada had worn her spine straightener every day. Now that she was older, she wore a corset. She wasn't sure quite how she had been slouching, given that her corset was tight enough to do lasting damage to her liver, but if her mother said she was, it must be true.

"Ada! I am glad to see you." Mr. Babbage stepped out of a nearby room. "My own exhibit is set up in here. Won't you come look? I wanted to make sure you were here before I shared it with anyone else."

Ada's face heated. She was flattered that the esteemed Mr. Babbage was singling her out tonight, although it was a tad inappropriate for him to call her by her first name in such a formal setting. But that was simply Mr. Babbage. She had been a student of his—sometimes he even privately referred to Ada as his protégé—since she was a child and her affinity for mathematics had started to attract attention. There was no math problem Ada couldn't solve, although Babbage did delight in finding ways to challenge her. Even through her illness he'd still endeavored to visit at least twice a month.

She glanced at her mother. "May I?"

"Go on, dear," Lady Byron said. "There's someone I need to speak with. I will fetch you shortly."

Ada adjusted her grip on her cane before following Mr. Babbage into a side parlor.

Even though there were several other people all standing about and whispering excitedly, Mr. Babbage escorted her forward, toward a sheet-covered object on a table. "This way," he said. "Get a closer look." He turned and grasped the sheet with both hands. A hush fell over the room as silk rippled to the floor, revealing a dancing figurine.

Everyone gasped in delight.

The dancer was beautiful. She stood in graceful arabesque, with one arm held aloft and a tiny bluebird resting on the tip of her delicate finger. The silk of her gown gleamed in the lamplight, all flowing green and white. She wasn't tall—only about the length of Ada's forearm—but she was exquisitely detailed, from the joints of her knuckles to the serene expression painted onto her plaster face.

"Before you mistake my silver dancer for a pretty statue— behold!" He turned a key in the wooden base, and inside, gears clicked and clicked and clicked. When he released the key, a simple melody began to play and the dancer gave a long opening curtsy before rising onto the tips of her toes.

Another gasp. A pattering of applause.

She was an automaton, and a remarkable one at that. (Automatons, in case you were wondering, were a precursor to robots. People had been making these sorts of machines for a long time, and they were only getting more complex.) The silver dancer pirouetted a full rotation before the crowd managed to put their responses together.

"It's uncanny," said someone nearby. "Her expression never changes."

"I feel like she's watching me," muttered another person.

But a thrill shot through Ada as she moved closer to the table, her eyes trained on the whirring and clicking ballerina. She'd made automatons before—on her own and with Mr. Babbage—but the detail in this one, the craftsmanship! This machine was exquisite.

"All those tiny movements," Ada breathed. "Every one of them imagined and scripted and built into the clockworks." Every bow, every bend of her arm, every flap of the bird's wings—each motion had been painstakingly planned and executed.

"Then you like her?" Mr. Babbage asked, pride making his chest puff out.

"She's stunning." She reached for the dancer but stopped short. "May I?"

"Be my guest," Mr. Babbage said.

Breathlessly, Ada bent to inspect the automaton more closely, now noticing the precise metalwork, the delicate gears, the finely tuned rods, all required for the dancer's movement. Her fingers itched to open the base and look at what was inside. But she would wait until the clockworks had run down.

Mr. Babbage was smiling widely. "I thought you'd appreciate her."

"She's remarkable," Ada said, looking into the automaton's eyes. It was true, they did sort of stare right through her, but that didn't bother Ada. "I can't believe you hid this from me!"

"I wanted her to be a surprise." Delight sparkled behind his green eyes as he walked around the table, pointing out his favorite details, like the way the dancer inclined her head in greeting every so often. "And I don't mean to brag—"

Ada snorted (only because her mother wasn't looming over her). Mr. Babbage loved to brag.

"Oh, Mr. Babbage!" A gentleman stepped forward. "Please tell me all about how you made this dancer. And . . . *why*?"

Mr. Babbage chuckled and glanced at Ada. "Excuse me."

Ada turned to watch the dancer again, but then she noticed a pile of papers, drawings and ideas scribbled by Mr. Babbage. Ah, his schematics, his calculations! Ada flipped through the pages of notes, and that was when she saw it: her own handwriting.

Calculations, sums and differences, written in tidy columns down the page. She remembered doing these tables in her dining room only three weeks ago, when Mr. Babbage had come for his bimonthly tutoring session. He'd often left sheets of math problems, so that alone wasn't strange. But here was her work on the table by his new automaton.

She glanced from the pages to the tiny gears on the bluebird's wings. She didn't have a ruler handy (drat!), but if she had, she was certain the length of each tooth would match that row of numbers there, and the diameter of the shafts would match this one here.

BOOM. Thunder rattled the house.

Another page of her math held the calculations for the dancer's pirouette, the length and speed of her turn, the timing of her arm movements.

Something hot and painful knotted inside Ada's chest. How could Mr. Babbage claim this dancer was all his when he'd used *her* calculations? Shouldn't he have acknowledged her part in the work? If not to his other guests, then at least to her. Maybe a "Hey, couldn't have done it without you!" or something. Was that too much to ask for?

Ada dropped the papers back to the table.

This didn't seem fair.

As Mr. Babbage drew his guests closer to the table, telling them all about how hard he'd worked on his silver dancer, Ada took a step back, frowning. But Lady Byron didn't leave her much time to brood over it, sweeping Ada back into the ballroom, where they found Mary Somerville and a young man who Ada didn't know by sight. (There were lots of people she didn't know by sight, what with hardly having left her house for the last three years.)

"Mrs. Somerville!" Ada pushed her anger at Mr. Babbage aside and embraced Mary Somerville, who had instructed Ada in math for years, and still came by every so often to see how Ada was progressing in her studies (and her health).

"It's so good to see you up and about," Lady Somerville said. "When I heard you would be able to attend tonight's party, I was beside myself with joy."

Ada smiled fondly. She wanted to get her former tutor alone and ask for advice on the automaton situation, but her mother cut her off.

"Ada, I would like you to meet someone special: Lord William King, future Earl of Lovelace. I think you'll get along famously." Lady Byron gestured to the young man who'd accompanied Mrs. Somerville.

"How do you do?" Ada curtsied, using her cane for support.

"Very well." William took her free hand and kissed it. "How lovely to meet you. I've heard so much about you."

"Have you?" A bolt of dread shot through her; most people knew about her because of her father, Lord Byron. They were always asking her to look at their poetry, as though she had inherited his genius. (She had not. Her mother would never have permitted it.) They wanted her to send their latest attempts to him, as though she had any idea where he was living these days. (She did not. Her mother had never told her.) Any time someone even mentioned Lord Byron, Ada froze up. Lady Byron, however . . . She always knew what to say, and wasn't afraid to say it loudly.

Fortunately, Lord William King didn't bring up Lord Byron, so Ada was (for now) spared the humiliation of both her own and her mother's reactions.

"Yes," William said eagerly. "Lady Somerville is a friend of my family. She holds you in very high regard, and now, meeting you, I can see why."

Approximately one-eighth of Ada relaxed (the part that had been worried about poetry), but the other seven-eighths tensed up as Lady Somerville smiled at her, wearing an expression that was both apologetic and hopeful.

Ada didn't see it, exactly, but she could have sworn that her mother slipped Lady Somerville some cash.

"While you were her student, she spoke about you all the time. Your mind for mathematics is unparalleled." William paused, his eyebrows raised expectantly, then tried again. "Unparalleled. Get it?"

Ada forced herself to smile.

"Of course she gets it," Lady Byron said. "Ada has a very quick wit. You'll have to work to keep up with her, Lord King."

Ada wanted to sink into the floor. This was why she'd been permitted to come to the party. Not for the science. Not as a reward for her hard work. But because her mother was scheming to marry her off to the nearest future earl.

"I feel quite up to the task, Lady Byron." William turned back to Ada. "I'd like to get to know you better. Would you do me the honor of a dance?"

Ada stiffened. At her side, Lady Byron stiffened, too. As did Lady Somerville.

"Oh dear," the math tutor said as everyone looked at the dance floor, where all the dancers were moving at top speed, their feet nearly blurring as they sashayed across the parquet.

Ada turned back to William, somehow managing to keep her tone even. "Normally, I'd be honored. But I'm sorry to report that I haven't been able to dance in years, and I'm not ready to take it up again quite yet." She motioned downward to her cane. (Her cane wasn't the reason she couldn't dance, of course, but she wasn't about to direct a strange young man's attention to her legs—which were, thankfully, concealed by layers of skirts and petticoats.)

"I—" William's face was bright red.

"She would love to dance with you," Lady Byron said smoothly, "once she is able. My dear Ada will save her first dance for you, Lord King, and that is a promise."

"Yes, thank you." William turned back to Ada. "Please, forgive me. I didn't even think about what I was saying."

"All is forgiven," Ada said. What else could she say? She was expected to forgive this gaffe, because it was increasingly clear that she was also expected to marry this man someday.

Lord King, Ada decided, was a lot like this rosewood cane her mother had chosen for her: worth a great deal of money, yet utterly impractical for Ada's needs. Ada would much rather have brought the cane she'd made for herself—lightweight aluminum, with a pivoting rubber tip, a padded handle, and a wrist strap—but Lady Byron had said it was too ugly to attend Mr. Babbage's party. Hence the new one.

This gold-tipped cane (which was so slippery!) was only temporary, though; as soon as she got home, she'd swap to her real cane. And she wouldn't need to use that one forever, either. She was getting stronger every day, nearly recovered from the mysterious illness that had weakened her legs three years ago. (Modern doctors would probably diagnose this as polio.)

She would dance someday. But not tonight.

During this moment of awkward staring at each other, the song ended, the dancing stopped, and William said, "Ah, well, it's a good thing you didn't say yes. Looks like the musicians are getting ready for a break."

Ada cringed. "Yes, good thing."

The lines of dancers fell apart as couples went back to the parlor, and—in that near magical way that good help could transform a room within minutes—servants appeared in the doorways with stacks of wooden chairs, which they began swiftly setting out in rows. Others wheeled a table into the room, and yet more carried sheet-covered objects to place on the table.

As the room's metamorphosis was completed, Mr. Babbage called toward the parlor, "May I have your attention? Please join me in the ballroom for a demonstration of the most thrilling nature, given to us by one of the world's most cutting-edge scientists in the field of electricity."

As the crowd of partygoers filtered into the room, Lady Byron turned back to William. "You simply must sit with us," she said.

Inside her head, where her mother couldn't hear, Ada screamed.

"I'd be honored," William said, smiling hopefully at Ada.

Ada could not force her face back into a smile.

Lady Byron pulled Ada toward the front row. "Sit here, where no one can see you sulking," she whispered. "And because I know you'll complain later if you don't have a good view."

Ada sat, as instructed, and tucked her cane behind her. It was true: she was frowning. (Learning that an entire party had merely been an excuse to introduce Ada to her future husband will do that to a person.) William sat beside her, and Lady Somerville next to him.

Lady Byron leaned toward Ada, keeping her voice low. "He's titled, my dear. Fifty thousand pounds a year. Try to be nice."

"Yes, Mother. Thank you for the correction." Ada said the words out of habit, but inwardly, she sighed. She was already fabulously wealthy—not that she was allowed to control any of her own money—and marrying for *more* money didn't interest her. Still, it could be worse. William King seemed nice enough. He was trying. Perhaps she should, too.

"What do you think this demonstration will be?" Ada asked William.

"Well, that man is Giovanni Aldini," William said in the tone of someone who was simply thrilled to be included. "Which means this is sure to be something amazing!"

"Indeed." In spite of herself, Ada couldn't help but be curious. This was science, after all.

The lights were dimmed. Mr. Aldini held up his hand. "What is life?" he asked simply.

An interesting question.

Ada leaned forward to hear his answer.

Mary ➔
THREE

From her seat two rows back, Mary also found herself leaning forward.

"It is a bold question, and one that has ever been considered a mystery," Mr. Aldini said in a vaguely Italian accent. "What makes a person—or a creature, or a plant, for that matter—*alive*? What spark animates us? But now, my friends, for the first time, we are beginning to understand."

Thunder rumbled outside. Mary shivered.

"I am the Great Aldini," Aldini continued. (Modesty was obviously not his strong suit.) "And tonight I intend to reveal, to your eyes only, *the secret of life*. But first, I would like to take a moment to thank our host—and my sponsor—Mr. Babbage." He gestured toward the back of the room. Obediently everyone twisted around to look for Mr. Babbage, but Mary couldn't see him through the throng of heads. The guests clapped for Babbage, and then they all turned back to Mr. Aldini, who had moved to the first item on the table and, with great ceremony, whipped off the cloth.

The object, at first glance, had the shape of a sewing machine. There was a large copper disc on one end of the base, and, on the other, a horseshoe-shaped magnet with its poles positioned on either side of the disc.

Shelley leaned close to Mary. "That's the Disc Dynamo," he murmured against her ear.

She nodded like she knew what that was.

Aldini began turning a crank on the device. The large disc rotated quickly, and within moments, sparks snapped between two smaller metal pegs set into the base. After he had cranked steadily for a full minute or so, Aldini attached two lengths of stiff copper wire to the Disc Dynamo. Then he picked up the wires, one in each hand, and touched the two ends together. A bright spark shot up between them, emitting a loud snap that made several of the ladies in the audience cry out in alarm.

Mary jumped in her seat. Shelley silently took her hand and squeezed it gently. It was a bold move, but it was dark in the room, and besides, no one was looking at them. She squeezed back.

Aldini continued. "You see, my friends, electricity is life. Like lightning from a storm." The storm flashed obligingly, then boomed. "It is a current that runs through each and every one of us, like we ourselves are only machines, powered by the energy of the gods." He drew the wires close together again and then slowly pulled them apart, creating an arc of silver electricity stretched between them, crackling and sizzling.

Mary felt the hairs on the back of her neck lift. She fixed her gaze, mesmerized, on the shifting tendril of light. It did seem alive. The light was reflected sharply in Aldini's eyes, an intense (some might even say maniacal) gleam.

He set the wires back onto the table. "What you are about to witness may seem like magic, but I assure you—this is science." He pulled away the cloth that had been obscuring the second object, which turned out to be . . . a dead frog.

"Is that all? A frog?" Jane asked wryly.

"Shh!" admonished Mrs. Godwin, elbowing her.

Mr. Aldini smiled, because of course he'd heard Mary's loud-mouthed stepsister. "Indeed, what you see here is but a common frog that you might find in any typical English pond." He lifted the board that the frog was displayed on, held down with a long bit of twine, presented belly up. (Think high school biology class.)

"May I have a volunteer from the audience to confirm its status?"

"Ooh, me! Pick me!" cried Jane, raising her hand.

No one else volunteered. Mr. Aldini reluctantly nodded at Jane, who rose from her seat and swept to the front of the room. She smiled brightly at the crowd. "What shall I do?" she asked.

"Look closely, my dear, and tell us: what is the status of this frog?"

Jane tilted her head to one side. "Its status?"

"Is the frog alive or deceased?" Mr. Aldini clarified. "Inspect it and tell us what you conclude."

"Oh." Jane's brow creased. This was not as pleasant a task as she'd anticipated, clearly, but she was committed now, so she did her best. She bent close to the frog, which remained completely still, and examined its body. She blew on it. It didn't move. She jiggled the board. Nothing. Finally, she removed her long silk glove and attempted to take its tiny pulse.

"This frog is dead," she declared at last.

That seemed obvious.

"Yes, but what is dead?" Aldini intoned dramatically.

"It's deceased," Jane explained. "It's passed on. It has met its demise."

Mr. Aldini nodded briskly. "Yes, yes, but what I mean to say is—"

"This frog has ceased to be," continued Jane, determined to give the right answer here. "It's gone to meet its maker. This"—she gestured grandly to the poor frog—"is a late frog. It's a stiff. It's bereft of life—it rests in peace. It sings in the choir invisible." She clasped her hands together, still only wearing one glove, as if she were reciting a poem.

"Right," coughed Aldini. "So we've established that it's—"

"Perished," interrupted Jane. "It's bought the farm, so to speak. Kicked the bucket. Shuffled off yon mortal coil. It has expired. This frog is no more."

"Yes, thank you, young lady," said Aldini. "You may sit down now."

Jane took a quick theater-style curtsy and returned to her seat.

"So the frog is dead," said Aldini. "But what makes a thing dead? Does it not still have the form of a frog? Does it not still possess all the flesh and organs of a living creature: a heart that can beat, lungs that can breathe, and so on? Why, then, is it not alive? What has left it?"

Mary bit her lip. She'd often wondered this exact thing.

Aldini went on: "I have long been fascinated by the thin line between life and death. For years, I have toiled, exploring the boundaries of science and chemistry, until I became myself capable of bestowing animation on lifeless matter."

He picked up one of the wires again, and, with a flourish, touched the end of the wire to the dead frog's body.

It was (even though he'd warned them that this was science) like a kind of magic. The frog's legs *moved*. They contracted, bending at the knees as if the frog were taking an enormous leap into the air. If it hadn't been fixed to the board, it might have hopped right off.

Aldini withdrew the wire, and the frog legs relaxed. He touched the wire to the metal again, and once more, they jumped, as if the frog were alive, although that of course was quite impossible.

BOOM went the thunder outside. *CRASH*.

Aldini removed the wire, and the poor frog went limp again.

31

Mary could not tear her gaze away. The whole thing was terrible and wonderful and spine-tingling. (And also, if your narrators are being honest, a bit gross.) *Electricity is life*, she thought. But in this case, that life was only fleeting. The frog was only alive when it was connected to the machine. But imagine, she thought, if more could be done. Imagine if the frog could be brought back to life for good.

And then, well, she did imagine it.

Later, when she was to think back on this event, she wasn't even sure it was she who had done it. All she knew was, one moment, she was staring intensely at the lifeless frog, *imagining* that it was alive, that it was doing more than simply kicking its legs, but it was shuffling right back onto yon mortal coil, its full essence restored to it. She *imagined* that it turned over and sat upon the board, slipping from its restraints, like a proper living frog would do. She even *imagined* it croaking.

Then she felt dizzy, momentarily disoriented, so much so that she swayed against Shelley, who was still covertly holding her hand. He turned to her in concern.

"Mary?" he whispered.

"I'm all right," she said, and then she fainted.

"Ribbit," quoth the frog.

Yes. The frog was actually ribbiting, and then suddenly there was a cacophony of noise, all around them people shouting, crying out incredulously, because the impossible had happened.

The frog was ALIVE.

FOUR

Tada

"The frog is ALIVE!" At Ada's side, William—along with most of the rest of the audience—surged to his feet, clapping so hard his hands must have been stinging. "Incredible! It's alive! Well done, sir! Very well done!"

"I can't believe that worked!" someone else cried.

"Electricity is life!" another person shouted. "I believe!"

"How magnificent!"

"Amazing!"

"Astonishing!"

All through the ballroom, people were clapping and cheering, shouting about the now-living frog. Even Mr. Aldini himself appeared a bit stunned. It was a miracle—no, it was *science*, the partygoers declared. One girl had even fainted, and now there was a cluster of people around her, fanning her, trying to wake her.

The shock swept through Ada, nearly startling her to her feet. But the muscles in her left leg protested, and she leaned back in her chair, staring at the frog. *How* had Mr. Aldini done that? Dead was dead, wasn't it?

Wait, wasn't it?

Yes, she decided. Dead frogs did not come back to life, no matter how much electricity a man zapped them with. Ada turned toward her mother. Lady Byron was still sitting primly in her seat, clapping politely, but she had an impressed tilt to her head as she gazed at the frog, which was sitting on the table as though confused by the crowd, the chaos, the noise. It croaked again—although considering its recent state, we should clarify that it did not die. It just made the frog noise. *CROAK.*

"Well, that is certainly a way to end the evening," Lady Byron said. "What do you think, Ada?"

Ada scowled. Surely her mother could see the truth. It hadn't taken Ada but thirty seconds to realize this Aldini man was a con. "It's clearly fake. Obviously the frog was in a drugged sleep, so deeply unconscious that it wouldn't wake until it was thoroughly shocked."

"You think this was some kind of magic trick?" Lady Byron asked. "Even after that girl's rather exaggerated insistence that the frog was dead?"

Before Ada could answer, Mr. Aldini held up his hands, trying (in vain) to quiet the applause. "Thank you!" he called. "Thank you. You are very kind. But this is a mere taste of what is possible. If you wish to see my full demonstration, please come to my show, which will be running for the next month at the Theatre Royal on Drury Lane. There, with all of my equipment available, I will be able to reveal even more wonders than these." He gestured grandly to the nervously croaking frog, but when his eyes landed on the small creature, he himself looked a little shocked.

"I should very much like to get tickets to his show," said a male voice a few rows back. "Wouldn't you?"

Ada looked at her mother. "You see? This was merely a ploy to sell tickets. The frog was alive the entire time. Mr. Aldini chose a girl who knows nothing about frog biology. Or perhaps she was planted there, instructed ahead of time to volunteer and tell everyone the frog was dead. After all, he spent most of his time talking about life and death and everything he'd ever thought about it, and only briefly showed us any actual science."

"Mr. Aldini is a respected scientist," Lady Byron said. "You should be more concerned with learning from him than criticizing him."

Ada knew where this line of conversation would end if she persisted: with her trapped in a closet, only a candle and a pile of Mr. Aldini's papers to keep her company. So she said, "Yes, Mother," and bit her tongue. Perhaps Mr. Babbage would like to discuss it with her later—except she was still miffed about the automaton. Drat.

"Thank you!" Mr. Aldini said again. "I will now take a few questions—"

Immediately, several members of the audience rushed to the table, surrounding the so-called scientist and his frog. But that, it seemed, was too much for the frog. The unfortunate amphibian gave a panicked croak, then leapt off the table, causing the crowd to part and shouts to begin anew.

People jumped back, chairs tipped over, and ladies shrieked.

Ada glanced toward William, to see if her future husband (sigh) had any thoughts about how obviously fake this all was, now that Mr. Aldini had revealed his true reason for being here, but Lord King was pushing his way to the table, eagerly asking about how one might try to replicate this experiment.

"Don't try this at home," Aldini advised.

Because it wouldn't work. Obviously.

Ada drew her cane from where she'd tucked it behind her, fought to get the blasted gold tip to stop sliding against the parquet floor, and finally (thanks for nothing, Lady Byron!) stood. There was only one piece of actual science on this table, only one part to this whole advertisement for a magic show, that interested Ada.

The Disc Dynamo.

She approached the machine, eager to examine the electricity generator that everyone else was ignoring.

"You don't want to look at the frog?" a man beside her asked. "Well, look *for* the frog, I suppose, now that it's escaped."

Ada shook her head. "What did the frog do? It came back to life—*if* you believe it was dead in the first place. No, the real miracle is this machine."

"Well, that is gratifying to hear. Thank you."

Ada looked up from the generator to see none other than Michael Faraday, the inventor of the Disc Dynamo. She nearly dropped her cane. "Oh, it's you."

Mr. Faraday smiled. He was young compared to many of the other men at this party, though still Ada's senior by a decade and a half. "Yes, Mr. Aldini had asked me to loan to him the Disc Dynamo for his demonstration. Or his elaborate scam to draw people to the theater, if that's your opinion." He gave a friendly chuckle. "And you are . . . ?"

"Ada Byron."

"Ah, the poet's daughter who prefers math."

"You've heard of me?" Ada felt like she, too, had been shocked by the copper wires coiled on the far end of the table.

"Certainly. Mr. Babbage speaks highly of you. He always says what a mind for numbers you possess."

Ada couldn't help the twinge of anger that flared up at the mention of Mr. Babbage, but she pushed it aside. This was her opportunity to speak with *the* Michael Faraday about his generator and she would not waste it. "I've read about the Disc Dynamo," she said, "but I haven't had the pleasure of seeing one in person before."

"Then you understand how it functions, correct?"

"I do. A person turns the crank here"—she pointed at the crank—"and the disc spins between the magnetic poles. This induces an electric current into these pegs, which can then be directed using wires of a conductive nature."

"Exactly right," Faraday said. "I've long believed that electricity and magnets are more connected than previously believed. I call it electromagnetism."

The name positively gave Ada chills.

"One could, with a direct current like this, perform any number of tasks—beyond terrorizing common frogs," he said. "Imagine machines powered with generators. Imagine what could be accomplished with such readily available electricity."

Oh, Ada could imagine.

Carriages powered by electricity, rather than drawn by horses, and entire houses lit by the glow of electricity along a fine wire, rather than illuminated by candles. There were endless applications for this technology, if only it could be harnessed and reliably generated.

A spark lit in Ada's chest. In came that near uncontrollable *need* to do science of her own. She would show Mr. Babbage that she could do better than him. She would invent something useful, something more than a pretty automaton to show off to her friends. She would create something that could change the world.

"I think you'll get along with William King very well," Lady Byron said during the carriage ride home. "He's handsome, you must admit that."

Ada hadn't really noticed.

"And rich. Fifty thousand pounds."

They'd discussed that already, but perhaps Lady Byron needed to say it again in order to convince herself that she was doing the right thing by marrying Ada off to some stranger.

"And he's . . ." Here, Lady Byron faltered. It seemed even she, with all her enthusiasm, could not come up with any more positive qualities about the young man.

"He likely isn't an axe murderer," Ada provided.

"Yes!" Lady Byron agreed. "He likely isn't an axe murderer."

Ada gazed out the window, watching the rain-soaked streets of London pass by as the carriage returned them to the Byron estate. It seemed unfair that she would have to marry this man, exchanging one gilded cage for another, but perhaps it wouldn't be all that bad. Lady Byron would no longer have absolute control over Ada's life. (No, that would be Lord King.)

Ada's reflection in the window looked back at her. Around the pale image, the reflection showed the box of the carriage interior, and her mother at her side. Mirror Ada was as trapped as real Ada.

Being trapped in a small space was actually Ada's first memory. When she closed her eyes, she could still feel the walls of the closet, the press of clothes above her, the doorknob that wouldn't turn. She could smell the stale air, the pungent mothballs. There'd been no light, beyond what shone around the door, and so Ada had whispered prime numbers to herself, as many as she knew—two, three, five, seven, all the way up to 2141, at which point she'd lost track—and then started on pi.

She remembered when Lady Byron had finally unlocked the

closet door, the burst of light, the sting of tears on Ada's sensitive eyes, and her promises never to do it again—though Ada couldn't actually remember what she had done wrong. Only that it had been bad enough to get her locked in a closet for hours.

Now, as the carriage rolled to a stop in front of the Byron estate, Lady Byron rapped Ada's knuckles. "Stop daydreaming. We're home."

Ada blinked up at the house, her eyes moving toward the dormer window of the third-floor attic. Lady Byron would go right to bed. She always did after parties. Which meant Ada would be free to do as she wished. Her mind turned away from her matrimonial future and back toward the thing that she would build, this thing that would change the world.

She already had an idea.

Mary

FIVE

Mary stared at the blank sheet of paper in front of her. Last night after the party (once she'd recovered from her rather embarrassing swoon) she'd felt inspired, brimming with all sorts of interesting ideas and seized by the desire to write them down. But now, as she gazed upon the pristine surface of the paper, she found that she was having trouble shaping any of her wild thoughts into coherent sentences. She picked up her pen and dipped it into the bottle of ink. Perhaps if she simply began to write something, the right words would come.

The tip of the quill hovered over the page. What to write? Something. She must write *something*.

A drop of ink fell from the quill and splattered onto the page. Mary sighed. Someone, she thought, really should invent a kind of pen that didn't need to be dipped into the ink over and over again. One in which the ink resided *within* the pen. That would be something.

But now back to writing.

Mary crumpled up the ruined paper and tossed it aside. Then she crumpled the next piece of blank paper and tossed it, too, just to get it over with. She glanced around. Her sisters were seated at the dining room table with her, Fanny to one side, Jane across, both of them writing. In the next room over, her father's study, she could hear his pen frantically scratching, punctuated by the occasional exclamations he made when the writing was going particularly well.

"Exactly!" he said just then. "Well done, me!"

He'd been on fire since a new idea had come to him last night in the carriage. A novel. Something about isolation, immortality, alchemy, the elixir of life, and the consequences of forbidden knowledge. He'd been writing all through the night. The only other person in her entire family who *wasn't* writing at that moment was Mary's wicked stepmother, who was sitting in the corner grumpily darning socks.

Mary chewed her bottom lip. She should write something about Aldini's demonstration—it wasn't every day that a dead animal was brought back to life right in front of you. The image of the scientist rose up in her brain—his resolute expression as he had touched the wires together, harnessing the writhing electricity between his hands. This man had used science to unlock the secrets of life and death. First a frog, but then what? The possibilities seemed endless.

She put her pen to the paper and wrote:

None but those who have experienced them can conceive of the enticements of science. In other studies you go as far as others have gone before you, and there is nothing more to know; but in scientific pursuit there is continual food for discovery and wonder.

Oh dear. That was terrible. Tedious. Boring. Why was writing so very hard? (We narrators are nodding soberly. We know, Mary. We know.) Perhaps, she thought, the treacherous doubt rising up inside her like some inevitable tide, she wasn't meant to be a writer after all.

Across the table, Fanny paused for a moment, stretched her arms, and then continued writing what appeared to be a letter. Her lips were pursed in concentration, her brow furrowed.

"What are you composing?" Mary asked.

Fanny gazed up at her, startled. "Oh. Just an account of last night. For my own . . . personal record. Of all the good needlework I've seen. And other things."

"I'm writing about how wonderful it was to dance with the illustrious Mr. Shelley," boasted Jane, who loved to tease Mary about Shelley in front of Mrs. Godwin. She grinned. "He's an excellent dancer. One of us should definitely marry him, I think. Should it be you, Fanny?"

Fanny's cheeks pinked slightly, even though she'd never shown the least bit of interest in Shelley. Or in any man, for that matter. "Well," she said softly after a moment. "Mr. Shelley's waistcoat last night *was* a thing of beauty."

"Fanny Shelley. That has a nice ring to it," Jane mused playfully.

Mrs. Godwin snorted. "Nonsense. If any of you girls is to marry Mr. Shelley, it should obviously be you, Jane."

"Perhaps," agreed Jane, darting another mischievous glance up at Mary. "Then I'd be Jane Shelley, which sounds equally nice."

Mary tried to kick her under the table and missed. Thankfully that was when Mrs. Godwin threw her socks down and swept out of the room, off to grumble while she did the breakfast dishes.

Jane turned to Mary. "Actually, I'm considering changing my name to Claire. Claire Clairmont. What do you think?"

"It's a bit redundant," said Mary, but somewhere in the back of her mind the words *Mary* and *Shelley* were coming together. Her spine prickled. Mary Shelley. She attempted to brush the name away, but it stuck like a cobweb. She decided to change the subject. "What is it that *you* are writing, Jane?"

"A letter." Jane tossed her glossy black curls over her shoulder. "I also had a fantastic idea last night. Did you know that *Lord Byron's* daughter was in attendance at the party? We were merely one degree away from a real celebrity! It's such a pity we didn't actually meet her. Apparently, she uses a cane to get about, just as her father does. She must be just like him!"

"How typical that all everyone seemed to notice about Miss Byron was her cane," Mary said. She had heard of Ada Byron— well, mostly she had heard that a person named Ada Byron, the daughter of the marvelous and scandalous Lord Byron, existed.

Mary, too, was wistful about not encountering Ada last night. She sighed. She wished she could meet her. She could relate to someone who was constantly being defined by their famous parent.

"Oh! You should send her some of your writing, seeing as you are going to be a writer someday." Jane gazed pointedly at the blank paper in front of Mary and the littering of crumpled papers around her.

"Right," said Mary slowly. But she had no intention of showing her dismal writing to anyone. "That's a very nice idea, Jane, but—"

Jane laughed. "Oh no, *that's* not my fantastic idea. My idea is that I'm going to write to Lord Byron and ask him to advise me in how I might become a famous actress."

Mary held in an incredulous snort. "You want to be an actress?"

Jane nodded. "I've given it a lot of thought—all this morning, in fact—and I've come to the conclusion that becoming an actress is the only proper way for a woman in my position to become financially independent."

Mary frowned. "But you've never even been in a play."

"And being an actress isn't exactly considered proper, Jane dear," Fanny added gently. (It's true: in the 1800s, being an actress was considered only a small step up from being a prostitute.)

"It is proper," insisted Jane. "And I'm pretty and very well spoken, and people generally like me as soon as they see me, and even more so when they come to know me."

"And you're so humble, too," Mary teased, but she couldn't really argue.

"All I need are the proper connections," said Jane. "Therefore I am writing to entreat Lord Byron to help me. Surely he must know some people in the theater circles."

"Yes, probably so, but why would Lord Byron—the most famous person in the world—endeavor to help you—some girl he's never heard of—become famous?" asked Mary.

Jane straightened. "Because I am acquainted with his daughter, of course. We are almost the best of friends. Also, it's well known that Lord Byron always endeavors to assist a damsel in distress. And I am in distress. It's clear that this family is in decline. I cannot live in this shabby little apartment any longer. I am destined for greater things than these!"

Again, Mary couldn't argue with her. Once upon a time, William Godwin had been a well-respected, prosperous man. The bookstore had been booming. They'd lived in a large, finely furnished house. They'd had servants. But that had been some time ago.

"It's a good idea, this actress thing," Fanny said softly.

Mary's mouth fell open. "What? Fanny!"

"Thank you," Jane said primly. "Oh. I almost forgot." She pulled something small and white from her dress pocket. "I was supposed to pass this along to you last night."

Mary took it from her. It was a folded paper flower, and inside she knew there would be a message from Shelley. She immediately gave up trying to write (thank heavens!) and retreated toward the bedroom she shared with her sisters.

"Wait, where are you going?" Jane called after her. "What did he write? You must read it to us!"

Mary firmly closed the door. Then she curled up onto her bed, where, at last, she began to unfold the flower.

The first row of petals held a line of poetry, written in Shelley's flowery script.

Sunlight clasps the earth, and the moonbeams kiss the sea.

A pretty good line, Mary thought. Why could *everyone* write but her, lately?

She pulled back the second layer of petals.

What is all this sweet work worth? If thou kiss not me.

Heat rushed to her face. Something so physical as kissing had not yet occurred between them, although not for lack of Mary desiring that it would. The problem with kissing Shelley was that they were never alone. They had but passing glances at each other in hallways, snatches of conversation between the bookshelves of the shop when no one else was paying attention, a stolen moment in a darkened, crowded room in which Shelley held her hand. They often took walks together, long, winding walks through the gloomy streets of London, lovely, transcendent walks in which she and Shelley talked about everything under the sun—poetry and politics, the merits of eating only vegetables (Shelley was an avid vegetarian), writing, art, and their mutual love of the natural world—but during all that time Jane was always plodding along behind them, not a chaperone in any sense of the word, but there. Watching.

Still, it was enough that Shelley wanted to kiss Mary. Their time would come. Of this, she had no doubt. Her lips meeting his felt as inevitable to her as death and taxes. She smiled and refolded the flower, tucking it with the others between the pages of her favorite book (*The Rime of the Ancient Mariner*, by Coleridge), where no one else would ever think to look for it.

Mary Shelley, she thought. It did have a ring.

She became aware, suddenly, of a faint knocking sound. Mary laid aside her book with a frown. How odd. Nobody in her house ever had the courtesy to knock—they simply burst in. Perhaps Mary had imagined the knocking.

But there it was again—louder this time. Mary went to her bedroom door and opened it, but found no one there. Very odd. She tilted her head to one side, listening. The knock came again, a sharp, insistent rapping, and that's when Mary figured out where it was coming from.

Inside the wardrobe.

That's also when she figured out that, behind the row of dresses and coats, there was *a door at the back of her wardrobe*.

For a long moment Mary simply stared at the door in wonder. Then another burst of knocking startled her to action. She curled her fingers around the knob and turned it. The door swung open, revealing a tall, smiling woman in a blue dress.

"Hello, Mary," the woman said. She had fuzzy red hair and smelled vaguely of sugar plums. "I'm Miss Stamp. How do you do?"

Mary was speechless. Then she realized she was being rude. "How do you—know my name?" she asked.

"Because I'm your fae godmother," replied Miss Stamp matter-of-factly.

That was not what Mary had been expecting her to say. Again, she couldn't think of how to reply to this seemingly ridiculous statement. For a long moment she just stood there opening and closing her mouth like a codfish. "I—I'm a bit old to have a fairy godmother, aren't I?" she managed at last. Miss Stamp did not, that Mary could see, have wings.

"Not fairy," Miss Stamp corrected her. "Fae. The word *fae* comes from the word *facere*, which, in Latin, means 'to create.'"

"Are you going to grant my wishes, then?" Mary asked. There was a part of her that was highly skeptical that this was even happening—a conversation with a strange woman who had appeared in a door at the back of her wardrobe? She must have fallen asleep while she was reading. She must be dreaming. But another big part of Mary was thinking, *Finally!* She felt like she'd been waiting all her life for something like this. Something magical. Something that would spirit her away from the drabness of her world. Or something that would enable her to become a real writer at last. Something exactly like a fairy—sorry, fae—godmother.

"No, my dear," said Miss Stamp. "I've been sent to teach you. Then you must see to your own wishes." She held out her hand. "Now will you please come with me?"

Mary pinched her forearm. It hurt sufficiently for her to

understand that she probably wasn't dreaming. Then, because she really didn't think she had anything to lose, she took a deep breath and followed Miss Stamp through the door at the back of her wardrobe.

On the other side she found not a magical snowy land full of talking animals (that hadn't even been invented yet) but a room full of . . . more doors. One door was white with pink flowers painted on it, while another was bright purple with a golden frame that surrounded the peephole. There was an official-looking black door with a silver lion knocker and the number ten posted to the outside. Another door was very tiny, like a door for a doll. Still another was round and green, with a shiny brass knob in the center. There were even a few doors in the ceiling.

Mary was impressed.

She was even more impressed when Miss Stamp marched over to an empty part of the wall, waved her hand with a bit of a flourish, and yet another door appeared. This new door was perfectly regular-looking, but Mary could only imagine what might be on the other side. A room full of windows? A flying castle, perhaps? But Miss Stamp pushed open the door to what seemed to be someone's attic, lined with various trunks and boxes, exposed beams on the slanted ceiling and a large dormer window on one side. Near the window was a worktable, and seated at the table was a dark-haired young lady of about Mary's age. The girl was taking apart a clock (gears and various pieces lay in neat piles all around her), her lips pursed in deep concentration.

Miss Stamp ushered Mary into the room and shut the door behind them. Then she cleared her throat.

The dark-haired girl glanced up. "Oh, hello, Miss Stamp. I didn't even hear you come in. Why did no one announce you?" Her eyes moved past them to the magic door. It was standing, alone and unsupported, in the center of the room. The girl's brow furrowed. "Wait. Where did that come from?"

"I will gladly explain," Miss Stamp said. "But first, introductions are in order." She gestured to Mary. "Mary Godwin, meet Ada Byron."

Byron. Oh dear. Jane's head would have exploded (metaphorically speaking) at this golden opportunity. But Mary felt instantly tongue-tied, stunned by the coincidence. She'd just been wishing that she could meet Ada Byron, and now she was standing in her house. Wait, *was* that a coincidence? "How do you do?" she stammered, and looked back to Miss Stamp. "Are you her godmother, too?"

Ada pried a spring out of her clock. "Of course not. My godmother is my aunt Augusta. Miss Stamp is my governess. Well, former governess. Mother fired her when she sensed I was becoming too close with her. As she does all my governesses. I've had ever so many governesses."

Her mother sounded *lovely*.

"What are you doing here, Miss Stamp?" Ada asked.

"I've come to teach you, my dear," Miss Stamp replied. "It's time."

Ada looked at Mary as if Mary could elaborate. "She told me the same thing," Mary said.

"Teach us what?" Ada finally set down her tools.

"How to be a fae."

"But I don't believe in fairies," Ada said.

"The fae are not fairies," Miss Stamp reiterated patiently. "We aren't sprites with wings, nor do we dance in toadstool circles or have an allergy to iron. Fae are just people—a very rare, special kind of people—who can do remarkable things. We can make what we imagine real."

"Like magic," Mary murmured.

Ada was frowning. "But I don't believe in magic."

"You will," said Miss Stamp. "It's something you were born to do. You'll see."

"Wait," said Mary. "You think I'm a fae?"

"I know you are," said Miss Stamp lightly. She patted Mary on the shoulder. "Your mother was one of the most powerful fae who ever lived, and the apple doesn't often fall too far from that tree. We have always suspected. But we didn't really know until last night."

Mary swallowed. "What happened last night?"

Miss Stamp smiled. "Surely you remember."

"You mean when . . ." Mary wet her lips. Why was her mouth so dry? She tried again: "You mean when Mr. Aldini brought that frog back to life?"

"That was fake," Ada interjected. "Obviously. I was there."

"Mr. Aldini didn't bring the frog back to life," Miss Stamp said.

"See?" said Ada triumphantly. "I told you."

"*You* brought the frog to life, Mary," said Miss Stamp.

Mary shook her head. "*I* did," she repeated incredulously. "No, I couldn't have."

"What were you thinking about, right before the frog—pardon my pun—hopped back into the world of the living?" Miss Stamp asked. "Think back. You were watching the demonstration. . . ."

"And Mr. Aldini was making the frog legs jump," said Mary. "And then I thought that it was sad that he wasn't *truly* bringing it back to life. It was cruel, even, him manipulating it that way. And then I thought it would be nice if the frog could really live again. I imagined—"

Miss Stamp caught her hand and squeezed it urgently. "You imagined it, Mary. That's right. You imagined it. And then it was real."

Mary shook her head again. "But—"

"And afterward you felt faint—drained, and it's no wonder. You had just given the frog a small part of your own essence. This is normally against the rules—bringing dead things to life, I mean—but naturally you didn't know, so we'll let it slide this once."

Miss Stamp bustled across the room and grabbed a chair from the corner. She flipped it over and directed Mary to sit. This was a good thing, because Mary's knees were suddenly feeling quite weak.

"It was me," she whispered. She looked up at Miss Stamp. "You were there? You saw?"

"Not me, directly. One of the other godmothers. A colleague of mine. But believe me, it was quite the feat for someone as young as you, and untrained to boot." She grinned. "You're a fae, Mary."

"Now hold on just a minute," Ada said. "You're saying that she's some kind of magical being?" Her lip curled on the word *magical*.

"Yes," said Miss Stamp bluntly. "And so are you."

SIX

Ada

"No, I'm not." What a ridiculous statement. This whole situation was ridiculous, in fact. "There is no such thing as magic, only natural phenomena that aren't yet understood."

Miss Stamp turned to Ada. "We've always known you would most likely be fae, my dear. Because of your father. That's why I was assigned to be your governess."

Ada leaned back in her chair, all the wind knocked out of her. "My father," she murmured.

She should have expected Miss Stamp to bring up Lord Byron, what with having brought up Mary's mother. Certainly *Lady* Byron was not fae. So it made a certain sense that Miss Stamp would pull Lord Byron into it, if these so-called fae gifts were inherited from a parent. Lord Byron was well known for his incredible imagination, the beauty of his words, the way he could spin emotion from nothing. To some, that might seem like a kind of magic.

But Ada hadn't ever met her father; he'd left the country when she'd been a tiny baby, off to the Continent to do whatever poets did. For years, that was all Ada had known about him, as poetry (especially his poetry) was expressly forbidden in this house. To Ada, Lord Byron was simply a name, a distant unknowable figure who meant nothing to her. Nothing at all.

"My father is fae, you say," Ada murmured, feeling *something* in spite of the nothing she had always preferred.

Miss Stamp nodded eagerly. "Yes. He was trained in the same way I intend to train you."

Ada let out a noise somewhere between a laugh and a cry of frustration. "So you are insisting that I'm some sort of"—she lowered her voice again—"poet like—"

"Oh *no*, dear!" Miss Stamp swept toward Ada and rested her hand on Ada's shoulder. "No, not at all." If anyone knew how dangerous the word *poetry* was in this house, it was Miss Stamp. "It doesn't work like that. You don't have to be a"—she, too, lowered her voice—"poet."

Mary's eyes were wide. "But I like poetry."

Miss Stamp nodded gently. "Fae specialize in many different fields. Some are writers, artists, and musicians, while others are inventors, architects, or brilliant engineers. It's about creativity, a sort of genius, the ability to see what could be, not simply what is."

Ada leaned her elbows on the table—then sat up tall again

as her eyes fell on the spine straightener that had been thrown in among the trunks and crates ages ago. "So you think I'm fae because my father is."

"Exactly." Miss Stamp smiled. "Look at all of this. How could you not be fae, my dear?" One by one, she motioned toward all the inventions that Ada had fashioned over the years: the butterfly automaton, a music box, and even Ada's cane.

Ada scoffed. "Those aren't magic. Those are science!"

Miss Stamp offered a patient smile. "Why not both?"

Clearly, Ada's former governess (now fae godmother) was not going to let this go. Ada decided to play along. "So if I am fae—and I'm not saying that I am—then why wait to train me until now? We've known each other for years."

"Fae abilities don't manifest until adolescence, dear," Miss Stamp said. "That's when training begins for every potential fae. Untrained fae can be dangerous. They do all sorts of things without realizing."

"Like bring frogs back to life," Mary said.

"An understandable mistake," Miss Stamp said. "One I'm sure you will not repeat."

"Shouldn't there be some sort of school?" Ada asked. "A centralized location where all fae students can learn?"

Miss Stamp's mouth pressed into a line. "There is—for boys."

Mary threw her hands into the air. "That is *so* unfair!"

Ada quite agreed. (Not that she was believing any of this. No, definitely not.)

"The godfathers run a boarding school for young men. It's very prestigious. It's also the only one." She sighed. "I haven't been there myself, but I've heard that there is chocolate cake for breakfast every morning. Wouldn't that be nice?"

Ada and Mary sighed as well.

"But I'm afraid there isn't a school for female fae. It's simply not acceptable for young ladies to go off to school like that. Unfortunately. No, I will teach you both here, in Ada's attic. It's how all of us must learn to harness our abilities, in small groups such as this."

"How will I get here?" Mary asked. "Will I be permitted to use the doors?"

"What doors?" Ada asked.

"No, no." Miss Stamp waved her hand at Mary. "I will come get you through the door in your wardrobe twice a week. We will come together. Both doors—this one and the wardrobe door—will remained locked at all times. The last thing we need is for one of your sisters to go wandering through."

"What doors?" Ada cried. Then she looked again at the one in her workroom. "How will I explain this to anyone else?"

"You'll figure it out," Miss Stamp said. "You already have all manner of strange things up here. What's a door that seems to lead nowhere?"

"A coatrack!" Mary provided. "Or a place to dry your socks."

Ada sighed again. "Mother will be angry if she finds out."

"Your mother is going to Bath," Miss Stamp said. "She won't be here to notice anyone coming in or out of the house."

"My mother's not—"

"Ada, darling!" Lady Byron called from below the attic stairs. She never liked to come all the way up, on account of the stairs being so steep. "Ada!"

"Um," Ada said to Miss Stamp and Mary. "One moment." She pushed herself up using the table for support, then grabbed her cane before going to the attic door to see Lady Byron at the foot of the stairs. She was wearing a traveling dress and leaning against a large black umbrella. Behind her, Pell wrestled with a giant bag. "Mother," Ada said, "are you going somewhere?"

"Yes, dear, how kind of you to notice. I'm going to Bath. I need to relax. These last few weeks have been so stressful, what with getting you ready for the party, arranging your meeting with Lord King . . ." She shook her head. "A mother's work is never done, is it? But for now, Mother needs a break."

Ada blinked at her. "Oh. Well. Have a lovely time, I suppose."

"Be good while I'm gone. Ta!" Then she spun and sauntered out of view, giving every impression of already being quite relaxed.

Ada turned and looked back at Miss Stamp, who appeared smug, and Mary, whose mouth had formed a small O.

"How did you do that?" Ada asked. "Did you use magic?"

"So now you believe?" Miss Stamp grinned.

"Now I don't know what to think, except that no matter what I say next, you and Mary will both show up in my attic twice a week, through this mystery door here." And the fact that the door had indeed appeared out of nowhere—that was convincing. But

Ada was sure there was some other plausible explanation. There had to be.

Miss Stamp picked up the broken clock Ada had been working on. "What happened to this?"

"It stopped winding. I think a spring—"

All at once, with only a wink from Miss Stamp, the clock was whole. Inside the brass case, the second hand tick tick ticked over the numbers. It even had the correct time.

Ada's mouth dropped open. "What did you do?"

"I imagined that it worked."

Ada took the clock from Miss Stamp and turned it over in her hands. "That's all? You imagined?" This was, she had to admit, pretty undeniable evidence.

"There's more to it than that," Miss Stamp said, "but in the simplest terms: yes, I imagined that the clock worked, and then it did."

And there'd been no poetry involved, none at all.

"All right. I'll believe. I'll train with you." Ada placed the clock into her pocket to investigate later. It would be a useful skill to have, the ability to make things exactly as one wanted them. Her eyes flickered to the stack of papers on her table, the sketches she'd drawn in the haze of inspiration last night.

"Wonderful," Miss Stamp said, opening the door. "Now I have to do some paperwork—to register you both as my students—but you should get to know each other. I'll return in an hour to take you back through the door, Mary." With hardly a goodbye, Miss Stamp stepped across the threshold and let the door swing shut behind her, all before Ada could get a peek at what lay beyond.

"It's unsettling," Mary said. "Watching her go through the door and not step out on the other side."

Ada made a circuit around the door, her cane thumping softly on the floor. She gave the knob a few twists. Nothing. It was locked, just as Miss Stamp had said it would be. "Drat," Ada muttered. Well, she'd work on the door problem later.

"What's all this?" Mary was standing over Ada's worktable, picking through the sketches Ada had been making last night.

Ada stopped beside Mary and let go of her cane; it stood, balanced on the four small rubber tips. (*So* much better than the one her mother had purchased!) "This," Ada said grandly, "will be my next invention."

"You're inventing a boy?"

Ada laughed. "No, something better. Did you see the automaton last night? The one Mr. Babbage said that he created all by himself with no help from anyone?"

Mary's brow rumpled. "Well, I did see the automaton, but I didn't get any of the rest of that."

"Never mind that," Ada said. "But he didn't do it all by himself, no matter what he tells the whole world—"

"I really don't think he told anyone that."

"And now I'm going to make an automaton of my own. A better one. A practical one that can actually be used to help people."

Mary leafed through the papers. "I liked the dancer. She was pretty."

"But can she"—Ada whipped a sheet out from the pile in

Mary's hands—"serve tea?" She held up the paper, which showed her automaton pouring steaming tea into a small cup.

"No," Mary admitted.

"And can she—" Ada tried to slide another sheet of paper out of the stack, but Mary's thumb was pressed too tightly. "This one," Ada said. "I'm trying to dramatically whip it from the stack."

"Oh, sorry!" Mary slid the paper forward. "Proceed."

Ada dramatically whipped the paper out. "Can the silver dancer play the pianoforte?"

Mary frowned. "I'll admit, I didn't ask to find out. But probably not."

"Can she—"

"She dances," Mary said. "I saw her curtsy and turn, move her arms around a bit. She was very pretty."

Ada rubbed her hands down her face. "That's the second time you've said how pretty she was."

"Because she was. I really don't know much about automatons. Are they difficult to build?"

"Incredibly. Every movement must be scripted. If even one calculation is off, nothing works. You could break the entire machine."

Mary's eyes—which were hazel, Ada noticed—went round. "This is all sounding quite ambitious. Have you ever built one before? Anything of this scale?"

No one had ever asked Ada that before.

Well, it wasn't like Ada had been permitted much company these last few years.

"Oh yes." Ada barely stopped herself from clapping her hands together. "I've built several automatons before, but the biggest is— Well, do you want to see it?" Suddenly, she was overcome with the urge to show Mary *everything* she had built.

"I would love to," Mary said.

Heart beating quickly, Ada took her cane and went over to the dormer window. She threw it open to reveal a long stretch of roof.

"Um, Ada?"

But Ada, in a series of practiced moves, had already shimmied out the window and buckled herself into a seat that was suspended from a wire. "This will take us directly to the stables. I'll send it back up, once I'm there."

"Is this safe?" Mary climbed out the window, too, onto the slice of roof between the dormer and the edge.

"Perfectly safe," Ada said. Then she pulled the release lever.

Mary ↝
SEVEN

Mary stared, open mouthed, as Ada disappeared down the zip line (she hadn't called it that, dear reader, but that's what we'd call it nowadays), the bright blue of her dress getting smaller and smaller as she was zipped away. Ada Byron was an odd girl, Mary thought—there was no doubt about that—but then again, wasn't odd generally so much better than boring? Watching her zoom down from the three-story house in under thirty seconds, Mary had a feeling that perhaps after today her life would never be boring again.

Now that she was a fae.

The line bounced. Ada must have reached the bottom. Then the wheel and pulley system next to Mary began to squeak. As she had promised, Ada was sending the chair back up to her.

She expected Mary to come down that way, too.

This was about the time that Mary realized she was afraid of heights. She'd never had the occasion to be up quite so high before. She glanced down. Gulp. Directly below the window was a hard stone courtyard. Her heart started to pound. She considered her options. She could just go back inside right now and exit the house the normal way—down the attic stairs, and beyond that, well, who knew; Mary hadn't come into this house in the typical fashion, and didn't actually know how to descend to the ground level. But she would find her way and arrive with her skull intact.

But then Ada would think she was a coward.

The little chair arrived at the top. Mary reached out and grabbed it. Ada was clearly a clever girl, maybe the cleverest that Mary had ever met, but not foolhardy. Ada had said it was safe. *Perfectly safe* was the exact phrase she'd used. And Mary was no coward.

She climbed awkwardly into the chair and fastened the strap around her middle as Ada had done. Then she swung herself over the edge of the roof and released the brake mechanism.

WHOOSH. The wind rushed at her, caught her hair and her skirt like a sail. She was flying. The air was cold and fresh against her cheeks. It smelled (not surprisingly) like rain. The ground loomed up below her. She would have closed her eyes, but she didn't dare. The line passed through an open space at the top of the stable. Then the air smelled (again, not surprisingly) like hay and horse poop. The chair jerked to a halt, and Ada was at her side again.

"Well done," said Ada, helping Mary to undo the strap. "It's quite the rush, isn't it?"

Mary stepped down from the chair and almost tumbled to the

ground. Her knees were feeling funny—wobbly, noodle-like.

"Are you all right?" Ada asked with a tiny smile. She helped Mary to sit on a nearby bale of hay. "You look a bit green."

Mary was about two seconds from bringing up her breakfast. She swallowed and took a few gulping breaths. "I'm fine," she croaked at last. "What was it you wanted to show me?"

"Over here," said Ada excitedly, and ushered Mary farther into the biggest, grandest stable Mary had ever seen—at least a dozen horses—with an adjoining carriage house that held a fine assortment of vehicles. But Ada led her past the horses and the carriages, to the very end of the building, where she stopped in front of the last stall. She stepped inside and, without any ceremony at all, pulled a sheet off a large object in the center of the stall.

It was a metal horse.

"Oh," said Mary breathlessly.

The horse was fashioned from iron, brass, and silver, which gleamed even in the dim light of the stables. It was a full hand taller than any actual horse Mary had ever encountered, solidly built, but there was also an artistry to its construction, a combination of elegant lines and a gentle face.

"Is it—" Mary reached out to touch it, but then pulled back. Her eyes roved over it instead. "And this is an . . . automaton? Not a sculpture?"

Ada snorted. "He's a machine, not some frivolous work of art."

"He's beautiful," said Mary.

"He performs a function according to a predetermined set of

coded instructions," said Ada. But then she admitted, "He is nice. His name is Ivan." Ada rested a hand on the horse's flank. He didn't react. "I wanted to keep him in the house, but my mother put her foot down. No horses in the parlor."

"Not even giant metal ones?" Mary made a scandalized face.

"Not even giant metal ones," Ada said mournfully. "But she did concede that I needed a stall for him, since he would rust any time it rained. Even with him living in one of the stalls, I have to oil him and clean off rust regularly." She gave the metal horse a fond pat. "While I was ill, poor Pell had to do it."

"While you were ill? Did you build him before then?"

Ada nodded. "I completed him on my thirteenth birthday. I'd wanted to add wings, but I couldn't make the math work to actually get him in the air. He's too heavy. The ratio of wings to horse, the overall mass—every time I work out the calculations, I find myself thwarted by gravity."

Mary, once again, was impressed. She was also curious about Ada's mysterious illness—what malady had befallen her, and was that why she required the cane to move about now? But they had only just met each other. Mary thought it might be rude to ask.

"What does Ivan do?" she asked instead.

"The tail is actually a crank." Ada led Mary around to the back side of the horse and demonstrated with a one-sixteenth turn of the tail. "Any more than this," Ada said, "and he'll go farther than we want—probably into that wall." Ada pointed at a section of the stables, which had obviously been repaired some time ago.

She released the tail, and the horse marched jerkily forward a couple of steps, clanking and whirring. Then the tail was back in its original position, and the horse went still.

Mary clapped her hands in delight. "Isn't he wonderful?"

Ada looked pleased with herself, a certain proud set to her thin shoulders. "He is, as I said, the largest one I've ever made." She bent carefully to pick up an oilcan from the floor of Ivan's stall and proceeded to give the horse a couple of squeezes into his leg joints. Then she sighed. "But he's not exactly useful, is he? After I gave up trying to make him fly—a child's daydream, I know that now—I thought he still might turn out to be some grand invention. A horse who will never need feeding or watering, who never gets tired, who never goes lame or gets old and dies."

"That would be something," agreed Mary. "I believe everybody would want one."

Ada nodded sadly. "Unfortunately, poor Ivan really isn't capable of much more than Mr. Babbage's pretty dancer. He's only for show. He's clockwork, for one thing. Even if he were fully wound up, he wouldn't go for more than two or three minutes before you would have to wind him up again. He needs something more sustainable to power him. And—" She blushed, as if she had remembered something deeply embarrassing.

"What?" Mary asked. "What's wrong with him?"

"He's got a fatal flaw. An oversimplification in my design," said Ada quietly.

"What kind of oversimplification?"

Ada muttered something too soft and quick for Mary to hear.

"What's that?" asked Mary.

"He can't turn around. He can't turn at all, actually. I didn't give him the proper kind of shoulder joints. He is only capable of going straight forward. He's not even very good at going backward."

"Oh, I see," said Mary. "Yes, that is a problem. But couldn't you just fix it?"

Ada crossed her arms over her chest. "That's easier said than done. I would have to take him apart completely in order to do that, and it would take loads of time, and he's so big and unwieldy and I'm—" She bent her head, a curl of dark hair falling into her face. "I'm not yet well enough to do that kind of work."

"I could help you." Mary sucked in a breath—she'd made the offer without thinking. Ada hadn't asked for her help. She didn't strike Mary as the type of person who was comfortable asking for help.

But Ada met Mary's gaze eagerly. "Perhaps you could, if you're indeed one of those magic fae people. If that's a real thing, although I am still not one hundred percent convinced that it is." She drew the clock Miss Stamp had fixed earlier out of her pocket and stared at it intently for a minute. Then she looked up at Mary again. "Would you try?"

"What, you mean *now*?"

"Why not now?" Ada returned the clock to her pocket and withdrew a small notebook and a tiny stub of a pencil. She opened the book and spent a few minutes fervently sketching. Then she turned the book to show it to Mary. "This is what I need."

It was a crude drawing of a mechanical horse's shoulder joint—a classic ball and socket—although Mary didn't know what to call it. She immediately felt that she was in over her head.

"Why couldn't you try?" Mary asked.

"I did already," Ada said briskly. "When you were deciding whether or not to zip down here. I attempted to imagine it—this piece of machinery replacing what's in Ivan's shoulder now, plus a small mechanism in his mane one could pull to engage it—like a turn . . . signal," she said. "But nothing happened, no matter how hard I thought about it. So now you could try. There's no harm in trying, is there?"

"I—" This all felt a bit premature. They hadn't even had their first fae lesson yet. And now here was Ada asking Mary to do magic? And it looked complicated, too. "I suppose you're right. What harm is there in trying?"

She took the sketch from Ada's hand and studied it. Then she moved to the side of the clockwork horse, up next to his shoulder, and gazed at the part of him Ada wished to transform. It was complicated, but it wasn't so difficult to picture the current shoulder joint becoming like the one in the drawing.

"Are you doing it?" Ada whispered.

"Doing what?"

"Imagining."

"Oh. Yes."

"And what are you going to do now?" Ada asked. "To make what you imagine real?"

Mary shook her head. "Maybe this isn't such a good idea."

"But you did it before," Ada pointed out. "With the frog."

"I thought you didn't believe in the incident with the frog."

Ada's chin lifted. "I am now willing to concede that it is possible."

Mary gave a small laugh. Then she closed her eyes and focused on the clockwork horse again. His shoulders. His mane. How *had* she done it before, with the frog? Was it really so simple as imagining a new joint? She took stock of her own shoulder—the way the bone was cupped inside the socket, the freedom it had to move in all directions. She imagined the gait of a real horse running along a road, a horse and rider coming to a bend. The rider pulling the reins and the horse turning, not just its shoulders but its head and neck as well.

There was a light thump. Mary opened her eyes. Ada was sitting on a barrel against the wall, her cane hanging by the strap around her wrist.

"You did it," she said dully.

Mary turned back to Ivan. Ada was right. He was different. The metal at his shoulder was a different color, for one thing, like polished brass. And his shape had changed.

"I did it," breathed Mary. "Did I?"

"Yes. I should have thought of reins," said Ada.

Mary stared at Ivan. Indeed, he was wearing reins now, which would help the rider to steer him.

Ada rose to her feet, shifting her cane to support her. There was a new light in her eyes that made Mary slightly nervous. "This fae business just might work out," the girl said.

BOOM. At first Mary thought the sound was thunder, which was a reasonable conclusion for her to draw. But then there was a shout from the other end of the stables.

"One of the carriages has collapsed!" exclaimed a groom.

"What?" cried the coachman. "They were in fine form yesterday."

Mary and Ada shared an alarmed glance and began to inch toward the exit. As they passed the carriage house they spied the coachman crouching down next to one of the carriages, which was lying in pieces on the floor.

"Blast!" yelled the coachman. "Our finest carriage!"

The groom crouched down, too. "Darnedest thing! It's like the axels have been taken apart and put back together again, but wrong."

The girls moved toward the door, Mary shortening her stride slightly to keep pace with Ada as they fled the scene of the crime. It had started to rain outside, the water coming down in sudden sheets. They shrieked and made for the house.

"Goodness!" exclaimed a portly, kind-looking woman as they burst through the door. "Miss Ada! Why are you—" Her eyes landed on Mary. "And who is this?"

"This is Mary Godwin," Ada said, drawing herself upright. "She will be visiting me regularly from now on."

The woman's mouth opened and then closed again. "Visiting you? Is that so? How often?"

"Twice a wee—" Mary began, but then Ada said, "Every day. Some days she can get here on her own, but on others I would like to send a carriage to fetch her. Our finest carriage—" Her brow rumpled. "Well, whichever carriage is available. But every day she should be here around noontime, so if you can prepare an extra meal for her, I would greatly appreciate it."

Now it was Mary's mouth that was open.

"But your mother, miss," said the housekeeper. "Does she know about this?"

Ada gave an impatient sigh. "No, she does not. And she does not need to."

The housekeeper's mouth pressed into a troubled line. "But—"

"Oh, come on, Pell," said Ada. "You're always saying that I should be spending time with young ladies my own age. This is my chance. Surely you wouldn't deny me that."

The housekeeper thought for a moment, and then relented. "All right, miss. At least while your mother's away."

"And how long is my mother going to be away?" Ada asked primly. "She failed to inform me."

"Oh. Well. She told me it would be a fortnight," said the housekeeper. (A fortnight, dear reader, was a span of approximately two weeks.)

"Good. Thank you, Pell," said Ada, dismissing her. "Oh, and can you bring us some towels?" She turned toward the grand marble staircase that would return them to the upstairs floors but suddenly stumbled and fell, emitting a frustrated cry of pain.

Mary rushed forward, but Miss Pell beat her to Ada's side, lifting her. "You've been overexerting yourself, miss," she scolded gently, helping Ada limp over to an upholstered bench along the wall. "You must take things more slowly."

"I am fine," Ada said. "I simply misstepped." She flexed her left leg out in front of her from under her skirts, winced, and then retracted it.

"Shall I call for Helix?" Miss Pell asked.

Ada's cheeks filled with color. She shook her head firmly. "No need. I only require a moment to rest. And those towels," she reminded Miss Pell. "Now, please. I don't wish to catch a chill."

Miss Pell hurried away.

The girls were silent for a long while as Ada continued to work her leg back and forth and Mary attempted to come up with something to say that wouldn't be completely awkward. Finally she settled on: "You wish me to come here every day?"

Ada glanced at the floor. "I'm going to construct the metal man, remember—the best automaton ever created. I thought you'd like to assist me. If that would be agreeable to you."

Mary nodded. "All right." It would be a chance to get out of her family's stuffy old apartment, after all, and experience something besides writer's block. Something exciting. And she could practice this strange new power.

Miss Pell abruptly returned with the towels and a tall, broad-shouldered man in tow.

Ada glanced up at him sharply. "Thank you, Helix, but that won't be necessary."

"Are you sure, miss?" persisted Miss Pell.

Ada's chin lifted. "Quite sure. I find myself sufficiently recovered now. Will you fetch me my cane?" She nodded toward the floor, where the cane had dropped when she'd fallen.

As Mary was closest, she bent and retrieved the cane. It had obviously been constructed from the same assortment of metals as Ivan the horse, with a worn flexible padding at the handle and some kind of pivoting joint at the base. Mary handed it to Ada, who shooed Miss Pell and Mr. Helix away, rolled her shoulders to stretch them, and stood to face the stairs again.

"Helix used to carry me sometimes, during my illness," Ada explained as she and Mary made their way slowly up to the second floor, Ada using both the cane and the banister for support. "I'm much more ambulatory than I was. But I'm still tired from last night's exertions. And today's."

Again, Mary restrained herself from asking about the illness. "I'm rather winded, myself." Her breath caught when she beheld the steepness of the final set of stairs—the ones leading to the attic. But then Ada popped out a little chair from against the landing that quickly and easily lifted her to the top. Mary trotted up after her.

Instead of resting, Ada looped the strap of her cane around her wrist and immediately walked over to the magic door that Miss Stamp had brought Mary through—and through which she'd soon return. "What's on the other side of this door?"

"Other doors," answered Mary, toweling her damp hair.

"What other doors?"

"It's a room entirely full of doors," Mary answered enthusiastically. "On every surface of every wall. Of all shapes and sizes." She rattled off descriptions of some of the doors she'd seen as she'd passed through earlier. "Who knows where they all lead to?"

"I should very much like to see that," Ada pronounced. She tried to open the magic door again. It was still locked. "Drat. Could you bring me that stool there?" Ada went to a trunk on the far side of the attic and rummaged around for a few tools, which she put into various pockets. Then she returned promptly to the door, balanced herself on the stool, and began to work on picking the lock. Because apparently that was a bit of a hobby of hers.

"I'll need to be able to send you messages," she said as she prodded at the door. Her tongue poked out for a second as she concentrated. "In case my mother returns earlier than expected. Or if there's anything you need to communicate with me. The messages should be relayed in a kind of code, for security reasons." Her expression brightened. (There was nothing Ada loved more than code.) "I'll get to work on it immediately. Well, right after—"

She didn't finish her sentence, because just then the door swung outward, knocking her off the stool, and Miss Stamp stepped out.

"Gracious," sighed Miss Stamp, gazing down at her student sprawled on the floor. "It's not that kind of lock, dear." She helped Ada to her feet and then back to her seat at the worktable. "What's this?" She touched the sketch of Ada's new automaton, the miraculous metal man.

Ada snatched the paper out of her view. "Nothing. Well, nothing yet."

Miss Stamp shrugged and then turned to Mary. "Are you ready to go home now?"

Mary nodded reluctantly. She had a strange thought then, like she would never really be able to go home again, because nothing in her world was the same as it was yesterday. It was a new world.

"And you girls got along all right?" Miss Stamp inquired.

"Yes," said Mary. She found that she liked Ada very much.

"We got along famously," agreed Ada. The girls exchanged a conspiratorial look that communicated that they would never, ever, definitely not tell Miss Stamp about the incident with Ivan and the now-broken carriage.

"I thought you might." Miss Stamp smiled broadly. "Mark my words: you two are going to become the best of friends."

EIGHT
Ada

Ada had never really had a friend before. Sure, she'd had governesses she'd adored (such as Miss Stamp), and tutors she especially enjoyed (such as Lady Somerville), but they'd inevitably been chased off by Lady Byron, who could not stand for Ada to have anyone in her life beyond a mother. Ada had certainly never had friends her own age, not even when she'd been a small girl, and definitely not while she'd been ill and more isolated than ever.

But now, with Mary sitting across the worktable, her brow furrowed and a strand of blond hair come loose from her braid, a piece of Ada locked into place, some vital part that had been lacking before. Having Mary here every day, Ada found that she liked having a friend. She looked forward to their hours together. And she thought, perhaps, Mary was feeling the same way, because every day for the last week and a half, Mary had shown up precisely on schedule, either by magic door or by carriage, but always wearing a smile, ready for lessons or work.

Ada glanced up—beyond Miss Stamp—at the tall, covered figure in the corner.

"It's important to remember," Miss Stamp said, "that even though it seems like you can create something out of nothing, that is not actually possible. It comes from somewhere."

"That's the law of conservation of mass," Ada said. "Nothing comes from nothing." It was an old idea—ancient Greek philosophy old—and had been supported over the centuries by scientists working in a number of fields, from chemistry to physics to biology. Now it was known as the law of conservation of mass, which basically stated that matter could not be created or destroyed, only changed.

"Precisely. So, while we can work more quickly than most people, fae magic follows the same basic rules. To build a house, you must have the materials. To prepare a meal, you must have the ingredients. The only difference is that you can put it all together with a thought, creating something huge and complex in a matter of seconds—if you know how it works. Which is one of the reasons we train in Ada's attic. There are always things to take apart and study here."

That was true. They'd gone through the trunks to find old gowns to learn how the shapes were cut, how the hems were stitched, how the brocade was applied. They'd found a pile of old portraits to disassemble, which taught them about the frames, backing, canvas, and paint. And they'd uncovered an old spinning wheel, which had come apart and gone back together several times by now.

"Now," Miss Stamp said, "knowing that your materials will come from somewhere, you must create responsibly. If you make something, you will destroy something else. If you add a piece to something, you will take a piece from another thing."

Like the carriage, Ada thought.

Mary scratched the back of her neck uncomfortably.

"You must always pay attention to the cost," Miss Stamp said. "If you don't gather your ingredients yourself, they will come from somewhere, and the effects of that will be random."

"And we don't like random," Ada said. "Because someone might notice."

"Which would put all fae at risk," Mary finished.

They had gone over *this* part at every lesson so far, possibly because Miss Stamp somehow knew about the carriage situation, but most likely because no one was supposed to know about fae. It wasn't safe for them if people knew what they could do.

"Very good. Now, how do you decide what the cost will be?" Miss Stamp asked Mary.

"Well"—Mary consulted her notes—"if you want to add something metal to, let's say, a metal horse, then you'll take something metal. You can look around and see what options there are nearby, what might cause the least amount of trouble for people if it's gone."

Miss Stamp nodded, eyeing Mary suspiciously.

"And once you've decided on, let's say, a pile of old horseshoes, then you'll put both things into your mind and draw a line between them. A mental line, not a real one with a pencil. You will imagine the horseshoes becoming the new shoulders for the horse."

"Well said, Mary. Now I'd like you to try it. Ada, make a key. Use those nails as your materials." She pointed to a small jar of bent nails that Ada had never been able to throw away, in case they were ever useful again. (And here they were! Useful!)

Ada spilled the nails onto the table and glared at them. She imagined the lengths of iron as a heavy skeleton key. She imagined the weight in her hand. She imagined the rough texture of the metal. And she imagined the way it would fit into a lock.

Nails. Key. Nails. Key.

Nothing.

She clenched her jaw and tried again, this time imagining the way all the nails would meld together and—

"Ada, you should breathe." Miss Stamp touched her shoulder. "Holding your breath won't help you focus. Your brain needs air."

Ada sighed and sat back. "I can't do it. I'm trying. I really am." She had never been a bad student in all her life, but at this, she was a monumental failure. "Perhaps I'm not actually fae."

But Miss Stamp was optimistic. "Some fae come into their abilities later than others, and some have to work harder at it. You should keep trying. I believe you will get it."

Ada was not so sure.

There was a clatter of nails rearranging themselves in the pile, and then a small thump. When Ada looked down on the table again, she found a big iron key, not quite like the one she'd been imagining but fairly close. Had she—

No. She hadn't even been trying, and Mary's face was suddenly red.

"Sorry," Mary said, sinking back into her chair. "I was imagining that Ada had done it, and suddenly the key was there and I promise I wasn't trying to show off."

"I know you weren't," Miss Stamp said.

Ada knew, too. Mary was a natural. She grasped this imagination business in the same way Ada understood numbers. Every exercise, every lesson, she *got* it in a way that Ada could not.

Miss Stamp sighed. "That will be all for today, I think. You've both worked hard. Mary, shall I take you home?"

Mary shook her head. "We're nearly finished with our project. I can take a carriage home, can't I, Ada?"

Ada nodded, relieved to get back to something that she was good at.

"All right, then I'm off. I'll see you next week, my dears." Miss Stamp went through the magic door, and then Ada and Mary were alone.

Mary pulled the sheet off the automaton and laid it aside. "Look at him," she said. "He's perfect."

Ada had to agree. The parts for the automaton had come from a variety of places, like an iron grate from the kitchen stove, the wheel of a broken-down sewing machine, an assortment of brass lamps, the pile of old horseshoes (that Mary had not used to fix Ivan), an aluminum washboard, and an assortment of other pieces of metal that Ada and Mary had found around the house. Twice, they'd had to flee Pell; once after she'd caught them taking her clothes iron, and another time when they'd raided the kitchen for the copper lids to her pots.

But the automaton looked nothing like any of those items. Over the last week and a half, in between Mary's visits, Ada had painstakingly designed every piece of this machine, every pin, every gear, every cam, every rod. She'd written out tables and tables of numbers, calculations for gear size, tooth length, and timing. Then she'd drawn precisely what was needed, down to the smallest detail—even the grit of the metal—and what material should be used to create it.

That had been where Mary came in. When they weren't having lessons with Miss Stamp, and when they weren't eating Pell's delicious lunches, Mary went through Ada's "to create" pile and created the exact items that Ada asked for.

Now, standing before them, their metal man gleamed brightly in the afternoon sun. (There was a rare break in the clouds, and Ada and Mary both found themselves squinting. What was this strange light?) He was tall and slender, with large silver-colored gears in all his joints, and graceful curves of metal protecting his insides. Where humans had bones and muscles, he had rods and pistons, practical parts for a mechanical boy. Some items, however, were purely decorative. Silver-plated kneecaps that spun when he walked. There was a storage compartment in his stomach (you never knew when you might need a secret storage compartment), a keyhole in his chest (where all his clockworks would be wound), and a control panel on his right wrist, where Ada could command him to perform any number of the tasks she was programming into him.

Yes, he was amazing. He had a great . . . body.

"He needs a head," Mary observed. "We should put it on."

"Not without a face."

"Mr. Babbage had a plaster face on the silver dancer. Will we do the same?"

"No. The other day, I put in an order for a lump of clay. It arrived this morning."

"A clay face? That sounds even scarier."

Ada snorted. "We'll make a metal face. One of the reasons that so many automatons have wax or porcelain faces is that it's time-consuming and expensive to make a metal one."

"Oh," Mary said. "I thought they just wanted automatons to be horrifyingly realistic."

"That, too. But *we* can mold the perfect face onto the clay, and you can replicate the shape onto the metal head." She motioned to the roundish piece of metal at the automaton's feet. The head had a neck hole, but no ears, and not even the suggestion of a nose or eyes. It was totally blank.

They worked together in companionable quiet for a while, with Mary shaping the clay into a head, pressing hollows for eyes, smoothing her thumbs up to create cheekbones, as Ada busied herself producing tools to draw the fine lines of his mouth and nose. By the time they were finished, the metal man looked like a whole and complete person, one whose features had been hiding in the clay, waiting to be brought to the surface.

"He's a piece of art," Mary announced.

Ada agreed. "Are you ready to put his face on his head?"

"I am."

Ada stood back, even though this shouldn't be explosive, and right before her eyes, the blank metal slowly came to resemble the clay face they'd fashioned. It was, quite literally, magical.

"Excellent," Ada said. "It'll take me a few minutes to attach it properly. Will you bring me a chair to stand on? And hand me tools? And stay close? My leg is hurting again and I don't want to fall."

When Mary came back with a chair, she wore that expression Ada was so familiar with—the inquisitive-but-not-wanting-to-be-rude look.

"You curious about my illness, aren't you?" Ada left her cane by the wall. Then she braced herself on the wooden back of the chair and climbed up, right leg first. When both feet were on the chair, she tested her balance before standing up straight. "I don't mind talking about it." Ada held out her hand. "Head, please."

Up came the head.

"One day, shortly after I turned thirteen, I awakened with a blazing headache, a fever, and my whole body felt sluggish. It took so much effort even to get out of bed." She held out her hand again. "Spanner." (In American, this is a wrench.)

Up came a spanner.

As she carefully placed the head atop the neck, minding all the delicate gears and shafts, Ada said, "That was a bad day. Mother sent me straight back to bed, instead of allowing me to see my tutors. But the next day was worse. By then, I wasn't able to move my legs at all." She put her hand down and started to ask for a pin, but Mary had anticipated her need and was already offering it up. "Even though I couldn't move my legs, I could still feel them. The pain was excruciating. I thought that would be the end of me, dead at thirteen, without ever having—"

"Kissed a boy," Mary sighed.

"Made a contribution to science."

"Oh." Mary blushed. "And that's why you're working so hard now?"

Ada locked the head into place. "Perhaps. Being sick was dreadfully boring, aside from the frightful pain. I spent all my time in bed, reading, solving math problems, trying to learn. I read every book on science that Mother would order for me. But even after I felt better, my legs were weak, and I couldn't get out of bed on my own. Mother wouldn't allow a doctor to help me with *that* part of my recovery, though, so I did it myself."

It had been difficult and painful work, first just persuading her legs to move, and later lifting and bending them to build up muscles. She would never say it out loud, but she'd sometimes felt her recovery had been intentionally slowed, thanks to her mother always wanting Ada all to herself. That was why no doctors had been brought to help her walk again.

Ada passed her tools back down to Mary. "After not being able to walk for so long, I'm grateful to be using a cane now."

"It does give you a rather dignified look."

Slowly, Ada climbed down from the chair.

They both looked up at the automaton, now with a head. His face was pleasant to look at: eyebrows lifted slightly in a neutral but kind expression, a fine, straight nose, and full, slightly parted lips—as though he were about to speak. His jaw and chin were a perfect balance between delicate and strong.

"How very handsome," Mary remarked.

"How very practical," Ada said. "I think that's what I'm going to call him, actually. Practical Automaton Number One. PAN for short."

"Number one? Wouldn't that be PANO?"

"No! One the numeral, not the word."

"So are you going to make a second automaton?"

Ada shrugged. "I might. You never know. Anyway, call him PAN. It's practical."

"I'm afraid to ask what Ivan stands for." Mary looked up at PAN again. "Is he finished, then?"

"Almost. I have a few tasks to program into him, but I can do that on my own. He'll be fully functional soon." Right in time for her bimonthly dinner with Mr. Babbage. "I suppose Helix is waiting to take you home now. It's nearly dark."

They looked out the window, where the clouds had gone back to their typical heavy looming. It was, indeed, dark. And raining. Again.

"Oh, before I go," Mary said. "I would like to invite you to a reading at the bookshop. It's tomorrow night. Do you think you could make it?"

"A reading?" Ada tilted her head. She was curious about the bookshop, because Mary lived there, and that seemed like an ideal home, but also because it would be quite a thing to see Mary in her natural habitat. "What . . . is being read?"

Mary's mouth formed a line.

Ada raised an eyebrow.

"Poetry," Mary mumbled.

Ada gasped and glanced around, but it was only the two of them in the room—and PAN, but he wouldn't tell anyone.

"I know," Mary said, "but if I can introduce you to my family, they'll be more accepting of my explanation as to where I'm disappearing to every day."

Ada frowned. "Who's reading? Anyone I've heard of?" The only poets she knew of were her father and his friends. The names Tennyson and Coleridge had been bandied about at the Babbage party, but she didn't know anything about them aside from the fact that they did some sort of writing.

"It's Shelley. Percy Shelley, I mean." Mary bit her lip.

"Why is your face like that?" Ada asked. "And why did you say his name like that?"

Mary gave a tiny shrug.

"Is he your beau?"

Another tiny shrug.

"Are you going to marry this Shelley poet fellow?"

"We don't believe in marriage," Mary said. "We just take walks together. And we talk."

"What do you talk about?"

"Oh, this and that," said Mary vaguely. "Sometimes we talk about the weather."

"Rain," supplied Ada.

Mary nodded, her eyes a bit dreamy. "We also discuss history and philosophy and the complexities of the human condition. And we often talk about writing." For some reason this made Mary blush. "He took my hand once. At the Babbage party, when we were watching Aldini's demonstration. It was dark, so no one else saw."

Ada held her fingers to her mouth. "He took your hand in front of everyone!"

"No one else saw!" Mary cried again. "But it was wonderful. It made me feel all fluttery inside."

"What about kissing?" Ada pressed, remembering how Mary had mentioned kissing earlier.

"No kissing yet," Mary said. "But soon, I hope. I'm certain it will be as lovely as those three seconds he held my hand."

"Better, ideally." Ada grinned. "Well, when it happens, you must tell me all about it. *I* will never kiss anyone."

"No?" Mary tilted her head. "I know there are vast differences between our stations, and there's likely to be no kissing in your future until you're married. But what about then? Won't you kiss your husband?"

"Nope." Ada lifted her chin. "All I want in life is to create science like no one's ever seen before. When I'm forced to marry, I shall simply lie back and think of electromagnetism."

"How wildly romantic," Mary said. "But about the poetry reading. Say you'll come."

Ada gazed up at the automaton, thinking. Her dinner with Mr. Babbage was two days from now, and she had four days before her mother was scheduled to return. Pell and the other house staff wouldn't tell on Ada. They all seemed so pleased that she had a friend her own age. And friends, well, they went out of their comfort zones for one another, didn't they? Look at all the work Mary had done on their automaton, even though she didn't know a thing about mechanical engineering.

"All right," Ada said. "I'll be there. What time is this"—she lowered her voice—"poetry reading?"

Mary

NINE

Mary checked her pocket watch for the umpteenth time. It was fourteen minutes to six (just two minutes from the last time she'd checked) and Ada still hadn't arrived. She peered out her bedroom window down into the street, which was deserted, the cobblestones gleaming with rain but not even a single person headed toward the bookshop. (This was not a good sign, dear reader, right before a book event.) Mary sighed and fiddled with the brooch at her neck, one of the only pieces of jewelry the Godwins owned that had not been pawned over the past year. The profile cut into the ivory was that of Mary Wollstonecraft.

"Is she here yet?" Jane popped her head into the bedroom. Jane had practically been bouncing off the walls since Mary had reluctantly informed her family that they were going to have a very special guest at tonight's reading: Miss Ada BYRON. Jane had squealed for a full sixty seconds after she'd heard that name, and then rushed off to decide what to wear to best impress Ada. Mrs. Godwin, on the other hand, had simply looked confused.

"You know Ada Byron? *You?*" she'd asked incredulously.

"Yes," Mary had answered with a slight edge to her voice. "I do."

"Hmph."

"How wonderful." Mr. Godwin had beamed at the idea of a BYRON in his bookshop. "I wasn't aware that you and Miss Byron were acquainted."

"We met at Mr. Babbage's party." This wasn't entirely accurate, but it had been Babbage's party—the frog demonstration, and what came after—that had led Mary to Ada, so Mary supposed that this was only a tiny white lie. "And afterward I was, um, invited to her house, and since then we've become friends."

At that, Mr. Godwin's smile had grown even brighter. "So that's where you've been disappearing to every day!" he'd exclaimed. "You see? I knew that party was going to improve our standing in the world. Well done, my dear."

He'd made it sound like she had befriended Ada on purpose in order to take advantage of her fame and fortune. And while Mary knew this wasn't true, part of her was quite aware that her association with Ada had created a marked improvement to her own day-to-day existence. She gained so much, spending her days with Ada. But what did Ada gain?

An invitation to a poetry reading in a run-down bookstore in a sketchier part of London.

"No," Mary replied to Jane's earlier question. "She's not here yet."

Jane gave an exaggerated pout and then flounced off.

Mary checked her watch again. Twelve minutes to six. But hark!—Mary detected the faint clatter of horse hooves outside. She rushed to the window. There it was: the Byrons' finest carriage, drawn by a pair of beautiful white horses. The footman had opened the door and helped Ada step down from the carriage.

Mary's stomach did a little flip of excitement. She didn't know why she was so nervous. She saw Ada every day. Ada saw her. But this felt different. This was Ada venturing into Mary's world.

Mary compulsively straightened her brooch and then slowly, making no sound or sudden movements that might alert anyone in her family to Ada's arrival, made her way out of her bedroom and to the narrow stairs that led to the bookshop. Then she walked swiftly to open the door just as Ada stepped up to the threshold.

Mary experienced that disoriented feeling you get when you see your high school English teacher at the grocery store. This Ada, resplendently dressed in gleaming white satin, jewels glittering from her neck and ears and fingers, her dark hair curled and coiffed, was not the Ada Mary was used to encountering. Mary knew Ada-of-the-attic, in her simple day dresses and her hasty, casual braid thrown over one shoulder.

Ada was staring at Mary, too. Color rose in her cheeks. "Oh," she said dully. "I'm overdressed, aren't I? This is the same gown I wore to the Babbage party. I don't have anything else to go out with."

"You're fine," Mary said. "Come in."

She ushered Ada into the bookshop. For a moment they simply stood near the door, taking in the rows of bookshelves housing the numerous books, the various comfortable chairs set around for people to read in, the flickering lamps.

"It's just a bookshop," Mary said. "But it's my home."

"I think it would be quite nice to live in a bookshop," said Ada, glancing around appreciatively. "You'll never want for something to read."

"Well, we don't live *in* the bookshop," Mary clarified. "We live above it." She didn't intend to show her new friend the apartments upstairs. Compared with Ada's extravagant house, the Godwin residence would seem very shabby.

"Still, it would be a wonderful thing to live in such close proximity to so many books," said Ada kindly. "Are any of them about mathematics? Or . . ." Her blue eyes brightened. "Science?"

"Yes," Mary laughed. "This way."

But before they reached the mathematics section, Jane stepped out from between two bookcases and cleared her throat loudly.

Drat. This part was going to be awkward. "Oh. Yes. May I present my stepsister, Jane Clairmont?" stammered Mary.

"How do you do?" said Ada politely.

"I'm considering changing my name to Claire," announced Jane.

Ada's brows furrowed. "So then you'd be Claire Clairmont?"

"Exactly."

"That's . . . nice," said Ada.

"And you are Ada BYRON," squealed Jane.

"Yes, I'm aware," said Ada wryly.

"I've written Lord Byron three letters this month," Jane said. "He hasn't written me back, but then it must take some time for a letter to go first to his publisher and then to wherever he is. Where is he, by the way?"

"I don't know."

"Oh." Jane was crestfallen.

"I'm sorry," Ada said.

Mary steered her away from her stepsister and toward the math books, shooing Jane away behind her back. "This was probably a terrible idea, you coming here. My family is somewhat mortifying."

"It's nice to see where you live," Ada said. "After all, you've been to my house often enough. Ooh, here's a book I haven't read about Pythagoras!" She stood her cane up beside her and clapped her hands excitedly. "And another one about Archimedes!"

Mary smiled. Maybe it wasn't a *wholly* terrible idea, inviting Ada over.

But then Mr. Godwin appeared beside them.

"Ah, this must be the illustrious Miss Byron," he said before Mary could get out any proper introduction. "I'm William Godwin, Mary's father. Your very presence, my dear, is a great honor."

Ugh, he was embarrassing.

"Thank you," said Ada. "I'm honored, as well."

"I've never met Lord Byron." Mary's father looked mournful. "I've met many great men, but not him. I've always wanted to meet him."

"I haven't really met him, either," Ada said stiffly.

"Anyway, Father . . ." Mary said somewhat desperately. She checked the pocket watch. Five minutes to six. "Isn't the reading about to start?"

"Our reader has not yet arrived," he said. "While you're waiting, would you like to see our art collection?"

Mary stared at him. What art collection? Then she realized that he probably meant to show her the painting of Mary's mother that was hanging in the parlor. Which would mean going up the steep and narrow stairs (which would no doubt be uncomfortable for Ada) and seeing just how shabby things were in Mary's regular life (which would certainly be uncomfortable for Mary).

"Oh, Father, I'm sure Miss Byron doesn't need to—" Mary protested.

"That's all right," Ada said quickly. "I've never really enjoyed art the way I ought to."

Mr. Godwin looked aghast. "You don't enjoy art?"

"I'm afraid not," Ada admitted. "Believe me, I've tried. A few years ago I was carted all over Europe to see the most famous paintings in the world, so that I might develop a taste for art. But I never could. I did like the windows," she added. "In Notre Dame."

Mary had never been to Paris, but she could imagine that Notre Dame had very good windows, indeed.

"And the architecture of the ceilings," continued Ada. "That was truly beautiful. That was art, I think."

Mary smiled. "I should like to see the windows in Notre Dame. And the ceilings."

"Interesting," said Mary's father distractedly. "Oh good. Shelley's here." He darted off to greet his protégé.

Thunder rumbled outside. Mary's pulse picked up the way it did every time she saw Shelley. She watched from across the room as Shelley ran his hand through his lustrous brown hair. He was talking to her father. He was smiling. He had such a perfect smile.

"So that's Percy Shelley," said Ada, following Mary's gaze. "Well, he certainly is handsome, isn't he?"

"Is he?" said Mary faintly. "I hadn't noticed."

"Ladies and gentlemen!" William Godwin called out. "Please join us in the reading room, where Mr. Percy Bysshe Shelley will delight us with some of his poetry."

Mary and Ada ambled into the reading room. Her father had (rather overambitiously) set out about fifty chairs, and there were exactly seven people who'd shown up for the reading, including Ada, but not including Mary's family. Which brought the total number of audience members to twelve.

Mary moved to sit in the front row.

Ada grabbed her arm. "What are you doing?"

"If we all sit in the front, it won't seem quite so empty," Mary explained.

Ada looked reluctant—she clearly preferred the back for such scandalous things as poetry readings, but she acquiesced.

In the front row, they were only a few feet from Shelley.

"Good evening, Miss Godwin," he said in a voice just for Mary, which made her feel warm all over. "How are you tonight?"

"I am quite well," Mary answered. Their eyes met. Held. "How are you?"

"Quite well," he murmured. "Now that I'm here."

"Hey, Shelley," said Jane, plopping herself down next to Ada.

"Hello, Jane," he replied. "Or should I say, Claire?"

Jane beamed. "I've been looking forward to hearing you read all week. Of course, I've already devoured your book. Your poems speak to my very soul."

"Thank you." Shelley looked at Mary again. "Have *you* read my book, young lady?"

"I've skimmed it," she teased. Of course she'd read his book. He knew quite well that she had. It was one of the things they'd talked about, in those conversations they'd had on their walks together. She'd soaked in every line of his book, because through it she could learn something more, however small, about Shelley.

Shelley's gaze flitted over to Ada. "And you?"

"I'm not allowed to read"—Ada glanced around—"poetry. In fact, if my mother knew I was here . . ." She shuddered.

"This is Ada *Byron*," announced Jane, leaning into Ada and clutching her arm like the two were the best of friends.

Mary closed her eyes for a moment in sheer mortification.

"Is that so?" Shelley said, his eyebrows lifting. "What a pleasure it is to meet you, Miss Byron. I've spent time with your father on several occasions. He's a great man, and a sensational poet. Perhaps the most influential poet of our time."

"So everyone tells me." Ada's expression tightened. Mary wondered what it must be like for Ada to hear people speak of her father. Perhaps the way that Mary herself felt when people mentioned Mary Wollstonecraft.

Mary's father approached the podium. "Ladies and gentlemen!" he cried again loudly, as if his voice had to carry over a large crowd. "Let us begin. It is with the greatest pleasure that I would like to introduce my protégé, Mr. Percy Bysshe Shelley. Mr. Shelley comes from a prominent family—his grandfather is a member of Parliament, as you must already know—and was educated at the very finest schools, where he began to write his stupendous poetry. . . ."

Her father went on, something about how Shelley's work was full of "love, sorrow, hope, nature, and politics." Clap, clap, clap, went the tiny crowd, and Shelley took a stack of rumpled papers from the inside of his jacket, cleared his throat, and began to read from *Queen Mab: A Philosophical Poem, With Notes.*

"The foreword is a bit about my favorite subject: love," Shelley said.

Ada gave a tiny, almost imperceptible groan. Mary leaned forward. Shelley began to read:

> *Beneath whose looks did my reviving soul*
> *Riper in truth and virtuous daring grow?*

In the book, Mary remembered, this part had been inscribed to someone named Harriet, but now Shelley's blue gaze swung to

Mary again. "*Dear girl, on thine,*" he read. "*Thou wert my purer mind. Thou wert the inspiration of my song.*"

She suppressed a delighted smile.

Shelley paused, signaling that this part was done. Jane and Mary clapped wildly. Ada gave the 1800s equivalent of a golf clap.

"Thank you," said Shelley. "And now for the actual book." He launched right into it.

How wonderful is Death,
Death and his brother Sleep!

He then read The. Entire. Book. Out. Loud. It was all interesting stuff, but the mix of purple language and Shelley's views of the world didn't really come to life when read out loud. And it took him like an hour and a half to get through it all.

By the end, even Mary was tired of hearing his voice.

At last, he got to the final line.

"*And the bright beaming stars, that through the casement shone,*" he finished, and smiled triumphantly.

"Oh, thank goodness," whispered Ada, clapping.

"And now I'd like to read another something that I've been working on," said Shelley.

"Oh drat," muttered Ada.

"'Ode to the Moon,'" Shelley read solemnly.

By now Mary was feeling rather sorry for Shelley. Nobody in the crowd had been particularly spellbound by what he'd written.

Or even very much entertained. If only there could be something to supplement his reading, Mary thought. Something to give the audience some visual stimulation. Something to spice it up a bit.

"*Art thou pale for weariness of climbing heaven and gazing on the earth,*" Shelley read.

Well, why not? Mary decided. She could help him out. It was what a good girlfriend would do. So right then Mary imagined the moon shining down on Shelley. It was much easier than converting a bunch of nails into a key. She only had to borrow the light from somewhere—say, one of the bookshop lanterns—and reshape it into a kind of hologram (although Mary wouldn't have known to call it that) of a bright orb glowing near the ceiling.

The moon.

The small crowd gave a tiny collective gasp.

Shelley paused for a moment, confused. Then he looked up, and also gasped.

Yes, it was the moon, all right, clear as—well, not day. Clear as the moon. At night. One could even see the little face on it.

Shelley coughed and glanced quickly back at his paper. He cleared his throat. "*Wandering companionless among the stars that have a different birth. And ever changing, like a joyless eye.*"

Mary imagined the moon shifting through its phases: first full, then waning, and then a sliver.

The audience murmured in approval as the moon changed. Mary felt a bit giddy. She was breaking the rules, using her power in public. What would Miss Stamp say? Mary glanced quickly at Ada, but her friend seemed as mesmerized as everyone else.

"That finds no object worth its constancy?" said Shelley. He paused again.

Everyone was still staring breathlessly at the moon.

Shelley fidgeted. "Uh. That's it. That's the poem."

Quickly Mary imagined the moon fading away, returning its light to the lamp.

William Godwin rose from his chair, cheering. "That was marvelous, my boy, simply marvelous! Did I mention that he's my student?"

"That was marvelous," agreed Ada softly.

"I know," whispered Mary guiltily. But it was such a small thing. No real cost. And nobody would guess that she had done it. Indeed, no one was even looking at Mary now. Everyone was still cheering for Shelley. They thought he had done it all, some clever illusion he'd pulled off.

"Thank you," he murmured. But now he was gazing at Mary. And he smiled.

Which kind of made it all worth it.

TEN

Ada

Well, thank God that's over, Ada thought as the poetry reading finally ended.

That was nearly two hours of her life she'd never get back. Two. Hours.

Everyone rose from their seats, excitedly discussing the moon and how gentle its light had shone over Shelley, how strange that was (moons did not suddenly appear at most readings, Ada surmised), and how excited they were to have witnessed such a thing.

"If you would like to purchase a copy of Mr. Shelley's book," Mr. Godwin said, wheeling out a cart full of copies of *Queen Mab*, "please form an orderly line."

Seven people—all six guests and Jane—shuffled to stand in front of the table, where Mr. Shelley sat and began setting out his pen and ink.

"How did you do the moon thing?" the first man wanted to know.

"Poetry is a kind of magic, don't you think?" Shelley replied.

"Have we all been drugged as part of an experiment?" the next man asked.

"Who can say what reality is anymore?" Shelley answered.

Mary drew Ada aside, behind a bookcase filled with Austen novels. "Well?" Mary's face practically glowed.

"Well what?" Ada asked. "The poetry? I'm in no position to tell if it was good or not. I have nothing to compare it to."

"No, I mean Shelley! What do you think of him? Isn't he wonderful?"

Ada peered around the bookcase to see Shelley signing a book to the third person in line—who must have also asked about the moon, because now Shelley was sending Mr. Godwin to find a drawing of the moon that he could copy into the book.

"He's very excited about poetry," Ada observed. "And you, I think. I believe you are a good match." It was clear that Mary loved the bookshop, but the reality was that the bookshop wouldn't be able to take care of her for much longer. She would, in spite of her protestations that she didn't believe in marriage, need to marry— same as Ada—and if there *happened* to be a boy she already admired, and he *happened* to be a baronet (and therefore rich), well, it seemed like this could be the ideal solution for her.

A blush rose in Mary's cheeks. "He's such a clever man. And a fine writer."

"So his poetry is considered good?" Ada tilted her head. "Huh."

"Wait, didn't you like it?" Mary gave a mock gasp. "I'd hoped you'd become a secret poetry fan, once you actually heard some. How scandalized your mother would be!"

Ada grinned. "My favorite part was the moon. I've been trying to figure out how you did it."

Mary pulled Ada even deeper into the bookcases. "How do *you* think I did it?"

Ada tapped her chin. "Well, it wasn't the real moon." She frowned, thinking through the ramifications of imagining away the actual moon. "If you'd taken the real moon, we would be part of a very different story right now. First, the gravity that pulls at our oceans would vanish, so all that water would come rushing down very quickly. As we live on an island, that prospect is most concerning. Assuming we survived the massive city-destroying waves, we'd have to endure the catastrophic consequences of a wobbly axial tilt, which would ruin our seasons and make the weather completely unpredictable."

BOOM! Thunder shook the bookstore.

"Ah—" Mary said. "I suppose it's a good thing I didn't accidentally take the real moon."

"Indeed," Ada said. "My other theory is that—somehow—you used candlelight as your material, rearranging whatever particles make up light, and shaped it into your moon. It was an illusion. So, on behalf of the entire planet, thank you for not causing a mass-extinction event."

"Let's not tell Miss Stamp about this."

"All right." Ada smiled brightly. "It was a very pretty moon."

Yet again, Mary had done something incredible.

And Ada hadn't been able to use her fae abilities even once.

She contemplated this for the entire drive home. Now, in the upstairs hall, she paused before a velvet curtain. It would seem strange to guests that Lady Byron had hung a green curtain in the hallway, but Ada hardly noticed it anymore. It had been here nearly all her life, hiding something Ada was not supposed to see.

A portrait of her father.

After the reading, Mr. Godwin had invited Ada up for tea, where a portrait of Mary Wollstonecraft had been prominently displayed in the parlor, so different from this one, hidden away like a shameful secret.

Ada fingers rested on the velvet curtain. Should she peek?

Her father had always been a mystery.

She thought back to a moment many years ago, when Lord Byron had performed his greatest feat to date: he'd died and come back to life.

Eight-year-old Ada had been calculating the airspeed velocity of an unladen swallow when the mourning bells began to toll. Word had spread like wildfire. People showed up at the Byron estate with candles. Finally, Lady Byron had come into Ada's attic and explained that Lord Byron had gone to Greece to fight in their war for independence. He'd been hurt in battle, and later died. But Ada was not to care about it. She was not to cry. Lord Byron had left them both, and she should have no feelings about his death, because he had not been part of her life.

But the rest of England had gone into national mourning. People read his poetry in the streets. A monument was built in his honor. Bookshops lowered their signs to half-mast. How, Ada had wondered, could all these people feel so strongly for her father? Why were they all permitted grief when she was not?

Shortly, a newspaper reported Lord Byron's final words. He'd cried, "Oh, my poor dear child! My dear Ada! My God, could I have seen her! Give her my blessing."

Little Ada had hardly known how to feel about that. It had seemed so unlikely. Performative. But there was part of her, one she wasn't supposed to acknowledge, that wanted to believe he truly had been thinking of her in those final moments.

Then, more news: Lord Byron was *alive*.

No one could say how he'd pulled through. He'd been declared dead. The proper paperwork had been signed. Funeral arrangements had begun. And then, suddenly, he was alive and well. It was the biggest mystery in all of England, and every time Lady Byron and Ada left the house, people wanted to know how he had survived. Where was he now? What would his next book be about?

Lady Byron avoided all those questions and more, and she'd coached Ada to do the same.

Ada had wondered if, now that he'd been given this second chance at life, Lord Byron would seek her out. But still, he did not visit. He didn't even write a letter.

Alive or dead wasn't something he could help, but *not present* was a choice.

"He left us" was something Lady Byron said any time her husband came up. "He's a useless poet, and he's not even that good."

Then why, Ada couldn't help but wonder, had Lady Byron decided to hang the portrait at all? Why cover it with a curtain?

Not for the very first time (but for the first time in a long time), Ada moved the curtain, revealing Lord Byron wearing a red-and-gold jacket of shining velvet, and holding a scimitar cradled in his arms. He stood against a sky of gilded clouds, his face turned at an angle. A red cap hid most of his hair, but Ada knew it was dark, like hers.

She'd inherited much from him. They were similar in appearance, and exactly alike in the way they went about their passions. Poetry for him; science and mathematics for her.

But what about this fae business? Miss Stamp insisted that Lord Byron was fae, and Ada must be, too.

"If I am fae," she whispered, "then I can make a jacket of my own, like the one you're wearing. I can use this curtain to make it. And some of the brocade from the trunks upstairs."

She imagined the jacket—green rather than red—and the way it would fit her, how warm such a garment would be. But when she tried to imagine the stitches, the precise cut of cloth, it all fell apart. Tailoring was not her strong suit.

So she chose something smaller, something she knew very well. A cane. Wood, like the one her mother preferred. Perhaps working with a single material would help, and there were plenty of wooden trunks in the attic. The lid of one, perhaps.

Ada took a deep breath and closed her eyes. She imagined the wood reshaping, all the splinters falling back into the grain, the metal re-forming. She imagined as hard as she could, remembering to breathe, as Miss Stamp had instructed. She imagined the way she thought Mary must be imagining, all the times *she'd* made it work.

But when Ada opened her eyes, the only cane was the one she'd made with her own two hands.

Her heart sank. She couldn't do it. She just couldn't.

And she knew, deep down, that she would never be able to do it. She was not fae.

She swept the curtain over her father. "I suppose I'm not like you after all."

Then, strangely disappointed, she sat in her little chair and cranked herself up to the attic. She didn't *want* to be upset. She'd never believed in magic before. She hadn't needed it—and she still didn't.

She set herself to finishing PAN. The dinner with Mr. Babbage was tomorrow, and she had every intention of showing him up—not with magic, but with science.

Her automaton was going to change the world.

Mary

ELEVEN

There was no doubt in Mary's mind that Ada's automaton was indeed going to change the world. PAN was a marvel. Mr. Babbage would certainly be gobsmacked by the mere sight of him, and that'd be even before Ada revealed all that he could *do*.

It was just too bad that Mary herself was going to miss it.

"But you should be there! You are his creator as much as I am," Ada had argued when they'd discussed it earlier. "You should be given credit."

"And how would you explain my contribution?" Mary had pointed out. "You designed him. You did all the complicated calculations. You provided the materials. I merely shaped some of those materials into the requested form using an improbable kind of magic that no one is supposed to know about. What would Miss Stamp say?"

Ada had frowned. "I suppose you're right."

Mary *was* right. (She took a moment to appreciate the rarity of a moment when she was right and Ada wasn't.) And this was why now, instead of being over at the Byron estate polishing up their miraculous metal man and preparing to reveal him to the world (er, Mr. Babbage), Mary was stuck here, at home, in the parlor with her sisters. Doing nothing.

Well, she supposed it wasn't nothing, *exactly*. For more than an hour she'd been attempting to write, but any real idea was still stubbornly eluding her. It was ironic, she thought, that she could so easily produce something using fae magic—she could imagine a thing and make it real—but she could not imagine a story.

Which made Mary wonder if she wasn't meant to be a writer, after all.

She sighed, set her writing materials aside, and moved to the sofa with a book. She hadn't even made it past the first page, however, when the door to her father's study opened, and Shelley appeared.

"Hello, Miss Godwin," he said, blue eyes beaming into her.

"Hello, Mr. Shelley," she returned.

"Fine day today, isn't it?"

She lowered her book and glanced at the window. The sky outside was a muted gray. Rain threatened. As usual. "Very fine," she said.

From beside her on the sofa, Jane also lowered her book—*How To Be A Respectable Famous Actress, Volume Six*. "Are you really going to talk about the weather?"

Shelley shifted his attention to Jane, smiling. "Perhaps you'd like to accompany me for a walk, Miss Clairmont? Being that it's such a fine day."

Here it was: the familiar ruse. Shelley asked Jane to walk with him. Mary volunteered as chaperone. Then, approximately fifty paces from the door of the bookshop, Mary and Jane switched places, with Jane walking behind at a considerable distance, to give Mary and Shelley a semblance of privacy.

"Well," said Jane, pursing her lips like she was thinking it over. "I am fond of walking, as you know. I walk all the time. It's how I get places."

"Excellent," said Shelley. He held out his arm. "Shall we?"

But then Mrs. Godwin, who'd been in the next room polishing the silverware, stepped into the doorway. "No," she said firmly, in much the same tone as one would use to admonish a hopeful dog. "No walk today."

This was a surprise. Mrs. Godwin had always approved of Jane walking with Shelley before. They made such "a fine pair," after all. But right now the look that the older woman was bestowing upon Shelley was decidedly cool.

Mary's breath caught. Had Mrs. Godwin noticed the way Shelley had seemed to address Mary when he was reciting that bit about love last night at the reading? Blast—they should have taken greater care to hide their affections. Mary felt a flash of dismay, but it was followed by a healthy dose of rebellion. So what if Mrs. Godwin knew about Mary's romance with Shelley? She was bound to find out sometime. And surely Mrs. Godwin could admit that Shelley taking an interest in any of the Godwin girls would be of benefit to their family. Financially and otherwise.

Jane tried to remedy the situation. "But, Mother," she protested. "I really do feel as though I could use a bit of fresh air. A walk would do me good."

Mrs. Godwin shook her head. "It would not be appropriate for you to walk with Mr. Shelley unsupervised."

"But of course we wouldn't be unsupervised," Shelley replied smoothly. "Mary will be our chaperone. Won't you, Mary?"

Mary nodded. "Of course. As I also quite enjoy walking."

Mrs. Godwin peered dubiously out the window. "It's hardly a lovely day. It looks like rain, in fact."

"It always looks like rain!" Mary exclaimed. "If we never went out when it looked like rain, we'd never go out! This is England!"

"We'll take an umbrella," said Shelley sagely.

"And I'll come along, too," murmured Fanny. You didn't even know she was there, did you? But she was, reading her own book—*The Best Embroidery Patterns of 18—Smudged Date*. Which she now set aside. "I also like walks."

"Hmph." Mrs. Godwin crossed her arms. "Nevertheless, I don't think it's wise to—"

"Oh, let them go, dear" came Mr. Godwin's disembodied voice from the study.

"Thank you, Father," they said in unison. Fanny distributed their cloaks and scarves. Shelley offered his arm again, and Jane took it. And off they went—Shelley, Mary, Jane, and Fanny, who all apparently loved walks—out into the gloomy gray day.

Which was suddenly, from Mary's point of view, looking much brighter.

"What was all that about with your stepmother?" Shelley asked as Mary took his arm a few minutes later, out of sight of the suffocating bookshop at last. Behind them, Fanny and Jane were chatting together merrily. (Well, Jane was chatting merrily. Fanny was listening.) So it was almost like Mary and Shelley were alone together. Almost.

"I don't know," admitted Mary. "She was acting strangely."

"Perhaps she didn't like my poetry last night," Shelley said. "Perhaps she's decided that I'm no genius after all, and therefore not fit company for her daughter."

"I'm sure that's not it," Mary assured him. "My stepmother doesn't have a smidge of literary taste, and besides, she doesn't care about such things."

"Then what does she care about?" Shelley asked.

"Money," Mary answered frankly. "Titles. Prestige. All of which you have."

"Oh." Shelley seemed troubled by this, but right then they arrived at their intended destination: St. Pancras's churchyard.

This was Mary's thinking place, a quiet tree-filled corner of her world—the one location she could come to get away from everyone else. But lately it had also become a rendezvous point for her and Shelley. (Yes, dear reader, Mary and Percy Shelley started dating in a graveyard.)

As they reached her mother's gravestone, Shelley reached to gently touch the letters: *MARY WOLLSTONECRAFT GODWIN. Author of A Vindication of the Rights of Woman.* "Good afternoon, dear lady," Shelley said softly. "It's good to see you again."

Mary stared at him, something squeezing in her chest. It was like Percy Shelley had been crafted from the ether specifically for Mary. Everything about him was exactly what she'd prefer. Even Ada with all her tinkering couldn't have come up with a more perfect boy—er, man.

"Really?" came Jane's voice from behind them. "You brought him to the graveyard? Again?"

Mary gritted her teeth.

"Do be quiet, Jane," hissed Fanny.

"My name is Claire," retorted Jane.

"No, it isn't," said Fanny.

Mary ignored them and pulled out a small wool blanket that she'd tucked inside her coat. She spread it out over a patch of grass. Then she and Shelley sat down under the twining branches of the oak tree beside her mother's grave. They had to sit rather close together, because it was a small blanket. Of course Mary didn't mind. One of her favorite things was to gaze deeply into Shelley's bright blue eyes.

"Please don't think me too forward," he said after they had been staring at each other for about three minutes straight, "but I find you to be absolute perfection."

Her heart skipped a beat. This was the most romantic thing he'd ever said to her, and he'd been saying many romantic things

lately. She couldn't think of how to reply, because "I was just thinking about how perfect you are, too" seemed glib. Instead she decided
to seize the moment. Why wait for him to act? So she picked up
the closed umbrella from where he'd set it beside them. Shelley
looked confused as she opened it—it wasn't raining at the moment,
strangely—but then she pulled the umbrella down, angled it so it
blocked them from view of her sisters, and leaned in to press her
mouth to his.

This was obviously forward of her. Unthinkable, really. Wildly
inappropriate. In a graveyard, no less. But she didn't care. All she
wanted in that moment was to kiss Shelley, as if to seal for posterity
the way they felt about each other. And what a kiss it was.

He made a startled sound that became a yearning little moan
and caught her by the waist to pull her closer. It turned out that he
was an excellent, naturally gifted kisser—as masterful with his lips
as he was with his words.

It was poetry, she thought, kissing Shelley. It was art and music
and thunder all in one.

(Or maybe the thunder was a separate thing.)

He touched her face gently. "Mary," he whispered against her
lips. "Mary, Mary."

"Shelley," she answered.

"Where have you been all my life?" he asked, and kissed her
again.

"Here," she answered. Kiss. Kiss. "Just here. Waiting."

It was getting pretty hot there, for England in the 1800s. But then Jane complained, loudly. "Can we go? I'm bored. And I'm getting cold."

"Oh, to be an only child," said Mary, and Shelley laughed. Mary reached to touch his cheek. "How fortunate we are to have found each other. As we're so perfectly matched."

"So true," murmured Shelley, but he looked troubled again. "Mary, I must confess something." He couldn't seem to get the words out. "Well, there's no easy way to say this. It was you, wasn't it . . . who created the moon?"

"Oh." She felt her cheeks heat. Should she admit it? But surely, after what they'd just shared, Shelley deserved her confidence. "That was . . . yes."

Overhead there was a faint rumble of thunder.

Shelley nodded. "So I deduced. It was you. My dear Mary."

Mary liked her first name shaped so intimately by Shelley's lips. And she also really liked Shelley's lips.

"Which means that you must be fae," he said then.

Drat. She'd been trying to think up some more rational explanation for the moon thing. Something involving papier-mâché and a candle and a bit of fishing line. Miss Stamp had but one firm rule: tell *no one* about the fae.

"You know about fae?" she asked Shelley hoarsely.

He nodded. "I got drunk with Lord Byron on the Continent one night last year, and he let it slip. Actually, we ran out of wine, and so Lord Byron simply *imagined* us having more wine, and we did. Then he was forced to explain the fae thing. After that he kept our goblets perpetually full of wine, just *whoosh* and voilà: more wine. It was magic." He cupped Mary's face again. "You're magic. But why did you make the moon at my reading? Did you think my poem was in dire need of some form of embellishment?"

Well, yes. But she couldn't say that. "Your poem was beautiful. Through your words I could see the image of the moon so clearly in my mind's eye that I couldn't really help myself. I'd never made an illusion like that." She gave a nervous laugh. "I was as startled as anyone."

He laughed, too. "I see. Well, it was the perfect way to end the evening. So thank you." He took her free hand (the one that wasn't still holding the umbrella) and interlaced her fingers with his.

"You're welcome," she murmured.

"Oh, Mary," he said fervently. "You're beautiful and intelligent and wise beyond your years. And your being fae is a bonus. It means that we would make the most wonderful team. With my genius and your power combined, I might be considered one of the world's greatest writers, someday. You will be a great writer yourself, I think, but perhaps after I've established *my* career." He rose up onto one knee, which was a bit awkward because she was still sitting down and also holding an umbrella. "Therefore, there's a question I need to ask you."

Oh dear. Mary's heart was beating like a drum. This was the moment. The question.

Things were really moving quite fast.

"Mary Godwin," he said. "Mary. My Mary. Will you do me

the great honor of becoming my . . ." He took a deep breath. "Writing partner?"

She blinked a few times. "Oh. Why yes, of course. I'd be honored to be your . . . writing partner."

His smile was luminous. "Excellent. I'm so pleased you agreed. We're going to do amazing things together." He took her hand and shook it, as if they were concluding some kind of business transaction.

BOOM went the thunder, and without any more ceremony, it started to rain.

Jane and Fanny rushed toward them. "Are you done snogging yet?" Jane cried over another rumble of thunder.

"You can make your own way home, can't you?" Shelley suggested. "I have some things to attend to just now, and to escort you home would take me farther away."

"We're fine," said Jane flatly. "Good day, Mr. Shelley."

"Good day." He bent and kissed Mary's hand. "Until next we meet, my love."

"Until then," she breathed.

He went off, whistling in the rain.

Fanny and Mary and Jane dashed back toward the bookshop, which was awkward because they only had the one umbrella between them.

"What was that about?" Jane asked as they ran. "It looked like he made some kind of proposition."

"Yes," Mary admitted. "Mr. Shelley has asked me to be his . . ."

"Yes?" squealed Jane.

"Yes?" Fanny said tensely.

"Writing partner."

Jane frowned. "His writing partner? Boo! What kind of proposal is that?"

"And did you accept his proposal?" Fanny asked.

"I did," answered Mary.

"Are you sure that's wise?"

"Why wouldn't it be? It's not like he asked me to marry him." She fought down a twinge of disappointment.

"Well . . . you don't know Mr. Shelley very well."

"I know him quite well," countered Mary indignantly. There was a more rational part of her brain that could concede that Fanny had a point. Mary and Shelley had only known each other for a matter of months, after all. But the heart wants what it wants (although Emily Dickinson wouldn't write those words for another *mumble mumble* years), and Mary's heart wanted him. "In some ways it feels as though I have always known him," she insisted. "We understand each other. We're the same."

"Sometimes people really do fall in love at first sight," argued Jane. "Or second sight. Or third. And Mary and Shelley have probably seen each other at least a dozen times. I, for one, am glad for you, Mary. First—fine, be his writing partner." She waggled her eyebrows suggestively. "And then be his something else."

At that moment, a gust of wind caught Mary's umbrella and jerked it from her hands. The girls watched helplessly as it spiraled away from them into the air. Within seconds they were drenched. They ran without speaking again all the way to the bookshop. Then, at the doorstep, Fanny gently touched Mary's arm.

"I'm glad for you, too," she said softly. "Just be careful. All right?"

"Did you have a nice time?" her father asked when the girls came back inside.

"Yes, Father," they replied in unison.

"Hmph," said Mrs. Godwin. "You're late!"

"How can we be late if we never set a time that we should be back?" asked Mary.

"Because you were with Mr. Shelley. If it had been up to me, you would never have gone out with him at all. All poets are charlatans and rakes, I find, sitting about all day thinking up pretty words with which to entrap unsuspecting reputable young ladies. It's unseemly."

Jane frowned. "Not all poets are bad, Mother. Think about Lord Byron."

Mrs. Godwin scoffed. "Lord Byron may be the worst rake of all."

"Yes, but isn't that romantic?" sighed Jane.

"Oh, speaking of Byron," said Mr. Godwin mildly. "A letter came for you."

Jane's mouth dropped open. "A letter . . . from Lord BYRON?"

Mr. Godwin retreated to his study and returned with an envelope. He handed it to Jane. "It would appear so."

Jane tore the letter open and read it right then and there. "He wrote me back! He gave me advice on how to—" She wisely stopped herself before she blabbed about being an actress in front of her parents. "He says I'm a charming girl, who he'd very much like to meet someday!"

"Ha!" laughed Mrs. Godwin sardonically. "That's unlikely."

BOOM went the thunder, which ended the conversation. Mr. Godwin went back into his study. And Mrs. Godwin went to see about dinner.

Alone with her sisters, Jane clutched the letter to her chest and grinned. "I'll read the rest later. But the point is, I have the interest of Lord Byron. Why, he's the most attractive, most intelligent, most famous man in the entire world. So much more famous than Shelley."

Well, that stung. But Mary was not about to let her sister deflate her Shelley balloon. "Yes, but Byron is far away. And he's old."

"He's not so old," said Jane.

"He's old enough to have a daughter our age!" Suddenly Mary was filled with the desire to see Ada—to tell her all about what had transpired this afternoon. Her first kiss! Sure, it had been in the company of her sisters, which was awkward. And in the presence of her dead mother. Sort of. In a cemetery. But she was sure that Ada would celebrate this milestone with her. Ada, at the very least, would understand how important it was. And then they could discuss this strange "writing partner" proposal of Shelley's, and what to do now that Shelley knew that Mary was fae. She really needed a proper vent session.

"With age comes experience," sniffed Jane, still going on about Lord Byron.

"Well, Shelley has done more than offer me a tiny bit of advice," Mary reminded her sister primly. "He's asked me to be his *writing partner*."

"Hmph." Mrs. Godwin was standing in the doorway again, holding an armful of plates. "The last thing I'd do is trust the word of Mr. Shelley. But then you've always been a foolish girl."

Mary felt hot with rage. "Foolish, am I? Less than a month ago you were going on and on about how perfect Shelley was as a match for Jane. You were determined to get him to marry her."

Mrs. Godwin's eyes narrowed. "That was before I found out what he is."

"What is he? A poet?" It really was about the poetry, Mary thought dazedly. Incredible. "You really don't understand anything about anything, do you? Percy Shelley's going to be one of the world's greatest writers someday! He's sensitive and clever and kind!" (And a really good kisser.) She was revealing too much. If her stepmother hadn't known that there was something between Mary and Shelley before, now she certainly would. But Mary didn't care. "He's wonderful," she said.

Her stepmother snorted. "He's not wonderful, you poor naive child. He's married."

All the air seemed to evaporate from Mary's lungs. "What? You must be mistaken. He's not— He can't be—"

"He is," insisted Mrs. Godwin. "He's not eligible after all, which I agree is a real pity. My friend Mrs. Lamb told me all about it this morning at tea. He eloped some time ago with a girl named Harriet Westbrook. His father was so furious that he disinherited him. So really, in spite of his fine manners and clothes and such, Mr. Shelley is a pauper. He's no use to any of us. Least of all you."

"He's married," Mary whispered, and there seemed to be nothing left to say.

Mary spent much of the day weeping into her pillow (as any of us would do), humiliated and horrified, but afterward felt oddly numb.

Shelley was married. Of course he was.

"Dinner!" Mrs. Godwin called through the door. She sounded surprisingly cheerful.

Mary sat up. She certainly couldn't tolerate sitting at the dinner table with her stepmother just now, who was bound to be smug and hateful. In fact, Mary decided right then that she could not stand to stay for even one more minute in this infuriating apartment with these infuriating people.

She got up. Walked slowly to her wardrobe. Pushed aside the dresses and coats. Grasped the doorknob and tried to turn it.

It was locked. Miss Stamp always kept it locked.

Mary tried to imagine it unlocked, but the fae magic didn't work. Perhaps there was a kind of counterspell or anti-fae thing on this particular door, to prevent her from using it in the off hours. She stamped her foot, but that didn't open the door, either. Then Mary tried to imagine another door to take her to Ada's—a new door—but that didn't work any better.

She'd have to get out the old-fashioned way.

Mary put on her coat. Then she crossed to the bedroom window and opened it. The street gleamed wetly below her. She told herself that it wasn't such a very big drop to the ground, and there was a tree (not a particularly sturdy tree, but she'd manage) and she could easily shimmy down. No problem. From there she would walk to Ada's house. She knew that Ada was about to sit down to dinner herself, with Mr. Babbage, an event that Ada had invited her to attend but Mary had declined. Now she wished she'd said yes. But she wouldn't make it to the Byron estate in time for dinner, anyway. Ada's house was halfway across London. It would take Mary hours to walk there. Which was too bad, because she was actually quite hungry.

She swung one leg over the windowsill, then the other, then stood precariously on the ledge of the window for a moment, clutching the sill, her eyes pressed closed as she attempted to summon some semblance of courage. The tree wasn't close enough that she could simply swing herself into its branches. This probably wasn't going to work.

But she had to see Ada. Talk it through with Ada. Now. (Or as soon as possible.)

So Mary opened her eyes, took a deep breath, and jumped.

TWELVE

Ada

"Is he here yet?" Ada could hardly wait for Mr. Babbage to arrive. She kept rushing back and forth between the parlor and the front hall, checking the windows, and shining PAN's face with a polishing cloth. He practically sparkled.

"Not yet, Miss Byron," Pell said from the dining room. "Although I should think you'd know before me." Since Pell had been cooking the dinner, setting the table, and tidying up every space their guest might see, she hadn't had time to look out every window in the front of the house.

Ada wished Mary had agreed to come. It made sense why she wouldn't, but having a friend here to help present would make this much easier.

"I suppose I do have you," Ada told PAN as she returned to the parlor.

PAN didn't respond. Obviously. Automatons couldn't speak.

She patted his arm. "I'm proud of you. You're a good automaton. The best."

A knock sounded on the door, making Ada's heart jump. It was time.

She scooped up a sheet. "I'm going to cover you now," she warned PAN. She wasn't sure why she felt so bad about it. She wasn't preventing him from seeing anything, because automatons couldn't see. Still, as she pulled the delicate sheet over PAN's head, she whispered, "Sorry."

"Ada! My dear." Mr. Babbage offered his hand, which she shook. "I've been most eager to ask what you thought about the party. Did you enjoy yourself? I'm sorry I was so busy that night. After the frog incident, I couldn't get away from everyone needing something. And Aldini is still trying to re-create the experiment. Fortunately for my house staff, no more frogs have come back to life." His gaze drifted up to the sheet-covered PAN. "What is this?"

"I've been working on something I hope you'll find interesting." Ada wasn't angry about the silver dancer anymore; she was about to one-up him.

"Ah, a new project. Yes, I'm very eager to see what's kept you busy these last weeks."

"Please, sit down." She motioned Mr. Babbage farther into the parlor.

"It's the kind of thing I need to be sitting for?" Obligingly, Mr. Babbage sat, leaning back in the chair, one leg thrown over the other knee. His elbows rested on the arms of the chair.

Ada went to stand beside PAN, who, at the moment, resembled a very tall ghost, with the sheet still thrown over him. Why had she made him so tall? Oh, right, to reach things on the highest shelves. "Technology is hurtling forward at a breakneck speed," Ada said. "Machines are becoming more plentiful, more useful—more necessary. Look at the textile industry. A bolt of fabric no longer requires a weaver working a loom for hours at a time; now, that same bolt of fabric is produced by a machine within minutes."

Mr. Babbage nodded.

"Agriculture is moving in the same direction," Ada went on, "as well as other major industries. The future is automated."

"That is a bold statement," Mr. Babbage said.

It was a correct statement. "With all of that in mind, I have been considering how automatization might affect our personal lives, how daily tasks might benefit from technology."

Mr. Babbage nodded encouragingly. Pell came to stand in the doorway, watching as well.

"Please allow me to present PAN: Practical Automaton Number One." She swept the sheet off the automaton.

PAN shone brightly in the lamplight. Every gear gleamed. He looked strong and precise, capable of every function Ada had programmed into him.

Pell clapped supportively. "Well done, Miss Byron."

Mr. Babbage shifted, leaning forward in his chair. "Well, look at that. He's certainly an impressive machine. And you're calling him PAN?"

Ada nodded. "He's a *practical* automaton."

"Indeed? Do you have a demonstration prepared?"

"I do." Ada took a chain from around her neck. On the chain hung a small key, which Mary had made from one of the silver spoons they'd found in the attic. The key went into the keyhole in PAN's chest plate. With a few turns of the key, PAN bowed and offered Ada his arm.

Mr. Babbage raised an eyebrow. "That must have taken a hundred equations to program."

It had actually taken one hundred and fifty-three equations. "Bowing is only PAN's most basic function. This is where the rest of his commands are given." Ada motioned to the control gears on PAN's wrist, which he still held out for her. She shifted him into walk mode and quickly calculated the number of steps he needed to take before his next action would occur.

PAN responded by walking toward the chair beside Mr. Babbage. Then he turned, sat in the chair, and crossed one leg over the other knee—sitting just as Mr. Babbage had been earlier.

Mr. Babbage jumped out of his chair. "Oh my. Well, that's certainly impressive. All those small movements, the way he swings his arms as he walks. It's so natural!"

"He's quite lifelike," Pell agreed from the door. She'd seen PAN earlier, when Ada had brought him downstairs. Before then, PAN had been in the attic, and often covered by a sheet (for modesty). "Why, as he was coming down the stairs, he even held the banister."

"Incredible." Mr. Babbage stepped closer to PAN. "Look at those parts. The materials are so fine. Did you have all of these pieces special ordered? I'm surprised your mother allowed it."

Ada held her tongue. She wasn't about to tell *anyone* that PAN was made with stuff she and Mary had found around the house, and then Mary had reshaped using only the power of her imagination.

"This is truly amazing work, Ada," Mr. Babbage said. "You should be very proud."

Oh, Ada was proud, though she wished Mary were here to receive her part of this praise. "Thank you. But the demonstration isn't over yet."

"There's more?" Mr. Babbage stepped away from PAN, giving Ada room to work the control gears again.

"PAN is programmed to perform a number of helpful tasks, such as pouring tea and writing thank-you notes," Ada said while she worked. "But that's not what I'm telling him to do now."

"Are you trying to put me out of a job?" Pell frowned. "Well, I'll never share my recipes with him. You still need me."

"I'll always need you, Pell." Ada stepped back as PAN took an embroidery hoop from the end table beside him, then dove into the activity she'd spent all night programming: needlepoint. His metal fingers were deft and precise as he drew the thread through the cotton fabric, continuing the intricate pattern of flowers and butterflies he'd been working on earlier.

Mr. Babbage gave a delighted, disbelieving laugh. "Oh, well done, Ada. Every single movement, the pressure he exerts on the needle, the way he works through this detailed pattern—truly! I've never seen anything like it."

"He's making a pillowcase," Ada announced. Her heart swelled with pride. PAN was the best automaton in the world. "This is only the beginning. I'm teaching him how to play Mozart's Concerto in C on the pianoforte, and he will also be able to open doors, set the table, and even take out the trash. I'd like to find a way to make him drive a carriage, but right now there are too many random variables in that. What if a child runs out into the road? Automatons can't see."

"So Helix's job is safe," Pell concluded. "He will be very glad to know."

"For now," Ada said. "PAN needs a part to enable artificial senses. Some kind of . . . sensor."

Mr. Babbage laughed. "Oh, that's a long way off, if such a thing ever becomes possible. But even so, I'd say you have plenty of job security, Pell. PAN won't replace you anytime soon."

"Well, he'd never replace Pell," Ada said. "No one could."

"I appreciate that, Miss Byron."

"But perhaps he could make Pell's job easier, taking some of the burden and allowing Pell to focus on the things that only trained housekeepers can do."

Here, Mr. Babbage's smile fell. He turned to Pell. "Miss Pell, do you know how to command this automaton?"

"Oh, no." She shook her head. "I'm afraid it's beyond me. But I quite like it. Him, I mean."

"So you would need to be trained to use him."

Panic flared in Pell's eyes. "I'd rather not."

"And how's your math? Because you'd need to specify every movement he makes." Mr. Babbage looked at Ada. "When you had him sit, you calculated the number of steps, the length of his stride, the way he would turn, how far he needed to bend to sit properly—yes?"

Ada gave a small nod.

"Is that something you could train Pell to do? Or anyone else?"

"I hadn't thought about it."

"And if PAN were to set the table, as you'd suggested, he'd need to be able to fetch the dishes, walk them over, put them in the proper places. But what if the dishes weren't in the correct place? What if he knocked over a glass?"

Ada frowned. "Then I could program him to clean it."

"I suppose," Mr. Babbage said, "I'm asking what would take longer: programming PAN with all these variables in mind, or Pell doing it herself?"

Ada's pride shrank back. "Um."

"So my job *is* safe." Pell visibly relaxed.

"How long does he run before he needs to be wound up again?" Mr. Babbage asked. "And how many activities can you instruct at once? Could you tell him to fold the laundry, then sweep the ashes out of the fireplace, and then dust the parlor?"

Mr. Babbage was asking an awful lot of questions here.

"Perhaps those aren't tasks I'd have him perform," Ada said.

"Indeed. It would be difficult for him to tell the difference between a towel and a sheet. Or a gown." Mr. Babbage gave Ada a sad look. "He is a work of genius. A marvel. But I fear he isn't as . . . practical . . . as you'd hoped."

Ada's fingers tightened over her cane. "He's only the first model. I could try again."

"I know your next attempt would be even more incredible. But machines are limited. PAN's clockworks will run down. He cannot learn. He cannot adapt. He can do only what you program—*exactly* what you program. And for him to be a truly practical automaton, others would have to be able to set his commands as well, which would require specialized training."

Ada swallowed back a lump in her throat. "I wanted to make a tool, not a toy."

"You should be proud," Mr. Babbage insisted. He was trying to be a good teacher—play the devil's advocate a bit. (To which your narrators say, STOP! No one likes the devil's advocate.) "I simply think you need to understand that, while it is amusing to see an automaton embroider with such apparent enthusiasm, I don't believe he is quite the revolutionary tool you imagined. In many ways, he's very like my silver dancer."

"Oh." Ada looked at PAN. "You're saying he has no purpose beyond entertainment—amusement."

"Entertainment is a purpose of its own, Ada. Otherwise, we'd have no novels, no plays, no art." He tilted his head as he, too, regarded PAN. "Your automaton *is* art. You put a lot of care into his design and inner workings. Don't tell your mother I said this, but PAN makes me think you take after your father as much as your mother. PAN is a kind of poetry in his own way. Metal poetry. The elegance, the simplicity. Your father would be proud."

Ada found she didn't have anything to say to that.

"Now," Mr. Babbage said, turning to Pell, "do I smell chicken?"

By the time dinner ended, Ada was both exhausted and energized. Mr. Babbage spent the whole meal talking about something *he* was working on—something about math, something about government funding, something about battleships. Ada wasn't paying attention. She could only think about her failings. As a scientist. As a daughter. As the benevolent creator of a metal boy.

Finally, Mr. Babbage took his leave—with only another "Good job on your delightful automaton" as he went out the door.

"Argh!" Ada cried. "I wish Mary were here."

She wound up PAN and set him to climb the stairs. It took three minutes of math, counting (and re-counting) stairs, and then fussing with all the control gears.

"This isn't very practical at all!" Then she thumped her cane on the stairs, using it to stomp since stomping still hurt her left leg. PAN, for his part, climbed pleasantly behind her. He really should not be so pleasant when she was feeling so rotten.

She threw open the attic door just in time to see the dormer window swing open, lightning crack in the distance, and a dripping figure lurch into the attic.

Ada screamed and brandished her cane like a sword. The figure screamed—in Mary's voice.

From below, Pell called, "Miss Byron, should I bring up some dessert?"

As the light settled and the dripping figure resolved into a dripping Mary, Ada lowered her cane. "Mary! Where did you come from?"

"Oh!" Pell shouted. "Miss Godwin is there, too? I'll bring extra!"

Mary was gasping, clearly trying to recover herself as well. "I pulled myself up the line. From the stables. I needed to see you."

Ada stumbled across the attic. "I needed to see you, too! This whole evening went horribly."

Mary wiped at her eyes. It could have been rain she was wiping away. That would have made sense. (But we know, reader, she was also wiping away tears.)

Ada didn't notice that Mary had been crying, however, as she was busy throwing her arm (just the left one, since she wasn't trying to bludgeon her friend anymore) around Mary and saying, "He said PAN isn't practical!"

"I hate men!" Mary declared with a noisy sob.

Oh good, Ada thought. Mary was properly upset about Mr. Babbage. "I hate them, too!"

"I have pie!" Pell called as she came up the stairs. "Oh, dears. Let's get you some towels. Then I need to finish cleaning up dinner, and I'll be off for the night."

A few minutes later found Mary (wrapped in towels) and Ada

with plates of leftover chocolate pie. PAN, who'd been wound up again, was sitting between them on the battered old sofa, back at work on his pillowcase.

"It's so frustrating!" Ada shoved another bite of chocolate pie into her mouth and chewed miserably. "I mean, I didn't think I was going to revolutionize science, but I didn't expect to be so thoroughly dismissed."

"That must have felt so—"

"Wretched!" Ada leaned on PAN's metal shoulder—but then stopped because he was metal and that was uncomfortable. Also, she didn't want her hair to get caught in his gears. "And what's worse—he's correct that there are limitations as to what PAN can do. PAN can't think or learn. He can't adapt. He simply does what he's told. He follows the rules."

"Unlike *some* boys!" Mary ate a bite of pie. "This pie is everything to me right now. Everything."

"And unlike *some* boys," Ada added, even though she wasn't sure why they were talking about other boys now, "PAN does needlepoint!"

They both looked at PAN, whose clockworks had just run out. He was no longer doing needlepoint.

"That was bad timing," Mary said around a mouthful of pie.

"I'm very smart," Ada said.

Mary didn't argue.

"I should be able to do this."

Do what was the natural question.

"I want a machine without limitations, one that can think and invent and talk. I want a machine that will do everything, without having to be wound up every ten minutes!" She thought back to Faraday's Dynamo Disc, the way electricity had sparked when the copper spun through the magnetic poles. The frog, when the spark had traveled into it, the way its legs flexed, its muscles constricted. The frog *before* Mary had brought it to life, when it was simply a (ceased-to-be) common frog responding naturally to energy.

If only she had a Dynamo Disc of her own.

FLASH! went the sky.

Ada sat up straight. Then, a few seconds later:

BOOM! went the sky.

Ada grabbed her cane and lurched to her feet, completely abandoning her pie.

"Can I have that?" Mary asked. "I didn't eat dinner."

"I have an idea." Ada bent in front of PAN and fiddled with his wrist until he stood up and stepped away from the sofa. "You two stay here." Quickly, Ada gathered her materials into her pockets and yanked open the dormer window, which led out onto the roof. Rain and cold wind lashed across her face, stinging her eyes.

"Ada, what are you doing?" Mary came rushing over, pie in hand. "You can't go out there."

"Oh, good, you're helping." Ada gave her a small spool of wire and a metal rod. "Pass this to me when I say."

"Wait." Mary took the wire. "Think about what you're doing. Is this wise?"

"I can't worry about your so-called wisdom. I need to get out there before the storm is directly over us."

"Isn't it already directly over us?"

"That's why I have to do this *now*."

FLASH!

BOOM!

That strike was closer. Much closer. Ada, already soaked from standing in the open window, started again to scramble out. She had minutes at best.

Mary grabbed her arm. "Tell me what you're doing so I know what to say at your funeral."

Ada was now straddling the window, one foot resting on the roof. This was, she could tell, what would eventually become known as a teachable moment. "Lightning is energy," she said quickly. "Energy is one of the things PAN needs in order to work. Right now, I turn the key to wind him up, but if I could use electricity to make him run, he'd go for longer than ten minutes at a time. He wouldn't need to be wound up."

Mary gave her a long, searching look, which we, your narrators, believe was one of intense doubt, but Ada took as complete comprehension.

"Good. Thank you." Ada thrust her cane into Mary's hand. "Hold this."

Now Mary was holding the cane, the spool of wire, and the pie. "Ada, wait—"

But Ada was fully out the window, moving carefully on the

rain-slicked roof with one end of the wire clutched in her teeth and the metal rod tucked down the back of her dress. (Reader, do not try this at home!) Before her illness, before she'd needed to be so mindful of her weakened legs, she had installed a series of small ledges that led to the very top of the roof. This was her destination.

FLASH! BOOM!

Frantically, she pulled herself up ledge by ledge, letting her arms and right leg do most of the work. When she'd reached the peak, she connected the wire and the rod and set the whole thing into a bracket that she'd mounted there for an entirely different experiment years ago. (Shh. Don't tell her mother.)

FLASH-BOOM!

Ada shrieked. That was close. Far too close. She didn't bother to check the connection again. She descended the ledges as fast as she could, shouting, "Drop the wire!" and tumbled through the dormer window.

Mary, who hadn't heard Ada, was still clutching the spool, the cane, and the pie. Without another word—there was no time—Ada tore her cane and the spool from Mary's hand and ran/limped over to PAN. She thrust the end of the wire into the keyhole in his chest and waited.

She didn't have to wait long.

FLASHBOOM!

Light engulfed the entire house, which shuddered and groaned. Ada and Mary screamed as electricity sparked down the wire and surged into PAN's chest.

The automaton began to embroider at (ahem) lightning speed. Flowers appeared within seconds and his whole metal body vibrated with excess power.

"It worked!" Ada blinked away light spots. "It worked! He'll do it all on his own now!"

At least until the energy dissipated. She had no way to store the excess power.

And anyway, what did this actually *do*? PAN could produce more pillowcases, bow extra bows, pour thrice as much tea, play Mozart even faster. But he still couldn't do anything Ada hadn't programmed. PAN still had every other limitation Mr. Babbage had named earlier.

"It's not enough," Ada whispered.

"What?" Mary looked aghast, which was emphasized by the way her hair was standing on end. Perhaps they'd been a smidge too close to the wire as lightning ran through.

Ada, too, felt like she'd been struck by lightning. Her mind whirred. "He needs a way to store the energy. He needs to be able to sense objects. He needs to see, to react."

"Ada, what are you saying?" Mary sounded even more concerned than before, but Ada could hardly hear her over the pounding of rain and the thoughts rumbling in her head.

"Use the magic on him. Imagine him with the ability to see what he's doing and respond accordingly. Imagine him with the ability to hear instructions—like *set the table*—so that his control gears aren't needed. Imagine him with the ability to calculate the number of steps he needs to take to go from one side of the room to the other." Ada returned to PAN. He was still embroidering; half the border was complete.

Mary had (wisely) backed away, and now stood on the far side of the room. She sneakily ate another bite of pie in case they both died. "That sounds like a lot of specialized knowledge."

"You can *imagine* it, though. It should be easy for you." Ada turned back to PAN. Her legs felt unsteady after all this scrambling around, but her mind felt sharper than ever. It was so clear what they had to do. "Mary, please! Imagine it!"

"I am!"

Ada was also imagining as hard as she could. PAN doing math. PAN solving logic puzzles. PAN helping her build more automatons. It couldn't hurt to try. She pressed her palm to PAN's chest, right over the keyhole to his clockwork heart. "Come on!"

That's when lightning struck again, in the same place it had before. (We know. What are the odds?) The force of the bolt threw them all backward: PAN to the sofa, Mary to the floor, and Ada slamming against the fae door.

She had the wind knocked out of her, and it took a minute to be able to breathe. Tears clogged her vision and her ears rang, but she forced her eyes open as another bolt of lightning lit up the workshop.

On the far side of the room, Mary struggled to her feet. Her hair was actually smoking this time. "No!" she exclaimed. "The pie!"

She'd fallen right into the rest of the chocolate pie. It was smeared all over her dress.

But Ada wasn't looking at Mary's dress.

She was looking at PAN.

Because PAN had stood up. And she hadn't commanded him to stand up. And he was turning his head to look at her. Which she hadn't programmed him to do, either. And there was a strange light in his silver eyes.

He was *seeing* her, she realized. It had worked. He had sensors—of some sort. Nothing like this had ever been invented before.

"Hello," he said.

And he was speaking. There was nothing in his construction that should have allowed for speaking. Another upgrade!

From across the room, where she was mournfully trying to scrape the chocolate off her dress, Mary looked up. "Did he—"

There was a soft whirring sound. Maybe it was only Ada's imagination, but he appeared to be thinking. "The correct greeting is *hello*, is it not?" he said.

Ada—perhaps a bit hysterically—began to laugh. "He's alive! He's aliiiiiive!"

"Oops," said Mary. "I did it again." Then she slumped to the floor.

THIRTEEN
Pan

Perhaps *hello* had not been the correct greeting after all.

He searched for another but found nothing in the database that had mysteriously formed when the blast of energy had surged through him, waking all his individual components, which were suddenly, magically integrated into a singular being. There was simply too much to process. He seemed to see, feel, and hear everything at the same time, unable to distinguish between the operation of his various senses. He put his hand over his eyes and darkness fell. When he let his hand drop, he saw one of the girls (the one who had not fallen to the floor) take a length of metal and rush to the other girl's side. The first girl began to softly slap the second girl. On the face.

"That is certainly not the correct greeting," he remarked.

"Mary," the first girl said loudly. "Mary!"

"Mary," Pan repeated.

The second girl's eyes opened. "Did he just say my name?"

"Is that your name?" Pan asked. "Mary?"

The first girl made an odd vocalization, a *ha ha ha*. "Yes. This is Mary. And I'm Ada."

Finally they were getting somewhere. "And who am I?"

The girls glanced at each other. "We've been calling you Pan," the one named Mary said. "Will that do?"

"Will that do what?"

Her mouth curved in what he'd later come to know as a smile. "Is the name Pan acceptable to you?" she clarified.

He didn't have a different name he would have preferred. "Yes. Pan will"—he paused—"do."

"Good." Ada helped Mary to her feet.

Mary tried to smooth her stained dress and lightning-frazzled hair. "How do you do, Pan?"

"How do I do what?" he asked, puzzled. There seemed to be a great emphasis on doing.

The other girl—Ada—was still looking at him, her head tilted to one side. He tilted his head to match hers. "How do you do everything? How do you speak? How do you move about on your own?"

He thought about it. "I was hoping," he said finally, "that you could tell me how I do."

"I'd like that. Say AH." Ada opened her mouth to demonstrate.

"AH." Pan opened his mouth and held absolutely still while Ada peered inside.

Then she gave a small hmph. "Let's see your eyes." She brought him nearer to a lamp and got so close to him that her breath fogged his face plate. "I don't see anything that would explain how you can see."

"Me neither," Pan said. "But I do see."

Ada pressed her ear to his chest. "I don't hear any clicking. You're not wound up."

"But I'm not wound down," he pointed out.

"You really are alive," Ada said, more to herself than to him, as she pulled away. "It was supposed to be sensors, a way to hear commands. But this is so much more. This is real. This is actual life. Mary, what exactly were you imagining? My instructions were clear."

"Oops," Mary said softly.

Pan put his hand over his stomach and felt the washboard there. His metal fingers clinked as he dragged his hand downward. Then he felt his face. "What is alive?" he asked.

The space between Ada's eyebrows pinched together. Pan wondered if this eyebrow pinch helped her to know the answer. He wished he could eyebrow pinch. "Life is a characteristic of something that preserves, furthers, or reinforces its existence in the given environment," Ada said.

"I do not understand," said Pan.

She began to list the qualifications for life on her fingers.

"Scientifically speaking, life involves homeostasis, organization, metabolism, growth, response to stimuli, and adaptation, which is the ability to change in response to one's environment."

Pan also counted off the words on his fingers: "I. Do. Not. Understand."

"It's being able to think and feel and move about and breathe," tried Mary.

Ada sighed. "That's a very basic way of looking at it, but all right."

He could think, Pan realized. (Then he realized that he had *realized* something.) "I can think," he announced.

"And what about feeling?" Mary asked, taking his hand in hers.

Ada leaned over to examine his hand. "Yes, can you feel that?"

"I meant emotionally," Mary said. "But I suppose either would work."

Pan *could* feel Mary's fingers on his hand. It was faint, but he could sense the pressure. It was . . . nice. He felt that he rather liked feeling. "Yes," he said at last. "To both."

"And we know he can move about," Ada said.

"Which leaves the question of breathing," Pan said. "What is that?"

"It's the process of moving air into and out of the lungs to facilitate gas exchange with the internal environment," said Ada.

Pan looked at Mary. He tilted his head.

"It's where you . . . um . . ." Mary's voice trailed off, and she demonstrated air moving into her nose and then out of her mouth.

Pan imitated her, a small fan in the back of his throat whirring. He could feel the air moving back and forth. "Is this breathing?" he asked breathlessly.

Ada shook her head. "Actually, you don't need to breathe. You don't have lungs." (She'd fashioned a decorative stomach and whirling kneecaps, but not lungs. Obviously an oversight.)

"I don't have lungs? Does this mean I'm not alive?"

Mary laid her hand on his metal shoulder. It was still nice. "You're definitely alive."

"Well, that's a relief," he said. "But how did I come to be alive?"

Again, the two girls looked at each other.

"Well. Mary?"

"I don't actually know," admitted Mary reluctantly. "I've had a rather baffling day. And then there was so much lightning and yelling, and you were saying that bit about how he should be able to see and respond and—"

Ada breathed in a short, sudden way. "Lightning! I need to take down the lightning rod!"

She crossed the room, using the metal implement to assist her walking. Then she hung it on a peg next to the window, sat on the windowsill, and rotated around so that she was outside. She closed the window behind her. Pan was concerned. Outside was water, which Pan instinctively understood was dangerous. One could rust in water. (Although your narrators are more concerned about the lightning.)

Pan followed her to the window. Then he stopped because

he had caught his own reflection in the windowpane. He lifted his hand to his face again. The reflection did the same. He tilted his head. "What am I?" he asked.

"You're what's known as an automaton," said Mary.

"Ah," Pan said, still looking at himself in the window. He touched the keyhole in his chest. He saw Mary's reflection appear next to his, and he spent a moment comparing the two of them. She was shorter, and made of a range of different colors, whereas he was mostly silver. She had eyelashes and impressively large hair. He touched his head. "I have no hair."

"I'm sure Ada could make hair for you, if you wished."

Suddenly, Ada's face appeared in the window, right inside Pan's reflection. He made a sound that could only be described as a robot scream and jumped back.

Ada burst through the window. "Oh. Did I startle you?"

"I thought I saw my inner self," Pan admitted. "But it was only you."

"I disconnected the lightning rod." Ada retrieved her cane from its peg and leaned on it. "No more getting struck by lightning tonight."

"You must dry off quickly," Pan advised. "Before you rust."

She made the *ha ha ha* noise again. "I'll survive." Then she shivered. "But I could really use a cup of tea."

Pan brightened. "I know just what to do," he said.

Twenty minutes later they were all down in the kitchen drinking tea. Well, Pan wasn't drinking, because he couldn't eat or drink, as it turned out. His stomach, Ada had explained to him, was only decorative. He would have been disappointed, but then Ada had also explained how the human body processes food and drink, and he'd decided his automaton body would suit him fine.

Mary lifted her teacup to her lips. Her mouth made a tiny slurping noise that Pan tried to imitate with his throat fan, but it wasn't the same. "It's very good tea, Pan," she said. "Well done."

He nodded. "Thank you," he said, which he recalled was the appropriate response to a compliment. "I was well programmed in tea making."

Ada, in the meantime, had finished her tea and was examining him again. She lifted up one of his arms and bent it, straightened it, and rotated it, then jotted down something in her little notebook. She reached for him again. He batted her hand away. "Excuse me. If you don't mind, I would rather you not do that anymore."

"I'm sorry," Ada said. "I shall try to respect your personal space. I'm merely attempting to learn more about how you've changed."

Pan had already learned so much about himself, and he'd only been properly alive for an hour. He already knew a great many things, more than simply how to make tea and embroider pillowcases. He knew customs such as hello, thank you, and excuse me. He knew pi to the one hundredth digit, perhaps more if he pushed himself. He knew that the earth was round and orbited the sun. He knew the days of the week and the months of the year. *How* he knew all of these things was still a mystery. The best Ada had been able to theorize was that, at the moment of his creation, Mary had copied some of her knowledge (and Ada's?) into him.

Still, there were obvious gaps that were vexing. But he was determined to learn.

He had already learned, for instance, that his name was Pan, and he was a living (if not exactly human) being, and that Ada had built him and Mary had brought him to life. And he had learned that they were not the only beings in existence, but there was a whole wide world outside Ada's house, and there were nearly a billion other beings (although strangely Ada couldn't tell him precisely how many) out there in that world.

"When can I see it?" Pan asked after Mary had finished her tea.

Mary and Ada exchanged glances again. "See what?"

"The world, and everyone in it. I should like to see that as soon as possible."

Ada smiled. "The world is incredibly big, Pan, and you can't see it all at once. Just bit by bit." She picked up her cane and started for the stairs. "Follow me."

She led them back to the attic and the dormer window, where Pan was alarmed to discover that she meant them to go outside. It had stopped raining, but outside still seemed dangerous. "I feel uncertain," Pan said.

Ada handed him an oilcan and an umbrella. "Here. These will protect you."

Pan swung open his washboard (it had hinges!) and put the oilcan inside his stomach for safekeeping. He felt that he had been given the most rare and valuable of gifts. "Thank you," he said. Then, as protected from the damp as he could be, he followed Ada and Mary onto the rooftop.

Rain still threatened ominously, but Pan suddenly didn't care. Because now he was learning about the sea of rooftops, the smoke that curled out of chimneys, the dancing chimney sweeps, the elegant dome and spire of St. Paul's Cathedral in the distance, and all the different shades of blue and gray and black he could discern in the clouds. And light. So many lights. They went on for as far as he could see, and each of them represented people. Families, Mary told him. Friends.

Pan felt very small, compared with all this, but somehow connected, too. Like he could be part of it. He could belong. "It's wonderful," he said.

"It is," Mary said with the same awe in her voice that Pan felt from the top of his hairless head to the gears of his silver toes.

"It is lovely," Ada agreed.

Pan stared out at all of London spread before him and whispered, "Hello, world."

PART TWO

(villainy)

PART TWO

Midlogue the First

We don't normally do this, dear reader, but we're going to pause here to focus on somebody else for a minute: Giovanni Aldini, aka the Great Aldini, aka the frog guy from chapters one through four. Aldini was a scientist (you already knew that), a physician (although currently his only patients were deceased amphibians), and the main villain of our story (you may have already guessed he was a bad guy, depending on how you feel about the zapping of poor, defenseless frogs).

But Aldini did have what (he believed) was a very good reason for the frog zapping, and it was this: *family honor.* Many years earlier, Aldini's uncle (an even more infamous scientist named Luigi Galvani) got into a really public science fight with another guy named Volta, about electricity and how many kinds there were. Galvani believed in animal electricity, which is basically the idea that creatures create a certain type of energy that moves through their bodies in the form of a mysterious fluid. Ew. Volta, on the other hand, was like, nah, it's just regular electricity that makes animals go. It was a whole big thing, and in the end Galvani was proven wrong, publicly humiliated, and then he literally died of embarrassment, which had haunted his nephew (Aldini, remember) ever since.

Aldini was determined to restore the family name to a place of honor in the scientific community. To this end, he decided to do what any reasonable scientist would do: a little light necromancy. He would use electricity to *bring people back to life*. But he couldn't do that at home, in Italy (for reasons), and he couldn't do that in France, because the French had a habit of beheading criminals and therefore those bodies were useless to him. But in England—well, the English hanged their criminals. To Aldini's way of thinking, a person might come back from that.

Still, it turned out that restoring life to the recently deceased is a difficult and complicated task. (Defibrillators—and the printed set of instructions for how to work them—hadn't been invented yet.) Aldini would have to start small, prepare the body properly, and determine the exact amount of electricity that would be required for true reanimation. He did this for a while—zapping frogs, over and over, but even when it looked like he'd finally done it, when the poor frog had seemed aliiiiiiiiiiiive, the effect only lasted a moment or two. After years of failure, his funding was cut, his family name smeared worse than ever, and Aldini was finally forced to face a sobering truth: dead is dead. Bringing someone back to life was impossible.

So he'd turned to show business. If Aldini couldn't bring back the dead, he could make people believe that he could. He always started with common frogs, as they were common, in fact, and easy to come by. Their twitching legs never failed to impress a crowd. And then—once the crowd was already excited by the twitching legs and sparks of electricity, he "brought the frog back to life." As in, he pulled a (living) frog out of his pocket and quickly swapped it for the dead one. (Which, yeah, meant he had a living frog in his pocket all night, and then later a dead frog. He got into the habit of saying "Excuse me!" every so often when the living frog ribbited.)

In theaters, where he had more space, he performed the frog switcheroo, and then he demonstrated the power of electricity on other things: a variety of animals and livestock that is simply too gross and morbid for us (your delicate-flower narrators) to go into here. But he couldn't exactly keep a whole cow in his pocket, could he? So he just said that he was getting closer and closer to succeeding with these bigger animals, and people clapped all the same. It wasn't fame and glory and the restoration of his family name. But it was a living.

Imagine, then, Aldini's surprise when his dead frog actually did come back to life, all by itself, at Mr. Babbage's party. *At last*, he'd thought, staring at the undead amphibian with a growing sense of shock and pride. *I've done it!* He didn't know exactly how, but that didn't matter. At last, things were going right for Giovanni Aldini.

At last, he wielded the power over life and death!

The only problem was, he hadn't been able to get it to happen again. Not back at his lab. Not with a hundred frogs. Which brings us to now.

ZAP!

"Still nothing?" Mr. Babbage asked.

Aldini shook his head. As any good scientist would, he had decided to re-create the experiment exactly as it had been under the successful circumstances, so he was here in Babbage's ballroom. He still had Faraday's Dynamo Disc, and the hundred or so dead common frogs, and everything—even down to the time of day, the position of the moon, and the height of the tides—was exactly as it had been before. (Well, as close as he could get, anyway.) The only thing that was missing was the audience.

"The audience," he murmured to himself. "Perhaps the audience is needed."

Babbage tilted his head. "Do you really think the presence of a few random people will make a difference?"

"No, it would have to be the right people." Aldini zapped another frog while he considered. The frog's leg muscles constricted pitifully. Its skin was looking a bit crispy, anyway. This frog was done. He removed it from the board and placed it with the other extra-dead frogs, then took a new dead frog and strapped it down for jolting.

"What do you mean the right people?" Babbage asked.

"I mean that I would need everyone who was in attendance at

the party, ideally wearing exactly what they wore to the party. But perhaps that isn't necessary. Perhaps merely the presence of only one person is required."

And then a terrible thought occurred to him. He didn't like it, but as a scientist, it was one he had to consider.

Perhaps he, even with all his knowledge and equipment, hadn't actually brought the frog back to life.

Perhaps it had been someone else.

Someone using a different method, one undetectable to him.

Which meant Aldini needed to find this someone else. At all costs, he had to locate this person and make them share how they'd done it. He had to possess the secret of life and death for himself.

And because he was, at heart, a nefarious villain, it also meant that he would need to eliminate the competition.

"Mr. Babbage," Aldini said. "I'd like to see your guest list for the party."

Mary
FOURTEEN

Mary was tired. First she'd (accidentally) brought *an entirely new person to life*, and then she'd walked halfway across London (again) in the rain (again), to get back to High Street by sunrise. At the bookshop she'd transformed the tree outside her window into a ladder, climbed it, and turned the ladder back into a tree. She had crawled through the window and straight into her bed and had fallen asleep the moment her head touched the pillow. But the moment after that, her stepmother was poking her in the side to wake her. Then Mary sat at the table, scribbling *all work and no play makes Mary a dull girl* over and over on a sheet of paper until Fanny had gently taken the pen out of her hand and suggested she take a nap. A nap had sounded great. She'd been asleep the moment her head touched the pillow again, but the moment after that Miss Stamp was knocking on the wardrobe door, ready to take her to the Byron estate for lessons.

"Today will be our last class for a while," Miss Stamp was saying now, "as Ada's mother will be returning home in two days' time."

Right. Ada's mother was coming home. Which meant Mary's daily excursions to Ada's house were about to come to an abrupt halt. A gloomy thought.

"With that in mind," Miss Stamp continued, "today I am going to teach you one of the most useful skills in any fae's toolbox: how to make a door that will take you wherever you wish to go."

Ada made her way over to stand beside Mary as Miss Stamp busied herself gathering the necessary materials for the lesson. Mary noticed that Ada was going slower than usual, leaning on her cane more. She was also very pale, with huge dark circles under her eyes.

Ada, of course, noticed Mary noticing her tired state. "How are you?" she asked softly. "You look as though you're about to topple over."

"I'll be all right," said Mary (also softly). "How are you?"

"Exhausted," Ada admitted. "PAN kept me up all night asking questions, difficult questions, too, like what is the difference between pie, the delicious dessert, and pi, the ratio of the circumference of any circle to the diameter of that circle. He's obsessed with homophones," Ada added. "You know, like *night* and *knight*, *bear* and *bare*, *sole* and *soul*, *exercise* and *exorcise*. And, most importantly, the letter *P*, the vegetable pea, and the act of pee. He wants to learn *everything right now*. It's like we've created a monster! He's a never-ending questions machine." She yawned. "Finally I just yelled 'Because!' and gave him a sheet of math problems to entertain himself while I got some rest."

"Rest," murmured Mary. "That sounds nice. Where is Pan now?"

"In my bedroom," Ada said. "I thought it prudent that we not reveal to Miss Stamp what we've done just yet."

Mary nodded. "That's probably for the best."

Miss Stamp returned to stand in front of them. "Now, before we begin such an important lesson," she said sternly, "what must we always, always, *always* be sure to do regarding our fae powers?"

"Create responsibly," Ada and Mary mumbled in unison.

"Good," said Miss Stamp. "Now the creation of a door itself is simple." She gestured to the items she'd piled beside her on the floor: a pile of old boards, a bucket of rusty nails, and a battered trunk. "Mary, if you would."

Mary rubbed her eyes. She focused on the materials, about to picture them coming together, but right then there came a series of thumping sounds from directly below them.

Pan was obviously walking about. And he had heavy feet.

Miss Stamp cocked her head to one side. "What is that?"

"Oh, nothing. Probably just Pell moving about my bedroom," Ada said quickly. "She does love to stomp. But back to the doors, Miss Stamp. Why can't we simple utilize the door we already have?" She pointed at the freestanding door in the center of the room, the one Mary and Miss Stamp had arrived through a few minutes earlier.

"That door already has an established connection that I would prefer not to undo," Miss Stamp said. She looked to Mary. "Go ahead, dear."

STOMP STOMP STOMP went Pan below them.

"Oh, that Pell," said Ada with a weak laugh. "I really must have a talk with her about being quieter when we are trying to work."

"It's quite all right," Miss Stamp said. "As fae, we must learn to be able to concentrate on our magic even when we're in the midst of distraction. Now, Mary: concentrate."

"Right." Mary tried to focus on the pile of boards. Imagine them making up a door.

"Imagine a door, if you will," said Miss Stamp after an extended period of absolutely nothing happening.

"I'm trying," Mary panted. "Did I mention that I'm quite tired today?"

STOMP STOMP STOMP went Pan's feet.

"I see," continued Miss Stamp. "Well. Adequate rest is essential for a heathy imagination." She turned to Ada. "How about you give it a try?"

Ada nodded miserably and gazed at the door-stuff for a long while. Again, nothing happened. Ada had never managed to do a single bit of fae magic in the past two weeks, so this wasn't exactly a surprise, but Mary felt bad for her anyway. Ada so hated to fail at anything.

"I apologize," Ada said finally, her jaw tight. "I really don't believe I have it in me, Miss Stamp. The fae, I mean. I've tried and tried. It's no use."

"Nonsense," said Miss Stamp. "You're a late bloomer, is all. And you look tired, too. What time did *you* go to bed?"

STOMP STOMP STOMP.

"Uh," said Ada. "Fairly late."

"You were up half the night messing about with one of your projects, I suppose?" Miss Stamp crossed her arms over her chest and made a tsking sound.

"Uh—" said Ada. "You see . . . I . . ."

"Very well. I can provide the doors this one time," said Miss Stamp primly. She walked to the center of the attic, then turned to look upon one side of the room with a tiny furrow in her brow. Immediately a door just seemed to snap itself into existence. She turned to the other side of the room and repeated the process (forehead wrinkle: door), using up the last of the materials she'd gathered.

She really did make it look effortless.

"Oh," Ada said, a bit disappointed. "We're just going to make a door from one side of the room to the other? We're not going to go anywhere interesting?"

"Baby steps, my dear," Miss Stamp said. "Now, in order to traverse from one door to another, you must first establish a mental connection between them, in the same way that you do when you connect an object you're creating and its source material. You must draw an invisible thread between the place you're about to exit and the place at which you wish to arrive. It must be exact, otherwise who knows where you might turn up? Distance is also a concern. Some fae are able to create doorways over vast distances, from one continent to another, even, but most of us can only accomplish smaller, more minor crossings. Your destination must also be a place you've been to and are familiar with—there's no closing your eyes and conjuring a doorway that opens to the Taj Mahal, if you've never been there. Also: it should be a private place, discreet, out of public view. No popping out of a random door in the middle of a crowd—that definitely would not be creating responsibly, would it . . . Mary, dear, are you paying attention? Ada? Oh, for heaven's sake. What is the matter with you girls today?"

Mary jerked upright. She hadn't actually heard any of Miss Pell's lecture, as she'd literally been asleep on her feet just now. Ada, for her part, had been staring intently at the floor, her eyes murderously tracking the continuous *STOMP STOMP STOMP* of Pan's feet below them.

Miss Stamp sighed. "Let's come back to the door lesson at another time." There was a clatter as the two doors on either side of the room were unmade again, returning to an orderly pile on the floor. She took both girls by their shoulders and led them to sit down at the worktable. "Each of you hold out your hands."

Ada and Mary both stuck their hands out in front of them, palms down.

Miss Stamp turned their hands over to palms up. Then she

dropped a bright silver shilling into each girl's right hand. "I want you to transform this coin in your right hand into a ring in your left hand. Take as long as you must." She crossed over to the dusty but comfy armchair Ada kept in the corner of the attic, reached into her satchel, and took out her knitting.

Mary stared down at the silver coin. She gave herself a little mental slap on the cheek and tried to focus. A shilling in her right hand. A ring in her left hand.

She tried to imagine it. What kind of ring? A simple silver band? Were there words of love engraved upon it? A line of poetry, perhaps?

"Mary," murmured Ada. "What's wrong?"

Drat. She was crying. Again.

She closed her fist around the shilling and wiped at her eyes. "I really shouldn't be as upset about it as I am."

"About what?" Ada said.

Oh, right. Mary hadn't actually told Ada about the thing with Shelley. Mary had certainly intended to tell Ada. She'd walked half-way across London to tell her. But then Ada had been caught up in her own bit of drama and then the lightning storm and Pan had happened and there hadn't really been a chance to discuss anything else.

Mary glanced up to make sure Miss Stamp was still thoroughly ensconced in her knitting. "It's Shelley," she said softly.

Ada scowled. "Oh no. Did he do something wildly inappropriate? He is a poet, you know. Therefore probably a rake."

Mary shook her head. "No, no, nothing like that. Well, yes, come to think of it. We did kiss. Although it was me who kissed him."

"You kissed him?" Ada's mouth dropped open. "But wait; I'm confused. I thought that's what you wanted."

"It was," Mary admitted. "But then I found out that . . ." She pressed her eyes closed. Her face burned with humiliation. The words were just too painful to say out loud.

Ada set her silver shilling down on the worktable and took Mary's hands. "What? What is it? I can't bear the suspense! What did you find out?"

"Shelley's married," Mary whispered miserably.

"WHAT?"

This came as a shout, which would have definitely attracted the attention of Miss Stamp, if not for another succession of distracting sounds that happened at the same moment: the word "HELLO," a terrified, bloodcurdling scream, followed by a *WHOMP*, coming from the room directly below.

Mary and Ada exchanged panicked glances.

Go, mouthed Ada.

Mary obediently barreled down the attic stairs and into Ada's room, Miss Stamp right behind her, Ada hurrying to the Stair-blaster (which is what Ada called the ingenious little chair that took her up and down the attic stairs). In Ada's room, Miss Pell was lying in a heap on the floor next to the bed. Her eyes were wide and frantic, and her normally ruddy complexion pale as milk. She'd clearly had a fright.

"Miss Pell!" Miss Stamp exclaimed, dropping to her knees beside the housekeeper. "Are you all right? Whatever happened?"

"I came in here to make Miss Ada's bed, as always," said Miss Pell. "And then the metal man, he . . ." She pointed a shaking finger over Miss Stamp's shoulder.

They all turned to look.

Pan was standing in the corner, perfectly still, like a good non-threatening automaton.

"Oh yes, I see. PAN can be quite startling if you come upon him unexpectedly," Ada said breathlessly, entering the room from behind them. "I don't imagine that you expected to find a metal boy in my bedroom, did you, Pell? Ha ha!" She tried to laugh but ended up sounding like she was being choked to death.

Miss Pell was still staring at Pan. "But he . . . he's ALIVE. He—"

"It's true. He is quite lifelike," Mary blurted out. "He does seem alive."

Miss Stamp rose to her feet and approached Pan. "Remarkable," she said, pushing her glasses up on her upturned nose. She got close enough that her breath left a fog of condensation on Pan's cheek. "This is the project that you have been working on?"

Mary and Ada nodded.

Miss Stamp rapped with her knuckles on Pan's chest, which made a hollow sound. Mary cringed. Pan's throat fan whirred, but thankfully he kept still. Then Miss Stamp poked at the keyhole in his chest. "He's an automaton?"

"Yes," said Ada hoarsely.

"What does he do?"

"Oh, um. All sorts of things, really," Ada said.

"He said hello to me," said Miss Pell with a shudder.

Miss Stamp's eyebrows lifted. "He speaks? However did you program him to do that?"

"Oh, well, that's a bit complicated to explain." Ada scratched at the side of her neck. When Miss Stamp simply waited for said explanation, she added, "I recorded a few common phrases such as 'hello' and 'goodbye' and 'how do you do?' using a conical horn to collect and focus the physical air pressure of the sound waves produced by my own voice. I then connected a sensitive diaphragm, located at the apex of the cone, to an articulated stylus, and as the changing air pressure moved the diaphragm back and forth, the stylus scratched an analogue of the sound waves onto a moving cylinder, which I'd coated in soft metal. Like a music box. Only better."

Mary didn't know how Ada had managed to come up with all of that on the spot, but she was impressed. And terrified.

Miss Stamp blinked a few times. "Oh. What else does he do? Please show me."

Ada stiffly approached Pan. It might have been Mary's imagination, but she thought she heard Ada whisper "I'm so sorry" as she lifted Pan's hand and pretended to fiddle with control gears at his wrist. "Stand back," she warned. "He's going to walk forward ten paces."

Obligingly Pan moved forward. He was perfectly capable of walking most smoothly in a human fashion (albeit heavily, as we've established) from one place to another. But he seemed to intuitively understand that it was very important right now that Miss Stamp not come to the conclusion that he was truly alive. He had to act like an automaton.

He was bad at it.

His steps were stiff and jerky, and at one point, he lost his balance and almost fell. He took eleven paces across the room instead of ten. Then, perhaps to impress Miss Stamp, he turned and did a little dance, moving his arms stiffly about his body at sharp angles (what we in modern times might call "the robot").

"Oh my," said Mary. "That is *too much*!"

Pan stopped dancing. He gave a stiff, formal bow. Then he said, "How do you do?" pronouncing each word clearly and separately, in a perfect metallic monotone. Then he went still again.

Miss Stamp clapped enthusiastically. "Bravo, Ada! What a marvelous creation! And Mary, you helped?"

"Uh, yes. I did contribute," Mary confessed.

"Excellent," exclaimed Miss Stamp. "You girls should be so proud of yourselves!"

"Oh, we are," said Ada.

They all stared at Pan again for a long moment. Pan didn't move, but Mary could hear the fan whirring in his throat, which meant that he was definitely having thoughts. Then Miss Stamp drew her pocket watch out of her dress and gasped. "Oh dear, look at the time. We've gone over. Can you be ready to go in a minute?" she asked Mary.

"I can find my own way home today," Mary said quickly. Hopefully not by walking.

"Good, good," said Miss Stamp. "Get some rest, will you? And keep up with practicing your skills. I will send word when we can begin training again." With that, she dashed out of the room and up the stairs to the attic. They heard the magic door open and close again. And she was gone.

All at once Pan relaxed. "Did I do well? I was trying very hard to act like I was not alive."

Unfortunately he'd forgotten that Miss Pell was still sitting next to the bed. She took the opportunity to scream again. "I told you!" she shrieked. "He's aliiiiiiiiiiiiiiiive!"

"Yes, we know, Pell," said Ada.

"But how?" she asked.

"I'm afraid we can't tell you that," said Ada. "And you absolutely cannot tell Mother."

Miss Pell's face went red again. "Now see here, young lady. I make allowances for you when your mother isn't here, but in less than forty-eight hours your mother will arrive back at this house, and she is not going to be all right with a metal boy, alive or otherwise, hanging about her daughter's bedroom. And what's more, I refuse to be caught in the middle of some kind of childish subterfuge. This is not some puppy that you'd like me to hide in the cupboard."

"What is subterfuge?" asked Pan. "I don't know this word."

Ada seemed to fold into her herself a bit at the mention of her mother. "Please, Pell," she pleaded. "You can't tell her."

"You're a clever girl. Find a solution. Because I need this job," Pell said as she huffed out of the room.

Ada met Mary's eyes.

"We'll figure something out," Mary said encouragingly. "We will."

Ada nodded. "Of course we will."

They had two days.

FIFTEEN
Ada

Ada wondered if, perhaps, just possibly, there was the slim chance that she was in over her head. Such a thing had never happened to her before, so it was an unfamiliar feeling, but it seemed like— perhaps—she needed help. Perhaps she even needed a grown-up: someone who would understand, someone who could advise her— and, most importantly, someone with the respect of her mother, who might be able to talk Lady Byron into accepting PAN.

Unfortunately that someone sounded a lot like Mr. Babbage.

"Come on, PAN," she said with a sigh. "We're going to visit a friend."

"A friend?" PAN's throat fan whirred. "Are you referring to Mary? I would very much like to speak with her again."

Ada checked her pocket watch. Mary had only been gone

for forty-seven minutes. "Perhaps later. Right now I have another friend in mind."

She still wanted to call Mr. Babbage a friend, even though he'd hurt her feelings terribly.

"All right," PAN said amicably, following her downstairs. "I should like to interact with more human beings." But at the front door he stopped. "It occurs to me that if we venture out there, my appearance may cause some alarm. Perhaps I could wear a hat."

"A hat, a large coat, some kind of dark glasses . . ."

"Ah, so you, too, have given this some consideration." PAN nodded thoughtfully. "I am glad. I would like to experience a coat." His throat fan whirred again. "Is there a way I might also obtain some hair? I find myself most envious of your hair, and Mary's hair. Especially her hair last night, when it was up to here." He held his hand above his head, indicating the way Mary's hair had stood straight up after the lightning. "Perhaps I could have big hair, too."

"I'll work on it." For now the best Ada could do was to offer him Pell's raincoat. It squeaked.

PAN clearly enjoyed his first carriage ride through London. He spent every moment clutching his umbrella and staring out the window, his gleaming silver eyes taking in the pedestrians working their way through market stalls, the other carriages drawn by snorting horses, and the enormous sky that stretched above them.

"Why is the sky yellow?" he asked as they turned onto Dorset Street.

"It's supposed to be blue," Ada said.

"I see," PAN said. "Why?"

Ada was about to launch into a lecture about light wavelengths and absorption, but that's when the carriage stopped and Helix came around to open the door. (Helix didn't appear to notice or care that a metal boy was getting in and out of the carriage, but that is the sign of an excellent driver: don't ask too many questions.)

"Act natural," Ada said as they climbed out of the carriage. She'd thought about telling him to act like a machine, but she'd already seen how that went. "And stay in the front hall until I come to get you."

PAN did as requested. The butler (who also didn't ask questions) led Ada toward the parlor.

ZAP!

Ada paused and walked backward a couple of steps to look through the double doors she'd just passed. One door was cracked open, and through that space, she saw frogs. Rows and rows of them, their little bodies splayed out on the parquet floor. Many of them looked freshly dead, but there were some that looked a bit—ew—crispy.

Then: *ZAP!*

A small ribbon of smoke drifted past the doorway.

Disturbed, Ada hurried on after the butler, who didn't say a word about the frogs.

Finally, they reached Mr. Babbage where he waited in the parlor, the same room where he'd displayed his silver dancer. But now it housed another device.

"Miss Byron to see you, sir," said the butler, before he left the room.

"Ada, come in." Mr. Babbage smiled. "What a pleasant surprise. Oh, you look tired."

No girl, not any girl from any century, wants to hear that she looks *tired*.

ZAP! The noise from the ballroom made Ada jump.

"But I'm glad you're here," Mr. Babbage went on. "I told you last night that I've been working on something big. Would you like to see it?"

Ada obviously wanted to talk to him about PAN first, but seeing as how she needed him to be in a good, helpful mood, she could humor him for a few minutes. "I'd be delighted," she said.

Mr. Babbage returned to the far end of the parlor, where his latest invention sat. "This is only a small piece of it, which I will soon present to the government board that is funding it, but for now, allow me to reveal"—he motioned grandly at the machine—"the Difference Engine."

It was a pretty good name, Ada had to admit, even if it wasn't the sort of engine that would (in the future) propel trains, or (even farther into the future) automobiles. Indeed, it would generate no motion at all. It was a series of columns, on which rested small cogwheels etched with the numerals zero through nine. A crank could be turned to activate the machine, and just like that, tables of numbers would be flawlessly generated. All of this would be invaluable for naval navigation (which was why the government was funding it), and anything else that depended on quick, error-free mathematics.

ZAP!

"The funding is quite generous," Mr. Babbage said casually. "Seventeen thousand pounds have been pledged to the completion of my machine."

Ada's mouth dropped open.

"Indeed!" Mr. Babbage said cheerily. "And now you, my dear, can say you saw it first."

"It's—" Ada moved closer. "It's magnificent."

Now this—this was the type of invention that could change the world. It was practical, in its way, but beautiful, and would require minimal training for the operator. No wonder all of that had been on his mind last night, when he'd been critiquing PAN, asking Pell if she'd be able to operate an automaton, and generally bursting all of Ada's bubbles.

(Wait wait wait. Reader, you may be asking what the Difference Engine actually does.

It subtracts.

Ada, well aware of this fact, was still quite impressed, because hey, a giant, beautiful machine that did math. But really? It subtracted. That's basically it.)

PAN could subtract, too.

Then she remembered: PAN! He was still in the front hall.

ZAP!

Ada jumped again. "Your machine is truly wonderful," she

said, interrupting Mr. Babbage as he began to demonstrate the Difference Engine. "But that is not why I needed to talk with you today. I, well, PAN—"

"Your automaton?"

"Yes. Well, the thing is, last night, I was thinking about what you said and—"

ZAP!

Mr. Babbage looked sheepish. "Oh dear. I'm afraid I might have come across a bit harshly. I've actually been thinking about it, too, and I feel I owe you an apology."

This was, in fact, exactly what Ada wanted to hear—just not right now. "That's kind of you to say, but the truth is, you weren't wrong. You made some very good points, which I took to heart. I was thinking about what you said regarding PAN's functions, who could operate him, how he could not learn or adapt, and I had this idea that I could make a few improvements, specifically to his run time."

Mr. Babbage's eyebrows lifted. "And what did you come up with?"

"Electricity, like Mr. Faraday's Dynamo Disc."

"Ah. Perhaps you were thinking of Mr. Aldini's frog, too?"

ZAP!

Ada jumped again.

Drat those zaps! They came randomly, not even at regular intervals. "Is that what's going on in the ballroom?"

"Yes." Mr. Babbage tilted his head. "The poor man has been

here every day for two weeks, trying to replicate what happened at the party. I thought he would give up after a while, but no. He's still here."

Two weeks! No wonder Mr. Babbage seemed so impervious to the zaps. "In a way, then, yes, I was thinking of the frog," Ada said, bracing for another zap. Nothing. Whew! "But I wasn't attempting to bring PAN to life. I merely wanted him to run for longer than ten minutes."

"Hmm. You'd need a way to store all that energy, though, to release it as it's required, rather than all in one burst."

"That is exactly the problem I ran into," Ada admitted.

"Wait, you tried this? Did you build your own electricity generator?"

"I used the lightning rod on my roof and ran a wire in through the window."

ZAP!

Ada startled again. This was no way to live.

Mr. Babbage was uncharacteristically quiet for a moment. "And your house is still standing?"

Ada nodded.

"And your automaton?"

"He's fine, too. Better than fine, actually." Oh, how to explain it. "He's a bit different than he was. More lifelike. More responsive. More inquisitive."

Mr. Babbage cocked his head. "Inquisitive?"

"That's why I came here. In two days my mother will be

home from Bath, and if she finds PAN—well, she will be most displeased."

"But you've made several automatons in the past."

"But I haven't ever brought them to life before." And, to be fair, *she* still hadn't brought one to life, but she wasn't going to tell anyone, not even Mr. Babbage, about Mary's involvement. (It was a difficult decision for her to make, because she really, really believed that Mary's contribution should be credited, but there were all those rules about not talking about fae magic.)

"To life, you say." Mr. Babbage clearly didn't believe her.

"I brought him here." She hesitated, but if she wanted Mr. Babbage's help, she couldn't hide PAN from him. "He's in the front hall."

"I suppose I should examine him, then." Mr. Babbage was already halfway out the parlor, and Ada hurried to follow. "You know that it is not scientifically possible for machines to be brought to life, don't you? Any illusion of life would be programming, like the way you programmed PAN to swing his arms while he walks."

No, there wasn't a scientific explanation for this. But there was a magical one.

"Perhaps one day, technology will have progressed sufficiently that we have difficulty seeing the difference between real life and artificial life, but that is centuries from now, if it ever becomes possible." Mr. Babbage led her past the ballroom and all the dead frogs. "But I should like to see what you've done— Huh."

As they approached the front hall, Ada (and Mr. Babbage,

apparently) became aware of voices. PAN's voice, and a man's.

"So you were born yesterday," the man said. "How interesting."

"I was brought to life yesterday," PAN corrected him. "I think that is different."

"And you think. Interesting."

"Many things are interesting to you," PAN said. "That is interesting."

Oh no! Ada brushed past Mr. Babbage, her cane thumping on the rug as she hurried around a corner to find PAN conversing with Mr. Aldini.

That explained why the zapping had stopped. Her heart sank. "PAN. What are you doing?"

PAN turned to her. "You said to stay here, so I have stayed here. This man wanted me to go over there"—PAN pointed down the hall, toward the ballroom—"but I told him I was to stay, so he came here."

Ada groaned.

"Oh my." Mr. Babbage stared, shocked, at PAN. "Ada! You really did it. You really did bring him to life. Or is it some kind of trick?"

Ada glanced at Mr. Aldini, wishing he'd leave, but she didn't know how to send him away without being impolite. (And young ladies *always* had to be polite.) "It's no trick," Ada insisted. "As I said, I was working late last night and—"

"I woke up!" PAN provided. "And now I want to learn all about everything."

Mr. Aldini turned to Ada, a fervent gleam in his eyes that made her involuntarily shiver. "And you did this? *You?* A female? A mere child? You are the one who creates life?"

Ada's chin lifted slightly. "I consider myself a scientist."

Mr. Babbage glanced between them. "Miss Byron is an undeniable genius, as you can plainly see, Mr. Aldini. I've always said she is my best student."

"But to bring an inanimate object to life," Mr. Aldini murmured. He waved his hands at PAN. "He walks! He talks! What else can he do?"

PAN rattled off the various tasks he could perform: tea serving, embroidery, dancing, complex mathematical calculations, ascending and descending stairs, holding an umbrella, wearing a coat. . . .

"Wait—you can do math?" Mr. Babbage asked.

"I am quite excellent at math." PAN listed several numbers, then added them. Then subtracted them. Then multiplied them. Then divided them.

Ada glanced at Mr. Babbage, whose face was slowly filling with color, because PAN could do more than subtract. So much more. Clearly Ada had spectacularly outdone her mentor. PAN made the Difference Engine look like a child's counting toy.

"*How* did you accomplish this?" Mr. Aldini demanded. "You must tell me everything. Every step. Every formula. Every last detail!"

"My techniques are proprietary," she said.

"Please, I must know your secret," Mr. Aldini said passionately. "It has been my life's work. Surely, you could tell me—"

"No," said Ada simply. "There is nothing I can tell you, sir, that would help you in your own scientific endeavors." That, and she did not actually wish to help this man. Every time Ada blinked, she saw the dead frog at the party, the way Mr. Aldini had taken credit for Mary's magic, and now—horribly—all the dead frogs on the ballroom floor. She had a bad feeling about what would happen if Mr. Aldini ever found out about the fae. (You think??)

"Come now, girl, there must be some arrangement we can come to." Mr. Aldini stared at PAN as if he was a specimen that he would like to take apart in order to see how he was constructed. "You were at the party, were you not? Your name was on the guest list."

Ada ignored him and turned to Mr. Babbage. "I am sorry, but I just remembered something else I have to do today. We must go."

"Oh, well, I won't keep you." Mr. Babbage still seemed a bit dazed and embarrassed. "And . . . PAN, it was quite . . . inspiring to meet you."

"I found it interesting as well," PAN replied.

With that, Ada and PAN hurried back to their waiting carriage and were soon riding away toward the Byron estate. Ada's leg hurt fiercely. She reached to massage the calf muscle through the layers of her dress, but her pain was small when compared with her fear.

Lady Byron was still coming home in two days. Mr. Babbage

was not going to provide a solution to this conundrum.

And now Mr. Aldini knew about PAN. How long would it be, then, before everyone knew? And what would happen to PAN when they did? They would always see him as a glorified science project, and not as a person.

He *was* a person, she thought. And she was responsible for him.

Ada felt that she'd taken a rather deft leap straight from the frying pan into the fire.

They were silent for a long while. PAN still strained to see outside, to get a glimpse of everything, but his enthusiasm had been dampened. (Speaking of dampened, PAN removed his oilcan from his decorative stomach and squirted some oil into his neck joints.) When Helix opened the door, both climbed out.

"Go upstairs," Ada told PAN as they walked inside. "I'll be up shortly."

PAN took off the raincoat and hung it back on its peg. "Are you going to do the important thing you told Mr. Babbage you remembered?"

"What? Oh, yes. I'm going to"—she thought quickly—"get something to eat."

PAN straightened—which shouldn't have been possible, because he was an automaton and already had perfect posture. His throat fan spun quickly. "Will you eat pie? And tea?"

"We can't subsist entirely on pie," Ada said, somewhat sadly. "But I probably will have tea."

"I understand. Do you expect me to serve it? As you know, I am quite good at serving tea."

"You are," she agreed. "But you aren't my servant."

He tilted his head. "I'm not?"

Ada took the key from around her neck. "This is what I used to turn your gears before."

His gaze fell on the key resting in her hand, and then he touched the keyhole in his chest plate.

"I think you should keep it. It's yours." She decided right there and then that even though PAN was her creation, he was not her property. He was an entirely new being. As such, it seemed only right that he should be in possession of every part of himself. "You're alive now. A person."

He took the key from her outstretched hand. "A person," he repeated thoughtfully. "Yes."

"Do you think Mary will come to visit me tomorrow?" PAN asked sometime later.

Ada shrugged.

"Maybe we could go see her," he suggested. "As a surprise."

What is it about Mary that draws PAN so? wondered Ada bemusedly. Perhaps it was the fact that Mary had literally given him life, and that had forged some kind of instant connection between them. "Pass me that spanner."

PAN handed her the wrench. "What are we building?"

"I don't know." Sometimes, when she felt anxious or uncertain, she simply put together bits of metal and hoped for the best.

"I was hoping," PAN said as he sorted through different bits and bobs on the worktable, "that you might call me Pan."

Ada tilted her head. "I do call you PAN. That's your name."

He nodded. "But you call me PAN with all capital letters. I can tell by the way you say it, like it's short for my original name, Practical Automaton Number One." He said this in an even more robotic voice than his normal voice. "But I want you to call me Pan, only the first letter capitalized."

"Oh." Ada hadn't actually realized she'd been capitalizing everything when she said his name. "All right. Pan it is."

"Thank you." He slid a small bolt to her—the exact item she'd wanted next.

Downstairs, a knock sounded on the door.

"Could it be Mary?" Pan asked. "Perhaps she has returned!"

Ada doubted that.

It was late, which meant Pell and the other servants had already gone home for the evening, so Ada grabbed her cane and started for the door. "Stay here," she instructed. "If it's Mary, I'll bring her up."

Pan nodded enthusiastically. "That is excellent, as Mary is one of my favorite people."

Ada hoped she was on that list, too. Considering how few people Pan actually knew, it would be a real blow to *not* be one of his favorite people.

Another knock sounded before Ada was even halfway down

the stairs, and then another as she was opening the door. It was Mr. Aldini.

Drat!

Ada frowned, and she considered shutting the door in his face, but her mother would be horrified if she found out, and Ada was already going to be in enough trouble. "Signore Aldini. I wasn't expecting you."

"I apologize for calling on you so late, Miss Byron. But I was hoping to speak about the PAN." Mr. Aldini looked genuinely hopeful as he stood there in Ada's doorway, his hat in his hands. "And the methods you used to animate it."

Ada stood her cane beside her so that she could cross her arms. "I gave you my answer before, sir. It was no. I have not changed my mind, nor will I."

"Please. As one scientist to another. Think of it as peer review."

Normally, Ada would be thrilled at the idea of peer review. But not this time. "Still no."

Mr. Aldini's face was growing annoyed. "Experiments must be replicated. You do understand this, don't you? What kind of scientist refuses to allow his—or her, I suppose—work to be tested? Are you a scientist, or are you a child?"

"A child, according to you. Now please go away." She started to close the door, but Mr. Aldini thrust his umbrella into the doorway.

"You are behaving very childishly now." He pried the door all the way open again. "We could have done this the easy way, you know. I would have interviewed you, studied your automaton, helped you gather everything you need to re-create your experiment. But if you cannot behave as a grown scientist willing to work with others, then we will have to do this the more difficult way. I *will* have my answers. You *will* provide the secret of life."

With that, Mr. Aldini shoved his way in and thrust a piece of cloth into her face.

A damp, sweet smell filled Ada's nose.

Chloroform.

Distantly, she heard her cane drop to the floor. Then she felt herself drop after it. And finally, horribly, nothing.

SIXTEEN
Pan

Pan turned the key over in his hands, studying the way the silver looked against his brass palm. He was a person, Ada had said.

But what did that actually mean?

Gingerly, he fitted the key into the keyhole in his chest, but he didn't turn it. His gears no longer needed to be turned by external forces. He knew the scientific definition of life (thanks, Ada) and the more straightforward definition (thanks, Mary), but what he didn't know was what to do with this life he'd been given. Before, when he'd been programmed to mindlessly bow and pour tea and embroider pillowcases, he'd had a function. A purpose.

Did he have a purpose now? And if so, what was it?

It was clear, after the utterly confusing incident with Miss Stamp and Miss Pell this afternoon, that it would not be safe for

Pan to stay at Ada's place of residence much longer. Earlier, both girls had seemed genuinely frightened by the idea that Miss Stamp would discover the truth about the nature of Pan's existence. Ada had also fearfully mentioned her mother several times since his creation, even going so far as to say that Lady Byron was going to *kill* her if she found out what Ada had done. (Pan had obviously not yet learned about hyperbole.) And even if they did survive an attack from Ada's mother, would Pan then be cast out into the wide, wet world with only an oilcan and an umbrella to his name?

Perhaps Mary would take him in, although last night, Mary had looked at her pocket watch and suddenly cried, "Three hours until morning! My stepmother will kill me if she finds out I've been out this late!" Then she'd rushed out with hardly a goodbye.

Mothers, step, god, and otherwise, were obviously something to be feared.

And clearly no solution for the mother problem had been reached by visiting Mr. Babbage.

Pan returned the key to the compartment in his stomach. He would make a use for himself, he decided. He would discover a purpose. For now, his purpose would be to assist Ada.

He crossed the room to inspect the object Ada had been working on before she'd gone downstairs. It didn't look like anything much, just a series of fourteen interlocking pieces that could be moved to create different shapes. Pan arranged it into a box and opened it. There was nothing inside. He closed the box and wandered over to the dormer window. There were so many people in the world—they filled the streets with foot traffic and carriages. Did each of them have a purpose? How had they discovered what it was?

An uncomfortable sensation welled up in his chest region. He took out his oilcan again and gave himself an extra squirt, but it didn't help the feeling of something not fitting right. He would have to ask Ada to look.

Thump!

The sound came from downstairs.

Followed by a louder *THUMP!*

Pan tilted his head to one side. He put the oilcan back into his stomach and went to the attic door, where he paused. Ada had very clearly instructed him to stay here. But that had been a concerning thump.

He creaked open the attic door. "Ada?" he called.

There was no reply.

Pan's throat fan whirred. She had told him to stay. But he also had a strong urge to go and investigate.

Should I stay or should I go now? he thought. *If I go there could be trouble. And if I stay there could be double. . . .*

"Ada?" he called louder. "Are you there?"

This time there was an answer. "Help! Please help!" came a voice. It was not Ada's voice, Pan knew at once. It was a man's voice. But it was calling for help.

Pan made up his mind. It was easy when he remembered that he was a person who could make his own decisions. So he decided. He would go help.

He moved swiftly down the stairs to the first floor, which came to an end in the entrance hall near the front door. Then he stopped abruptly.

Because he saw Mr. Aldini.

Mr. Aldini was leaning over Ada, his fingertips on her throat. And Ada was lying on the floor. Her eyes were closed.

Mr. Aldini looked up. "Oh good. PAN, you must help."

Pan hurried to Mr. Aldini's side. His silver eyes scanned quickly over Ada. She was not moving. Her cane lay beside her. "What is wrong with Ada?" he asked.

"I'm afraid poor Miss Byron has fainted," Mr. Aldini answered.

Pan nodded. "Mary did that before, when I was first alive."

Mr. Aldini glanced at him sharply. "Who's Mary? Well, never mind that for now. One thing at a time."

"Should we try to revive her?" Pan peered down at Ada. "Have you tried slapping her on the face and saying her name loudly?"

Mr. Aldini looked confused. "I tried to revive her, but to no avail. We must take her to a doctor at once. Can you lift her?"

Pan easily lifted Ada (and her cane) into his arms. "Where must we go to find a doctor? And also, what is a doctor?" He held in his mind an image of a man in a white coat, from some part of his mysterious knowledge base, but he didn't understand what it meant.

"A doctor is a man who fixes people," Mr. Aldini explained.

"Oh, like Ada would be capable of fixing me if something were to break," Pan said. "Yes, we should get her to a doctor at once."

"This way." Mr. Aldini held the door open for Pan to carry Ada out of the house. He gestured at his waiting carriage. "Let's get her in there. Quick. It's about to rain!"

"I should retrieve my umbrella!" cried Pan. He could see it right there in the umbrella stand, but he couldn't take it without dropping Ada. "Will you get it for me? It's the yellow one."

"No time for that," said Mr. Aldini, and literally pushed him out of the house.

When they reached the carriage, Mr. Aldini again opened the door. Pan set Ada down gently onto the seat, then climbed in himself (quickly, before any rain could get on him) and sat across from her. Mr. Aldini jumped in and called to the driver to go. "Hurry!" he shouted.

The carriage lurched forward. Pan clutched at the side to keep from tipping over. Ada's hair had fallen across her face, and Pan reached to brush it back. He wished she would open her eyes.

"Ada!" He touched her cheek gently, afraid to slap because he knew that he was very strong, and she was very fragile. "I do hope she will be all right," he said softly. "Mary woke up quickly when it happened before."

"Tell me about when it happened before," Mr. Aldini said as the carriage continued to careen through the darkened London streets. "What was it that caused this—Mary, did you say her name was—to faint? The doctor will surely want to know."

"I'm not certain," Pan said. "I was so very new at the time. I was only learning to use my eyes. I don't have eyelids, you know."

"Yes, I noticed. But back to what happened before. . . ."

"Well." Pan took a moment to remember. "Ada said, 'He's aliiiiiiiiiiiive' and then she made this sound: HA HA HA HA HA HA! and then Mary fell very slowly to the floor."

"Interesting," said Mr. Aldini. "And what happened before that?"

"I wasn't alive yet," Pan said. "So how should I know?"

"But clearly you have some idea of how you came to be alive," Mr. Aldini said.

"Not really," answered Pan. "It is all very mysterious." He fixed his silver eyes on Aldini. "Do you know how *you* came to be alive?"

Mr. Aldini suddenly seemed uncomfortable. But Pan didn't notice because the carriage had jerked to a stop.

"Have we reached the doctor?" Pan asked.

BOOM went the sky.

"Yes," said Mr. Aldini. "You'll need to carry her inside."

If Pan could have trembled, he would have been trembling. Go out? In the rain? He would surely rust immediately. But he must do it, he decided. For Ada.

"All right." He scooped Ada up again. In his arms, her head lolled back limply. It was deeply unsettling. But then she gave a small moan. "Ada," Pan said. "Oh good, you're alive. Are you awake now?"

"Hurry!" Mr. Aldini urged him. "In here!"

They dashed from the street into a building, where Mr. Aldini led him down a long hallway until they came to a door.

"How fortunate." Pan watched as Mr. Aldini unlocked it with a small key. "You have the key to the doctor's."

"Um, yes." Mr. Aldini opened the door. "Bring her in here."

Pan brought her in there. *In there* was a large room with dingy white walls and two long tables. One was occupied by a sheet-covered object. (There are a lot of sheet-covered objects in this book, aren't there?) Near the tables, there were various tools: a saw, a small knife, and a hammer.

"What are those things?" Pan asked, drawing Ada closer to him.

"Those are the doctor's tools," Mr. Aldini said. "For fixing people."

Pan caught sight of a human toe peeking out from the sheet-covered table. "And this toe?"

"Replacement parts," Aldini said smoothly. "Put Miss Byron down on this table."

Pan placed Ada on the table and leaned her cane against the nearby wall. She would need it when she got up. But that uncomfortable feeling had returned to his chest. He hoped Ada wouldn't need any of those replacement parts. "Where is the doctor?"

"He'll be here shortly. Now you must go to the waiting room."

"I do not wish to leave Ada," Pan said.

"You must wait in the waiting room," Mr. Aldini said firmly. "You cannot be in here while the doctor is working. Come with me."

Pan touched Ada's throat, as he'd seen Mr. Aldini do before. Under his fingers he felt the slow, steady pulse of her heart. But he couldn't tell if anything had changed. He had to trust that the doctor would help. He followed Mr. Aldini out of the room and back into the hallway.

"The waiting room is here," Mr. Aldini said, and unlocked the door to the next room over.

Inside, there were a number of tables pushed against the walls, with mirrors hung behind them. The room was quite untidy; the tables were strewn with various hats, wigs, and small tubes and tins, but what purpose they were meant for, Pan didn't know.

"May I have one of these?" he asked, pointing to a wig. "For the whole day that I've been alive, I've desired hair."

"Certainly," said Mr. Aldini.

Pan lifted the wig and placed it carefully onto his head. He gazed into one of the mirrors. He was a blond now, with dozens of ringlet curls. If he could have smiled, he would have. "Do you suppose Ada will like it? After she is fixed and wakes up?"

"She undoubtedly will," Mr. Aldini said. "I think she'd also like to see you wearing clothes. Why don't you choose something nice to try on while you wait?"

Pan started to nod, but it made his wig slide across his head. "All right."

"Step right over there." Mr. Aldini pointed Pan to a gap between two racks of costumes.

Pan did as he was told, moving between the racks to find a

small, empty space walled off by more racks. No, wait, those were something else. Bars made of metal. He turned around, but Mr. Aldini was already swinging more bars toward him. "What—"

Mr. Aldini slammed the door of the cage and locked it. "You'll wait here."

Mary ↷
SEVENTEEN

Nothing even a little bit exciting had happened last night. Mary had gone to bed early, but all night she'd tossed and turned, pondering Pan's predicament (what was to be done for him when Lady Byron returned?) and pondering her own (what was she going to do about Shelley?) and pondering her own predicament yet again (what was she going to do with *herself* now that she couldn't go over to Ada's house every day?). In fact, today was the last day before Ada's mother returned. Shouldn't she and Ada (and Pan) spend the day together? But it was after lunch now, and Ada hadn't sent for her. (At the moment, dear reader, Ada was tied up.)

Perhaps she has no need of me anymore, Mary thought glumly.

Fanny's hand came down lightly on her shoulder. "Are you all right, dear?"

Mary wiped at her cheeks. "I got something in my eye, was all. It's quite dusty in here."

Fanny nodded, her eyes full of sympathy. "Do you want to talk about Shelley?"

No, Mary definitely did not want to talk about Shelley. It was just too humiliating.

"Let's talk about you." Mary gestured to the embroidery hoop in Fanny's hand. "What are you working on?"

Fanny held up the hoop. Embroidered in the center was the image of a well-dressed man with a large red X drawn across him. Under the man, in exquisitely beautiful cursive, were the words, *Men are villains.*

"It needs more flowers," Mary said dully.

Fanny nodded. "I thought so, too."

"Oh, look!" came Jane's voice brightly from across the room. "I have received another letter from Lord Byron! I can't wait to read what it says. Probably something about how very alluring he finds me."

Mary stood up. "I'm going for a walk."

"But it's raining," said Fanny, frowning gently.

Mary grabbed an umbrella. "It's always raining."

Outside, her feet directed themselves naturally toward St. Pancras's churchyard. But she didn't want to go there, as now her memories of that place also involved Shelley—so she deliberately stopped and walked the other way. She ended up in a seedier part of town getting her umbrella stolen by a street urchin named Oliver

Twist. (Mood.) Then she got lost for a while and had to stop and ask for directions. A kind-eyed man named Bob Cratchit set her back on the correct path toward home, but when she came into sight of the bookshop, her thoughts were as muddy as they had been when she started, and now she was cold and wet and her feet hurt.

She stood in the street for a long moment, staring up at the warm-lighted windows of their apartments. She could hear the faint tinkle of Jane's laughter from upstairs. She sighed.

BOOM went the sky, and right then someone grabbed her arm and pulled her into the alley.

Mary began to scream until she realized it was Shelley.

"Oh, my love, you're drenched," he observed.

She should say something. Something scathing. Something that would put Shelley in his place immediately. Something that would wound him the way that he had wounded her.

"Of course I'm drenched. Oliver Twist stole my umbrella," she said sharply.

"Who's Oliver Twist?" He took off his coat and pulled it around Mary's shoulders. Which was kind of him. Gentlemanly. But that was not the point.

"You're married," she said, even more sharply.

Shelley bent his head and gazed guiltily at his feet. "Ah. So you know."

"You should have told me."

He ran his fingers through his lustrous hair. "If I had told you, would you still have allowed me to sweep you off your feet?"

"Well . . . no," Mary answered.

"Therefore I couldn't tell you. I had to be with you. My heart demanded it."

"Your heart," she repeated woodenly. "What about *my* heart?"

"I love your heart," he said. "I love you, Mary."

He *loved* her? Hearing those words was a bit like getting struck by lightning. (And Mary would know exactly how that felt. Her hair still hadn't fully recovered from the other night, in fact.)

"BUT YOU'RE MARRIED," she calmly screamed.

He shook his head. "Yes. But it's not what you think."

"What I think is that you're MARRIED. To Harriet Westbrook!" Mary began to pace, which sucked because her feet still really hurt. "I should have known the night of the reading, when you read the foreword of your book and you left out her name. I should have known when you asked me to be your writing partner, and not your . . ." She stopped and pointed an accusing finger at him. "You, sir, are a villain!"

Perhaps Fanny was right. Perhaps all men were villains.

Shelley shook his head wildly. "Harriet and I have an arrangement. We've agreed that we're free to see other people. Well, I am, anyway. Harriet isn't interested in seeing other people, as it happens. But we have an understanding."

Mary crossed her damp arms over her chest. Water dripped into her eyes. "An understanding," she repeated slowly.

"I was very young when I married her," Shelley said. "Young and stupid! I was only seventeen."

"I'm seventeen!"

"I was a very stupid seventeen," he backpedaled. "Not like you. You're quite intelligent for a seventeen-year-old."

"You were seventeen only three years ago," Mary pointed out. "Perhaps you're still stupid."

Shelley's blue eyes flashed with pain. "That was hurtful, darling. Please. Allow me to explain. I only married Harriet in order to rescue her from her abhorrent family situation. I won't bore you with the details, but trust me when I say I was trying to assist a damsel in distress. I never truly loved her, and she never loved me, either. She only loved the security I could give her—my wealth and my good name. She never understood me, not the way that you do."

"I'm beginning to think that I don't understand you," Mary said, although with less fire than before. "Perhaps I don't know you at all."

Shelley grabbed her hand. "Oh, but you do. You have always seen me, Mary. And I have seen you. I truly do love you. You've given me the moon, my dear Mary. I could not bear to be parted from you." He pressed an ardent kiss to her knuckles.

"But how?" Mary's voice trembled. "How can we be together, Shelley, if you're married?"

He squeezed her hand. "Surely you, of all people, don't believe that such an antiquated institution applies to us? We're forward-thinking individuals. We don't believe in marriage. Even if I were free to do so, I wouldn't dream of marrying you. It'd be like putting a wild and beautiful bird into a cage."

Oh. Right. That.

Shelley kissed her hand again. "You are the one I'm meant to be with. I know this in my soul."

She gave a helpless sigh as her anger dissipated. What remained was a sort of ache. He was right that she didn't believe in marriage. How had she forgotten that? She was her father's daughter, after all.

She shook her head. "I don't know, Shelley. I feel—"

"Please give me a chance," he begged her. "Trust me, Mary."

She realized that there were two paths before her. On path one, she could reject Shelley and go on being upset that he was married, smothered by Fanny's pity and Jane's bragging about stupid Byron, and her wicked stepmother's disdain. On path two, she could have everything back—handsome, intelligent Shelley and his wondrous kisses and his love. His *love*.

Her choice seemed clear enough. "All right, but—"

"All right?" Shelley's eyes lit up. "So we're agreed?"

She nodded almost shyly. "But I still feel—"

"Oh, Mary," he cried. "My love, my only, my one. You are my sun, my moon, my starlit sky. Without you I dwell in darkness." He spun her around. "Mary, Mary."

"Shelley," she said, smiling in spite of herself. "I suppose I love you, too. I couldn't have hated you so much all day yesterday if I didn't love you."

"Of course you do." He grinned.

"But you still should have told me—"

"I'm so sorry, darling. I'll make it up to you. Let me make it up to you . . . tonight." He drew her closer to him, gazing down at her lips. She shivered. Her stomach gave a little flutter.

"Tonight?" she breathed. Oh dear.

"Go inside and put on a dry dress. Something nice," he instructed. "Then meet me back out here in fifteen minutes."

Mary nodded. She was becoming more and more adept at sneaking out of her house.

He kissed her, his lips soft and hot against hers. It was enough to make it feel like the world was spinning, everything else lost but Shelley and his amazing magnetic lips. It was enough to silence the tiny warning voice in the back of her head.

(Reader, your narrators here. We just want to give a small public service announcement about the tiny warning voice in the back of your head, the one that whispers that you might be about to make a mistake. We're here to tell you there's a 99.8 percent chance that the voice is right. Please listen to the tiny warning voice. No matter how good a kisser he is.)

Shelley pulled away. "The sooner you go, the sooner you can return," he said, and shoved her gently toward the bookshop.

"You seem to be in a better mood," Fanny said as Mary brushed by her on her way to the bedroom to change. "Did you have a nice walk?"

"Yes, it was most satisfactory," Mary said. Although that wasn't entirely true. Things—like her heart—had been mended during her talk with Shelley. But they hadn't really talked to each other, so much as *at* each other, so the whole thing still felt a bit unresolved. But she'd have time to work that out.

There were new things to consider. Like tonight.

She put on a fresh dress and dried her hair. Her shoes were still wet, but there was no helping that. Then she had to accomplish the most difficult part of her task—getting past her family again. The trick, she thought, would be to act like she had every right to simply walk out the door. No sneaking. No skittering. Just walking like she had somewhere to be.

Because she did.

"Where do you think *you're* going?" her stepmother said as she passed the parlor.

Drat.

"I forgot to lock the shop door when I came in," she said.

"How negligent of you. Go at once and lock it," demanded her stepmother.

"Yes, stepmother," Mary murmured.

Nobody noticed when she grabbed another umbrella on her way out.

When she returned to the alley, Shelley took her by the hand and led her up the street to a waiting carriage. Her heart was pounding as they climbed inside. "Where are you taking me?" she asked a bit tremulously after they'd ridden for a while. Because if marriage was off the table, what exactly was on the table right now? Did Shelley mean to take her to some private room where they could . . . express their feelings for each other?

"You're going to love it," Shelley said, picking up her hand and entwining his fingers with hers.

BOOM went the thunder. (And also Mary's heart.)

She hoped she would love it. She didn't entirely know what *it* entailed, if she was being honest. She'd heard rumors. She was fairly certain of what parts it might involve. Which was exciting. And terrifying.

Maybe they should simply talk tonight, she thought. They had much to discuss. Maybe just talking and of course some kissing would suffice. They could wait for the rest.

"I can't believe I've waited so long," Shelley said.

"Oh?" Mary said weakly.

"You're going to be thrilled," he said. "Ecstatic! When you feel the power of it, it's like nothing else. It's transcendent. Of course, as you well know, it can be a bit jolting. But you're not the kind of girl who's faint of heart."

As she well knew? What kind of girl did he think she was?

"No, I'm not," said Mary faintly. "I can't wait to—"

"We'll have to do this regularly from now on," he said.

CRACK went the sky.

The carriage came to a sudden stop.

"Oh good," said Shelley. "We're here."

He flung open the carriage door and stepped down, then turned to help her out. She blinked a few times as her eyes adjusted to the bright lights. They were standing in front of—not a hotel, or a boardinghouse like where she knew Shelley lived, but . . . a theater.

SIGNORE ALDINI'S DEMONSTRATION OF ANIMA-TION read a banner spread over the doors in big block letters.

"I've seen his show numerous times since we encountered him at Mr. Babbage's party!" Shelley cried excitedly. "You remember that, don't you? The frog?"

Mary remembered.

"But tonight he's really going to do it," Shelley said. "He's going to bring a human being back to life!"

KAPOW! said the sky.

"Oh," said Mary, and a nervous prickle moved down her spine. (Reader, also listen to the spine prickle.)

"You're going to love it," said Shelley again.

EIGHTEEN
Ada

Ada couldn't move.

At first, she thought it was because she was groggy. Well, she *was* groggy. Her eyes wouldn't focus quite right, and her thoughts were as substantial as clouds. But when she tried to lift her hand to rub the sleep from her eyes, her hand wouldn't move.

No, that wasn't right, either. Her hand received all the orders from her brain—sort of. She could feel her hand. Her fingers twitched and curled into a loose fist. Her elbow bent. But no matter how she tried, her hand would not be raised.

Was she sick again? What would happen to her if she'd lost the use of her arms? Her hands? She wouldn't be able to build anything. It seemed so much worse a fate than losing her legs. Panic seized her—but even that was foggy. *Breathe*, she told herself. *Breathe*.

She took a deep breath, in and then out. Slowly, she registered a band of pressure around her wrists, *preventing* movement. She wasn't sick again after all. She'd been restrained.

She struggled to dig through her memories and find her last clear moments. Leaving Pan upstairs in the attic. Answering the door. Mr. Aldini. Her sluggish heart thumped faster. Mr. Aldini had done something to her. He'd taken her. But where?

She tried to look around, but her head was restrained, too. Out of her peripheral vision, she could make out the candle wax dripping and pooling on every surface. There were glass flasks, vials, sketches of human and animal skeletons, and shelves of books and jars of unidentifiable substances, which glowed eerily in the flickering light.

This was . . . definitely not good.

There was also something beside her, a large and hulking shape that she couldn't quite make out. She gathered her strength and forced her head to turn, losing a few strands of hair to the restraints and some kind of metal bowl over her head. But finally, she could see the second table, this one with a sheet draped over whatever object rested on top of it.

The object was human shaped. Not strapped down.

A faint noise worked its way up her throat. She was in some kind of laboratory. With a corpse.

(Well, that got dark fast. We, your faithful narrators, will be sleeping with the lights on tonight.)

A door creaked open.

"Excellent." Mr. Aldini entered the room. "You're awake."

"Wha—" Ada meant to say *What do you want?* or *Why am I here?* but her mouth was as slow as her thoughts.

Mr. Aldini turned a crank, and Ada's whole body tilted up. It gave her a better view of the room—the vials and scales and piles of notes—but the thing that repeatedly drew her eyes was the corpse on the other table, flat on its back. A foot stuck out of the sheet.

Ada's breath hissed. But even as scared as she was, she knew that this wasn't right. It wasn't enough. Her fear had a strange, detached quality to it, like looking at a thunderstorm through a glass window; she could see and hear the rain, but she wasn't getting wet.

That, too, sent another jolt of numbed alarm through her.

"What—" She caught her breath and tried again. "What did you do? To me."

Mr. Aldini gave her that same creepy smile he'd given at her front door. "Nothing that you can't recover from, my dear. A small dose of laudanum. Well, first the chloroform, to get you here. Then the laudanum, when the chloroform started to wear off. You've been in and out since last night."

Since last night? Surely Pell and the other servants would have raised an alarm if they couldn't find Ada in the morning. But no one would ever think to look for her *here*. (Wherever here was.)

"Are you going to kill me?" Ada asked, her mouth slow and cottony.

Mr. Aldini laughed. "No! People would miss you."

"Where is Pan?" She glanced around the room again, but she was alone with Mr. Aldini.

"The automaton is fine," Mr. Aldini said. "As I've said, I'm primarily interested in how you brought this metal man to life. I did ask nicely, but I'm afraid that you're simply a bratty little girl who doesn't like to share her toys. After your second refusal, I came to realize that if I wanted your help, I'd have to *make* you help me. So here we are." He produced a notepad and pencil. "When you're ready, my dear."

Ada said nothing.

He sighed and put the notepad and pencil aside. "Very well. We'll discuss your process later. For now, as I'm on a tight schedule, perhaps you would be so kind as to simply *do* it. As a sort of demonstration for me."

Ada shook her head.

Mr. Aldini tapped his pocket watch. "I have a show coming up, and I've promised the public that, during that show, I will bring a man back to life." He motioned to the corpse. "Our friend here is a criminal, hanged about an hour ago. I won't ask you to resurrect him yet. We'll save that for the show. For now, we'll start small. I only want to see that you can do it." He produced (you guessed it) a dead frog. "Restore life to this, if you will."

Where was he getting all these dead frogs? It was really quite disturbing.

"It's not that simple," Ada said.

"Well, what do you need? I will procure it for you."

"Nothing," Ada said.

"But you must have done something before, made some sort of preparations."

Ada frowned. "I truly don't know what you're talking about."

"You were at Mr. Babbage's party; I remember seeing you at my demonstration, the one where I—well, everyone assumed it was I—brought the frog back to life. Even I believed, for a time, that I had finally done it. But after all my attempts to re-create that singular success were met with failure"—his nose wrinkled at the word—"I understood that it hadn't been me. Someone else must have done it. I was certainly not looking forward to interviewing everyone on the guest list, but then, like magic, you appeared at Mr. Babbage's house with your shiny metal man, and I immediately understood that it was you, all along." Mr. Aldini thrust the frog toward her. "So tell me what steps you took, how you timed it, how you made it appear as though I had been successful. Were you trying to humiliate me or help me?"

"I can't tell you," she said hoarsely, "because I didn't do anything."

"I think you will change your mind, once you understand the consequences of refusal. I'll make this simple for you, since you may not be thinking clearly after that laudanum." Mr. Aldini reached up and tapped the metal bowl over her head. The sound echoed around her, like her head was trapped inside a bell. "Electricity is a wonder, isn't it? Some time ago, I discovered that it doesn't only affect dead frogs and other creatures, but it can pass through the skull of a person and affect the brain as well. I've used it on patients for years. It helps clear the mind and steady the emotions. Sometimes, I do it on myself. Perhaps it will help you, too."

He moved around behind her. Metal clattered and scraped as a second crank was turned.

ZAP!

A shock zinged through Ada's head and body, all the way down to her toes. Stars burst in her vision. Her skin buzzed. She felt her jaw clench and her eyes squeeze shut, both against her will. Something popped and her mouth filled with the taste of blood where she'd bitten her tongue.

Then it was over. It had lasted only a second, but all the hairs on her arms were standing up straight.

"Refreshing, is it not? That is but a sample, my dear." Mr. Aldini came back into view. He smiled and lifted the dead frog. "Now, have you changed your mind about helping me?"

So it was to be torture, then.

She wished that she had the fae power, that she could imagine herself out of these restraints. But no. Even as she tried again and again, in her time of greatest need, the magic did not come.

"I can't." The words scraped out of her. The muscles in her jaw ached with every movement, and forming words hurt her tongue where she'd bitten it. "I can't help you."

"Miss Byron, I am not asking you for anything too difficult. You've done it before. Now do it again, or I'll be forced to give you another little jolt."

Mr. Aldini disappeared behind her again. The crank turned.

Another burst of electricity shocked through her head, worse than the first.

As her vision cleared, Mr. Aldini came back around. "One or two treatments can be very beneficial," he said conversationally, "but too many applications—well, let's say I've seen it go wrong more often than I'd like to admit. The patients who've had a bit too much electricity to the brain can become sluggish. Mentally, I mean."

Ada swallowed a lump in her throat.

The frog came back into view. "Help me help you," Mr. Aldini encouraged her.

"I can't," Ada rasped. "I can't bring your frog, or your criminal, back to life!"

Mr. Aldini sighed. He disappeared behind her. The crank turned. A third shock ripped through Ada. "Unpleasant, yes? I wonder if I've just zapped a year of your life away. It would be a shame to damage that lovely brain of yours any further."

Ada really liked her brain. She had to give him something. "I did it with lightning," she blurted out.

"Go on."

"I connected Pan to a wire and a lightning rod. But that's all. I didn't do anything else. The lightning struck, and he came to life. I don't know exactly how. I cannot replicate it."

"Lightning, you say. That's very similar to my own technique."

"Yes, lightning." Her heart pounded. Did he believe her?

"What about this Mary person?" he asked.

Wait, how did he know about Mary?

Her expression must have betrayed her surprise, because Mr. Aldini smiled. "Ah, yes. Mary. She did help. Or, perhaps, she is the one responsible for this miracle of life?"

Ada shuddered.

"Who is this Mary?" Mr. Aldini asked. "There were several Marys in attendance at Babbage's party. It's a frustratingly common name."

Thank goodness for common names, Ada thought. Mary, at least, was safe.

(Mary, right at this moment, was taking her seat in the audience.)

"Well?" Mr. Aldini said. "Who is she?"

Ada hesitated, and Mr. Aldini smiled in that way that meant he was about to shock her again. "She's nobody!" she cried. "Mary is my lady's maid, is all. She's just a girl." (Later Ada would be proud of her quick thinking here. Especially given that thinking was so very difficult with her electrified laudanum brain.)

"How was she involved?" Mr. Aldini pressed.

"She wasn't. She didn't do anything. She didn't even touch Pan."

"I heard she fainted."

"Wouldn't anyone? A machine had just started talking."

"Hm. I suppose. Women have such delicate constitutions." He didn't look as though he fully believed her, but then he checked his pocket watch again. "Oh dear. It's nearly time. We'll have to continue this after the show. And I suppose I'll have to change my plans for tonight. If you won't—or cannot—help me with this corpse, then different arrangements will need to be made. My fans demand entertainment."

"What will you do?" she rasped.

"I'll make use of what I have," he said ominously.

Pan. He meant Pan. "Where is he?"

"I'll bring him to you," Mr. Aldini said, suddenly agreeable. "But first . . ." He fastened a long strip of cloth around her mouth to gag her. "I'm sure you have many valuable things to say, but in my experience, women always want to dominate the conversation, and I can't have that." He left the room, and then a few minutes later, Ada heard him in the hall saying, "Remember, she's been quite ill."

"I still do not understand why you locked me in that cage," Pan said. "Did I do something wrong?"

"It was for your own protection." Mr. Aldini's voice was louder now as he pushed open the door. "Here she is. All fixed, as promised."

Pan rushed into the room. "Ada!" He paused. "Why are you wearing a metal hat?"

Her heart lifted to see him. Strangely, a blond wig hung limply off the side of his head, but otherwise he seemed unharmed.

Mr. Aldini slammed the door closed. "Let's have a chat." He motioned to a stool beside Ada.

Pan tilted his head to one side. "If you wish for us to chat, why does Ada have something covering her mouth? Will that not make speaking difficult for her?"

"I wish for you and me to chat," said Mr. Aldini. "Miss Byron should rest."

Ada tried to tell Pan to get out of here, but since she was gagged, it came across as "Mmmm mmmm mmm!"

Mr. Aldini patted the stool. "Please sit."

Pan's throat fan whirred, but he perched his metal behind on the tiny stool. "If Ada is fixed now, I should like to take her home as soon as possible."

"Ah, but then you would miss this wonderful opportunity," said Mr. Aldini. "Do you realize what a unique specimen you are? You are what is known in my area of science as an animated inanimate object."

Ada protested again, but she still couldn't speak around the gag.

"See?" Mr. Aldini said. "Miss Byron agrees."

Pan looked at Ada, but because of the restraints, she couldn't shake her head.

"I'm sure you've heard of my show," Mr. Aldini said.

"Actually, no," Pan replied politely. "I'm not even entirely sure what a show is."

"It's an exhibition that people come to see in order to be entertained and educated. I can assure you that my show is the best in London. We're sold out every night. In fact, there's a line of people waiting outside right this very moment, hoping to get into the theater and see my spectacular demonstration."

"So this is not a doctor's office?' Pan asked. "Why would you tell me that it was a doctor's office if it is, in fact, a theater?"

"It's a bit of both," said Mr. Aldini. "Theater, office, laboratory, all together. I really do need to acquire a larger space."

Ada struggled against the gag and restraints again, but they were completely secure. If only she had fae magic. She could have made her restraints into something else. She could have freed them both. She could imagine them somewhere safe.

"I am quite disappointed that I will not be able to bring this man back to life tonight," continued Mr. Aldini. "But now you've come along. Yes, you're only a machine. But you look like a man. And you're alive. Well, almost."

"I am all the way alive," Pan said softly.

"Indeed," said Mr. Aldini. "Ideally, Miss Byron would tell me how she came to make you that way, and I could replicate it. But it seems that she's unwilling to share." He glared at Ada. "So the debt for the doctor's visit remains unpaid. But you could pay it." He turned to Pan. "Miss Byron cannot go home until the debt is paid."

"How would I do that?" Pan asked.

"You could be in my show. People will pay good money to see you."

"I do not want to be in your show," Pan said.

"Ah, but you will be."

"I can make my own decisions," Pan said.

"And you will decide to be in my show. If I tell you to jump, you will jump."

"How high?"

"Never mind. But that's the right attitude. You will do exactly as I say."

"Mmm mmm!" Ada tried again. *Don't do it!* she wanted to scream. *Run away!*

"See?" said Mr. Aldini. "Miss Byron would like you to do as I say. So you can both go home."

Pan glanced between Ada and Mr. Aldini. "Are you sure that's what she's saying?"

"Oh yes. I spend a lot of time with gagged patients. I'm very good at understanding the mmms."

Pan looked from Mr. Aldini to Ada and back again. "I do not believe you," he said. "I think this is an example of subterfuge. I only recently learned what subterfuge is, but I believe that is what you are attempting to do here."

Mr. Aldini sighed and pulled a small device from his pocket. "Well, if you're going to make things difficult, fine. Let's be done with the pretenses, shall we?"

Pan's fan whirred. "Wait. What are pretenses?"

Mr. Aldini ignored him and held up the device. "If I push this button"—he showed them the big red button in the center of the silver box—"it will produce a surge of electricity in Miss Byron's new hat."

"Like lightning?" Pan asked, aghast. "But that could hurt Ada!"

Mr. Aldini nodded. "It would most certainly damage her. It could even kill her."

Ada squinted at the device. It wasn't connected to anything, no wires that she could discern. There was no way to remotely crank the generator, although that was an interesting idea. Mr. Aldini was bluffing, but she couldn't tell Pan. The only thing she could say was more, "Mmm mmm mmm!"

"So what you're saying," Pan said slowly, "is that if I do not agree to be in your demonstration, you will harm Ada."

"Yes." Mr. Aldini smiled his creepy smile. He pulled out his pocket watch again and checked the time. "Goodness, it's almost curtains up. So you must make your decision, PAN. Who will pay the debt? You or Miss Byron?"

Outside, there was a crash of thunder.

Ada closed her eyes. She had never felt so useless. So helpless. So lost.

Pan lowered his head for a moment, his fan whirring steadily. Then he looked up at Mr. Aldini. "I will do as you ask."

NINETEEN
Pan

The stage had a painted black floor and ended in a heavy red velvet curtain with gold fringe. Mr. Aldini instructed Pan to stand in the exact center. From there, Pan could hear so many new and interesting noises coming from the other side of the curtain: the hum of voices and shuffling of feet, the squeak of hinges and rustles of fabric. Mr. Aldini busied himself for several minutes speaking to another man, who finally nodded and disappeared into the gloom backstage. Mr. Aldini then came to Pan and began to polish him—which was rather uncomfortable. When he was satisfied that Pan gleamed as brightly as possible, he checked his pocket watch again.

"Showtime," he said.

Pan felt his insides tense as if he'd been wound up much too tightly.

"I still do not wish to do this," he said to Mr. Aldini. Although he wasn't quite sure what Mr. Aldini was going to ask him to do. Besides jump. And he still didn't know how high.

Perhaps Mr. Aldini meant for Pan to be his assistant with the frogs.

Mr. Aldini reached into his pocket and pulled out the device that could electrocute Ada. "But you will do what I say."

"I will."

"Excellent," said Mr. Aldini cheerily, and put the device away again. "On with the show!"

"Wait. I have a question," Pan said.

"Just do exactly what I say," Mr. Aldini instructed. "It will all be over soon."

"What do I do?" Pan asked. "First, I mean."

"First, don't move at all, no matter what." Mr. Aldini nodded to someone in the wings, and there was a rolling noise, drums—although Pan couldn't see where it was coming from—and the velvet curtain lifted to reveal the front half of the stage. The lights there were brighter than any candle Pan had ever seen. He wanted to cover his eyes, but Mr. Aldini had said not to move.

Slowly, his eyes adjusted to the bright light, and he could perceive the rows of chairs that seemed to stretch on and on before him. In each one a person. And they were making a strange motion with their hands, banging them together, which made a noise.

"What are they doing?" Pan asked quietly.

"I said not to move," Mr. Aldini said. "That includes not

speaking. But they are applauding. It means they are happy."

Pan didn't move or speak.

"Ladies and gentlemen!" Mr. Aldini declared. "I am the Great Aldini!"

The crowd grew louder with their applause.

Mr. Aldini bowed. Pan thought he had not done very much to deserve all the applause, but then again, he had barely learned what applause was, so maybe it didn't mean what he thought it meant.

"I know that I promised that I would bring a man back from the dead," began Mr. Aldini. "But unfortunately, that is not possible tonight, as I have not been able to locate a proper specimen."

The crowd deflated a bit. One man even called, "Boo!"

Mr. Aldini held up his hand. "Please. I assure you, no one feels this disappointment more than I. But not to worry. Tonight I present to you something even more extraordinary. Something truly amazing."

Pan wondered what that could possibly be.

"It will blow your mind," Mr. Aldini said.

That didn't sound safe, Pan thought.

"It will make you reconsider all in this world that you believe to be possible!"

Pan already believed a great many things to be possible. What else was there?

"And here it is!" Mr. Aldini held his arm out toward Pan.

Did he mean Pan? Pan wanted to look around, to see if there was someone behind him, but Mr. Aldini had said not to move, so he didn't move. Pan wanted to *ask* if Mr. Aldini meant him, but Mr. Aldini had said not to speak, so he didn't speak.

So far, being in the show was simple but highly confusing.

"Ladies and gentlemen, meet the PAN. Over the past several weeks, I built him to be a fully functional and practical automaton. But the PAN is simply a machine. A marvelous machine, a breathtakingly elegant machine, but a machine nonetheless. He is not alive."

The audience murmured, not quite sure where this was going. Pan would have asked for clarification, too, if he could have, because Ada and Mary had made him—he knew that to be a fact. So Mr. Aldini was saying something that was not true.

There was a word for that. Something related to subterfuge.

"Before I begin tonight's demonstration," Mr. Aldini said, "I would like a member of the audience to join me on the stage, to confirm the nonliving status of the PAN."

Half a dozen people raised their hands, and Mr. Aldini pointed to a woman in a large yellow gown.

The woman ascended the small staircase to the right of the stage, and Mr. Aldini offered her his arm as he guided her to where Pan stood in the center. It took all of Pan's focus to remain still. He really, really wanted to run away.

"Now, my lady, please take a look at the PAN. Tell me, does he show any signs of life?"

The yellow dress disappeared beyond Pan's vision, and he couldn't track the woman without moving, so Pan stared straight ahead, into the bright lights. When the dress—and then the woman—appeared on the other side of Pan, he kept perfectly still.

Then she stood up on her toes and gazed straight into his eyes. Hers were brown, with darkened lashes, and when she blinked, her eyelids were a different color than the rest of her face. She looked and looked, her breath fogging across his face plate.

Pan didn't move. Not a gear.

At last, the woman stepped away. "He's an automaton," she announced. "There's no life in those eyes."

An unpleasant stabbing feeling rushed through Pan, but that was good, wasn't it? That she'd believed he wasn't alive?

The woman and her giant yellow dress were escorted down the stairs once again, and she vanished back into the audience.

"Now," Mr. Aldini said, "the moment you have been waiting for."

Pan waited a moment. Then he waited a moment more. Which of these moments was *the* moment? It was impossible to tell.

Mr. Aldini rolled a cart onto the stage. The cart held a machine, with a horseshoe-shaped magnet and a large copper disc that spun between the poles. It was like the device in the room where Ada was being kept, but the wires on this one were connected only to forceps, not a metal hat/bowl. Pan started to relax, but then the whole device moved behind him and he couldn't see it anymore.

"Now," Mr. Aldini said loudly, "I will bring the PAN to *life*!"

The crowd gasped. Pan would have gasped, too, if he could have. He was already alive! What did Mr. Aldini intend—

"You're doing an excellent job," Mr. Aldini said quietly. Something—one of the forceps?—clamped onto Pan's shoulder plate. "Keep pretending that you are not alive until I say the words."

What words were those? But Pan could not ask without putting Ada at risk.

The second forceps clamped onto his other shoulder plate.

Mr. Aldini stepped out in front of Pan. "What is life?" he asked the mostly silent crowd. They were all watching, leaning forward, as though hungry for the answer.

Pan was most eager to hear the answer to this as well.

Mr. Aldini started going on about exploring the boundaries between life and death, something about creating life, something about harnessing the power of the gods. (You, reader, have heard all this already. Pan hadn't, though, so he listened intently, even though none of it was actually useful to him.)

"Electricity is life," Mr. Aldini said.

Electricity is life, Pan thought.

But he didn't have much time to ponder on it as the crank began to turn on the Dynamo Disc.

At first, it was nothing but noises—the creak of the crank, the squeal of the disc spinning—but then:

ZAP!

Electricity shot through the wires and forceps and burst through all of Pan's metal. It jolted into him, making the copper in his body burn and itch, making the iron ache, making the aluminum light up. Everything, every single one of his components, felt like it was on fire.

The gears in his joints began to turn, the clockworks all wound up, the springs tightened. It didn't hurt, exactly, as Pan's nerves were not as sensitive as human nerves. But it was most unpleasant. Still, he didn't shout, because Mr. Aldini hadn't said he could.

Finally, Mr. Aldini cried out, "He's alive! He's aliiiiiiiive!" and Pan recognized those words. Those were Ada's words, and Pan's cue to act naturally again.

Pan jerked away from the Dynamo Disc, ripping the wires from the machine. The electricity stopped.

Everyone in the audience gasped, and people were shouting. Some were clapping. A few had gotten to their feet, as though they might rush the stage, but Mr. Aldini stepped forward and held out his hands, pushing downward as though he—with the power of his mind—could make them sit again.

And it worked. People in the audience returned to their seats.

"As you can see," Mr. Aldini called over the noise of the audience, "I have brought the PAN to life. But I suppose you would not be satisfied with this simple demonstration of him walking forward. I suppose you will want more."

"Yes!" the audience cried out. "More!"

"Very well." Mr. Aldini turned to Pan and unclamped the forceps. "Now, PAN, if you will . . ." Mr. Aldini did a twirly thing with his hand. Pan didn't move. "Turn around," Mr. Aldini whispered.

Thinking of poor Ada, Pan turned around.

More gasps came from the audience.

"Turn back around," Mr. Aldini said.

Pan did as instructed.

"Now, introduce yourself, PAN."

Pan hesitated for a moment. Then he said, "Hello. I am Pan."

The audience erupted in raucous applause. Pan turned to Mr. Aldini. "Am I done? Can I see Ada now? Can we go home?"

"No," Mr. Aldini said. "These people paid to see a show."

"Is that not what we just did?" Pan said. All his metal parts—which was all of his parts—still tingled from the electricity. He didn't want to do anything else, but now that he knew how terrible it was to be shot through with electricity while he was alive, he knew exactly how much it would harm Ada if Mr. Aldini pushed that button. And *she* was not made of metal. Human flesh seemed so much more delicate. Pan couldn't let her be hurt like that.

"The show requires more of you," Mr. Aldini said.

Pan would have frowned if his face could have moved that way.

But then Mr. Aldini ordered Pan to put his left hand in, then his left hand out, then his left hand in and shake it all about. Pan did as he asked, but he didn't know what was happening.

Mr. Aldini told him to dance.

Pan did. (He only knew the one dance—the robot—but the audience seemed to like it.)

Mr. Aldini told him to recite the alphabet. Pan was relieved to discover that he knew the alphabet. He could recite it both forward and backward.

Then Mr. Aldini instructed him to stand on his head.

Pan obeyed, although it made his oilcan and key clang horribly inside his iron stomach, and Mr. Aldini gave him a curious look.

"Open your stomach," he said when Pan was right side up again.

"In front of everybody?" Pan whispered.

"Now," said Mr. Aldini.

Pan really wished he did not have to do that, but he did. For Ada. He would do anything for Ada. So he swung open the hinges of his washboard abs to reveal his stomach. And then he withdrew the oilcan and the key.

Mr. Aldini's eyes were bright with mischief. He put the key into the breast pocket of his coat. Pan could do nothing to stop him. There was a new feeling rising in Pan's chest, a big feeling, powerful, like his gears were misaligned and he was going to overheat. Everyone was still applauding, clapping and clapping, and he should be happy, too. He had learned so many new things today, about doctors and theaters and subterfuge. He had desired to have a purpose, and now he found that he had been given one.

But he was not happy.

Because he had come to understand a simple, terrible truth:

Not all people were good.

Mr. Aldini forced him to dance again. Pan's heart—his metaphorical heart, anyway—began to fill with despair. Couldn't all these people see how humiliating this was? Didn't they care? Were they all like Mr. Aldini?

Pan looked down into the crowd and felt a jolt when he saw a familiar face. Mary's face. Her eyes were open wide, her hand covering her mouth.

And she was not applauding.

Mary
TWENTY

Mary stared in horror at the familiar metal boy on the stage. Beside her, Shelley was clapping feverishly. Everyone around Mary, in fact, seemed charged with a strange, terrible energy at the sight of Pan— poor Pan!—parading about up there, doing exactly what Aldini told him. There was no expression on Pan's metal face, but Mary could almost tangibly feel his pain and humiliation and sadness. Her heart squeezed for him.

"Rub your stomach," Aldini commanded, and Pan obliged, his metal fingers clanking along the ridges. "Now pat your head *at the same time*! Now hop on one foot!"

"Isn't it amazing?" Shelley exclaimed. "I have so many questions!"

Oh, Mary had questions, too. Her mind churned with them,

question upon question, but underneath them all, the most important question: where was Ada?

Because Mary knew, down to her bones, that Ada never would have agreed to this monstrosity of an act. Ada wouldn't have given Pan into Aldini's care voluntarily.

Which meant that Ada was in trouble.

Which meant that Mary had to find her. Right now.

She started to stand up, but Shelley's hand came down on her arm. "Are you all right, my love?" he asked, all sweet concern.

"I have to go . . . powder my nose," she explained.

He frowned. "At a time like this? When we are witnessing one of the marvels of the modern world? Surely your nose can wait."

He was adorably dense sometimes. But she didn't have time to explain to him what "powdering one's nose" actually meant, and besides, that would be somewhat indelicate. Instead she said, "I'm afraid I'm having female problems."

Shelley's hand dropped from her arm, his expression suddenly horrified. "Oh. Well. You'd better go, then."

Unimpeded, Mary slipped past a dozen people and into the aisle.

"Are you all right, miss?" asked an usher as she entered the lobby.

"Is there a place where I can powder my nose?" she asked demurely.

The usher gazed at her blankly.

"I'm having female problems," she said.

"Oh dear God." He directed her to a washroom. From there she shimmied out the window and into the alley, then ran along the building until she found what she'd been looking for: a side entrance. But the door was locked.

"Drat," she muttered under her breath. She tried to call up the image in her mind of a key, a heavy brass key with a ragged edge.

The key instantly materialized in her hand. Mary smiled. She really was a natural at this fae stuff. (But she had forgotten to account for the cost, and somewhere in the nearby audience, dear reader, someone's key disappeared from his pocket. It was going to cause all kinds of problems for him later. But this story isn't about him.)

Mary tried the key in the door.

It didn't fit.

"Double drat," she said. Of course it would be difficult to imagine the exact key for this exact door. She'd have to try something else.

Very well. She imagined the locking mechanism inside the knob, the pieces of metal that would turn to unlock it. She pictured it moving. She willed the movement to be real.

Click went the door. (And unbeknownst to Mary, another door in the theater suddenly locked.)

Mary hurried into the building. She was standing at the end of a darkened hallway. Somewhere close by she could hear Aldini's loud voice booming out. It sounded like he was wrapping up. She must hurry.

She dashed down the hallway until she came to another three doors.

All locked.

This time she didn't even bother saying drat. She mentally jimmied the lock of door number one the way she had before. (Behind her, in response, the original door locked again.) This room was a dressing room, with props and costumes strewn about it, but what drew her eye immediately was the large, ominous cage set back in one corner. A person-size cage.

She gulped as she looked at it. But now she had to focus on finding Ada.

She tried door number two. Behind this door was a striped cat who hissed at her fiercely. Mary shut the door quickly.

She furtively hoped that Ada would be behind door number three.

Click.

And (hooray!) Ada was.

She was gagged and strapped down to a table—this was less of a cause for celebration—with a strange metal contraption on her head. Her eyes were closed, her face pale in the dim light. She didn't move. And beside her, under a sheet, was an actual corpse, which was also ominous.

Mary rushed to her friend's side. "Ada!" she whispered urgently. "Ada, wake up!"

She felt a stab of relief when Ada's eyes opened. Two little bumps appeared over Ada's eyebrows as she frowned. "Mary?

What are you doing here?" she asked.

But what came out was "Mmmmm mmmmm mmmmm?"

"I was about to ask you the same question," Mary said, frantically removing the gag and unbuckling the straps over Ada's arms. "Do you think you can walk?"

"Absolutely." Ada swung her legs off the table and then slumped immediately toward the floor. Mary caught her. "I'm not doing much better than the corpse," Ada observed. She cringed. "The corpse is really disturbing, wouldn't you agree?" She straightened in alarm. "Where's Pan?"

"He's performing." This was not the time to tell Ada that Aldini had electrified poor Pan in front of the entire audience. "Right now we have to get you out of here."

"We need a door," said Ada, blinking several times as if to clear her clouded vision. "If only we'd been paying attention to the lesson about the doors!"

"A door?" Mary turned to look at the door she'd come through. Ada was right. She couldn't remember a single thing Miss Stamp had told them about the door business. Drat drat drat. "Well, I guess I'll give it a try. What's the worst thing that could happen?"

"We didn't get to that part of the lesson," Ada slurred. "But I suppose we could end up in a wall. Inside a floor. Under the ocean. Trapped in the nothing space between the doors forever."

"Do stop talking," Mary said. Then she remembered a single thing Miss Stamp had told them about the door business. "Miss Stamp mentioned something about an invisible thread, from the door you wish to exit from and the place you wish to go."

"I'd like to go to my bedroom," Ada said. "That would be lovely, wouldn't it? To be home in bed. I never thought I'd say this, but I quite miss my bed."

Mary immediately turned her efforts into picturing a door in the center of this room. Her hands clenched into fists. Sweat popped out upon her brow. This fae stuff was hard work. After a long, arduous moment of imagining, *POP* went the air in the center of the room, startling both girls (but not the corpse), and there was a door.

"Well done!" said Ada warmly.

Mary hurried to open the door, which—thank goodness—was unlocked this time. It swung open to reveal the attic workshop in Ada's house. "I'm more familiar with the attic," Mary said.

"It will have to do," said Ada as Mary grabbed her under the armpits and dragged her unceremoniously through the doorway.

"My ears popped. A pressure change," murmured Ada. "That makes sense." Then she sat up abruptly. "Wait. What about Pan? We can't leave Pan."

"I'm going back," said Mary resolutely. "I'll get him." Only she had no idea how.

Once back at the theater, Mary destroyed (*POP!*) the door to Ada's house. It wouldn't do to leave it there while Mary tried to retrieve Pan. What if Aldini were to find it?

Mary retraced her steps: back down the hall, out the side door, in the washroom window, out into the lobby, and back into the auditorium, where the show was ending and everyone was standing up now, clapping and clapping.

She slid in breathlessly next to Shelley.

"Mary! Where have you been? Are you recovered?" he exclaimed. "I've missed you."

"Sorry," she said. "There was a line for the washroom. But is the metal man still—"

"A marvel!" he said, and remembered that he was supposed to be applauding.

"Take a bow, PAN," Aldini ordered Pan, and Pan bowed stiffly.

Mary's mind raced. "I should very much like to meet this metal man," she said to Shelley. "Personally, I mean. Do you think we could arrange that?"

"Of course!" Shelley smiled because he knew this would impress her. "I am Percy Bysshe Shelley, after all. I will ask."

"If you'd like to meet the PAN in person," called out Aldini, "please line up along the left side of the theater, and, for a small extra fee, you can touch him and speak to him. There is also an artist on hand, who can quickly draw your picture next to the PAN, as a memento."

"I'd like a picture," said Mary, and ran to get in line.

It was awful, waiting, watching people poke and prod at Pan like he was an expensive toy for them to play with. And still she had no idea how she was going to get Pan away from Aldini and all these people and back where he belonged, with Ada.

Mary was nearly in tears by the time she and Shelley had reached the front of the line.

"Ah, Mr. Shelley," said Aldini, shaking Shelley's hand. "So glad you could make it tonight. What did you think?"

"It's an absolute wonder," said Shelley. "You've outdone yourself."

Pan turned to look at him. "What has he outdone?"

Shelley clapped Pan on his metal shoulder, making a clanging noise. "Why, he's created you, my fine chap."

"Mr. Aldini did not create me," said Pan in an offended tone. "I do not know why he said that. I was created by—"

Then Pan finally saw Mary standing just behind Shelley.

"I'm pleased to meet you, sir," she said quickly. "*For the first time.*"

Aldini and Shelley both smiled condescendingly at her attempt to be polite to an automaton.

Pan's throat fan whirred. "Oh. Subterfuge."

"I can see your young lady is quite taken with my machine," Aldini said with a laugh.

"Yes," said Mary, "he is a marvel."

"I wonder if we might have a private audience with the automaton," said Shelley, bless him. "I'd like to inspect him more thoroughly. In the interest of art."

"Oh now, I'm afraid this is as private as I can allow," said Mr. Aldini.

Drat. Drat drat. Mary needed an idea.

But then there was a hullabaloo from the lobby.

"The front door is gone!" someone screamed.

Oh dear. Mary had not been creating responsibly. It was a good thing Miss Stamp wasn't here.

"What is the meaning of this? Where is the door?" cried a second voice.

"We can't get out!" yelled a third.

"What? What's this about the door?" Aldini scowled. He pointed at Pan. "Stay right here," he commanded, and then turned and dashed off to the lobby.

Mary glanced around. Everyone, all the people in line, and even Shelley, were now moving toward the lobby to see about the missing door situation. (She must have destroyed the door when she created the door to Ada's house. It really had been quite brilliant of her, come to think of it.)

She grabbed Pan by the arm, then spotted the two black marks on his shoulder plates where the clamps had been. Poor Pan! "We have to go." How, she still wasn't exactly sure.

But Pan didn't move. "Mr. Aldini said to stay here."

"Yes, but Mr. Aldini is a villain," she pointed out.

He nodded. "Yes," he agreed. "Oh, Mary. Not all people are good!"

"I know."

"But if I don't do as he says, he will kill Ada. He has a device that will electrify her brain in a very unsafe way!"

"Ada's not here anymore, Pan." Mary shook her head. "I got her out."

"Where? Where is Ada?" he asked.

"Home."

"That is very good news," Pan surmised. "I, too, should like to go home."

"I'm working on it." Mary bit her lip. She looked around. There wasn't any clear way to exit the theater. It wasn't like they could simply walk through the door. For multiple reasons.

If only Pan weren't so conspicuous. Everyone (especially Aldini) would see her attempting to escape with a shiny metal man on her arm. She wondered if there was a way to disguise Pan. If only, she thought, he could look like a real boy.

If only.

And then she thought, *Well, why not?*

It was going to be tricky, she knew that at once. It would not be enough to simply imagine Pan as a boy. There was the cost to consider. (This was the first time all night that Mary had stopped to consider the cost.) To make Pan look like a human boy, she had to make something else—someone else, she realized—look like Pan. And she couldn't do that to some random stranger, no matter how desperate she was to set Pan free. She wasn't *completely* irresponsible.

But then Mary remembered the corpse. She hadn't seen more than its foot, but she didn't need to see more, did she? It wasn't a direct transference—the corpse's likeness for Pan's. It would be enough to simply make Pan look like a person, and make this (dead) person look like Pan.

"Mary?" Pan asked gently. "Are you having thoughts?"

239

"Yes, dear. I'm having so many thoughts."

She didn't have time to give the situation too many thoughts, however. She clasped Pan's smooth brass hand in hers and stared up at his face—this face that she and Ada had so meticulously crafted. First she imagined his eyes—those silver eyes of his—as human eyes, with an iris and a pupil. She imagined his body with real bone and muscle and sinew, covered by skin, not metal. She imagined clothes on that body—a fine suit, like what all the men here were wearing. She imagined hair on his head. She imagined his heart beating.

And then—and then!—it was so. Her vision seemed to blur, and when it cleared, PAN the metal man was gone. And Pan, the real boy, was standing before her.

He blinked a few times. His eyes were still silver in color, but very human.

Real.

"What just happened?" he asked, and his voice sounded like Pan's, but with a new timbre to it. "I feel strange."

Mary could only stare at him.

"AHHH!" screamed a voice from the lobby. "What happened to my suit? Where are my clothes!"

Pan's hand in Mary's was warm. He lifted it carefully, gazing at it in wonder. "I have fingernails," he breathed.

"You have everything," she said, and laughed. Then she nearly fell over. She was so tired, so very, very tired.

Pan caught her by the waist. "Are you all right? Are you about to faint? Because I don't know if I can handle that again."

"I'm fine," she said. "Everything's fine."

From the lobby they heard a tremendous crash. Mr. Aldini had located an axe (one of those in-case-of-no-doors, break-glass axes), and was chopping a hole in the wall where the door should be.

"Let's go home," Mary said.

They walked arm in arm to the lobby, where people were streaming out of the impromptu door hole. They were almost through it when they were stopped by Shelley. "Mary!" he cried, grasping at the arm Pan wasn't holding. "Are you still feeling poorly? Where have you been? And who exactly is this?"

"I'm P—"

"Peter!" Mary shouted.

Pan frowned. He could frown now. His lips could move. It was remarkable. "I'm Peter? But I quite like the name Pan."

"He's Ada's cousin," Mary said quickly. "I just happened to run into him. I was feeling a bit faint—"

"Oh no!" cried Pan. "But you said you weren't going to faint! You said you were fine! Why does everyone not say what they mean?"

"I was fine. I am fine," Mary insisted. "I was just caught up in all the excitement, I suppose, and got a little wobbly there, and Peter assisted me."

"Oh," said Shelley, gazing at Pan appraisingly. "I didn't know Miss Byron had a cousin. So you're related to Lord Byron?"

Pan tilted his head. It was clear that he didn't know what a cousin was. "I'm Pan?"

"Peter Pan," Mary jumped in with again. "He's Ada's cousin on her mother's side."

"I see," said Shelley. "Well, thank you for taking care of Miss Godwin, Mr. Pan, but I can handle it from here. It's late. I should get her home." He pulled at Mary's arm.

"I, too, should like to go home," said Pan, not letting go of Mary's other arm. She was being stretched between them most uncomfortably.

"Do you think we might give him a ride?" Mary asked. "He's staying with Ada. Which is on the way, isn't it? I'm so bad at direction." (Reader, in no way was Ada's house on the way to Mary's. But Mary was doing the best she could.)

"Why not?" said Shelley jovially. But then he seemed to remember something. "But what about the automaton?"

Mary and Pan froze. "What . . . what about him?" gasped Mary.

"I thought you wanted to see him in private," said Shelley.

"Oh. I . . . did," said Mary.

"She did," agreed Pan.

"Hmm. Well, I'm sure I can see him again at another time," said Shelley. "So let's away."

They all started for the door hole. There was a terrible moment as they passed Aldini on the way out. He was trying to calm a man in his underwear. He did not give them a second look.

Whew. Within moments they were in the carriage, hurtling through London. Shelley had out a piece of paper and was writing a poem, probably about the automaton. His eyebrows drew low over his blue eyes. *"Oh shiny, rapturous contraption!"* he murmured. His expression darkened. "That's not it. Oh, why is writing so hard!"

"Well, keep trying. You'll get it," Mary said. Then she let him go back to being absorbed in the poem and turned her attention to Pan.

He gave a great sigh using his new lungs. He lifted his hand to touch his chest. "I'm feeling something new right now," he said. "What is it?"

"Relief," answered Mary. "Because you are free."

Pan smiled. It was a nice smile. "I am free," he repeated. His eyes met and held hers. "Thank you, Mary."

"You're welcome, Pan," she said, and then she leaned her head upon his shoulder, which was now warm and squishy the way a real boy's shoulder should be, and slept all the way to the Byron house.

TWENTY-ONE
Ada

In the Byron house, Ada awakened, shivering.

A thin blanket covered her legs up to her waist, and through the fading fog in her mind, she could hear rain pattering on the roof and window.

It was dark, but even without a light, she knew the shape of her own attic workshop. There was the fae door Miss Stamp used. There was the dormer window Ada climbed in and out of, lit every so often with a flash of lightning in the distance. And there was the worktable with her piles of notes and drawings, tools and trinkets, and the logic puzzle she'd been making for Pan. A clock tick tick ticked but she couldn't see it from here. Even so, the stillness (aside from the storm) gave her the sense that it was either very late at night, or very early in the morning.

She had only faint memories of coming home. There was something about Mary. Then something about doors. Followed by something about going to rescue Pan.

Pan!

Ada sat bolt upright, gasping as she swung her legs over the edge of the sofa. Memory and dread flooded into her, because Pan was still with Mr. Aldini. Ada grasped around for her cane and started to push herself up just as a complete stranger walked in.

"Ahh!" Ada raised her cane to bludgeon him.

The boy froze, wearing an expression that Ada would have called deer-in-the-headlights, if headlights had been invented yet. (Deer had, though.) As it was, he looked shocked and uncertain what to do. "I apologize! Don't hit me!"

"Who are you? What do you want?"

"I wanted to bring you tea." He held up a tea tray.

She lowered her cane, staring at him. He was a young man, no more than seventeen or eighteen, with copper-colored curls and silver eyes. And even though Ada was absolutely certain she'd never seen him before, there was something familiar about the way he looked at her, that kindness and innocence of his demeanor. And then there was the way he placed the tea tray on the table.

"Pan?" she asked shakily. But it couldn't be, because Pan was metal. This boy was . . . not.

His worry melted into a faint smile. "Hello, Ada." His voice sounded like Pan's, but without the slight metallic, echoey quality from before. "One lump or two?"

Now *that* sounded like Pan.

"Pan!" she shouted.

"Ada!" he shouted back.

"You— You're—" Was there a polite way to tell someone they suddenly looked human? "What happened to you?"

He nodded emphatically. "I know! I look different. I have clothes. And hair of my own."

Ada crossed the room to inspect him. Two arms. Two legs. Definitely a head. All the parts were there. (All the parts she was willing to look for, anyway.) "But how is this possible? How did you become . . . ?"

"Real?" He held out his hands, studying them with a kind of wonder in his eyes. "Mary did it somehow. I'm not sure about her exact methods, but I have skin now!"

"You do," she agreed. "It's very nice." Indeed, his hands were smooth and probably quite soft, as he hadn't yet developed calluses or chapped spots.

He beamed. "Thank you. I'm quite proud of it."

He poured her a cup of tea, which she took gratefully. Tea helped everything.

As she drank, warmth flowing through her body once again, Pan told her the story of Mary's brave and daring rescue last night. "And then I became a real boy," Pan concluded.

Ada rested her empty teacup on her lap, thoughts whirling. "What about Pell and Isosceles and Helix? The other servants? Do you know if they're all right? Did Mr. Aldini hurt them?"

Pan dug through his pocket and produced a crumpled note.

I've gone to stay with a friend for a few days. Don't worry about me.

—Ada

It wasn't even in Ada's handwriting. So why had no one come looking for her? (Actually, Pell had been out all night peering into every ditch and checking every hospital for Ada, after she'd tried to file a missing persons report with Scotland Yard, but it turns out that missing persons reports hadn't been invented yet, and even if they had, the police would have assured Pell that teenagers took off all the time, and they had to be missing for more than twenty-four hours in order for anyone to truly be worried. Poor Pell was beside herself.)

Ada put the note aside.

"Not all people are good." Pan took the empty teacup and stared into it for a long moment. Ada sensed that something significant had changed inside him, as well as outside. What had happened with Mr. Aldini had stripped away Pan's innocence. And now he was a boy. A real boy. One who knew that the world could be cruel and take advantage of gentle souls like his. Pan looked up again, his jaw set. "Now what do we do? Can we go visit Mary?"

Oh, all right. Not that much had changed.

Ada shook her head. "No. I mean, maybe. Somehow Mr. Aldini knows there's someone named Mary involved." Ada had told Mr. Aldini that the Mary in question was her lady's maid, but there was no way to know if he'd believed her.

Pan looked down. "It was I who told him about Mary. I didn't realize there were people who couldn't be trusted."

"It's all right." Ada touched Pan's arm. "You didn't know. But we're still in danger. Mr. Aldini will have figured out by now that we've escaped." Ada could have kicked herself. Here she'd been sleeping off the laudanum and drinking tea when she should have been worrying. She lurched to her feet. "When he can't find us at the theater, this is the first place he'll look. And who can say what he would do to get us back?" The man had a *corpse* stashed in his office, for goodness' sake.

Pan took a deep breath. "So what do we do?"

Ada rubbed her temples, pushing away the forming headache. This whole situation was too big, too impossible. "I'm not sure."

"It should be against the rules," Pan muttered. "There should be a rule that one person can't go to another person's house and take them away to hurt them."

"It *is* against the rules!" Ada cried. "You're brilliant, Pan."

"Am I?" He grinned. "So what happens if you break that rule?"

"Well, Scotland Yard comes to arrest you. There's a trial—people judging your innocence or guilt based on evidence, that is—and if you're found guilty, you get locked into a small cage for a long time."

Pan's expression darkened. "Mr. Aldini locked me in a small cage. I did not even break any rules."

"He is not a good man," Ada confirmed. "Locking you in a small cage was also against the rules. So was electrifying you." She paused, considering their options. "We can tell the police about what happened, but the part where you became a real boy is going to be difficult to explain. Plus, we don't have evidence. Who would believe us?"

"What would count as evidence?" Pan asked. "Something to prove that you were there, in the theater?"

"Yes, but there's nothing like that."

"Only your cane," Pan said.

Ada looked down at her cane, which she'd laid on the table. It was the rosewood one, though, with the gold tip. She'd noticed, of course, which one she'd been using, but she hadn't thought about it too much yet. She'd needed a cane and this one had been nearby. "Where's my good cane?"

"I believe it's still at the theater, in the scary room with the spare parts."

"That's evidence, Pan!" Ada sat up straight. "I'll go to Scotland Yard, tell them that I was kidnapped, that I escaped, but that my cane is still there."

"Will Mr. Aldini also be in trouble for kidnapping me?"

Well, that was harder. "I'm not sure how to explain you to the police. When you came to life, you became your own person. But as far as the police are concerned, you were my property, since I built you. It *is* against the rules to take something that doesn't belong to you—that's called stealing—but I'd have to prove that, too."

"There were many people who saw me at the theater," Pan reminded her. "And Mary and Mr. Babbage know that you built me. Wouldn't they help you?"

"Perhaps," Ada murmured. "Now that you look like a regular boy, there is no automaton to recover. But that's all right."

"So that's our plan?" Pan said. "When do we go to Scotland Yard?"

"Immediately, I think. This could fix everything, Pan. Going to the authorities will solve all our problems."

Suddenly, the front door slammed and a familiar voice called out, "Ada, darling! I'm home!"

"Blast!" Ada cried in horror. "It's my mother!"

Footfalls sounded on the stairs. "Ada? Are you up there?"

Panic startled Ada into action. "Quick!" she hissed. "Hide."

Pan hurried into the corner of the attic and threw a sheet over his head. Which wasn't quite what Ada'd had in mind, but it would do for now.

Ada finger combed her hair, which had the distinctly crispy quality of having survived two close encounters with electricity. The footsteps grew closer until, approximately ninety-two seconds after her mother had yelled, the door to the attic burst open and Lady Byron stepped in, wearing a deep frown and a traveling dress.

Ada stopped moving. "Hello, Mother," she said softly. "You're home early."

"I'm right on time," Lady Byron said, "and you know that. Now, good heavens, what are you wearing? What has happened to you?"

Ada glanced down to get a look at her dress. It was the same one she'd been wearing yesterday, but completely rumpled, creased where she'd slept on it, and stained in a few places.

"You look a fright!" Lady Byron declared. "PELL!"

Ada cringed, only because her mother wasn't looking.

"Pell, get up here right this instant!"

Pell, who had dejectedly arrived back at the Byron estate only moments before, hurried up the stairs. "Oh, Lady Byron, I'm so very sorry, but I don't know where—" Pell stopped speaking when she stepped inside the attic, her eyes immediately falling on Ada and taking in the state of her appearance. "Oh."

A hundred emotions passed over Pell's face, from abject tearful terror (which she'd been wearing when she'd walked into the attic) to acute relief, and then her face settled somewhere between the two extremes. Which was fair. Ada was back, after all. And Ada did, as her mother had said, look a fright.

Lady Byron stalked toward the poor housekeeper. "What have you been doing these past two weeks? You haven't been taking proper care of Ada at all. Look at her."

"Yes, Lady Byron," said Pell quietly. "I'm sorry, Lady Byron."

Ada tried to catch Pell's eye, but the housekeeper was busy looking at her shoes. Poor Pell. She needed this job and couldn't afford for Ada to go off getting kidnapped.

"Yes," Lady Byron said stiffly, "you should be. My poor, neglected daughter. You must go draw her a bath right away. I cannot bear to see her like this." Lady Byron paused. "And while you

251

are drawing baths, get one ready for me, too. The road from Bath is so filthy."

Pell gave a quick nod and exited the attic, not giving Ada another look.

Lady Byron spun and took Ada's hands. "Oh, Ada, my dear. This is why I can never go away again."

"No?" Ada squeaked.

"I leave for five minutes and the staff has you looking like a small, rain-soaked mouse. Your hair is an affront to fashion. How long have you been wearing this dress?" She held up a finger. "Wait, don't tell me. I couldn't bear to know the depth of Pell's neglect. My dear, you look exhausted. Absolutely wretched. When was the last time you bathed?" She turned and bellowed, "PELL, HURRY UP WITH THAT BATH!"

By this point, Ada had a white-knuckled grip on her cane. "Please, don't blame Pell," she said. "None of this is her fault."

"None of what, dear? What exactly happened while I was gone?"

"Nothing!" Ada said quickly. Perhaps too quickly. "I mean, nothing has happened. I've been working on a new project, that's all."

"Oh, really?" Lady Byron glanced around. Her eyes settled on the tall figure under a sheet. "Is that it? I'd like to see." She took a step toward Pan's hiding spot.

"Not yet!" Ada said. "It's not finished. But, um, I'll finish soon." Drat. She was going to have to make another automaton, wasn't she? In case Pell mentioned Pan the impractical automaton she didn't know how to use.

Whew. Lady Byron coming home was already a lot of work.

"Oh, my dear. You mustn't be so shy about your efforts. You're so clever. You know I love looking at your inventions."

And judging them. And saying they weren't good enough. And sending her into a corner by herself with a sheet of math problems.

Ada wished Lady Byron would go back to Bath.

"Never worry, my dear. I won't leave you again. We'll soon get you married to Lord King, and then he will also take care of you." Lady Byron gave Ada one of those loose hugs that were mostly air, as though she didn't actually want to touch her daughter. "PELL, THAT BATH!"

Ada's ears started to ring.

Pell reappeared at the attic door.

"Oh, good." Lady Byron straightened. "The bath?"

"Not yet, Lady Byron. But there's a man at the door for Ada." Pell's eyes cut to Ada, worry filling her gaze. "A Mr. Aldini, ma'am."

Ada's whole body went cold. She couldn't breathe.

Fortunately, Lady Byron didn't seem to notice. "Mr. Aldini? The galvanist who did that vulgar frog demonstration at Babbage's party? What on earth does he want with Ada?" Lady Byron shot Ada a warning look. "You stay here. I'll deal with this."

With that, Lady Byron swept out of the attic.

Pell followed, but not before she, too, looked over her shoulder at Ada, her eyes filled with warmth. "I'm glad you're safe, miss," she whispered, then hurried after the lady of the house.

Footfalls sounded on the stairs, heading down toward the first floor.

"You can come out now." Ada went over to Pan and pulled the sheet off him.

He slouched, gasping for breath. "That was terrifying. Your mother— Are all mothers like that? I would have helped, but— And then I thought she might see me!"

Ada put her finger to her lips, then beckoned him to a loose board in the wall. She pulled aside the board, revealing a flared tube of metal, like the loud end of a trumpet. The sound of voices came through. It was Ada's secret hear-what-my-mother-is-saying-about-me-in-the-parlor listening device.

"Lady Byron!" the low, accented voice of Mr. Aldini intoned. "What a surprise to find you here. And a delight, I mean."

"Mr. Aldini." Lady Byron's voice was cold. "Whatever could you possibly want with my daughter?"

"Ah, straight to the point. I like that in a woman. No beating around the bush. No rambling on before saying what she wants. Just the facts."

Awkward silence.

"Well," Mr. Aldini said, "I simply came to see to Miss Byron."

"Oh?"

"Yes, indeed."

(No indeed, reader. This was actually not why Aldini had come to the Byron estate. He'd come to blackmail Ada into returning to the theater. But upon seeing Lady Byron, he'd quickly realized he needed to change tactics.)

"Last night, I held the greatest demonstration of my entire career," Mr. Aldini went on. "You see, I brought a metal man to life!" Paper rustled. (Ada couldn't see it, dear reader, but Mr. Aldini was holding up this morning's newspaper with the headline THE GREAT ALDINI GIVES LIFE. A drawing accompanied the article, one of Pan—still metal—and the forceps clamped to his shoulder plates, and electricity sparking all around him. Below that was a review, a glowing five-star review, the kind that used the words *magnificent* and *masterpiece* and *life altering*. As far as reviews go, it was a pretty good one. It might have even been enough to help restore a family name.)

"You brought a metal man to life," Lady Byron said dubiously.

"Yes, indeed!" Mr. Aldini said again, a manic pitch to his voice. "And I would like more than anything to continue my presentations with my living metal man, but, well, I do hate to tell you this, but I'm afraid your daughter—"

"What about my daughter?" Lady Byron said slowly.

"She has broken my machine."

Lady Byron gave a sharp, indrawn breath. "Ada? *My* Ada was at that theater on Drury Lane? No, sir, you must be mistaken. Ada is much too responsible and respectable to visit the *theater* like some commoner. And now you accuse her of breaking something that belongs to you? No, it must have been someone else."

"It was her," Mr. Aldini said. "There was some hubbub because of the doors last night, and when I returned to my automaton, it was broken. Completely useless."

(Wait, you might be asking. What automaton was he talking about, being that Pan was right there beside Ada, listening to every word, every indrawn breath? Well, Mr. Aldini means the corpse. You know the one. When Mary had imagined Pan into an actual human, all those parts had to come from somewhere. Magic has a cost, if you'll recall, so as Pan had gained skin, eyes, real hair, and so on, the corpse had become metal. Now it *looked* like an automaton, but it didn't function. It certainly wasn't alive.

So Aldini had gone into the laboratory, discovered Ada missing, found an automaton where the corpse had been, and assumed—in the way anyone who didn't know about fae would— that Ada had broken Pan and made off with the corpse . . . possibly to resurrect it at a show of her own. It was hard to say what a teenage girl might want with a corpse. Anyway, he didn't care about the corpse nearly as much as he cared about getting Pan operational again, given that he had more shows to put on.)

"If you built the machine, you should be able to fix it," Lady Byron was saying. "Ada certainly isn't responsible for it. Besides, she's not even allowed to leave the house unaccompanied."

"Oh." Mr. Aldini paused. "I think perhaps she was accompanied by her lady's maid? A girl named Mary. Perhaps we could speak to her?"

Ada and Pan exchanged worried glances.

"Well, now I'm quite sure you are mistaken, sir," said Lady Byron. "Ada does not have her own lady's maid. In fact, we have no one employed in this house by the name of Mary. Now, I find it inappropriate for you to be here, accusing my daughter in this way."

Mr. Aldini cleared his throat. "I see. My apologies, madam. But then, to whom should I return this cane?"

Ada stifled a gasp. Her cane! Her good cane!

Lady Byron made a flabbergasted sound. She did not like to be contradicted. Ada could picture the exact shade of red that was currently filling her mother's face. "How did you get this?"

"As I said, Miss Byron was visiting the theater, and I simply wish for her to fix what she broke." He paused. "Lady Byron, I can see that you are concerned for your daughter's reputation. Please, don't worry. I won't tell anyone that she was present at my theater. I would never. You have my word as a gentleman."

"Leave. Leave right this instant."

Ada and Pan exchanged looks again. "The cane," Pan whispered. "What evidence do we have now? And what will your mother do now that she thinks—"

The door slammed. "ADA! Come down here and get in this closet *immediately*!"

Ada gulped in a breath. How long would she be locked in the closet this time? A week? A month? And while she was doing random equations in the dark, waiting to be let out, bad things would most certainly happen to Pan.

And like that, Ada decided that she wasn't going to take her mother's abuse anymore. She would not allow things to return to the way they'd been before Mary and Pan had come into her life. No.

Ada shoved the loose board back into place. "Quick," she said, "block the door." According to her calculations, they had approximately ninety-one seconds until her mother reached the attic and all hell broke loose.

"Block the door? Why?"

"To prevent my mother from getting inside."

Pan's eyes went round. "What is she going to do? Will she"— he lowered his voice—"kill us?"

"Just bar the door." Ada grabbed a satchel, then hurried to the side of the room with the trunks and threw in the box of spoons she'd been using for Pan's silver parts. In they went with a noisy clatter. A notebook followed, a pencil, and other items she gathered from her work area.

Meanwhile, Pan had dragged the sofa in front of the door and was watching Ada move about the attic.

The knob rattled. "Ada?" Lady Byron's voice squeezed around the door. "Ada, what are you doing in there?"

"I'll be out in a minute!"

Pan looked alarmed, so Ada shook her head. "Subterfuge," she whispered. Then she looped the rosewood cane into the satchel and headed toward the dormer window. It was raining, but the sky was a light yellow-gray by now, and Ada could see most of the way down to the stable.

"What are we doing?" Pan asked. "We aren't going out there, are we?"

"It's that or the closet." Ada shimmied outside and slung the bag over her shoulder. "Come on. We need to go."

Bang, bang, bang. The attic door shuddered under Lady Byron's fist. "Ada, what are you doing? I demand that you open this door at once!"

"But it's raining," Pan said.

"Is there a boy in there?" Lady Byron shouted.

"No, Mother!" Ada called. Then, softer: "Hurry. We have to go now."

Pan gave the rain a wary look, but finally scooted out onto the roof as well. He cringed every time the rain touched him. (Which was a lot. It was pouring right now.)

The seat attached to the zip line was only meant for one person at a time. There was no way for two people to strap into it at once, even if Ada had wanted to sit on Pan's lap. But they didn't have time to take the zip line down individually and send the chair back up in between.

"On a scale of one to ten," Ada said, "how strong do you think you are?"

"I experienced no difficulties moving the sofa."

"Wonderful." Ada handed him the rosewood cane. "Hook this over the wire. We're going down."

Pan looked even more alarmed than before.

Ada wasn't sure whether what they were about to attempt was

mathematically possible, but there was simply no time to do the exact calculations. She climbed onto Pan's back and looped her arms around his neck.

"Uh," said Pan. "I can't breathe."

"Then you'd better get us down there quickly."

With that, they zipped down the line, rain stinging them in the face, and dropped into the pile of hay that Ada had at the bottom of the zip line for emergencies.

Ada's legs were wobbly as she took her cane back from Pan. "There, that wasn't so bad, was it?"

"A tiny piece of wood has lodged itself into my skin!" Pan held out his hand to show her. "It hurts!"

Ada plucked the splinter free before dragging Pan along. They had to keep moving. Who knew how long the sofa was going to keep her mother at bay? "Let's go."

"Where are we going?" Pan looked up at the sky as they hurried away from the stables. "And how long do we have before the rust sets in?"

"We're going to see Mary."

"Finally," Pan said.

TWENTY-TWO
Pan

The bookshop where Mary lived was apparently *Closed*. "May I knock on the door?" Pan asked. "I've always wanted to be the one who knocks."

"Knock yourself out," Ada said.

Pan stared at her, aghast—but when a faint smile touched her mouth, he realized it was one of those human figures of speech he hadn't yet learned, and she was teasing him. The muscles (he had muscles!) in his shoulders relaxed somewhat, but only somewhat, because Pan understood that they were still very much in danger. From Mr. Aldini. From mothers. And most immediately, from the rain.

He balled his fist and then knocked on the door, feeling so very human. But it rather hurt his knuckles.

"Can't you read?" said a chilly voice on the other side. "We're closed. And if you can't read, what are you doing here?"

Pan didn't know what to do, so he knocked again.

A stern-looking woman opened the door and glared at them through narrowed eyes. "Oh," she said. "Miss Byron. What can I do for you?"

"Hello, Mrs. Godwin," Ada said brightly. "I'm here to see Mary. Is she available?"

Pan felt a jolt of panic. This was Mary's stepmother. Pan scanned the woman for a weapon of some sort. There, a rolling pin in her hand. She might use it to bludgeon them.

"Ada," he murmured, "be careful."

"Mary is unavailable," Mrs. Godwin said. "She is, in fact, being confined to her room right now. No visitors allowed." (Yep, dear reader. Mary was grounded.)

Ada's eyes went wide. "What? Why?"

"Not that it's any of your business," Mrs. Godwin sniffed, "but it has come to my attention that Mary has been sneaking out, unattended, to do who knows what, with who knows who, at any time she pleases. She didn't return last night until nearly morning."

"Oh no," said Ada. "I'm afraid there's been some kind of mis-understanding. Mary was with me, all last night."

Pan swung his gaze around to regard Ada. What she was say-ing was not entirely true. Ada hadn't been with Mary *all* last night. In fact, Ada and Mary had spent very little of last night in each other's company. Ada was obviously attempting some form of sub-terfuge. How exciting!

"Hmph," said Mrs. Godwin. "And what were you doing all last night, then?"

Ada cleared her throat as if something was stuck in it. Pan patted her gently on the back. "Thank you," she said. "I invited Mary to come with me to the theater. I got last-minute tickets."

"Is that so?" Mary's stepmother crossed her arms over her chest. "Well, that's even worse. Mary should have asked for permission. Which I wouldn't have given her. The theater is not a proper place for young ladies. I'm shocked that your own mother would allow you to go."

"I'm very sorry," Ada said contritely. "It won't happen again. I promise."

"I hope not," added Pan. "The theater is a bad place for anyone."

Mrs. Godwin's gaze settled on Pan. He took a small step backward.

"Please, Mrs. Godwin," Ada pled before they could get into explaining Pan. "I need to speak with Mary rather desperately. It will only take a few minutes."

"Please," Pan echoed.

Mrs. Godwin turned her narrowed eyes on Pan again. "And who are you, young man?"

"Did someone say young man?" A girl's voice sounded from behind Mrs. Godwin. "Ooh, hello. I'm Claire."

"My name is Pan," Pan provided. "Peter Pan. I'm Ada's cousin."

Ada gave him a curious look. Pan raised his eyebrows as if to say, *See? I can also do the subterfuge.*

"Peter Pan?" Claire pushed herself into the doorway, her gaze moving up and down Pan in a way that for some reason made him uncomfortable. "Well. It's such a pleasure to meet you."

Pan wasn't sure yet if it was a pleasure to meet her, so he remained silent.

"Ten minutes," Ada pleaded. "That's all we need."

"Jane," Mrs. Godwin snapped, "go up and fetch Mary."

"But, Mother!"

"Now!" Mrs. Godwin said.

Mothers truly were the most terrifying of people. And why had she called the girl Jane, when she'd said her name was Claire? Pan was confused.

"You can have five minutes," Mrs. Godwin said. "But that is all."

"Thank you," Ada breathed.

Finally, they were admitted into the bookshop, where Mrs. Godwin deposited them in a small back room.

"I've never seen so many books," Pan whispered.

"This isn't a library," Ada said. "You don't have to whisper."

But whispering felt right. There was something very special about all these books, something that made a strange feeling of reverence build up inside him. "I wish I could read them all."

Mary came into the room and closed the door behind her. "There's never enough time to read all the books we want to read."

"Mary!"

Ada and Mary threw their arms around each other with a fierceness that alarmed Pan until he understood it to be some kind of friendly greeting. Pan was uncertain of what the appropriate action for him would be, so he finally placed his arms around them both.

Mary pulled back, laughing. "You look much better than you did last night," she said to Ada. "And you," she said to Pan, "look much the same. I still can't really believe it. You have hair!" She lifted her hand as if she would touch his coppery locks, but then stopped herself. Pan took this to mean that touching another person's hair without permission was not polite.

"I always wanted hair," he said. "And now I have so much. Not only on my head, either. I've found small, fine hairs on my arms and curlier hairs on my legs and even some—"

"That's all right, Pan," interrupted Ada, her face reddening. "We've all got hair, but it's best not to dwell on it. Anyway, I have to talk to you, Mary, and there's a lot to cover in about four minutes and thirty seconds."

Quickly she summarized their predicament: Mr. Aldini was after them. Lady Byron was after them. They were officially *running away*.

"And we have about two minutes for you to tell me what we should do now," Ada said.

Mary's eyebrows lifted. "Me tell *you*? You're the genius here."

"But you're the hero. Your quick thinking saved us all last

night." (And Ada was kind of right. Mary has the title of this book and everything.)

"All right, all right," Mary said. She bit her lip. Pan wondered if that hurt. Then her eyes lit up. "We should ask Miss Stamp! Surely she would help us."

"But how are we going to do that in under ninety seconds?" Pan glanced fearfully at the door, where he knew Mrs. Godwin was about to reemerge.

"Right, Pan! The door!" Mary said. "*You're* the genius!"

"Hey, now," protested Ada.

"Am I?" Pan asked.

Mary stared intently at the door of the back room. "An invisible thread," she muttered to herself. "Invisible thread." She crossed to the door and opened it, revealing the bookshop with its rows of shelves and oh so many books. Pan tensed. He could hear Mrs. Godwin's footsteps on the stairs. Coming closer. (If we could, dear reader, we'd insert the theme of *Jaws* in the background. But you'll have to imagine it.)

"She's coming back!" he cried. "We're going to need a bigger door!"

Mary slammed the door closed. She did a strange pursing of her lips that reminded Pan of Ada's eyebrow pinch. Then she opened the door again, but—Pan gasped—what was on the other side was an *entirely different room*. "Go!" said Mary, shoving Pan and Ada through the magic door. "I'll be right up."

She shut the door again.

Pan looked around. They were in a larger room than the back room of the bookshop, but not by much. There were three small beds. One large wardrobe. A vanity with a mirror. And a girl.

"Oh, hello, Fanny," said Ada. "We were—uh—"

Fanny said nothing. Had she seen what was behind them as they'd crossed through the door? It was impossible to tell. Being that she said nothing.

"My leg was hurting," Ada said quickly. "Mary said I could come in here to rest."

Fanny looked meaningfully at the chair in front of the vanity. Ada sat.

An awkward silence followed.

"This is awkward," Pan announced.

Fanny got up and left the room.

"That was also awkward," Pan said.

Finally, Mary entered. There was the sound of the door being locked behind her. "Sorry. My stepmother didn't believe me when I said you'd left. She wanted to search all through the back room. But then she was satisfied that you were gone, and she told me to go to my room for the rest of the day." She smiled. "So how can we call upon Miss Stamp? I've never tried, have you?"

Ada shook her head. "She just appears."

"Same," Mary said. "How does one summon a godmother? We could try wishing on a star."

Everyone looked out the window. It was daytime. And cloudy. Not a star in sight.

"We could try the wardrobe," Ada said.

"The wardrobe?" Pan asked.

Mary opened the wardrobe and pushed aside the clothes hanging there.

"There's a door in the back of the wardrobe!" exclaimed Pan. "This is unusual, is it not?" He really had no idea what was normal anymore.

"Yes, Pan. It's unusual." Mary rapped loudly on the magical door.

Pan stared intently at the wardrobe. "And now we expect Miss Stamp to immediately appear?"

"This door leads into a room that is full of other doors," Mary explained. "But I do not think it's being constantly monitored. We will have to hope that someone eventually hears us knocking. It could take quite some time."

Right then the door burst open, and Miss Stamp emerged.

"Or we can expect her to immediately appear," said Ada.

"Girls!" said Miss Stamp breathlessly. "Whatever are you up to?"

Both Mary and Ada started talking at once. It was loud. Pan was tempted to cover his very delicate fleshy ears. Miss Stamp, however, simply nodded and waited and nodded some more. Then Ada and Mary finished speaking at the same time and stared at their teacher expectantly.

"Well," huffed Miss Stamp. "Isn't this a mess? I'm disappointed in you girls. What have I told you and told you about

CREATING RESPONSIBLY? What a fine kettle of fish!"

"I do not see what fish have to do with anything," Pan said.

Miss Stamp looked at him, softening. "You poor lad." She turned to the girls again. "This is why we have the rules. I specifically told you, no bringing things to life."

"You said dead things," Ada pointed out. "You never said anything about inanimate things."

"Obviously the same goes for inanimate objects. When you imbue something—anything—with life, you give it some of your own. Remember, there is always a cost." Miss Stamp sighed. "Generally, if a person brings something to life using fae magic all willy-nilly, *which you did*, without specifying the exact amount of life they wish to give, they instinctively give very little. Days or weeks, only." She tapped her finger on her chin. "How long has it been? When exactly did you bring him to life?"

Mary and Ada started talking at the same time again. Something about lightning. Something about how men are villains who don't tell you the most important information you need to know and how that naturally would upset anyone past the point of thinking clearly. Something about how time is meaningless.

"It's been two and a half days," Pan said. He wanted to ask her "How long do I have?" but he found he was afraid to hear the answer. Days or weeks. So really, he could stop being alive at any time.

The girls had gone quiet.

"Can I give him more?" asked Mary softly.

"I'd give him some, too," said Ada.

But Pan shook his head. "I would not wish for you to cut your lives short on my account. No matter how much that I like being alive."

"We'll discuss the possible solutions—and consequences—later," said Miss Stamp. "For now, you must come with me, Pan. And Ada, you should return home."

"But Mr. Aldini is still out there and—" Ada shuddered. "My mother. My mother is going to be quite upset. She hasn't even heard the part where I went to a poetry reading."

"Indeed," said Miss Stamp grimly (as she was well acquainted with Ada's mother), "but at least you will be safe at home. Surely Mr. Aldini can't abduct you right from under your mother's nose. And, as far you've told me, he doesn't fully know of Mary's involvement, outside of there being a person of interest named Mary, and we all know how excessively many Marys there are in the world." She pointed at Mary sternly. "So you, too, should stay in your room. Now say your goodbyes."

But Pan didn't want to say goodbye. Instead he said, "No."

"I'm sorry?" said Miss Stamp.

"I am my own person, and I make my own decisions," he said. "And I decide that I will not be parted from Ada. Or Mary. I refuse."

"And I'm not going home," Ada said, crossing her arms over her chest. "You can't make me."

Mary shrugged. "I'm already locked in my room."

"Fine." Miss Stamp sighed again, a deeply aggravated sigh. "I will go discuss your situation with the other godmothers. I'll be back in an hour." She gave them the sternest of looks. "Don't do anything irresponsible, in the meantime. All of you, stay here."

With that, she bustled out through the back of the wardrobe.

Ada immediately began to pace, her cane thumping the floor. Her eyebrows were doing the pinch thing again. "Where can we go? Where can we go?"

"Wait," said Pan. "Miss Stamp said to stay here."

"And then she'll be back, likely with other godmothers. Her plan won't change just because an hour passed. She'll have *backup*."

Oh. That seemed likely, now that she said it that way. And Pan wondered if, when Miss Stamp returned with the other godmothers, they would find a way to unmake him somehow. A fate he would very much like to avoid. "So where can we go?"

"We can't stay in London," Ada said. "Mr. Aldini will find us."

Pan shuddered.

"We have to leave town," Ada murmured. "We have to go somewhere he won't think to look."

"What you need," Mary said, "is someone who has a vested interest in protecting you. Someone who wouldn't condemn you for the magical part of it. Someone open-minded, who won't care so much about propriety."

"Yes?" Ada prompted. "Do we know anyone like that?"

Mary's eyes suddenly widened. "Your father."

"You have a father?" Pan turned to Ada, astonished.

"Everyone has a father, Pan," Ada said. "Well, almost everyone."

"Who? What? Where? When? Why? And how?" Pan asked.

"It's a long story," said Ada. "And no, I couldn't possibly go to my father. I don't even know him."

"But don't you wish to know him?" Mary asked. "And perhaps he desires to know you. And I can't think of anything else, and we don't have a lot of time here, so take it or leave it."

"Take what? Leave what?" asked Pan. "I'm confused."

Ada was scowling. She clearly hated this idea. "I don't hate this idea," she said. "But it won't work, on account that I have no notion of where my father is."

"Jane's been corresponding with him," Mary said.

"Jane?" asked Pan.

Ada looked confused. "Your sister's been writing to my father? Whatever for?"

"She's a damsel in distress," said Mary. "And he is supposedly rescuing her from the tedium of her mundane existence."

"Ew," said Ada.

"Agreed," said Mary. "But the important detail here is that Jane always sends her letters to his publisher in Paris. You might not know where to find Lord Byron, but they will."

"What is Paris?" Pan asked. "Is it far?"

"It's in a whole other country, Pan," said Mary. "But it's not so far."

"It's where we'll have to go," Ada said resolutely. "It seems there is no other alternative."

Mary knelt next to one of the beds and pulled out a worn carpetbag with a broken handle. Then she hurriedly crossed to the wardrobe and withdrew a spare dress, which she handed to Ada, after which she went to the door and somehow unlocked it using only the power of her mind. (Mary was amazing!) She went out briefly, and came back with a hunk of bread and some cheese, a flask of water, and two changes of clothes: one for Pan to wear now (since he was still dressed in the rather conspicuously fancy and ill-fitting suit she'd conjured onto him at the theater last night) and one for later. For some reason the girls turned around while he changed.

"I don't have any money," Mary said then after he was presentable again.

Ada clutched her satchel to her chest. "I have Mother's spoons."

"Spoons? Are spoons a form of currency?" Pan asked.

"They're made from real silver," Ada said. "It's more than enough to get us to Paris."

"You should go," Mary said. "Miss Stamp will be back soon." There was sadness in her hazel eyes, and Pan suddenly understood that Mary didn't intend to accompany them on their journey.

"Come with us, Mary," he said impulsively. "Please."

Mary's mouth opened and then closed again. "Oh, Pan. I wish I could—"

"But why can't you?" he asked.

Ada and Mary exchanged glances. "Because we're running away, Pan," said Ada finally. "And as young ladies, if we run away, even for one night, our reputations will be ruined. And then we can never come back."

It was only then that Pan fully understood what Ada was doing for him. "But, Ada—"

"Thank you," Ada said to Mary. "For all of it. Truly. Be well."

"You're welcome," Mary said. "Be safe."

They threw their arms around each other, Pan once again placing his arms around them both, and then Mary hustled them out the window and down a ladder that suddenly appeared. This was Pan's second time today sneaking out a window, and he was not a fan.

It was still raining outside. Mary tossed down an umbrella. Mary really was wonderful.

"Now what?" Pan asked.

"We get a carriage," Ada said. "And go to Dover."

"I thought we were going to Paris."

"I don't know if I've explained this to you, Pan, but we live in a place called England."

"I thought we lived in London."

"Indeed. London is a city in England. And England is an island." Ada paused to draw the shape of Great Britain in the dirt with her cane. Then another shape. "And this is France, beyond this large channel of water."

"Oh." Pan clutched his umbrella closer. "So much water."

"The best place to cross the channel is a city called Dover," Ada explained. "So that's where we'll go first."

"All right," Pan said. "I'm ready." But he paused to stare up at the bookshop. "Are you sure this is the best course of action? As it's going to ruin your reputation and possibly therefore your life?"

Ada's face pinkened. "I've decided something important today, Pan. I would like my life to be my choice."

Pan nodded. That, at least, he understood.

She took his hand. "Let's go."

Mary

TWENTY-THREE

"Please pass the potatoes," sighed Mary.

Her father passed her the bowl. She scooped a large portion onto her plate, then sat staring at the lumpy mass of mashed potatoes with resignation.

"Hmph. She should be sent to bed without supper," sniffed Mrs. Godwin. "As a punishment for gallivanting off last night."

"Ada told you. I went to the theater."

"What theater? To see what?" Mr. Godwin asked.

She might as well tell the truth. "To see Mr. Aldini's latest demonstration," said Mary.

"You went out," sniffed Mrs. Godwin. "At night. Without a chaperone."

"I had a chaperone," said Mary stiffly. "As you know perfectly well, I was with Ada." Mary wished she was with Ada now, and Pan—dear, sweet, and earnest Pan. She couldn't stop thinking and worrying about Pan. Mary didn't know how much time she'd given him the night she'd brought him to life. A month? A year? Miss Stamp had said it probably wasn't very much. But how much was it?

Mrs. Godwin tsked her tongue. "Two unchaperoned girls at a theater, of all places. What must Miss Byron's poor mother think?"

Mary shuddered.

"I wish *I'd* gone to Mr. Aldini's demonstration," said Mary's father glumly. "All of London is talking about it. Apparently he brought a metal man to life in front of everyone. One who could walk and talk and think for itself. Imagine the implications."

"Himself," Mary corrected him softly.

"It was probably a charlatan's trick," harrumphed Mrs. Godwin. "Like that automaton a few years ago who was said to be able to play chess, but then it turned out that it was a man hiding underneath it making all the moves, using mirrors and such."

"Well, he did that thing with the frog, didn't he?" Mr. Godwin said. "That was real." He waved around a piece of roast beef on the end of his fork. "The frog, remember? We all saw it."

Mary smiled a secret smile.

"In any case, I should like to have seen this metal man myself," Mr. Godwin said.

"I wish I'd been there, too," said Jane grumpily. "It must have been most exciting. Why does Mary get to have all the fun?"

It *had* been exciting. It had been the most exciting night of

Mary's life, up to then. (Before that, the most exciting night of her life had been the previous night, when she'd brought Pan to life.)

"You're entirely missing the point," said Mrs. Godwin. "Mary left this house without telling any of us where she was going and did not return until the dead of night. Who knows if this was the first time she'd stolen away from us?"

Mary gasped in outrage. "How dare you!"

"Perhaps Miss Byron has merely agreed to cover for you," continued Mrs. Godwin. "For all we know, she spent last night with a man."

Mary swallowed guiltily. She avoided Fanny's gaze. Fanny had been peering out the window when Mary had returned home last night, and had seen Shelley help her down from the carriage and kiss her good night.

"And for all we knew at the time," continued Mrs. Godwin, savagely cutting at her slab of roast beef, "Mary had run off and been debauched."

Mary's jaw tightened. Of course when she'd gone off with Shelley last night, the idea of her "debauchery" had been a real possibility, perhaps even an exciting one. But now she was quite offended at the suggestion.

"In which case," Mrs. Godwin went on, "her reputation, her future prospects, *her entire life*, would be utterly ruined!"

Mary threw down her fork. "My reputation?" she burst out. "What reputation is that? What prospects, Stepmother? What life?"

"Mary," said Mr. Godwin gently.

Mary pushed back from the table and stood. "I'm sorry, Father. Please excuse me. I find I'm no longer hungry."

Then she fled to her room and threw herself down on her bed. (She may have cried some bitter tears, dear reader, but we don't know. We left her alone for a minute, because she really did deserve some privacy as she was railing against the unfairness of the world.)

Sometime later, after she'd rather emotionally wrung herself out, Mary heard a noise. A tick . . . once, and then a few seconds later, again. She sat up and wiped her eyes, straining to listen.

Tick. Pop.

The sound wasn't coming from the wardrobe, not that she expected anyone to come through there anytime soon. Miss Stamp had been quite irate when she'd returned from her meeting with the other godmothers to discover that Ada and Pan were gone. She'd given Mary a stern talking-to. (Mary was getting in trouble with everyone at this point.)

Bang. Clatter.

The noise was coming from outside. Mary sprang from her bed to see what was the matter. Away to the window she flew like a flash, tore open the shutter, and threw up the sash.

At that point two things struck her as odd. One: it wasn't raining this evening. The sky overhead was a brilliant orange, the sun setting behind the rows of buildings across the street. And two: Percy Shelley was attempting to climb the little ash tree next to the bookshop, and apparently having a devil of a time at it, since the tree wasn't nearly big enough for climbing (which Mary already knew). As she watched, one of the branches bowed under his weight and dumped him to the ground.

"Shelley!" she called as loudly as she dared, hardly more than a whisper.

He scrambled to his feet, smiling at the sight of her. "Mary!"

"What are you doing?"

"Climbing this tree to your window, of course. I've been trying to speak to you all day, but your father won't let me in. I've fallen out of his good graces, which seems hypocritical to me, because of who he is and what he's written about marriage and the like. He desires me to go away forever and have nothing more to do with any of you. But I can't stop thinking about you. I do not wish to be parted from you, Mary."

Her heart fluttered at his words. "I do not wish to be parted from you, either," she whispered. "But—"

"Run away with me, Mary," he said then. "Tonight."

Her breath caught. What was with everyone asking her to run away with them today?

"I don't have much to offer you," he said. "It's true that my father has cut me off, and I am woefully without funds until my grandfather dies, which could be any day now, but probably won't be, as he is, last I heard, in decent health. But I can offer my heart. My very self. And we will have such great adventures together. We will have art and music and poetry. Oh, Mary, I will write poems about the sunshine gleaming from your golden hair. I will write entire sonnets about the taste of your lips."

She shivered. She had not forgotten what an excellent kisser he was.

"Oh, Percy," she sighed. "I—"

He held out a hand to her. "Don't answer now. Take some time to think about it. It is the greatest decision that you shall ever make, and if you decide to come with me, to be with me, then meet me at midnight at St. Pancras's churchyard. I'll have a carriage waiting there."

"Mary?" There was a gentle knock on her door, and her father's voice.

"I must go," she gasped at Shelley.

"Midnight!" he whispered.

"Midnight," she agreed. She closed the window and hastened to open the door. Her father was standing on the other side. He took in her disheveled appearance and her flushed face.

"You've been weeping," he said. "About Mr. Shelley?"

"How did you know?" she asked.

He scratched at the back of his neck. "Jane may have let something slip about the truth of your relationship. Are you all right, my dear?" he asked.

"I'm fine," she said dully.

"I very much doubt that." He took her by the hand and drew her over to sit on her bed. He sat down beside her. "You've had your heart torn asunder, my dear, and it's all right to cry about it. It happens to us all."

"I'm not really so heartbroken as all that," she admitted.

He patted her hand. "I suppose you thought yourself in love with Mr. Shelley." He sighed. "There is nothing so keen as young love. And young love thwarted, well. That is terrible indeed. I was quite fond of Shelley myself, before I discovered that he didn't have any money. I am beginning to believe that he came solely for the purpose of seducing one of my daughters."

Mary stiffened. "I'm sure Shelley's intentions were honorable, Father. He does hold you in great esteem. That we developed feelings for each other in the meantime, well, I don't think that could be helped."

He smiled. "It's sweet of you to think the best of him. But I do believe, my dear, that it is time to put Mr. Shelley out of your mind. No good could come of a relationship between you. Surely you must see that."

"But you don't believe in marriage, Father," she said.

"That's true. I don't, in theory. In the ideal world, the world that I imagine, we would not be so constrained. But we don't live in an imaginary world, my dear. We live in the real world. And the real world has rules and consequences. Which is why I married your mother, and why I married your stepmother, so that we might have a life together in the real world. And that is why your being with Mr. Shelley is quite impossible."

Mary frowned and looked into her lap. "I suppose so." But she was thinking of all the things Shelley had said, how they would see the world together, and conquer it, in their way. Kisses and poems and music and art. Adventure. Love.

"You are so like your mother," her father added softly. "But you are also wiser than she was. Your mother was all passion. She was like a wild flame, burning out of control. You are steadier, my little Mary. You have a quieter, more steadfast heart."

"Thank you, Father," Mary murmured. But didn't he know that she wanted to be like her mother? Her mother's life, if nothing else, had been extraordinary.

"So no more hand-wringing over Mr. Shelley, all right?" her father said.

"All right."

He patted her hand again. "Good girl. I knew you would see reason. You're the sensible one."

Mary had always thought Fanny was the sensible one.

"Good night, my dear," he said, and kissed her on the forehead. "I left a portion of dinner in the cupboard for you. Can't have you going hungry."

He was a good father, she thought, trying to smile up at him. "Good night, Father."

Naturally, she had a most difficult time falling asleep. It really was, as Shelley had said, the greatest decision of her life.

What her father had said about the real world was accurate. She knew that. But she also knew that she didn't entirely live in that real world that he spoke of. Mary could exist in a world of imagination. She could literally bring her dreams to life. Surely, with such a power, she could bend the real world just enough to get by.

And Shelley loved her. And she supposed she loved him too—not like a wild flame, exactly, but when he was near, her heart always raced, her stomach twisted in anticipation of what might happen between them, her palms became a bit sweaty, her knees indeed felt weak. That was love, wasn't it?

And her father was wrong: Shelley was no villain, merely bent on seducing her for the sake of debauchery. Last night he hadn't taken her to some darkened room to take advantage of her. He had merely brought her to one of his favorite places, so that she might share in his passions and pursuits.

She turned onto her side. Then turned the other direction. Then kicked off the blankets and lay flat on her back. Then got cold and drew the blankets back over her again.

She knew that Shelley was occasionally vain. And he was a hopeless dreamer, a romantic in every sense of the word. But she would be a grounding influence on him, would she not? That's why, as he himself had said more than once, they would make such a good pairing.

Her steadfastness to his flightiness.

She sighed. *Should I stay or should I go?* she wondered up at the ceiling, weighing again and again the pros and cons.

And sometime, at half past eleven, to be exact, she came to a conclusion:

One didn't live an extraordinary life by being sensible. She was missing out on one adventure, with Ada and Pan. She hadn't even really had time to think about going with them. But here was the universe, giving her another chance.

She sat up and reached for the clothing she'd left next to her bed.

From the bed across the room came Fanny's gentle voice. "No, Mary. You shouldn't go."

"I must go," said Mary.

"Of course you must. I'm coming, too," said Jane.

Mary lit a candle. That's when she saw that her sisters were both still dressed.

"Did he ask you to meet him at midnight?" Jane asked.

Mary's mouth dropped open. "How could you possibly know that?"

"It's straight out of a romance novel." Jane checked the pocket watch on her nightstand. "Oh, that doesn't leave us much time. We should go." She reached under her bed and pulled out what appeared to be a rope ladder constructed out of bedsheets.

Fanny started to put on her shoes.

"Wait," said Mary breathlessly. "I am the one who's running away. With a young man!" She lowered her voice so as not to wake the parents. "This is hardly the kind of situation that calls for one's sisters."

"It's exactly that kind of situation," Jane argued. "You need us to watch your back."

"Shelley can watch my back."

"He'll be busy watching your front," Fanny countered, then blushed. "Oh, you know what I mean. If you're going to insist on running away, we must come with you."

"But Stepmother is right," Mary said. "Running away will ruin your reputation."

Jane scoffed. "Like you said, what reputation? The reputation of being poor and desperate and insufferably boring? No." She flounced her black curls stubbornly. "I am not missing out this time. I am not throwing away my shot!"

Fanny nodded. "So it's settled. We're going."

"Oh, no. You are absolutely not going," said Mary.

"This is already so exciting!" exclaimed Jane as the three girls made their way toward St. Pancras's churchyard. They were all wearing long, dark cloaks and carrying carpetbags stuffed with their belongings. As they came in sight of the cemetery, Mary saw a carriage with a pair of fine white horses parked to one side of the street.

Her heart began to race. There was no clap of thunder this time, but once again she felt electrified. The air was hot and muggy. She could hardly catch her breath.

Just as they reached the door of the carriage, it was flung open and Shelley peered out. His smile was luminous, rapturous joy. "Oh, Mary!" he cried. "I knew you would come! How happy you have made me!"

Then his gaze traveled to the two other people behind her. "Oh," he said, his brow furrowing. "You, uh, brought your sisters?"

"I couldn't leave them behind," said Mary.

"Couldn't you, though?" Shelley said dubiously.

"No. I really couldn't," she said. "I hope that's all right."

She could practically see the wheels turning in Shelley's head. He ran his fingers through his hair. Then he seemed to come to a decision. "All right, then," he said. "The more the merrier, I suppose." He jumped out and held the door of the carriage open for them.

Fanny climbed in without a word. Jane squealed and threw her arms about Shelley, then disappeared into the dark chamber of the carriage after her sister. Mary moved to follow her, but then, as her foot touched the step, she hesitated.

The small voice in the back of her brain said, *No. This is not the way.*

"My love?" Shelley kissed her hand.

She forced a smile and sternly but silently told the small voice to mind its own business. "Let's go," she said, and climbed inside.

The carriage was a bit crowded and extremely stuffy. They opened the windows, and the breeze of air as they moved helped a little, but not a lot. For a while they were all quiet, contemplative, as the carriage bumped along.

But finally Jane could hold it in no longer. "I say, where are we going?"

"Uh." Shelley rubbed the back of his neck. "I got a room for us at an inn at the edge of town. It might be a bit cramped, considering that there are four of us." He cleared his throat. "And then tomorrow I thought we'd be off to Dover."

"So we're going to leave the country," said Fanny.

Jane clapped her hands together. "We're going to leave the country!"

"Yes," said Shelley gallantly. "And when we reach the

Continent we can go anywhere that your heart desires, my Mary. We can walk the streets of Rome. Or Vienna. Or Florence."

"Have you ever been to Paris?" Mary asked.

His blue eyes twinkled. "Of course. Many times. I would love to show you Paris."

"But I thought you didn't have any money," said Fanny.

"We don't need much, do we?" Shelley countered. "We've got all that we require. The clothes on our backs. Our own two feet. The rest is just details to people like us."

Mary gazed out the window, only half hearing Jane list off all the places they should go and things they should see, then move on to instructing them all to introduce her as Claire to everyone they should happen to encounter. The carriage was passing a part of London that was greatly familiar to Mary, on account of all the times she'd gone to the Byron house. In fact, they were passing quite close to Ada's house itself.

But Ada wasn't there anymore. She was off on her own adventure.

The right *adventure* said the voice in the back of her head.

And this time, Mary listened to the voice. She didn't belong here. She belonged with Ada and Pan, helping them, throwing her fate in with theirs as she should have done earlier today. She had to help Pan. Find him more life. Or give him some more of hers. Something.

"Stop the carriage," she said.

"Whatever for?" Shelley asked, his eyebrows drawing together adorably in concern.

"I must— Please stop the carriage," she repeated.

He frowned but leaned out the window to order the driver to stop. The carriage rolled to a halt, and Mary immediately stepped out. The moment her feet touched the ground, she felt better. She took a few deep breaths, and then turned to look at the three faces peering out at her from the carriage window.

"I can't go with you," she said. "I'm sorry, Shelley. But I can't."

Fanny grinned. Jane's mouth dropped open.

Shelley looked wounded, but he swallowed and bent his head. "Why not? Don't you love me?"

"I do, but . . ." She worked to find the right words. Why could she never find the words when she needed them? "I simply can't go with you, Percy. There's somewhere else I have to be. Please try to understand."

There was a long moment when he seemed like he would protest, but then he slumped. "All right," he said miserably. "I understand."

Jane and Fanny scrambled out of the carriage.

"But I hope this is not goodbye," Shelley said.

"No. Just goodbye for now, I'm sure," Mary replied. "And I shall write to you, if you'd like."

"Of course," he said, and there were actual tears brimming in his eyes. "Of course, dear Mary. I shall await your letters."

"Thank you. Be well, Shelley," she said.

"Be happy, my love." Then he signaled to the driver, and the carriage pulled away.

Mary thought he had taken that rather well. Perhaps even a bit too well. But then, she hadn't actually broken it off with him, had she? No. She'd just asked for some space. And he'd given it to her. He was a gentleman, after all.

"He could have at least seen us back to the bookshop," said Fanny as they were literally left in the dust.

Jane coughed. "Now we have to walk all the way home?"

They wouldn't need to walk. If she wanted to go home, Mary could make a fae door, she realized. It would be as simple as that. But:

"If you want to go home, I can send you there," Mary informed them. "But *I'm* not going home."

She walked briskly to the entrance to the Byron estate, her sisters trailing behind her, greatly confused. The large iron gates were locked, but Mary made short work of that.

Click.

"But . . ." Fanny had not quite caught up to Mary's line of thinking. "But Ada's not at home, Mary. Is she?"

How did Fanny know that? "She's gone to Paris," Mary said. "To find Lord Byron."

"Lord Byron!" cried Jane.

"Oh dear," said Fanny.

"And that's where I'm going, too." Mary pulled open the door to the stables.

"Mary, you can't mean to steal a horse," Fanny said. "I don't approve."

"I'm not," Mary said, beaming, as she reached the stall where

Ada kept Ivan. "Not a real one, anyway. Ada won't mind." She bit her lip. What she was considering was against the rules. Again. It was not responsible creation. Again. And apparently it would suck some of her life away. Again. But she didn't need this to be a long journey. Surely she could afford to lose a week or two.

She laid her hand on the smooth bronze shoulder of the mechanical horse.

"Mary!" Fanny cried sharply. "What are you doing? Wait!"

But Mary was done waiting. She wanted to get on with the adventure.

She imagined Ivan running, his gears spinning, responding to her directions. (Reader, she imagined Ivan like a car.) She closed her eyes.

"*Live*," she whispered.

PART THREE

(all about
the spoons)

Midlogue the Second

Us again. This time we'd like to take a break from our regularly scheduled program to tell you more about Mary's favorite hottie: Percy Bysshe Shelley.

About a year before the Babbage party, after he'd eloped with Harriet, and Lord Shelley (Percy Shelley's dad) had declared, "Off with his allowance!" young Shelley was forced to look for alternative ways to keep living his posh lifestyle. So he did what any guy would do to make some quick cash: he wrote a book of poetry.

Fortunately, it did pretty well! Unfortunately, it turns out poetry is not the best way to get rich fast. Shelley, undeterred, took the next logical step: he decided to do a bit of ladder climbing. "Networking," some would call it. Shelley went to hang out with all of the most famous and successful poets he could find. Which eventually led him to one fateful evening spent in the company of Lord George Gordon Noel Byron (aka Ada's dad).

You already heard the part in which Shelley told Mary that Lord Byron had told him about the fae. We seem to remember something about a never-ending cup of wine. Actually, the wine was pretty important, because it was due to the drinking of all this wine that Lord Byron became tipsy enough to enlighten Shelley about this magic fae stuff that Byron wasn't supposed to share. Shelley knew this because Byron kept saying, "I shouldn't have told you that."

But naturally Shelley had some questions. "You can make anything you can imagine? *Anything?*"

Byron shrugged. Then hiccuped. "Well, almost anything," he said. "But there's a cost."

"What's the most fantastic thing you've ever imagined?" Shelley asked.

Byron's expression took on a tragic air. "I imagined once that I was alive," he slurred mournfully.

Shelley didn't know what to make of that. "So you're a fae," he said. "And who else?"

Byron glanced around and lowered his voice. "Well, I'm really not supposed to say. It's a secret. But Chaucer, right? And obviously Shakespeare."

"Obviously."

"I heard a rumor that Jane Austen was fae." Byron drank, and drank some more.

"Is it only writers and artists, then?" Shelley asked. "Imaginative types?"

Byron scoffed. "No, no, those are merely the fae that interest me." He drank until the cup was empty and then magically refilled it. "Let's see. Isaac Newton, the bloke with the apple falling on his head, and Alexander Hamilton—that American fellow everyone always goes on and on about. But he wasn't clever enough to imagine himself alive, now was he?"

This was all fascinating information to Shelley. "Who else?"

"Oh!" Byron snapped his fingers. "Mary Woll—Wollstone—Wollstonecraft! She was definitely fae. I was at a party with her once when she made a man's pants disappear." He and Shelley both laughed in a dude kind of way. "But seriously. They were my pants. And they literally disappeared." (We, dear reader, are really trying hard not to picture this.)

Shelley choked on his wine. "What a party that must have been."

"It was wild," Byron agreed. "But we're not supposed to talk about all this fae business. And we're certainly not supposed to go around telling people the identities of fae. It can lead to problems, you see. With vampires."

"Vampires?" Shelley gasped. "Those are real?"

Byron pshawed him. "I am being metaphorical. By vampire, I mean the sort of person who exploits fae for his own personal gain. A leech, to speak metaphorically again. He sucks out the fae's creative energy. Like with Dante and Beatrice. Or Vermeer and the girl with the pearl earring. Do try to keep up, Shelley, my boy. But seriously, I shouldn't be telling you any of this. You'll keep it a secret, right?"

Rrrrrright.

A short time later Shelley was knocking on Mr. Godwin's door looking for an apprenticeship (and the daughter of Mary Wollstonecraft). And you were there, dear reader, not long after that, when Shelley and Mary were watching a frog be resurrected at Babbage's party.

Indeed, it seemed things were going pretty well for Shelley. After Mary made the moon at his poetry reading, there'd been no doubt in his mind that she was fae. She'd even confirmed it for him. And then she'd agreed to be his writing partner! It was unfortunate that she'd learned about Harriet, but he'd meant it when he'd said he wanted to be with Mary. Mary had magic. Inspiration. Stories that could make him as famous as Lord Byron.

Harriet had none of those things.

Of course, then Mary had gotten out of his carriage in the middle of their running away together, and though he had considered forcing her to remain in his company . . . well, he was no brute. Plus, that would have been difficult on account of her sisters.

But Shelley was sneaky. So when Mary and her sisters disappeared into the Byron estate, Shelley told his driver to stop (again) while he got out and waited for them. Shortly, they emerged, all three of them riding a large metal horse. Clearly, they were going somewhere on their own, and Shelley had to go after them. Mary, after all, was his ticket to fame and fortune.

He got back into his carriage. "Follow that horse," he said, "but stay back so they don't see us."

The driver followed that horse. No questions asked.

Unbeknownst to Shelley, he was not the only one watching the Byron estate.

Aldini had also been keeping tabs on the place, watching for Lady Byron to leave, or—better yet—Ada. (He hadn't seen Ada and Pan zip-line out the back window, because, hello, *back* window. He'd been across the street.) So Aldini was watching from a carriage of his own when Mary (and Jane and Fanny) emerged riding a giant metal horse. (*That* sure got Aldini's attention. A giant metal horse that walked on its own!) And Aldini was still watching when Shelley hopped back into his carriage and started after the horse.

At which point Aldini did what anyone would do. He signaled to his driver and said, "Follow that carriage that's following that horse. But stay back so they don't see us."

The metal horse was an interesting development. Perhaps he didn't need Miss Byron after all.

TWENTY-FOUR
Ada

"I wish Mary had come with us." Pan sighed mournfully and stared out the coach window. If he cared that they'd traveled all the way to another country—they were on their way from Calais to Paris now—he didn't show it. "If Mary had come, I'd have someone to talk to."

"What am I?" Ada peered across the compartment. "Chopped liver?" (Reader, this phrase wasn't commonly used until much, much later, but Ada's superpower was being ahead of her time. Whatever time that actually was.)

Pan shot her a quizzical look. "No. You are more than your liver." Before Ada could explain, Pan turned toward the window again. "And I appreciate your company, but you're not Mary. She's special."

Ada stuck out her tongue at him, but he wasn't looking. He was back to staring at the French countryside rolling past, so green and rain-drenched.

The truth was, Ada wished Mary were here, too. But it was impossible. Mary couldn't leave her house in the middle of the night and ride off on a whim. Still, Ada missed her friend.

"I've been thinking about what Miss Stamp said." Pan didn't look away from the window. "About how my days are numbered, how I'll run out of the life Mary gave to me. It won't be much longer, will it?"

"I don't know," Ada admitted. "No one knows exactly when they'll die, but I suppose if Miss Stamp is right, we do have some idea with you."

"But is it death?" Pan glanced at her. "If I wasn't born, can I really die? I had imagined I would stop, like clockworks running down."

"Isn't it the same thing?" Ada asked.

"Whatever it is, are you sure running away is worth it to you?" Pan bit his lip. "I may live only another week or two. Then what will you do?"

Then she would be on her own, without very much to her name—unless they found Lord Byron quickly. And even when they did find him, she'd need him to take them in. She'd need him to support them, to help them when Lady Byron inevitably came looking, as word *would* get out that Lord Byron's daughter had come to live with him.

"Perhaps it isn't too late for you to go back," Pan said. "I could go on my own. See what there is to see before . . . And your reputation could remain intact. If Miss Stamp is correct, your mother might punish you, but you'd be safer in so many other ways."

"We're in this together, Pan. I won't leave you."

"And I won't leave you." His smile was sad. "Until I have to."

"Let's not dwell on that," she said. "Let's focus on getting to my father. He'll know how to help us. He might be able to help you, too. Remember, he's fae, and he used his fae powers to live, even after the whole world had thought he was dead."

Pan brightened. "That is a story I would be most interested in hearing."

Ada didn't know how her father had done it—what with fae powers being secret—but they would certainly ask.

BOOM. Thunder rattled the carriage and storm clouds loomed threateningly above. Ada's heart sank. Mud on the road was already making their carriage slide and jerk; another storm would only make the drive worse. And slower.

"What do you think he will be like?" Pan asked.

"I've heard him called 'mad, bad, and dangerous to know.' But Lady Caroline Lamb said that, during their affair." Ada paused. "It probably is significant that none of his romantic partners have anything nice to say about him."

Lady Byron certainly didn't.

"I wonder—" Pan yawned so hard his jaw cracked. He stayed like that, mouth open in horrified silence, and looked at her with wide eyes. "What was that?" he asked, but since he didn't close his mouth, it sounded more like, "Aught ahs hat?"

Ada laughed. "That was a yawn. You can close your mouth. In fact, please do. I can see your tonsils."

Carefully, Pan closed his mouth. "I was afraid my jaw would fall off. Is that a possibility?"

"A very unlikely one."

He frowned. "What does it mean?"

"The yawn? It means you're tired. You should sleep." She motioned for him to lie down on his bench. "You've had a long day."

"How is one day longer than another?"

"I have a lot to teach you about language."

Pan sighed. "Mary would be good at that."

Ada smiled. "Yes, she would. Now, close your eyes and go to sleep. I'll wake you when we reach Paris."

Obediently, Pan closed his eyes and—within moments—was snoring softly. Sleeping for the first time.

BOOM went the sky, but Ada had long ago given up jumping at crashes of thunder. She closed her eyes, letting the storm and the sway (and jerk and slide and squelch) of the carriage lull her. Maybe she could rest now, too.

"No!" Pan startled up, kicking, arms flailing, and then he threw himself to the floor of the coach.

Suddenly, Ada wasn't sleepy anymore. "What? What is it?"

Pan was shaking as he looked about their space. Finding nothing dangerous, he climbed back onto the bench across from her.

His eyes were round and haunted. "I think I have fae powers."

"What?" How could Pan have fae magic? Unless Mary had managed to pass it on to him somehow, when she'd brought him to life. (Now there was a question: could Mary imagine *Ada* with the magic?)

He gave a very serious nod. "I see things. In my *mind*. When I'm sleeping."

"Oh!" Ada released a nervous giggle. "You were dreaming."

"No," Pan insisted. "It was so real. So vivid. I was there."

"Where?" Ada used her cane to brace her while she crossed over to sit beside him. "Tell me what you saw."

Pan's breath was still heaving. Haltingly, he said, "There were automatons that looked human, like me. But they were being hunted. People hated them. People feared them."

Ada took his hands. "You were dreaming. Sometimes, in our dreams, our minds try to make sense of the events in our lives. After what you've been through, this really isn't a surprise. Besides, you *are* human now. It makes sense that you'll dream."

Pan squeezed her hands. "I haven't even told you about the sheep. They were *electric*."

"Like automatons?"

Pan shrugged. "It was so frightening. Are you sure it wasn't real?"

She shook her head, biting her lip to keep from smiling. He'd changed so much since he was created. To suddenly be human—it must be quite an experience. "It was only a dream. Dreams can't hurt you."

All the frightened energy seemed to have drained out of him now, and when he signaled that he wanted to lie down again, Ada moved back to the other side.

"How long until we get there?" Pan asked.

"Hours." Ada looked out at the yellow-tinged clouds, which spat rain over the hills and forests and distant villages. "I won't be surprised if we have to ride through the night."

Pan closed his eyes. "I wish Mary were here. I think she'd like hearing about my dream."

"I think so, too," Ada said. "Remember it for now. When we get to Paris, I'll buy you a notebook, and you can write it down and show her when we see her again."

If they ever saw her again.

In the bookshop, Lord Byron's books took up three entire shelves, in addition to the elaborate table display near the front door, and also the small stack of books on the counter where the clerk was reading (you guessed it) one of Lord Byron's collections.

A crowd of young women huddled between the bookcases, each with a volume of Byron's work clutched to her chest. There was giggling. There was quoting. There was even a bit of swooning.

"Are you sure this is a good idea?" Pan asked.

They were standing on the other side of the bookcases, peering into the Byron aisle and listening to the aforementioned swooning for one very good reason: it was Ada's only idea.

"We need to know who publishes his work so that we can go to their office." Admittedly, this had been a pretty serious oversight. When they'd stepped out of the coach and onto the busy Paris streets, Pan had asked which way they should go now. And Ada hadn't known the answer. Mary had said Jane was writing to Lord Byron via his publisher in Paris, but Ada had forgotten to ask for more specific details than that, what with running away from home. So here they were. In the bookshop.

"All right," Pan said. "Go over there and get a book."

"I think you should do it."

"He's your father," Pan countered.

"That's exactly why you should be the one to do it," Ada said. "They'd eat me alive if they realized who I am."

Pan looked at her sharply. "I had no idea life was so perilous."

Ada nodded.

"Perhaps if we go together, we can fend them off." He peered between the books once again. "Do you think any of them are mothers?"

"It's impossible to tell," Ada said. "But you're right. We should both go."

"Very well. But first, I have a concern."

Ada waited.

"They sound like they're speaking, but I can't understand a word."

That, at least, Ada had the answer to. "They're all speaking French. It's another language. Not everyone uses the same one. There's also German, which they speak in Germany. And Greek, which they speak in Greece. And Spanish, which they speak in Spain."

"Ah," Pan said. "And we speak English in England. I understand!"

"And in Belgium, they speak Flemish. And French. And German."

"Oh." Pan slumped. "Now I don't understand anymore."

Ada patted his arm. "I know. Just when you think you know something, the world proves that you don't know anything. Well, best not to delay anymore." As boldly as she could, Ada stepped around the bookcase and plucked the first book off the shelf. It was covered in green cloth and gold ornamentation, and in the center, with golden olive branches twining through the large gold lettering, it read BYRON.

"Ooh!" One of the young ladies broke off from the group. "Another fan! You should come have brunch with us and talk about how masterful his writing is."

The other girls nodded in agreement. There were five of them. Ada and Pan were vastly outnumbered.

They glanced at each other. Pan shrugged, because the girl was speaking French and he still didn't know French, so Ada was really on her own here.

"Um," she said eloquently. (In French, that's still "um.")

"Oh, I see you are struck by the magnificence of his poetry. I know that feeling well." The girl took the book from Ada's hand. "*Tales and Poems.* I love this one! I've read every one of his tales. And his poems. But *Childe Harold's Pilgrimage* is my favorite. It's autobiographical, you know."

"I didn't know," Ada finally managed to say. Curiosity kindled in her chest. "Which one is that?"

The girl turned toward the rest of her friends. "Which one is that?" They all laughed, but not in an unfriendly way. "Ah, my new friend, you are in for a treat. There's nothing like it in all the world. It's so romantic, so insightful. His poetry speaks to my soul."

Curiosity got the better of her, and Ada found the first volume of *Childe Harold's Pilgrimage* on the shelf. After a furtive glance around (no sign of her mother), Ada flipped through the book. Something about boredom with a life of pleasure, something about traveling across Europe, something about wars.

Nothing about a daughter.

"Isn't it wonderful?" the girl asked. "You should read the whole series. They get better and better."

"I don't really like"—Ada glanced around again—"poetry."

"What? Why not? Why are you even here?" The girl stepped back into her group and hugged the green book to her chest. "Poor Lord Byron. Poor, poor thing."

Poor Lord Byron? As far as Ada could tell, there was nothing poor about him. Here were dozens of his books, printed and guarded by packs of roving fangirls. He was wealthy, successful, and loved by all. (Except Lady Byron. And Lady Lamb. And his other exes.)

Frowning, Ada flipped to the title page and scanned down for the publisher: Lagardère. It had the address and everything.

"What is that?" Pan pointed above the publisher name, to a squiggle of ink that didn't match the rest of the lettering. "Did someone write in it?"

Ada's breath caught. "It's signed," she whispered in English. "He was here. Holding this book." And now she was holding it, this "autobiographical" book about his life that didn't include her. She wasn't sure how to feel about that, so she returned the book to its shelf and backed away from the five girls who were glaring daggers at her, as though she had personally injured their Lord Byron.

When Ada and Pan stepped out of the bookshop (having purchased a small notebook for Pan to write down his dreams), Pan popped open his umbrella and offered Ada his arm. "Which way?"

Ada's leg was sore, stiff from the long ride to Paris, so she swapped her cane to her left hand and took Pan's arm with her right. This way, they could share the umbrella, and it would be harder for them to get separated. (Also, Ada really missed her own cane, the rubber tips, the loop, the padded handle; her fingers hurt from gripping this one.)

"North," she said. "No, east." Fortunately, the publisher's office was on a major street, one she knew from her previous visit to Paris (and her study of maps when she was bored), but it was always disorienting to move about in a foreign city. What she needed was some sort of moving map, one of those "you are here" pointers that tracked you as you move and guided you along the route to your destination—a system that always knew your position, globally speaking.

Well, never mind all that. They started north. No, east.

"I think I need to learn French," Pan commented over the drum of rain on their umbrella.

"Why is that? Aside from the practical reasons, I mean."

"Because you seemed very upset about what happened in the bookshop, and I want to be able to help if something like that happens again. Will you teach me French on the way to the publisher?"

"It's a complex language, one that takes years to master, but I suppose I could teach you a few words before we get to Lagardère." As they walked, she started with the basics, like *hello* and *goodbye*, *where is the restroom*, and other important phrases. Pan picked them up immediately, and several minutes later, when they reached the large office building, he was having basic conversations with her in French.

Pan pulled open the door to the office for her, then shook rain off his umbrella and folded it away.

Ada stepped up to the front desk, where a receptionist was sorting through piles of paper. "Hello," she said in French. "My name is Ada Byron—"

"I'm sure it is. And what can I do for you, *Miss Byron*?"

"I'm looking for my father, actually, and I was hoping you might be able to tell me where he's currently living."

"Oh, really?" The man raised his eyebrow. "You think I'd tell you? You think *I* know?"

"Well, my friend has been corresponding with my father and her letters have been coming through you. So I was hoping—"

"That I might give up the location of our most famous author?" he said. "That I, personally, might know where to find him and tell you? That you, some stranger off the street, might be believed to be Lord Byron's daughter?"

"None of that is very nice," Pan said in perfect French. "Ada is his daughter, and she needs to find him."

The receptionist glared at Pan, then Ada again. "Prove it," he said. "Prove to me that you are Anna—"

"Ada," Ada corrected him.

"Byron, and then I will consider going to my boss and asking them if they could unlock the vault where we keep Lord Byron's current address so that I can give it to you. Of course, if you are Annette—"

"Ada," Ada said again.

"Byron, then you should already know where to find him. Well? Where's your proof?"

Ada looked at Pan, who shrugged.

It wasn't as though Ada had any kind of identification on her. She had run away, after all. And aside from somewhat inheriting his appearance, Lord Byron hadn't given her anything else—not even his fae magic, it seemed.

Sigh.

The man behind the desk motioned to the door. "If you cannot produce any irrefutable evidence that you are who you say you are, you'll have to leave. Sorry not sorry."

Glumly, Ada and Pan stepped back onto the street.

"He was very mean," Pan commented.

Ada didn't argue.

"If they won't tell us where your father lives, what do we do now? How will we find him?"

"I'm not sure. I need to think." Then they rounded a corner and Ada caught sight of a proud Gothic spire that reached above the rooftops, and she knew what to do. It wouldn't solve their how-to-find-Lord-Byron problem, but she set that aside for now. She grabbed Pan's arm. "This way."

Pan hitched their bag higher over his shoulder and hurried along. "What are we doing?"

"I want to show you something special."

TWENTY-FIVE
Pan

Pan stared up, and up, and up. He and Ada stood in the very center of the nave of Notre Dame, necks arched back, raptly taking in every detail. Pan's eyes traveled slowly over the ceiling of white stone, along the lines that stretched toward the center like fingers—or ribs. His fingers trailed down his own ribs. Indeed, the cathedral felt like a body, a stone giant sleeping, and Pan was standing in its heart.

His gaze lingered on the faint blue-and-purple glow where sunlight touched the stained glass windows below the ceiling. And below that, the stone took on a rose-colored hue as it divided into a series of playful arches, shifting to golden as they stretched down in huge columns until they met the checkered black-and-white stone floor.

"Humans built this?" He felt that he could not speak any louder than a whisper in this place.

"Yes," Ada said. "In the eleventh century. Hundreds of years ago."

"Did they use magic?" He couldn't imagine how else such a feat would be accomplished.

"No," Ada said. "They used math."

He gulped in a breath. It was like those first moments when he'd seen London from the rooftop—but instead of sensing how small he was compared to the enormousness of the world, he felt something different, as though time itself was just as huge and unknowable, and he was merely a flash of life in the infinite span of existence.

Ada was touching his shoulder. "Are you all right?"

He managed a nod. His eyes burned mysteriously. He placed his hand at the center of his chest. There was so much here: the overwhelming vision of the cathedral but also its sounds—the voices of men singing that seemed to float all around him, the murmur of people talking in French and the soft scuff of their shoes on the stone floor, the deep rich sounding of a single bell in the background, marking the hour. He could smell candle wax and incense and the musty smell of stale water. He could feel the cool, almost tender touch of the air in this place. "Tell me about how it is constructed," he said after a time.

"Well." Ada pulled herself up taller. "You see those lines on the ceiling? Those are the six-part ribbed vaults. They are what help keep the ceiling from collapsing on us right here and now."

"Are we in danger?"

"No." Ada laughed. "Not at all. The ribbed vaults serve to transfer the weight of the roof downward to the supporting pillars and buttresses."

"Buttresses," Pan repeated. "I like that word."

"Everyone likes big buttresses." Ada grinned. "You can see the flying buttresses when we go outside again."

"I remember them," Pan said. "Those buttresses are so big. And what about these arches? Do they help redistribute the weight of the stone as well?"

"Yes," Ada said brightly. "Everything here is designed to be functional as well as beautiful. It's really quite something." She was quiet for a moment. "This is one of my favorite places in the whole world. I'm glad I could share it with you."

Pan was glad, too. He hadn't ever conceived of anything so grand. And the idea that *people* had built this—without magic—was more than he'd anticipated. What was stopping him from learning how to do something like this, too? He could understand the math. He could imagine arches and buttresses and columns arranged in pleasing yet functional ways.

Perhaps he could build something that would last centuries, even if he himself would not.

That knowledge stabbed at him again. There was so much to explore. So much to take in. But at any point, the days or years Mary had given him could run out. He could . . . stop.

"Come look at this." Ada guided him through the cathedral until they came to an enormous circular window, which was made of smaller interlocking circles and colors. It was so intricate and beautiful, with glass panels that radiated outward to resemble a flower.

"The rose windows," Ada murmured.

"How do you say *it's beautiful* in French?" he asked.

"C'est beau," she said.

Pan repeated the words. He liked French and the way it sounded. He pointed to the smaller stained glass figures beneath the circular part of the window. "Who are they?"

"Saints." Ada's mouth quirked into a smile. "They're people who sacrificed themselves for what they believed in."

Pan studied the serene faces of the saints. "They must have been very good people, for someone else to make a window out of them."

"Yes." Ada gazed at the window for a moment longer. Then she turned and led him through the cathedral again. They walked slowly, partly because it seemed as though Ada's legs were tired of carrying her for so long, but mostly, Pan thought, for him. He found himself reluctant to leave this space, and she must have known it. It felt safe. Secure. Magical.

"Have you figured out what we're going to do yet?" Pan kept his voice soft. "About getting the publisher to tell you where your father is?"

Ada nodded. "My plan is fairly simple. You're picking up French quickly, which is fortunate."

"I like languages. If your plan relies on my knowing French, I think we will succeed."

"Wonderful," Ada said. "Because you're going to have to be a man."

"What?" His shout echoed through the vaulted nave. Then he lowered his voice. "What do you mean? I only became a boy a few days ago. Now you want me to be a man already?"

Ada touched his arm. "The man at the publishing house dismissed me because I'm a young woman. But he'd make more of an effort for a man. Men respect other men more than they respect women."

"That doesn't make any sense!" Pan cried. "I'm not so sure I want to be a man."

She glanced down. "I'm sorry to ask this of you. But I don't know of a better way."

The important thing, he knew, was to find Ada's father. To go where they would be safe. And Ada had given him so much: form, friends, and possibility. For her, Pan would attempt to do anything she required. "I'll do my best," he said. "Tell me how to be a man."

Ada gave a faint half smile, as though she understood that this was difficult. "The problem is, I don't actually know many men, so they are something of a mystery to me. I know Isosceles and Helix. And Mr. Babbage."

"And Mr. Aldini," added Pan, frowning.

"No," Ada said firmly. "You should not model any behavior on Mr. Aldini. He is not a good man."

Pan's gaze flickered back to the saints in the window. "I would like to be a good man."

"Well, I think you're already on your way there. You're polite. You listen. You ask questions. And you respect people."

Warmth filled Pan's chest. "Thank you."

Ada tapped her chin. "I'm not well acquainted with any *young* men. My mother has done quite an admirable job of keeping me away from anyone my own age." She smirked. "Up to now, anyway. I met Michael Faraday once. And there's Shelley, I suppose."

Pan dramatically ran his fingers through his hair. "There— that's my Shelley impression."

Ada snorted. "That's accurate. Well, I suppose we'll have to start with the exterior appearance of men. There are many customs that men adhere to in order to maintain a good standing among their peers," she went on. "For example, when men greet each other, they will often shake hands, like this." She held out her hand.

Pan held out his hand and shook it.

Ada laughed. "No, I mean"—she took his hand in hers—"like this. They grasp hands and then give them a shake." She demonstrated the rest of the hand-shaking ritual.

"I see. Why do they do this?" Pan asked as they shook.

"Nobody knows," Ada said.

(Reader, we know. It was a practice that started in ancient Greece. It was a sign of peace, and to let the other person know you weren't carrying a weapon. But this was not something Ada had studied.)

"They just do it," she added.

They practiced a few more times, but Pan thought he got it right the first time. It was not at all difficult. He felt that he might actually pull off this whole "being a man" endeavor.

"You'll also want to say things like 'How do you do?' and 'It's a pleasure to meet you.'"

"Even if it isn't a pleasure?"

"Yes," Ada sighed. "Unless you intend to be rude, it's expected that you'll say it's a pleasure to meet someone."

Pan frowned. "Very well."

"If you're wearing a hat, you might have to tip it." She demonstrated with an imaginary hat. "Now you try."

Pan, who wasn't wearing a hat, either, mimicked her movements.

"Very good." Ada grinned and motioned for him to come with her. "Now, you'll have to practice saying a few sentences in French, such as, 'I would like to arrange an interview with Lord Byron for the newspaper article I am writing.'"

Pan followed her toward the great doors that led outside.

"We can practice a bit more before going back to the publishing house," Ada was saying as they walked. "Perhaps we should rest tonight and go back tomorrow. We might be lucky enough to find a different clerk—one who won't remember you. Otherwise we might have to fashion a disguise of some sort."

Pan loved the idea of a disguise. He assumed it would involve a real hat.

As they started to leave the building, Pan cast one last look inside. It was so beautiful. Wondrous. As long as he lived (which, again, might not be a very long time), he would always remember the way standing inside this sleeping giant had made him feel.

Then they stepped outside, where sunlight (it was sunny for the moment) made him squint and blink back tears. He rubbed at his eyes. All at once he felt drained and overwhelmed. It was so much louder out here, a cacophony of clanging and voices.

"Look at that!" people were saying (in French, of course).

"I've never seen anything like it," others said (also in French).

His eyes adjusted to the brighter light. He looked across the square to see that a crowd was forming around a large metal horse. "Ada, look!" he called, catching at Ada's arm, because he thought she would probably enjoy seeing a thing like that.

"That's strange," she murmured. "I have a horse exactly like that back at home. Oh!"

Pan searched to find what else had caught Ada's attention, and quickly he spotted a familiar-looking young lady. Golden hair. The slender, graceful figure. A thoughtful expression on her face.

But it couldn't be. Ada had explained exactly why it wasn't possible, something about the ruination of her reputation and her life. Nevertheless, Pan's heart swelled at the sight of Mary standing near the horse. Without another word he started across the square toward her.

Their eyes met as he approached. She smiled. The sun gleamed off her pale hair. Her cheeks were a dusty pink. Her hazel eyes were warm and full of laughter. That was when Pan realized something else, something that he felt should have been obvious all along.

People could be beautiful, too.

Mary TWENTY-SIX

Mary tucked a strand of flyaway hair behind her ear. Pan came dashing over to meet her, running like a gangly teenage boy now, which was new, but he brought himself up short in front of her, his silvery eyes roving over her from head to toe as if he could not believe that she was here.

She was having trouble believing that herself. She, little Mary Godwin, in Paris, France.

"Mary," Pan gasped. "You look . . ." His voice trailed off and he suddenly glanced away, as if he couldn't bear to look directly at her anymore.

She flushed, embarrassed. She knew she must look a mess, travel worn and rumpled, a bit sunburned, completely scraggly. She probably even smelled. She tried to smooth her hair again, but didn't get a chance, because at that moment Ada nearly bowled her over.

"Mary!" her friend gasped, her cane clattering to the cobble-stones as she hugged Mary, released her, and then hugged her again. "You're here!"

"I'm here," Mary agreed breathlessly.

"But how?"

Mary turned and gestured at Ivan, who was standing perfectly still even as various French men, women, and children ran their hands all over him and exclaimed to one another (in French, so Mary couldn't be exactly sure of what they were saying, but she guessed it was something along the lines of "Mon Dieu! Sacre bleu! What an amazing invention this is!"). "He's one of your more inge-nious ideas," she said to Ada. "A horse that never tires and never needs to be fed. We made excellent time, except when we had to get on the boat." That part had been iffy. Ivan weighed quite a lot, it turned out. For a few precarious moments it had seemed like the boat they'd hired would capsize and Mary and her sisters and the boatman would all end up at the bottom of the English Channel.

Ada shook her head. "But . . . how? Ivan can't go more than a few paces before he—" Comprehension dawned in her blue eyes. She gasped. "You brought him to life," she whispered fiercely. "Mary! That is definitely not creating responsibly! Miss Stamp is going to be so steamed!"

At the words *brought to life*, Pan's head swung around toward Mary again. (He had been studying Ivan.) His eyebrows pinched together. (He would have been so excited if he'd realized he could do the eyebrow pinch at last, but sadly his attention was now focused elsewhere.)

"The horse is alive?" he asked softly. "Like me?"

Mary tried to act casual about it. "Nothing's like you, Pan. I don't think I gave him much besides the ability to run." If she'd thought it through a little better, she would have altered Ivan before she'd animated him, given him a more comfortable seat, for example. It had been quite the uncomfortable journey riding all this way with her sisters clinging behind her, being bounced continuously upon Ivan's metal back.

Her—ahem—buttresses were quite sore.

"But you gave him some of your life," Pan murmured.

"Not so much of it," Mary replied, although it was hard to say how much, really. It wasn't like there was a way to quantify one's life. But this did not appear to console Pan. He merely looked stricken in a different way.

"Peter!" cried Jane then, rushing the poor boy and embracing him like they were old chums. "Oh, Peter! I'm so glad Mary was right, for once. You *are* here!"

Right. To Jane, Pan was Peter Pan.

"Thank heavens," gasped Fanny, coming up beside them, too. "I don't think I could take another mile on the back of that horse."

"Oh good, you brought your sisters." Ada suddenly tilted her head to one side. "Wait. How did you know where to find us in Paris?"

Pan tilted his head too, an action that caused Mary to stifle a smile. "I've been wondering that myself. Paris, I have recently learned, has a population of more than 650,000 people. It seems quite unlikely that you'd be able to locate us among such a number."

Mary allowed her smile then. "It was an educated guess. You once told me you liked Notre Dame. It was the one place you talked about. So I thought it wouldn't hurt to check here, anyway. But I was afraid I'd miss you."

"Well, you were right on time," said Ada, stooping to retrieve her cane and leaning on it. "Unfortunately, the man at the publishing house refuses to tell me where to locate my father. But not to worry. I have a new plan now." Still, Ada looked a bit worried. "It involves Pan acting like a man."

"Subterfuge," whispered Pan.

"Wait. Did you say you wish to find out where your father is?" asked Jane abruptly. Because she could never mind her own business when it came to other people's private conversations.

Mary elbowed her. "Where did you think we were going?"

"You simply said we were going on an adventure!" Jane exclaimed. "Not to see Lord BYRON. I would have packed a better dress!"

"Yes, but did you hear the part about us not knowing where to find him?" said Ada.

"Oh, that's not a problem," said Jane with a toss of her curls. "I've been corresponding with Lord Byron for weeks, you know, and I'm getting letters straight from him now, instead of having to go through his publisher like before." She looked excessively proud of herself.

Mary could have shaken her sister. "So where is he, Jane?"

"He's renting a house on the shore of Lake Geneva. Villa Diodati, it's called. That's where we'll find him." She clapped her hands together. "Hooray! We're going to Switzerland!"

"Hooray. Where is Switzerland?" asked Pan. "Is it far?"

"Yes, Pan. It's far," Ada said.

"This would have been wonderful information for us to know *yesterday*," said Mary.

Jane sniffed. "You never want to hear about my letters with Lord Byron."

"I am not riding to Switzerland on the back of that horse," Fanny remarked pointedly.

"It's been a long day," said Ada. "We'll work out our travel plans tomorrow."

Mary nodded. "Now. I would like to see these windows inside Notre Dame, please."

Pan's face lit up. His silver eyes fairly danced. "Oh, I would very much like to show you. May I?" He offered Mary his arm.

She laughed and took it. "You may."

They passed a most wondrous hour or so inside Notre Dame (in which Mary was properly awestruck by the windows and the architecture), and then they found a restaurant close by for an early supper. There they discovered another wonder: French food.

Pan wanted to try it *all*, so each of them ordered a different dish and they passed the food around between them: salade Niçoise, coq au vin, boeuf bourguignon, ratatouille, and confit de canard, plus all the accompanying bread and cheeses. Mary enjoyed the food, of course, but mostly she enjoyed watching Pan enjoy the food.

Each lift of his fork was a moment of keen anticipation. With exquisite care he would bring the morsel to his mouth and chew it slowly, taking his time to fully appreciate each taste and texture. Right now, for instance, he was trying the confit de canard. He'd asked how it was prepared, and the chef himself had come out to inform Pan that in order to make this dish, the duck had first been marinated in salt, garlic, and thyme for thirty-six hours and then slow-cooked in its own fat at low temperatures.

Mary had already had some. It was really, really good.

Pan took a bite. His eyes closed. "Oh," he said.

Mary found herself blushing. Which was silly. He was only eating. But he was enjoying it *so much* it was almost indecent to watch him. It seemed too intimate. She took a sip of wine.

"That was . . . beautiful." Pan's eyes opened again. "Is *beautiful* the right word?"

"Delicious," Mary provided. "But I think food could be described as beautiful, too."

"I am learning that many things are beautiful," said Pan. "But I will call this delicious. May I have more?"

Ada pushed the plate over to him. "Have it all."

"Will that be everything?" asked the waiter.

Mary felt a flutter of guilt. The meal had been, well, delicious—the best meal of her life, in fact—but it had also been expensive. And Mary had no money—none at all—to pay for it. She was now relying completely on Ada's charity. Ada, for her part, seemed happy to accommodate them. "Good thing I have a great quantity of spoons!" was all she'd said concerning the cost of things.

But Mary still felt guilty. She'd brought in three more mouths to feed, after all. And Ada hadn't actually asked her along on this adventure. Pan had asked, but he hadn't known any better. So Mary had basically invited herself.

"Do we want anything else?" Ada asked, looking at Pan.

"There's more?" His eyes widened.

"I'm stuffed," said Mary.

"That was all very good," said Fanny.

"What do you have for dessert?" asked Jane.

Oh, reader. French food is delicious. French dessert is truly beautiful. Now there was chocolate soufflé and strawberry tarts and macarons and crepes and crème brûlée and orange-cardamom madeleines.

And by the end of that, Mary really was stuffed.

"I'm so full I could burst!" sighed Jane.

Pan looked alarmed. "Is that a possibility?"

Ada paid the bill, and the group ambled back into the street. They came to a man playing a violin and stopped to listen.

"Beautiful," Pan said when the song had faded away. "I am glad I got to hear that."

Pan was constantly changing, each day growing more and more human. He was understanding more and feeling more and having more complicated thoughts. But one of those thoughts was clearly concerning how much life he had left to live. She could see it in his eyes every now and then—a flash of pain. It was unfair, she thought, to offer him the world this way, life and all that came with it, but in the midst of all this wonder in the fact that he was alive, he had also learned that he was going to die.

Mary touched his arm. "I am glad you got to hear it, too," she said, and she imagined that some of her life, a small bit, flowed from her and into him.

They walked along the Seine for a while, and Ada decided that she would have Pan make the travel arrangements for them tomorrow at a nearby travel agent, now that he'd been learning to be a man. "I am becoming more adept at the walk," Pan said, and demonstrated his interpretation of how a man was to walk, his shoulders back and chest out, his head high, his eyes fixed on his destination.

"Very nice, Pan," Mary said.

"Yes," agreed Jane, who'd been behind him the whole time. "Very nice."

Mary shot her sister a warning look.

Pan tilted his head. "The actions are simple enough: hand-shakes and hat tips, the way of speaking, but . . ." He almost subconsciously ran his fingers through his hair. "I'm afraid my appearance isn't very man-like. I am still mostly boy. Do you think I will grow?" He fastened his gaze on Mary again, as if she, the one who had made him real, would be able to answer this crucial question.

"I don't know," she admitted.

"I have acquired three hairs upon my chin," he said, and stuck his chin out to her so that she might behold these three small reddish hairs. "So maybe there's hope." Suddenly he stopped walking and looked at Ada, who'd been strolling along a few paces ahead of them.

"What is it, Pan?" Mary asked.

"I'd like to inquire about the signs," Pan said.

"Signs?"

"The ones that are posted intermittently around the city," he explained. "The ones that read, *Beware of pickpockets*. What is a pickpocket? And why must we beware?"

Mary smiled. He was always so curious, but also somewhat fearful. She wondered sadly if that came from his experience with Mr. Aldini. "A pickpocket is a thief. But not to worry. We don't have much in our pockets to pick," she said.

"But do they also take things from bags?" Pan asked. "Because I saw a little boy reach into Ada's satchel. And now he is walking away."

Mary gasped. "Ada!" she cried. "Watch out!"

But it was really too late for that now. Ada turned and stared at her. "What?"

"Stop! Thief!" Mary shouted, pointing at the boy.

Ada's hand immediately went to her bag. Then she was shouting, too. "My spoons!" she cried. "That boy took my spoons!"

The boy grinned and took off running. Mary took off running after the boy. Pan took off running after her.

"He's very quick, isn't he?" gasped Pan as he and Mary chased the little bugger up one street and down another. They had to struggle to even keep him in their line of sight.

"It's a necessary part of his occupation, I suppose," Mary panted.

"But why would he want to steal Ada's spoons? Is he in need of cutlery? Or money?"

"Whichever it is, we need them more," said Mary, and ran faster.

The boy had ceased smiling by this time. Usually when he stole something, no one even noticed until it was too late. In the cases in which they did notice, they rarely gave chase for more than a block or so before he outran them. But this kid hadn't accounted for Mary's endurance (from all the walking) and Pan's basically brand-new pair of human legs. Inconceivably, they were gaining on him. And even more inconceivably, he hadn't been able to lose them no matter how many twists and turns and passes through crowds he attempted. Pan—and his keen eyes—always saw where the boy went.

"He's made a crucial mistake," Pan said after the boy made another sudden turn.

"That's right!" exclaimed Mary. "He's stolen from the wrong

person this time!" But she was beginning to tire. That, and she had a side ache, because let's remember that right before this she'd consumed a great deal of food.

"I meant that this way is a dead end," Pan clarified. "May I run ahead and catch him now?"

This made Mary wonder if Pan had been keeping pace with her for the entire chase just to be polite. "Go! Get him! But be careful, Pan. He might have a knife."

Pan nodded and pulled out ahead. (He also had brand-new lungs and a brand-new heart; he could have run for ages.) Mary watched as, moments later, he deftly caught up with the boy. Then Pan gave a great leap and tackled the kid. They both rolled over the cobblestones. The boy released the box of spoons, which broke open and burst onto the street in silver flashes. The boy sprang to his feet and ran away again.

"Pan!" Mary yelled as Pan started to give chase. "The spoons! Get the spoons!"

But again, she was too late. The boy might have abandoned the spoons, but the other people on the crowded street had definitely noticed them. There was a rush and jumble of bodies as a dozen people at least darted in to grab the stolen spoons. Mary ran as fast she could, but she only managed to snag one before all the others simply vanished, along with the people who'd absconded with them.

"Oh no!" she wheezed. She bent at the waist and tried to breathe. Then she straightened. Pan was standing in front of her, clutching another single spoon. They lifted their spoons and touched them gently together, as if the act might somehow restore the others.

Two spoons. Mary was light-headed at the thought.

"This is not good," Pan said.

TWENTY-SEVEN

Ada

No, this wasn't good at all, Ada thought as they trudged through the streets of Paris, looking for somewhere to rest for a few minutes.

The last time she'd been to Paris, with her mother and Miss Stamp and a small army of servants, Ada hadn't had to think about things like pickpockets. She'd been able to simply enjoy the sights and sounds and take in all the grand history of France. Oh, and the food. She was quite full *now* (the cheese! The bread! The *chocolate*!), but what about later tonight? What about tomorrow? Two spoons would only last them so long—and they certainly wouldn't get them to Switzerland.

"I can't believe how foolish I was," Ada moaned. "I should have kept a better watch over our spoons. I should have got a lock for the box." She sighed.

"There, there," Jane said. "Perhaps if we tell the travel agent who you are, they'll give us a line of credit. Surely Lord Byron will pay for the trip, once we arrive at Villa Diodati?"

Ada snorted. "It's unlikely that anyone will believe I'm Lord Byron's daughter. Apparently that's a ploy that many young ladies have used to attempt to find my father." She glanced meaningfully at Jane.

"There must be something we can do," Mary said. "Perhaps I could imagine us some form of money—"

"No," said Fanny.

Everyone (except for Ivan) swung their heads around to look at her. Ada had almost forgotten Fanny was there.

"I only mean," Fanny said, "that using your imagination to acquire money seems like stealing. Isn't it true that there's a cost?"

Ada sighed. "You're right. Our situation isn't so bad that we need to resort to crime."

"There must be something else, then," Mary said. "Something that would land us immediate money, enough money to reach Geneva."

"I could audition for that play over there." Jane pointed to a nearby theater where women in very tiny garments waved to passersby.

"That's not a play, Jane," Mary said.

Ada looked over at Pan, who was walking with one hand resting on Ivan's flank. He kept looking over the metal horse, as though checking for rust or worn spots.

"All right," Ada said, "we need a plan. Money. On three,

everyone say a way we can acquire some capital. One, two, three."

Somewhere off in the distance, beneath the bustle and hum of the streets, beneath the clank and whir of Ivan, crickets chirped.

"I see," Ada said grimly. "No one has any ideas? Not any of us?"

"I already offered one," Jane said shortly. "No one appreciated it."

"I don't do theater," Pan said.

"Maybe we could wash dishes at that café," Mary suggested.

Fanny simply held up her embroidery hoop. It had ten flowers on it and a bluebird. "Will embroider for food," she said.

Ada sighed (again!), casting her eyes over the street in front of them. There had to be some way to get money very quickly. All she needed was a sign.

RACES TODAY
BEAT THE ODDS
WIN LOTS OF MONEY VERY QUICKLY

Ada gasped. "I know what we need to do!"

Everyone followed Ada's gaze.

"Gambling?" Mary sounded dubious. "Oh, Ada, I don't know."

"I think it sounds wildly exciting!" Jane announced.

Fanny didn't say anything. Neither did Ivan.

"Do you mean for Ivan to race?" Pan asked warily. "I like him a lot, but I don't think he can win against experienced racers. He's too heavy."

"Too bouncy," Mary added.

"Too squeaky," Jane said.

"I didn't ask you to steal my mechanical horse and then complain about a free ride," Ada said. But she was smiling. "No, there's no need to make poor Ivan race. They already have horses, and I'm not sure they'd allow a metal one to run, anyway."

"That seems unfair," Pan said, abruptly changing his position. "Ivan should be able to race if he wants to."

"I've been to the races before," Ada said. "When I was here years ago, I begged my mother to let me see the horses. We weren't allowed to gamble, but I remember seeing other people do it. All I need is to understand the odds and work out the math on which horse will win. Then we will win, and be able to afford to book passage to Geneva."

Mary looked intrigued. Jane looked delighted. Fanny looked skeptical.

"Someone will have to stay behind and mind Ivan," Pan said. "Now that we know people will steal from us, we need to protect him. He can't protect himself, after all."

Indeed, even as they were discussing who should stay and who should go, several more passersby wandered up to pet the metal horse.

"You're right," Ada said. "We can't lose Ivan."

Pan sighed in relief.

Shortly, it was decided that Ada and Mary would go to the races, while Pan and Mary's sisters would stay behind to guard Ivan.

"I'm glad we're getting time alone together," Mary said, once they'd entered the racetrack grounds. Everything was crowded and noisy, and filled with the scent of sweat and, uh, horse stuff. There was still another hour or so of sunlight, which struggled through the yellow-gray clouds. "So much has happened since we last had time to catch up."

"I know," Ada said. (Reader, she didn't know the half of it.) "I really am glad you decided to come along. It wouldn't have been a proper adventure without you. And your sisters, I suppose."

"I couldn't leave them behind, no matter how hard I tried," Mary said.

Ada laughed. "I think Pan is happy to have them. He and Fanny can talk needlepoint."

"Jane keeps looking at him," Mary grumped. "But she doesn't know anything about him."

"Someone sounds jealous." Ada grinned.

"I'm not jealous," Mary said. "It must be so difficult for him, knowing that his life comes at such a steep cost, and not knowing how long he has. I see him trying to make the most of every moment, but I see, too, how it also hurts."

"Oh, Mary," Ada said. "How long do you think you gave him?" She didn't know which was worse—Pan not having long to live or Mary having cut her own life short.

Mary twisted her skirts in her fingers. "I'm not sure. When I did it with Ivan, I was more conscious of it. I only gave a little. But with Pan . . ."

Ada nodded sadly. "So we have no idea when he might—"

"Correct."

Ada pressed her palm against her heart, as though that could stop it from hurting so much. The thought of losing Pan was too horrible to think on. "Perhaps the godmothers will figure something out. But they don't know where we are."

"Not to mention, we've been breaking all the rules fairly regularly." Mary's face was pale. "That is, I have. They might not wish to help us anymore. Miss Stamp was quite angry when she came back through the wardrobe to find that you had gone."

"Don't tell Pan," Ada said. "He's already afraid of her. Did she tell you what the other godmothers had decided about him?"

"No," Mary said. "She simply muttered 'Fiddlesticks!' and stamped back through the door."

Ada nodded glumly. "Is that what made you change your mind about coming with us?"

"Oh. That was Shelley, actually." Mary bit her lip. "He asked me to run away with him. And I did, for a minute."

Ada stopped walking and stared at Mary, shocked that this was the first time she was hearing about this. "What? When did this happen? Shelley's still married, is he not?"

"He is." Mary blushed bright red. "But I don't believe in marriage?"

Ada gave her a sidelong glance. "It's one thing for *you* not to believe in marriage, in principle. But he has to. You have to believe in marriage *if you're married.*"

Mary was looking at her feet. "He did explain himself quite well, the other night. He said that he was too young to fully understand what he was doing when he married her. And he said that he did it to rescue her from a terrible home situation, and that they never truly loved each other. And he said they have an understanding now, in which he's free to see other people."

Ada screamed in her head. Then she went ahead and screamed out loud. "Balderdash!"

"Excuse me?"

"That is nonsense," Ada said plainly. "Can't you see? Shelley's a rake! He's making up excuses, and they only serve himself. What about you? How does any of this help *your* situation?"

Mary looked up, an angry fire in her hazel eyes. "He loves me," she said softly.

Ada was tempted to say that this didn't really sound like love, but there were the beginnings of tears in Mary's eyes. Dragging Shelley wouldn't help anything. Mary had made the right decision, in the end. She hadn't run off with Shelley. She'd run off with Ada.

So Ada threw her free arm about Mary's shoulders and hugged her. "I'm sorry."

Mary tried to laugh it off. "It's all right." She wiped her eyes. "I needed some space from Shelley, to decide what I actually want from my life."

"Well, now you certainly have space. I still think he might be a rake. But I suppose you can't help your feelings."

"Right," Mary murmured. "My feelings."

"You're my friend, and I'm on your side. I'm also sorry that I've been so wrapped up in my own problems that I haven't paid the proper attention to yours."

"You did build a whole boy, get kidnapped, and go on the run to find your estranged father," Mary said generously. "We've both been busy."

"I suppose. And now we both have time to do some reflecting about our situations." Ada led them through the crowd until they could see the racetrack below. There was no sight of the horses yet, but she could hear their snorts and whinnies over the din. She found, as they walked, that she was quite excited for the races to begin. (She also found she had the creeping sense that she was being watched. But when she glanced over her shoulder, there were only other people there to bet on the races.) She smiled at Mary. "You have the entire English Channel between you and Shelley, and once we're off to Geneva, it will be months before you see him again. You can decide what to do later."

"Much, much later," Mary agreed. (Reader, it wasn't going to be as much later as she thought.)

Ada nodded. "For the time being, let's win some money."

They spent the next quarter hour interviewing people, asking about the horses and their performances over the last few races. So far, Ada had learned that a horse named Odor in the Court had stumbled in his last race, but had been tended by one of the best horse physicians in France. She'd also learned that a thoroughbred called Ghostzapper was the favorite for tonight, while Late for Dinner was the hungry newcomer everyone had their eyes on.

Ada had been scribbling in her notebook for several minutes, carrying the five, dividing by thirteen, and calculating the exact curve of the track. There was math. Lots and lots of math. Your narrators tried to keep up, but really, all you need to know is this: Ada—being a genius—came up with an algorithm that would predict which horse would win each race.

As they walked up to the booth to place their bets, Ada explained every detail of the math to Mary, somehow failing to notice the way Mary's eyes glazed over.

"So," Ada said, "are you ready to win?"

"What? Oh, yes. Definitely. Let's win."

Ada had the feeling that Mary hadn't been paying all that much attention.

Finally, it was their turn with the bookie. He gave Ada a skeptical look before seeming to decide that her money was as good as anyone else's, and he passed her a card to fill out.

"I don't have any money," Ada said.

The bookie took the card again. "Then no betting."

"But I do have these silver spoons." She pulled them out of her pocket. "How much would you give me for them?"

The man shot her another skeptical look, but he took the spoons and weighed them. "I'll give you twenty-five for each."

Thunder rumbled overhead.

"They're worth at least thirty-five each," Ada said.

"Thirty," he said.

"Thirty-five."

"Do you want to bet your spoons or not?"

Ada sighed. "Fine. Thirty." Muttering curses under her breath, Ada filled out her card. She would bet on three races, doubling her bet each time. So, for her first bet, she'd put down sixty—both spoons—and then, when she won the first race, those winnings would go to the second, and when she won *that* one, her bet would double again and the last race would gain her two forty.

It wasn't as much as she'd originally had, with all those spoons, but it should be enough to get them safely to Villa Diodati.

"Are you sure about this?" Mary asked as Ada finished writing down her bets. "I don't know about a horse called Hoof Hearted."

"Hoof Hearted has good odds," said the bookie. "He's blown through the finish lines of his last three races."

Ada knew. "He'll win this race, too. Math never lies."

The bookie raised an eyebrow, but he took Ada's card without any extra unwanted commentary. Then Ada and Mary went to find their seats as the races began.

The first race was thrilling. The horses all shot from the gate, flying over the track so quickly that Ada could almost feel the thunder of their hoofbeats in her chest. (Or maybe that was real thunder.) She and Mary cheered as the horses hurtled toward the finish line with their tails flagged and sweat streaming behind them. The crowd vibrated with excitement.

Ada's pick crossed the finish line first. She cheered and hugged Mary.

"Four spoons!" Mary cried.

"Math!" Ada agreed.

When the next race began and the horses exploded from the gate, Ada's next pick pulled ahead and stayed ahead—crossing the finish line long before any of his opponents.

"Eight spoons!" Mary shouted.

"Math!"

One more race to go. "Come on, Hoof Hearted!" Ada screamed as the third and final race began. As soon as Hoof Hearted crossed the finish line, they'd have sixteen spoons. They wouldn't have to worry about money again.

The horses careened around the track, sweat beading, breath rushing. Ada and Mary were on their feet, jumping and cheering as all the horses kept pace. There was no clear leader yet.

"Go, Hoof Hearted!" Mary cried. "Run faster!"

"My math believes in you!" Ada shouted.

But when the horses all crossed the finish line, it wasn't Hoof Hearted who'd pulled ahead, but another one—a dark horse called Under the Dog.

Hearts beating wildly with shock and disbelief, Ada and Mary dropped back to their seats.

Now they had zero spoons.

TWENTY-EIGHT
Pan

The group managed to secure a small room for the night in a hostel in a shabbier part of the city. (This was where Pan learned that not all smells are good, either. This district of Paris smelled like urine and rotten apricots, which was not the most pleasant of combinations.) To pay for the room (and a stall for Ivan), Ada sold a fine gold chain that had been a birthday gift from her mother. Ada and Mary both seemed especially downcast, and Pan wished he had more knowledge about how to bring comfort to people. But he didn't know what to say or do that would help them.

He also didn't know how they were going to get to Switzerland now, without any spoons.

"I don't understand how I got it wrong!" Ada kept muttering to herself. In this way she passed the entire evening by going over her calculations again and again, trying to find the flaw in her algorithm. Jane/Claire (Pan wasn't sure which she should be called) called dibs on the single bed and went directly to sleep. Mary sat in a corner, staring dully at a blank page in her notebook. And Fanny started a new needlepoint project, so Pan sat next to Fanny and they chatted quietly about their favorite threads and stitches until the wee hours. (Fanny had a great deal of needlepoint experience, while Pan's was quite limited, so he felt he had much to learn from her.)

In the morning, they still had zero spoons.

There was no breakfast and still no plan. The group wandered aimlessly away from the hostel, Ivan clanking along with them. It was decent weather, although the metal horse did seem to be suffering from some rust; Pan wished he had his oilcan with him, but Mr. Aldini had taken it, along with the little key.

Pan touched his chest.

That was when a strange sensation began to prickle at the back of his neck, as though someone were watching him. He looked around, and sure enough, there were a lot of people watching their group—and Ivan.

Then he spotted a child poking his grubby fingers into the empty spaces in Ivan's chest.

"Stop it!" Pan cried, and the child scurried away.

But he was hardly the only curious child. Indeed, several more had gathered around, including grown-ups who gawked at Ivan in a way that all felt horribly familiar to Pan. "They're treating Ivan like he's some kind of show," he complained to Ada.

Ada stopped walking. She gasped. "Pan, you're a genius. That's it!"

"What's it?" Mary glanced from Ada to the people following them. "Oh. Are you thinking what I'm thinking?"

"I'm thinking about food," groaned Jane/Claire.

Pan didn't know what anybody was thinking, but he got a sinking feeling in his stomach when Ada whispered something to Mary. Mary smiled and nodded and instructed the crowd to form a line, and when Ada began to collect the money and Fanny helped people climb onto Ivan's back, Pan wasn't completely surprised.

The rides were five minutes each, and for a handful of coins, anyone could take a bouncy trot up and down the street. At first, it was only children who wanted to ride, but then there were couples and friends, people young and old, smiling and laughing as Ivan, without complaint, performed his duty.

It was a reasonable plan, Pan had to admit, even if it unsettled him. By lunchtime they'd gathered enough money to purchase a baguette and some cheese for everyone in their party. Pan still enjoyed the taste and texture of the food, although this meal wasn't nearly so grand as the one they'd eaten the night before.

The girls were in a better mood after that.

"We're making progress," Ada said more cheerfully as they walked farther into the city—toward a nicer district, where they could charge more money for rides on Ivan.

Pan had made it his job to check Ivan for damage after each

ride, and to stop people from banging on or kicking the mechanical horse.

"Are there people inside of him?" they asked. "Making him move about?"

"Does he run on steam?"

"Does he wind up?"

Pan answered each of these questions ("No," "No," and "No"), but he was unsure of what to tell them about how Ivan did work, seeing as even Mary and Ada didn't seem to comprehend it fully. And then someone in the line would inevitably ask the hardest question of all:

"Is he real?"

Pan's breath caught every time they asked the question. His body felt strange, a combination of yearning and restlessness and anger that he didn't understand. Finally he snapped, "Are *you* real?" to the little girl who'd asked him.

She shrugged. "Of course I'm real."

"How do you know?" he pressed. "Perhaps you are a machine, too."

She ran off crying.

Pan suddenly felt so weary he sat down on the cobblestones and rested his head in his hands. His eyes drifted closed. He took a deep breath and let it out slowly.

He knew without even having to open his eyes that Mary was now sitting beside him. "Are you all right?" She touched his shoulder, and instantly Pan felt a bit better. He lifted his head and tried to smile at her, to show her that he was fully operational.

"I'm fine," he said.

But then Ada approached them, and her expression was cross. "What did you say to that girl? Pan, it is important that you—"

"I did not mean to make her cry," interrupted Pan sharply. "But I don't like this. It's wrong."

"We need money," Ada said. "If we don't have money, we'll go hungry. And we can't stay here, Pan. We must get to Switzerland."

Pan sighed. "I know." And he knew Ivan was not alive in the same way Pan had been alive when he'd first awakened, but this felt too close to what Mr. Aldini had tried to make Pan do. He didn't know how to explain that to Ada without hurting her feelings. Mr. Aldini had injured her, too, after all.

The next conflict came when a tall man in a suit approached Ada and said, "That's a fine invention you've got there. I'd like to buy it. Five hundred."

Ada rocked back on her heels, her expression shocked.

"Five hundred," Pan repeated. "Spoons?"

Now the man looked confused. "What?"

"Not spoons," Ada clarified. "Livres. I must confer with my friends," she told the man. Then everyone huddled together.

"That would more than cover our—your expenses," Jane/Claire said bluntly. "We could be at Villa Diodati in no time."

"I agree," said Fanny. "Ivan's drawing too much attention to us, anyway. We can't hide with a giant metal horse."

"It would be a shame to lose him," Ada murmured. "I built

him when I was a child, you know."

Mary bit her lip. "I don't think we should sell him."

Everyone looked at Pan, who looked at Ivan. "No," Pan said. "Ivan may be made of metal, but he's one of us. We don't sell our friends." It was bad enough that they were selling rides. "In any case, we don't know this man at all. We have no idea how he would treat Ivan. What if he's like Mr. Aldini?"

Ada nodded grimly and went back to the man in the suit to turn him down. He went away after that, grumbling in French.

After another hour of collecting money and leading Ivan around the streets of Paris, Ada announced they had enough to try the travel office.

"Pan will have to do the talking," Ada went on. "Just like we practiced."

"Before I do any of that," Pan said, "I think we should buy an oilcan for Ivan. He's the one who did all the work today."

"That's not true," Jane/Claire said. "I kept everyone orderly and plied them with small talk while they waited in line."

"Which you wouldn't have been able to do if Ivan hadn't been giving rides," Pan argued. "Oilcan. Or I won't speak to the travel agent."

Ada's eyebrows lifted, but she nodded. "You're right, Pan. Ivan will need the oil regardless, but we definitely need to treat him nicely after the day he's had."

The knot in Pan's chest eased.

"Mary, take this and buy some oil." Ada passed Mary a few

coins, and when Mary was gone, she turned to the others. "Jane and Fanny, hang back here with Ivan. Pan and I will try at the ticket office."

Pan didn't want to admit it, but he felt a small thrill as the group moved toward the ticket office. He was going to be a *man*.

Ahead of him, Ada stopped abruptly. "Quick!" she cried. "Duck!"

Pan's stomach rumbled as he thought of the confit de canard he'd had yesterday, but that didn't seem to be what Ada was referring to. The whole group skittered toward a side street. One at a time, they peered out, and through the window of the ticket office, Pan spotted the somewhat familiar face of a tall, red-haired woman. "Miss Stamp!" he gasped.

In the back of their group, Fanny gasped, too.

Everyone swung their heads around to look at Fanny.

"Oh, um." Fanny's face turned red. "That name sounds dangerous. Does she like to stamp people? And how do you know her?"

Pan frowned. "She's Ada's godmother."

For Ada's part, her face was pale and frightened. "I'm not worried about Miss Stamp." She glanced around the corner again. "We've got bigger problems. The woman standing with her is *my mother*."

That sent a bolt of terror through Pan's insides. "Your mother!" He'd never actually seen Ada's mother before. In the attic he'd had the sheet over his head. And then they'd fled for their lives.

"If only we could get closer," Ada whispered. "I need to know what they're saying." Her eyebrows did the pinch thing. "I can't go. Pan can't go, as Miss Stamp has seen him. Fanny? You're quiet. Go listen to them."

"Oh, no," Fanny said. "That's a terrible idea."

"I'll go." Jane/Claire stood up straight and threw back her shoulders. "I'm the best actress anyway."

Pan, Ada, Fanny, and Ivan waited in tense silence. When Jane/Claire returned several minutes later, she looked sober.

"Well, it's not good news," she reported. "The conversation went something like this." Jane/Claire began her best impressions of Lady Byron, Miss Stamp, and the travel agent:

Lady Byron, dramatically: "I simply must find my daughter! She is so precious to me! Tell me, my good man, have you seen my precious child?"

Ticket agent, irritatedly: "No."

Miss Stamp, pointedly: "We know she's in Paris."

Ticket agent: "A lot of people are in Paris."

Lady Byron: "How dare you use that tone with me? Don't you know who I am?"

Ticket agent: "No, and I don't care."

Lady Byron, offended, huffing: "I am Anne Isabella Noel Byron, eleventh Baroness Wentworth and Baroness Byron. My husband is Lord Byron. You might have heard of *him*."

Ticket agent: "That scoundrel!"

At this point, Jane/Claire paused in her performance to explain what she'd uncovered about the ticket agent's motivation:

the poor man had had a terrible experience that time he'd met one of history's biggest stars. You see, Lord Byron had come here to Paris recently on his way to Lake Geneva. But Byron wasn't content to take a regular coach. Instead, he'd commissioned a brand-new vehicle, one crafted from the finest mahogany. Inside, the coach boasted a writing desk and the 1800s equivalent of a minibar. There was also a dining service and doctor, as someone such as Lord Byron regularly needed midnight snacks and a cure for his hangovers. The construction of the coach had taken weeks, and Lord Byron (or one of his people) was in the travel office every day, asking for updates, demanding faster work, and requesting various upgrades.

"It was a nightmare," Jane/Claire said, resuming her role as the ticket agent. "Go away! I will not lower myself to speak with another Byron. [passionately] I despise you all!"

Lady Byron (slipping the travel agent a hefty wad of cash): "You should know that I'm nothing like my husband. I, too, despise Lord Byron, even though we're married. Please, tell me if my daughter books passage anywhere! Here's where we are staying. Call upon us immediately should my daughter appear. Oh, how I miss her!"

Travel agent: "Sure, lady."

"And then," Jane/Claire said, "as Lady Byron and Miss Stamp left the building and started for that hotel over there"—she pointed—"Lady Byron asked Miss Stamp if she was certain that you were here in Paris, and Miss Stamp said yes."

"How does Miss Stamp know where we are?" Pan asked.

"Probably just a guess," Fanny suggested.

"She said she was certain," Jane/Claire insisted.

"Well done, Jane," Ada said. "Perhaps you should consider a career as a spy."

"Perhaps I will," Jane/Claire replied. "But for now, what are we going to do? Your mother knows we're here, and now we can't get to Switzerland. The jig is up, I think."

"Not yet," Ada said. "I have an idea."

Later, right before the travel office was set to close, Pan and Ada strolled into the building. (They'd left Fanny, Jane, and Mary—who'd returned with the oilcan—with Ivan.)

"Miss Byron, you say?" said the travel agent when Ada introduced herself. "What a great pleasure to meet you. An honor, truly. Whatever can I do for you? Where would you like to travel? Tell me everything."

He was in much better spirits than he'd been earlier. Obviously because of the cash Lady Byron had slipped him. And the prospect of more, once he reported that he'd encountered her daughter.

"Thank you," Ada said demurely in French. "It's been such a treat seeing your beautiful city. But now I need two tickets."

"Oh?" The travel agent leaned forward. "*Two* tickets, you say?" His eyes roved curiously over Pan.

"My cousin and I would like to visit somewhere else now. Somewhere equally beautiful. With history. With excitement."

Ada was quite the excellent actress herself, Pan observed. But then Ada excelled at everything she tried.

"And where would that be?" asked the agent eagerly. He picked up his pencil to write it down.

"Romania," Ada breathed. "That's where we desire to go."

Obligingly, the travel agent pulled a map from inside his desk and opened it for them. "Yes, yes, that's such an excellent choice. Where in Romania would you like to travel? Exactly, I mean."

Pan gazed down at the map, drinking in all the details. The blue lines to indicate rivers. The brown lines to indicate mountains. The black lines to indicate roads. And there, right in the center of Romania, was a red dot.

"Oh," Ada was saying, "there are so many options. Romania is such a wonderful place. I don't know. . . ."

"Transylvania." Pan pointed to the red dot on the map. "Bran Castle."

There. He'd done it. He'd come up with his own subterfuge.

He didn't know whether he should feel guilty or proud.

(We, as the narrators, are really glad that this was a lie. Not because we have anything against Transylvania, per se. But because that would be an entirely different story.)

They watched as the ticket agent tried to spell *Transylvania* in the note he was making for Lady Byron. "Wonderful. I will begin to work on your travel arrangements right away," he said.

Pan was a bit disappointed that he hadn't gotten to use his man training to get things done. But this was just as good. They had accomplished their true mission, which had been to throw their motherly pursuers off their trail. Because when the ticket agent informed Lady Byron and Miss Stamp that he'd encountered Ada, he'd send them in a completely different direction while our heroes made their way to Switzerland.

"But we still have a big problem," Jane/Claire complained when the group gathered again on the street. "Because now we can't use the travel office! How are we actually going to make it to Villa Diodati?"

Just then a carriage rolled up to them, and a familiar young man leaned out.

Jane/Claire squealed and clapped her hands. "It's Shelley!" she cried.

Fanny heaved a beleaguered sigh.

"Drat," Pan heard Ada mutter under her breath.

But Mr. Shelley seemed not to hear them. He was only focused on one person.

"Hello, Mary," Mr. Shelley said.

Mary

TWENTY-NINE

"What are you doing here?" Mary asked.

The corner of Shelley's mouth quirked up, his gaze warm and blue as ever. "I was about to ask you the same question." He glanced briefly over the group: Fanny and Jane, Ada, Pan and Ivan, then back to Pan (who shifted uncomfortably at the sudden scrutiny), and once again at Mary. "When we last parted I assumed you'd be going straight home. And yet here I come upon you in Paris."

Ada crossed her arms over her chest, her cane dangling. "You didn't answer Mary's question," she said sharply. "Why are *you* here, Mr. Shelley?"

"I was in the neighborhood," he said lightly, but then he murmured, "I've come for Mary, of course." He met Mary's eyes. "Your father is worried sick about you and your sisters. He sent me to

357

bring you back to London." (This, reader, was a lie. But as well as being a good kisser, Shelley was quite the adept liar.)

Mary found that her heart was pounding—the way it did every time she encountered Shelley. "You spoke to my father?" She was under the impression that her father was no longer on speaking terms with Shelley.

Shelley nodded. "We've come to an understanding, he and I. He's agreed to mentor me again. All is mended."

Mary nodded thoughtfully. If Mary's father could come to accept Shelley, even though he was broke and married, then perhaps her father would accept the idea of Mary and Shelley together. But . . . Mary's conversation with Ada yesterday flitted through her consciousness . . . she wasn't sure that's what she wanted anymore. Being with Shelley had once felt so right, but now it felt . . . well, wrong.

But how could she say this to him? "I—" she began.

"Perhaps Mary does not wish to go home," said Ada. Mary cringed at the way she was glaring at Shelley, clearly making no attempt to hide her feelings about him. "And how did you find us?" Ada asked. "You can't really expect us to believe that you happening upon us just now is a coincidence. That is mathematically quite improbable."

"It's no coincidence," Shelley admitted. "I ascertained that Mary was with you, Miss Byron, as you are such dear friends, and therefore I followed Lady Byron and the governess here to Paris in their pursuit of you."

(That was also, dear reader, a lie. As you'll recall, Shelley had followed Mary at a distance, with Aldini following *him* at a distance. And since we know you're wondering where Aldini is at this point, well, he's over there, hiding behind that shrub.)

"And how, exactly, did my mother know I was in Paris?" Ada wanted to know.

Shelley ran his fingers through his hair. "I've no idea. Perhaps you left a trail of some kind. In any case, I've come to entreat you, Mary: please, come with me. Come home."

Home was a funny word, Mary mused. When had the bookstore on High Street ever felt like a real home? Home was where the people you loved were, and so many of the people Mary loved were standing right here with her now.

"Perhaps we should go, Mary," Fanny whispered then. "For Father's sake."

"Out of the question!" exclaimed Jane with a flounce of her curls. "I'm not going to miss out on my chance to meet Lord Byron! No offense, Shelley, but we're in the middle of having a grand adventure here. Don't rain on our parade!"

As if on cue, there was a sudden flash of lightning in the distance, followed by the low rumble of thunder, and it started to rain.

Shelley held out his hand to Mary. "Come on inside, girls, where it's dry, and we can talk about it."

Fanny stepped toward the carriage. Jane hesitated and then stayed where she was.

But Mary herself stepped back. There was really nothing to

talk about with Shelley. This wasn't only a matter of family. It was a matter of responsibility. She turned and met Pan's earnest silver eyes. She had made Pan alive, made him real, made him a person in every sense of the word. She could not abandon him, or Ada, or even Ivan. She knew her family would never understand that, but that didn't change the way things were. She had to see this particular adventure through.

She shook her head. "Please tell my father that I love him dearly, and I am safe, and I will return when I can."

"I could go with you," Shelley suggested hopefully. "I could even take you there, wherever you're going."

"Lake Geneva," piped up Jane, brightening. "That's so extremely generous of you, Shelley. And that looks like a spacious and comfortable carriage."

Mary looked then to Ada, who gave the smallest shake of her head. Her friend's jaw was set, her eyebrows drawn low over her blue eyes. She was never going to accept a ride from Percy Shelley.

"No, thank you," said Mary softly. "We'll find our own way."

Jane's mouth dropped open.

Shelley closed his eyes for a moment. Sighed. "How many times, my Mary, will you end up breaking my heart?"

"I'm sorry," she said. "Please believe me when I say it's not my intent to hurt you."

He nodded and sighed again. "Very well. But what will you do about Lady Byron? She's relentlessly seeking you, and she will not stop until she finds her daughter and brings her home again."

"We've already handled the situation with my mother," said Ada stiffly. "That's none of your concern. Good day, Mr. Shelley." She stood up straight, ignoring the water that was dripping into her eyes.

"Good day," he said, and gave Mary a final sad and longing look. Then he said a word to the driver of his carriage, and in a moment both he and the carriage had disappeared from view.

"That's just wonderful!" sniped Jane. "There goes our ride!"

"What are we going to do now?" sighed Fanny.

At first, Mary tried to procure them a form of transportation using her fae magic. She managed to turn a pumpkin into a coach, which seemed very impressive for all of ninety seconds before it was discovered that the "coach" was really just "coach shaped" and not something that any of them would wish to ride around in. The wheels didn't roll very smoothly, it was slimy inside, littered with pumpkin seeds, and it smelled bad.

Then it was decided that they would walk to Switzerland. Being that five people could not all possibly fit on the back of the miraculous metal horse. (Even three people had been most uncomfortable. Mary's buttresses were still quite sore.) With the money they'd made giving rides earlier that day, Ada was able to purchase a small cart that could be pulled behind Ivan, into which the group piled their meager belongings and in which they took turns, when they tired, riding along—Ada more than everyone else, for good reason. Her fancy rosewood-and-gold cane made a terrible substitute for her modified version, which was, as far as anyone knew, still in Mr. Aldini's possession.

Mary enjoyed the walk. Even though the journey was nearly three hundred miles. Even though it would take them almost two weeks to reach Switzerland at the rate they were going. Even though it rained on them most days, and the road was eternally muddy.

At one point Ada asked her, "Do you want to discuss what happened with Shelley?" and Mary very firmly replied, "No." Instead, Mary spent the journey getting to know Pan better.

He seemed so determined to make the most of this adventure himself, to see and touch and smell everything that it was possible to perceive. He constantly looked up at the sky, so much so that he often stumbled over things at his feet. He was fascinated by the shapes of trees and clouds, the flight and sounds of birds and insects. He asked Ada and Mary for the proper names of every species of living thing he came upon, learned the difference between the song of the sparrow and the thrush. He also spent much of his time walking right alongside the horse, an oilcan in his hand with which he regularly lubricated Ivan's gears.

"I am fearful for him," he said, peering up at the clouds that perpetually threatened rain. "What if he should rust?"

"He won't," said Mary. "Because you are taking such excellent care of him."

They walked along in silence for a time. Then Pan said, "I have been meaning to thank you, Mary, for changing me into a human. For making me real."

Mary put a hand to Pan's arm, felt the warmth of it under his simple cotton shirt. "I did not make you real, Pan. I merely made you appear real. What I mean is, you already had thoughts and feelings. You were human. Before."

He considered this and then smiled. "I've been thinking about what kind of man I'd like to be. If I get time."

"And what kind of man have you decided on?"

"I should like to have a job," Pan said. "It seems to me that most men employ themselves in some way."

Mary nodded. "And what sort of employment are you considering?"

"I should like to design and build great structures," he said. "Like Notre Dame."

"You want to be an architect," Mary said.

Pan's eyebrows lifted. "Yes! And how would one go about becoming an architect?"

"It takes many years of study," Mary said.

Pan's smile faded. "Oh. Then I do not suppose I will have the time for that. I must be content then to appreciate what others have built."

Mary's heart squeezed for him. Her hand was still resting on Pan's arm, and without really thinking about it, she once again imagined a small bit of her life moving from her and into him. Then she grew dizzy for a moment and lost her footing on the road.

She almost fell, but Pan caught her and righted her. "Even if I cannot be an architect, I should like to be a good man, on the inside and not simply on my exterior," he said, and then for some reason he blushed. "I would like to be a good man. In your eyes."

"Oh." Mary also blushed.

Pan pulled back from her, his arms dropping to his sides. "Is your father a good man?"

"Yes," she said. "He is."

"And what makes him good? Is he a saint?" Pan asked.

A laugh bubbled up inside Mary. "He is definitely not a saint. We all have flaws. But my father is kind. He cares about more than just himself. He sees Fanny and Jane as his daughters, even though they aren't related to him by blood. And he has tried to treat us, as his daughters, with dignity. He's educated us, and never talks down to us, and he tries to offer us as much opportunity as we would have if we were his sons."

This was all making her feel increasingly guilty. Her father *was* a good man, and she was a terrible daughter for doing this to him.

Pan began walking again. "Why are women not treated as equals to men? It doesn't seem right. Perhaps I am not understanding because I don't yet know the difference."

"The difference?"

"Between men and women." He stopped again. "From what I can discern, males are typically larger than females. And they are shaped differently. I, for example, have wider shoulders. And you—" His gaze dropped to her chest.

Mary crossed her arms. "Uh . . ." Oh dear. She did not feel qualified to have this conversation. She was tempted to tell him to go ask Ada, but she supposed that was the cowardly way out. "As you've noticed, what makes a man different from a woman largely has to do with one's body parts." Mary bit her lip, dissatisfied with her own explanation. Was that truly what made them different? It seemed like there was something more, but she couldn't put it into words. Why was Ivan, for instance, characterized as male when Ada had certainly not given him any genitals?

"What body parts?" Pan asked.

Drat. Mary's face was beet red at this point. "Our . . . uh . . . nether regions."

Pan immediately looked down at his crotch. "Oh, that *thing*?" he said. "I didn't have that before, when I was made of metal. I find it most amusing and befuddling. So you created that thing for me, Mary?"

Mary wanted to jump into a deep, deep hole. "Yes. I . . . yes." She supposed she was glad that she'd sneaked into her father's office once and read a book on anatomy, otherwise she would never have been able to imagine such a . . . thing.

"Wait," Pan said, "so you don't have a thing?"

"No."

"Do you have something else?"

"Yes."

"Can I see it?"

Oh, to die, to die, before she had to answer. "No. Those parts are considered private, Pan."

"Oh." He nodded as if he understood now. Then he shook his head. "So me having one thing, and you having a different thing, means that I am more deserving of respect and education and consideration?" His jaw tightened. "But you are real. You have thoughts and feelings the same as I do. Why should our parts dictate what we can do?"

"I know. It makes no sense."

"It makes no sense!" he agreed enthusiastically. "It's not fair." He stared off into the distance, thinking again. He was quite attractive, she observed. Not in the way that Shelley was, of course, but nice to look at. His copper curls suited his complexion well. His jaw was at a perfect angle for his face. His ears were very comely. His eyelashes were spectacular against his startling silver eyes.

She'd done a fine job, she reflected, imagining a real boy. A man.

"So you and Pan had quite the little talk this afternoon," Ada whispered as she and Mary settled into bed that night. Pan (using his man-thing-power) had easily procured them a room at an inn in the small French town of Dijon (which Mary would later remember as a series of charming stone bridges and would never, as your narrators do, immediately think of mustard). In the next bed over, Fanny mumbled in her sleep (something about her doing her duty) and Jane was snoring softly. For his part, Pan had chosen to sleep in the stables with Ivan. Not that Ivan required sleep. But the first night of their journey, someone had attempted to steal Ivan, so Pan preferred to remain with the horse to guard him. "He came to me with some follow-up questions. That was unbelievably awkward."

"I know," Mary said. "But I feel that he deserves to know everything. This is his life, after all."

Ada's brow furrowed. "Speaking of his life, I saw what you did. You gave him some of your life. You were so pale and weak this afternoon."

"Only for a few minutes," Mary protested, but then she sighed. "I can't help it. I am so afraid that he'll just . . ."

Ada sighed, too. "It doesn't make sense to me, this notion that we all have a set amount of life given to us, unknown but finite. But it's clearly unsustainable—you constantly pouring little bits of life into Pan won't work long-term. What if one day you both just . . ."

Even Ada, who normally was able to speak her mind just fine, couldn't say the words.

"I know," said Mary.

"And worst of all, I can't think of a solution," Ada said.

"Your father will help us."

Ada's blue eyes clouded with worry. "I hope so. Oh, Mary, I am terrified to see my father."

Mary reached for Ada's hand and clasped it tightly. "I'll be with you. We will figure it out. When we're together I find that we are quite brilliant. We can solve any problem that we are presented with."

"I'm so happy that you didn't go with Shelley," Ada said fervently.

"So am I," Mary said.

Suddenly, Jane, from across the room, gave a tremendous

snort. "Why hello, Lord Byron!" she called out flirtatiously. "Fancy meeting you here! Oh yes, I, too, am quite delighted to make your acquaintance in person!" Then she began to snore again, loudly.

"But did you have to bring your sisters?" Ada said, and then she and Mary both fell into girlish giggles, and then fell into sleep.

The next morning it was discovered, to everyone's dismay, that Ivan had stopped working. There was no longer any light in the horse's eyes, no movement in his body. He was like a bronze statue of a clockwork horse.

"Can you bring him back?" Pan asked Mary.

She bit her lip. To bring Ivan back, she knew, would take a great deal of energy, and she wanted to save all her energy for Pan.

"No." It was Ada who spoke. "You cannot give more of your life, Mary. Not for this."

Pan accepted this decision, but he was very upset. He was even more distressed when Ada decided that they would trade Ivan for a donkey at the inn.

"But we can't simply leave him here!" Pan exclaimed.

"We can't bring him," Ada said. "I'm very sorry, Pan. But it's the way it must be. We must still get to Switzerland."

"We can come back to visit him," Mary said.

Pan stared at Ivan's frozen body. "But what if he rusts, without me here to oil him?"

"He's in the stable, out of the rain," said Ada. "He'll be fine."

"And we can leave the oilcan with the innkeeper," said Mary.

Finally, with much cajoling, they convinced Pan to continue on with them. It was raining hard all day, and Pan walked next to the donkey with his umbrella over both of them, out of habit more than anything. Mary's heart was broken for him. She understood that this was a death, to him, and she could not think of what to say to ease his pain.

"My eyes keep leaking," he said during a moment when they all stopped to rest. He looked so stricken that Mary couldn't help but come up beside him and take his hand. "Why?"

"It's called crying," Mary said. "It happens when we are sad."

"Do men cry?"

"We all cry," she said. "I am so sorry you are sad, Pan."

"Are you not sorry for Ivan?" His gaze moved over her face. "You are not crying."

"I *am* sorry for Ivan," she said. "But I always knew that his time was short."

"Like my time," said Pan quietly. "I am like Ivan."

She shook her head. "You are not like Ivan. When I made Ivan come to life, it wasn't the same as when I made you. I only imagined the horse with the ability to run, because I had no money and I needed something to carry me to you and Ada. He did not have the ability to have thoughts and feelings. He was not real in the way that you are real."

"If I cease to function, will you leave me?" he asked almost bitterly.

She pulled him into her arms to hug him. "I would never leave you, nor would Ada. You are very dear to us both, Pan."

He was stiff for a moment, unyielding, and then he relaxed against her. His hand came to rest at the small of Mary's back. He bent his chin to the curve of her neck. He smelled of straw and, inexplicably, of lilacs. Her cheek found its way to his chest, where she could feel the steady beating of his heart.

Just a little more, she thought, because she couldn't bear the idea of this sweet heart stopping. *We're almost there*. Then she gave him another small portion of her life.

His arms tightened around her.

"This is pleasant," he said softly. "I find it immensely comforting."

"Can we go to Switzerland now?" asked Jane loudly. "Or are we all going to simply stand about hugging?" She hooked her arm through Pan's and pulled him away from Mary. "It's time to start thinking some happy thoughts, Peter Pan, no matter how attached we were to the clockwork horse, and I, too, was very attached to Ivan, I assure you. But we must pull ourselves together. Stiff upper lip, my boy."

Pan's eyes sought out Mary's. "I did not understand any of that."

"She means," clarified Mary, "that it's time to move on."

It was several days later that they arrived in the desired part of Switzerland. They passed the night in Geneva, as it was by that time too dark to make their way to Villa Diodati—even though it was only an hour's walk from the city. Mary tossed and turned all night. She thought she kept hearing a strange, persistent noise from nearby—a zapping sound—but she told herself that it was probably just the usual lightning and thunder. Or a troubled dream.

(Reader, it was not a troubled dream. It was definitely Aldini, as he still believed Ada was the one who possessed the ability to bring things to life. And he was still trying to bring frogs to life on his own.)

The next morning was unusually sunny (although there were storm clouds on the horizon) and the light played and danced upon the waters of the lake in the most breathtaking way. Beside Mary, Pan was silent, his silver eyes open wide, taking in the view.

"Are you all right?" she asked him. He'd been quieter since the incident with Ivan.

He nodded briskly. "There's just so much beauty," he said. "I am glad I got to see this part."

"Are you still feeling terrified?" Mary asked Ada as they walked along the shore of the lake, toward where the people in the town had informed them that they could find Villa Diodati.

"I'm fine," said Ada, although she was decidedly not fine. She had that pain-weary look she got when her leg was bothering her. And she was obviously very tense about meeting Byron.

"Would you like to hug?" Pan offered.

"Not now, thank you, Pan," said Ada.

In a little while the villa came into view. It was a large and stately three-story house a couple hundred yards back from the lake, with a red roof and shutters and a series of columns all around the outside. Pan parked the cart and tied the donkey to a tree. Then the group stopped for a moment to look at the house.

"I knew Lord Byron would live in a place like this," breathed Jane. "It's right out of a storybook, isn't it?" She began to practically skip toward the entrance. They hurried to catch up with her, Mary and Pan staying behind to walk with Ada.

"Wait!" Mary called as Jane reached the door. "Ada should be the one who knocks."

Jane pouted, but she stepped aside, taking the moment to smooth her hair and pinch some color into her cheeks.

Ada stood in front of the door, took a deep breath, and raised her hand. To knock.

THIRTY
Ada

She could do this. All she had to do was knock. Put her knuckles to the door a few times and wait. And she *would* do it. Any minute now.

Aaaaany minute now.

"Do you think she is malfunctioning?" Pan asked quietly. "She's not moving."

Ada was practically knocking already. Practically.

Mary put a hand on Ada's shoulder. "It's only a door."

"I don't see what the big deal is," Jane said.

Nothing at all, Fanny said.

Ada brought her fist down on the door. Once. Twice. Three times. Then she considered running away, behind those bushes over there.

But before she had a chance to flee, the door creaked open,

revealing not a butler, as Ada had expected, but a tall, dark-haired man they all (except for Pan) instantly recognized. Ada's eyes roved over his face, taking in the cleft in his chin (like hers), the bump along the line of his nose (she'd clearly gotten her nose from her mother), and the faint scar that cut across his left eyebrow (how had he gotten that?). He'd changed some since the curtain-covered portrait in Ada's upstairs hallway had been painted. His mustache was fuller, his mass of curly dark hair quite obviously receding, leaving a widow's peak, and his cheeks were thinner than they had been.

The group stared at him, stunned. They'd been expecting to find him here, but it was still a shock.

Here he was, in the flesh. Lord Byron. The most famous man in the world.

Ada's heart was galloping. She opened her mouth to form some kind of greeting, but no words emerged.

"Why, hello." Her father's blue eyes (exactly the same shade as hers!) flitted from Ada to Jane to Mary to Fanny. "Ladies."

Pan cleared his throat.

Lord Byron glanced at Pan. "And sir." But then he went right back to scrutinizing the young women who'd shown up on his doorstep, pausing on Jane, the prettiest. He smiled. "Hello in particular. What can I do for you? Are you lost?"

"We're exactly where we wish to be," Jane said, gazing up at him from underneath her lashes. Ada calculated that in another 3.5 seconds, Mary's sister would launch herself straight into Byron's arms, and he would clearly enjoy it. Ada had to work up the courage to speak. Right now.

She stepped between her father and Jane. "I should introduce myself. I'm—" Ugh, why was this so hard? Well, maybe because her mother would simply kill her if she knew what was happening right now. Or maybe because her father was checking out her friends. "I'm—"

"Ada," he said softly, his eyes widening. "You're Ada. My daughter."

She let out a long breath. He knew her. He saw himself in her. He recognized her as his daughter. "Yes," she said.

He was smiling again, a slightly different smile than he'd had earlier. Moments dragged on, and she thought she ought to say something else, but her heart had crawled up into her throat and she couldn't find the words for what it meant to see her father for the first time.

Finally, she thought.

Then he glanced down and saw her cane—and Ada realized that he was leaning on one, too. "Like father, like daughter," she joked weakly.

"Are you going to hug now?" Pan whispered.

Lord Byron opened his arms, and, though Ada had never felt she needed anything from him, she found herself stepping into his embrace. Against her hair, he said, "Ada, my dear. My daughter. I have longed to see you, and now, at last, you're here."

Ada felt strangely disconnected from herself as she hugged him back. As if she were having some improbable dream, and any moment now she would wake. She couldn't truly believe it.

"Well," Lord Byron said abruptly, pulling away, "let's get you inside. And your friends. Please, introduce me."

The group filed into the villa and stood awkwardly in the front parlor while Ada made introductions. "This is Mary Godwin, my best friend."

Mary's cheeks flushed, but she nodded politely to Ada's father. "How do you do, sir."

"Miss Godwin." Lord Byron bowed slightly. "I've heard so much about you."

Now Mary's cheeks went from flushed to bright pink. "You— You have?"

"You're Mary Wollstonecraft's daughter. I knew her a bit, and I'm very admiring of her book. And you are already a writer, are you not?"

"I wish to be," Mary said softly.

Lord Byron nodded. "And so you shall be." And because he was who he was—the greatest writer in the world—this pronouncement seemed irrefutable.

"This," Ada said, moving on before Mary passed out under the pressure, "is Pan. He's—" Well, how to explain Pan? "As far as anyone outside this room is concerned, Pan is my cousin."

"Oh," Lord Byron said, eyebrows raised. "What an interesting introduction. I cannot wait to learn more."

"How do you do." Pan smiled. "I'm Peter Pan. Ada's cousin."

"These are Mary's sisters," Ada continued. "Fanny Imlay."

Fanny gave a quick curtsy and then faded into the background.

"And Jane Clairmont."

"*Claire* Clairmont."

"Right," Ada said, trying not to roll her eyes. "Sorry. This is Claire."

Byron's welcoming smile became a bit wooden. "Oh yes, dearest Claire."

Jane squealed and ran in for a hug, practically knocking Lord Byron off his feet. "We've been writing to each other for so long!" Jane cried. "It's only right that we meet at last!"

"Yes," Lord Byron said weakly. "At last."

"We are two souls languishing for each other," she said quickly.

"Oh, well, *languishing* is such a strong word," said Lord Byron. "But I certainly found your letters charming. You're quite an interesting young lady who is friends with my daughter."

"*Friends* is such a strong word," said Ada.

Jane, undeterred, disengaged herself from the one-sided hug with Lord Byron and got right to business. "And now that we are together, I'd like to demonstrate my acting abilities for you. First, I'll do my damsel in distress. Ahem." She cleared her throat and shook her shoulders and arms to loosen them. "Oh woe," she cried loudly. "Woe is me!" She clasped her hands beneath her chin. "Won't some strong man come to save me from my life of misery and despair?"

"Ja— I mean, Claire." Ada spotted Mary making cutting motions over her throat. "Perhaps we should put our bags down before we talk about acting."

Lord Byron seemed grateful for the redirection. "Leave your things here while I give you a tour of the house."

"That would be lovely," Ada said quickly. She was starting to feel almost sorry for her father. Yes, he'd abandoned her before she could even crawl, and yes, he had the kind of reputation mothers warned their daughters about, but it was hardly his fault that people kept throwing themselves at him, literally. He was famous, and everyone wanted something from him.

Ada knew how that felt, in her own way.

They placed all their meager, damp belongings in front of the fireplace to dry, then followed Lord Byron through the house as he showed them the ballroom, the conservatory, and the library (which held an unusual number of candlesticks, a painting of a mysterious woman in scarlet, and probably a secret passageway or two).

Ada, who had spent all her life in one grand building or another, was impressed but not surprised that this beautiful place was where her father had holed himself away to write. There was inspiration all around (if—*whispers*—poetry was your sort of thing). Mary, Jane, and Fanny spent the tour admiring the artwork, the bookcases, and the chandeliers. Pan kept pointing out archways and windows he liked. There were numerous views of the lake, each more spectacular than the last, although the window glass was pocked with raindrops now.

"And here we come to the drawing room." Byron motioned to the door with a smile. "I think you'll all be pleased. A surprise waits within!"

"Ooh," cooed Jane. "I adore surprises."

Ada wasn't sure she could handle surprises, but even though her instinct told her to go back downstairs and curl up in front of the fire with their bags, she followed their small crowd through the door and into a warmly decorated drawing room, complete with stuffed bookcases, a blazing hearth, and an incomplete game of chess.

And there, on the plush sofa, sat Percy Shelley, his feet propped up on the table as he lowered the book he'd been reading. And he didn't appear at all surprised to see them. "Mary," he said, sitting up straight and placing the book on the table. "You're finally here."

"Shelley!" Jane cried happily.

Mary's mouth had fallen open. "Weren't you going back to London? To tell my father that we're fine?"

"I sent word to your father," he said, rising to his feet. "But then I thought I might be able to be of some assistance to you here, as Byron is a friend of mine. I didn't expect it to take so long for you to arrive. What took you?"

"Our horse stopped working," explained Jane. "And the donkey wasn't nearly as fast."

Pan gazed at the floor.

"What a shame," said Shelley. "Oh, Byron, you would have delighted to behold this mechanical horse your daughter built. It was a marvel. I've never seen the like."

"Is that so?" said Lord Byron. "Perhaps you could make another one, Ada darling. For me?"

"No," Ada said quietly. "I don't think I could."

Upon seeing Shelley (the rake!), Ada's first thought had been to go back to the library for one of those heavy candlesticks. But now, with Shelley talking about how long he'd been here, waiting for them to arrive, her anger had faded because she realized the truth: her father hadn't simply recognized her—he'd been expecting her. Shelley, who'd traveled much more quickly in his carriage, had warned Lord Byron that Ada and the others were on their way.

Shelley crossed the room to Mary. "I do hope you're at least a little glad to see me," he said softly, taking her hands in his.

Barf, thought Ada.

Mary nodded and smiled faintly. "Of course I'm glad. I'm just surprised, is all."

"She keeps leaving you, and yet you persist on popping up again and again," said Ada tersely. He was like a bad penny. "And again."

Mary's hazel eyes flashed, which Ada took to be best-friend code for: *Shut up; I can handle this.*

The corner of Shelley's mouth curved upward in what was meant to be a charming lopsided smile. "I can't seem to stay away," he said, lifting one of Mary's hands to place a gentle kiss to her palm. "Perhaps you'll come to understand my predicament, Miss Byron, if you ever fall in love yourself."

Ada sucked in a breath. She was considering the various levels of blunt-force trauma her cane could inflict upon Shelley's fluffy-haired skull when she suddenly became aware of Pan's expression—the way his gaze had zeroed in on where Shelley's lips touched Mary's skin, the tension around Pan's eyes, and the flash of hurt—and she realized what he'd been trying to tell her for weeks, but she hadn't truly understood. Maybe even he himself hadn't understood.

He was in love with Mary, too.

"Ada," Lord Byron said. "Might we speak for a moment?" It had been two hours since Ada and her party had arrived at Villa Diodati, and Ada still hadn't spent any time alone with Lord Byron. "I'll be right back," she told Pan, who was sitting across from her. She'd been attempting to distract his thoughts concerning Mary by teaching him the rules of chess, which he'd grasped quickly, and then some of the more basic tactics. He didn't always understand the point—which was to prevent her from moving forward, and to take her king—but when she'd explained that the game was meant to sharpen the mind, he'd seemed more eager. "Keep studying the board," she said, "and when I return, show me how you'd win in the next five moves."

Pan nodded and she rose to follow her father out of the drawing room.

For a moment, it was just the two of them in the hall, moving quietly, the thumps of their canes on plush rugs the only sound. Then Lord Byron cleared his throat.

"I should like to start by saying that I am delighted that you are here," he began, and Ada's heart lifted. "When Shelley arrived and told me that you were seeking me out, I was stunned, naturally, but most eager to make your acquaintance. I've always thought of you, over the years. My daughter. My child. And now here you are, the mirror image of myself. It's astonishing, really."

Ada was torn between elation at her father's words and the remnants of anger she'd carried all her life. He had never even written to her, never expressed an interest, except for maybe that one time when he died for a minute.

Lord Byron continued. "But Shelley also told me that you're running away from your mother."

Oh.

"Is that true? Are you in some kind of trouble? I have . . . complicated feelings concerning your mother, but I don't doubt that she cares very deeply for you." He pushed open the door to the library and motioned for her to go inside first. "Why would you flee from her?"

Ada stepped into the library. "I do not wish to malign Mother, as she has done the best she could on her own." (Maybe this wasn't exactly true—not locking Ada in the closet so many times would have been nice.) "Still, Mother isn't equipped to help me through some of the problems that have recently arisen in my life. I was hoping you might be better suited."

"Me?" Lord Byron sat in a large chair and leaned his cane against the arm. "What makes you think I could do better?"

Ada sat across from him, resting her cane across her knees. "I know what you are."

Her father quirked a smile. "I am many things to many people. You'll have to be more specific, I'm afraid."

"You're fae," Ada whispered. "I know all about the fae. I have my own fae godmother."

"Do you?" He smiled warmly. "And are you as talented as I think you are?"

She *was* talented, but she wasn't a fae. But she didn't want to admit that out loud. Not to him. Not yet, when he seemed so pleased that they might have this in common, too. "Mary is the talented one," Ada said. "It comes so naturally to her."

"But not to you?" He tilted his head, curious. "I would have assumed, given that you're my daughter . . ."

She looked out the window. Dark clouds were gathering on the horizon, threatening to transform this light rain into a genuine storm. "Perhaps I should start at the beginning."

"Does this have something to do with the boy you introduced as your cousin?"

"It has everything to do with him," Ada said, and when Lord Byron nodded encouragingly, she found herself telling him the entire story—from the party at Mr. Babbage's house, to the lessons Miss Stamp was providing for her and Mary, to that fateful night when they'd brought Pan to life, and to the terrifying day Ada and Pan had spent as Mr. Aldini's captives. "Now Mr. Aldini wants to electrocute my brain, Mother is furious about my reputation, and Pan could drop dead at any minute. We need help. And I thought you must—since you survived the war in Greece—have some knowledge, some way that you used your fae powers to keep living."

"And you hoped that I might impart this knowledge to you," Lord Byron concluded. "On Pan's behalf."

"Yes." Ada leaned forward. "I cannot bear to lose him. There must be some way."

"Hmm," said her father, frowning. "That is a predicament."

"Are you going to scold me now?" Ada wondered what the closets were like at Villa Diodati. Probably very comfortable.

"Scold you? Whatever for?" her father asked.

"For not creating responsibly?" said Ada. "For running away and perhaps forever damaging my reputation and future prospects? For stealing Mother's spoons? For losing them so foolishly? For gambling?" It really was quite the long list.

Lord Byron shook his head. "No, my dear. I do have questions, but I won't be scolding you. I believe you've had enough of that from your mother."

"So you know a way to help Pan?" Ada asked.

"There's a very good reason I couldn't stay with your mother. She left me first."

Ada's chest tightened. "What? But you left the country when I was only five months old."

Lord Byron smiled sadly. "That is true, but when you were not yet one month old, your mother spirited you out of the house, in the middle of the night. She refused to have any contact with me—or allow me to have contact with you—thereafter. I left the country because I couldn't bear knowing you were so close, but out of reach."

"Why would she do that?" Ada had never heard this side of the story before.

"Who can say? But since then I've come to believe that it was for the best. I am not the most responsible of men. We who are wild at heart should not be caged," he said. "Not by someone like your mother. She doesn't understand people like us."

Ada bit her lip.

Lord Byron seemed to recognize her discomfort, because he reached for her hands. "Perhaps I should have fought for you. I've regretted it ever since. But what would I—a wanderer, a writer— offer an infant? How could I possibly take care of you? At least your mother provided you some stability, while I would have presented only chaos."

Ada's heart began to soften. "So you didn't leave me because you don't—" She stopped herself before she gave away her fear that he didn't love her.

"My dear." He squeezed her hands. "I'm sorry. I know I should have come for you sooner. I almost did, actually—but I heard that you'd fallen ill, and I knew your mother was better prepared to help you recover."

Pain twinged up Ada's leg, and she wanted to say that her mother had done her best to *prevent* Ada's recovery. But that was a conversation for another time, perhaps, when they got to know each other better.

"But now you are here, and you're asking for my help. And of course I will help you. I will keep you safe. Everything will be fine now. I promise." Then he smiled hopefully. "And I know I may not deserve it, but I hope that one day you will consent to call me *father*."

FLASH! Lightning flared in the window. A moment later: *BOOM!* The entire villa rattled under the thunder.

"Father," she said softly, testing out the word. "Thank you."

"I will protect you," he said. "I'm so sorry that I wasn't there for you before, but you can trust me now."

"Thank you," she repeated quietly, wanting to believe that it was true—needing it to be true.

FLASH, BOOM!

Outside, the storm was growing closer.

THIRTY-ONE
Pan

Pan was feeling a great many emotions today. He felt relief, now that they'd finally made it to their destination, and hope, that Lord Byron would be able to provide the assistance that Ada so desperately wished for. He felt weary, as their journey had been long and strenuous, even for a body as brand-spanking-new as Pan's, and a prickling fear, that his weariness was not ordinary fatigue but a sign that he was running out of time, and soon—too soon—he'd stop completely. There were things he still wanted to do before he stopped. And things he felt he should say. To Mary, especially. And now he was feeling confused, because Shelley was there, too, vying for Mary's attention, and annoyed, because for some mysterious reason he found Shelley extremely annoying.

It was a lot of feelings.

But currently what Pan was feeling most of all was hungry. He'd had only a scant piece of bread with cheese for breakfast that morning, as the group had been eager to be on their way from Geneva, and in the excitement of their arrival at Villa Diodati, they'd somehow missed lunch. His entire body now had an unpleasant emptiness, and if Pan could have rapped upon his stomach, he expected that it would have made a hollow sound even though it was no longer made of iron.

So as the group sat down for dinner, rain drumming ever harder on the windows, Pan added a few more emotions to his list: anticipation. Considering the opulence of Villa Diodati, he could only imagine what delectable consumables might be served here. And if Pan had learned one thing about himself over the course of his brief life, it was that he loved food. (No surprises there. Pan was a teenage boy, after all.)

Then he was feeling disappointment, on account of the seating arrangements. Before they had taken their chairs, Shelley had called dibs on sitting beside Byron, with Mary, Fanny, and Jane/Claire in the middle. That left Pan sitting next to Ada on the far end of the table.

"I'm happy to sit beside you," Ada said, staring forlornly across the table toward her father.

"And I am happy to sit beside you," Pan agreed, gazing toward Mary. Happy was not one of his current feelings, although he understood now that saying he was happy was meant to communicate to Ada that he valued her company, so it wasn't a hurtful untruth.

He looked at Shelley, who was already pouring wine into his and Byron's goblets, laughing loudly, running his fingers through his undeniably impressive shiny brown hair, and suddenly Pan felt oddly angry. And still quite hungry. (There really should be a word, he thought, for a combination of hungry and angry. Why was language so very limited?) He frowned. Why did he dislike Shelley so?

Lightning flashed outside the window, throwing Shelley into silhouette. Thunder crashed, making the entire house shudder, and Jane/Claire gave a nervous laugh. "Some weather we're having!"

Fortunately, the servants chose that moment to place a large silver platter in the center of the table. Pan's stomach rumbled. His mouth watered. He eagerly picked up his fork. A servant whisked off the lid of the platter, and the steam cleared, and then . . . the only thing inside the serving dish was a dark green leafy substance.

What? That had to be wrong. Surely there was something else.

Pan glanced about wildly. No more dishes were forthcoming, and around the table, every smile fell. Well—every smile except for Byron's and Shelley's. When the servants filled their plates with the limp vegetable, the two men were all grins.

"What is this?" Pan whispered to Ada.

"It's steamed kale," she whispered back. (Yes, dear reader, kale was a fad for hipsters even before the Victorian era.)

"Is this food subterfuge?" asked Pan.

Ada shook her head. "I think they're serious. This is it."

Glumly, Pan accepted his kale. More disappointment. It

wasn't that Pan disliked vegetables. He'd had some really excellent vegetable dishes in France. But kale was—

"I adore kale!" exclaimed Shelley. "Do you know that I once composed an entire sonnet about the merits of kale? It's called, 'Ode to Thou Leafy Green.'"

Pan experienced more annoyance at Shelley. Beside Pan, Ada made a faint gagging noise.

"Wine, sir?" a servant leaned in to ask Pan. He shook his head. He'd tasted wine in Paris and found it didn't suit him. He noticed that the women were also abstaining, except for Jane/Claire.

Shelley lifted his goblet of wine. "To the arrival of the ladies." He drank deeply. "Finally."

Byron chortled. "To Ada, my daughter!"

They drank.

Shelley toasted again. "To Mary, my partner and my love!"

They drank again.

Something funny was happening with Pan's jaw. A clenching. A grinding of his teeth. That probably wasn't healthy.

The group focused on eating for a while. Mary smiled at Pan from across the table but said little during the meal, chewing her kale in silence. Ada, who was normally loquacious, especially if you got her going about math or science or astronomy, was staring out the rain-lashed window, deep in her own series of thoughts. Fanny was always quiet, so nothing had really changed there. But even Jane/Claire seemed uncharacteristically subdued. She had one elbow on the table with her chin propped in it and was alternating between chugging her wine and glumly picking at her plate, shooting the occasional resentful glance at Lord Byron. The only people conversing were Byron and Shelley, and they solely seemed interested in speaking to each other.

Pan wondered if this was normal behavior. As Shelley and Byron drank and laughed and talked, Pan picked up from their conversation that the two men had been spending all their time together since Shelley had arrived at the villa a week earlier. They'd gone fishing on the lake. They'd spent every afternoon in Byron's study, writing poetry side by side at identical mahogany desks. And now they were sitting together at supper, chatting away as if they were the only two people in the room. (The term *bromance* hadn't been invented yet, dear reader, but this describes what had been going on between Byron and Shelley to a T.)

"Ah, Byron! You must be the cleverest man alive!" Shelley exclaimed after laughing heartily at one of Byron's jokes.

"I must be," Byron agreed. "Which is why the smartest thing you've ever done, my boy, is to talk me into being your mentor!"

The tiniest wrinkle had appeared between Mary's eyebrows, Pan noticed, at the mention of Byron mentoring Shelley.

After a time Byron motioned for a servant to clear the table, signaling that the meal was at an end. "You'll all be pleased to know," Byron said, "that I have a most entertaining evening planned for us, now that we're all together at last."

Beside Pan, Ada sat up a bit straighter. The others looked interested, too.

"Yes, indeed," Byron said. "Let us now recite some POETRY."

"Drat," Ada muttered. She laid her fork beside her plate. "But don't you think we should talk about how to help Pan?" She hesitated a moment. "Father."

Byron gazed fondly at Ada. "We should have that talk tomorrow, my dear. You've had a long day. I think you would like to rest first, wouldn't you? Relax a bit?"

Ada looked uncertain. "But we've been resting most of the day. I thought we might talk about how you . . ." Her eyes darted to Shelley. "How you survived the war in Greece. In private, if you'd prefer. But we don't know how much time we have before . . . I think we would all like to see to Pan's situation as soon as possible."

Pan agreed.

Byron's eyebrows pinched in the same way Ada's always did. The resemblance was uncanny, although there were different things going on behind Byron's eyes than when Ada did it. "Is it really so urgent as all that? Do you think your precious Pan is going to drop dead right now?"

Everyone looked at Pan, and heat rushed to his face. He didn't like the way their eyes felt on him, like they were judging, trying to measure how much life he had left.

Ada glanced meaningfully at Mary. "No, of course not. Not tonight."

Mary cast her eyes downward, and Pan could tell something was wrong, something unspoken passing between Ada and Mary, involving the continuation of Pan's existence.

"What's all this about Mr. Pan dropping dead?" Shelley took a long pull of wine as he looked at Byron. "I came here to have a poetry party, not a funeral."

"Mr. Pan!" Ada's father laughed as though Shelley had told a hilarious joke. But it was just Pan's name he apparently found funny. "Ah, Shelley. Hasn't Mary told you? She and Ada—but mostly Ada, my brilliant daughter—built Pan out of spare parts. Quite genius, really. He was an automaton. And now he's walking about like a real person."

"The automaton?" Shelley's eyes widened. He stared at Pan. "You are the PAN? It was you, that night at the theater?"

Pan didn't answer, but then Shelley turned to Mary, who nodded slightly.

"But why didn't you tell me?" he said. "And how did you—"

"Wait, wait, wait," interjected Jane/Claire, setting down her wine goblet a little too hard. "You're saying that Mary and Ada *made* Peter Pan? They crafted a boy using that imagination magic? Like what Mary did to the metal horse?" She turned to Mary with a grin. "Can I put my order in now?"

"We're not supposed to talk about it," Byron said. "But yes—there's a very powerful and ancient magic that only the rarest and most special of individuals possess. Did I mention that it was Ada who did most of the building on the automaton? The apple clearly doesn't fall far from the tree."

Ada was frowning. "Father," she said.

He waved his hand at her. "Oh, not to worry, Shelley already knows all about the fae." He didn't seem to consider Mary's sisters a threat.

"Yes, Byron let me in on the secret some time ago," Shelley murmured, his eyes locking on Pan. "I found it most fascinating, and since then, I've devoted my time to learning all I could about fae and magic. Learning about fae has been extremely beneficial for my art. It has caused me to question everything I believed to be true. Now I know that anything is possible, including, apparently, building a man from scraps and bringing him to life."

But Byron looked bored. "Enough about the boy. We'll deal with him tomorrow." He pushed himself back from the table. "Now. Back to the subject of poetry. Shall we move to the parlor?"

Ada looked as though she meant to protest, but she said nothing.

"Of course," said Shelley, and smiled.

In the parlor, Byron got out a pipe, and he and Shelley passed it back and forth between them, which filled the room with a musty, smoky smell that made Pan want to cough.

Byron started reading first. He read from the book he was writing now: the latest volume of *Childe Harold* (aka the adventures of a genius poet living on the edge of a lake): *"Dear mountains! my own beautiful lake! how do you welcome your wanderer?"* he began passionately. *"Your summits are clear; the sky and lake are blue and placid. Is this to prognosticate peace, or to mock at my unhappiness?"* He shook his fist at the ceiling, lowered his head to signal he was done for now, and then glanced around for their reaction.

"That was most wonderful, Byron!" Shelley leapt to his feet, clapping and clapping.

Pan put his hands together once, but that was all he could manage. He disliked clapping. It reminded him of Mr. Aldini's show.

"Thank you, my dear Shelley," Byron said jovially. "And now you should read from what you're working on."

Shelley withdrew a small stack of papers from his jacket. He cleared his throat. "'Ode to a Fish,'" he read loudly.

The poetry wasn't so bad as Pan had been led to expect. He found that he liked the occasional moments in which Shelley's words conjured an image, like a kind of magic in itself, the silver slip of a fish moving through Pan's mind like it did through the water of the lake. But then Shelley seemed to shift from the description to some kind of a political diatribe about the plight of fishes, and how human beings are all like fishes, entangled in some kind of eternal net, and Pan felt that he had missed something.

There was more clapping. So much more clapping. Pan wished they would stop.

"Bravo!" cried Byron. "What a marvelous poem. You, my friend, are going to be one of the greatest writers of your time. A Romantic poet! My protégé!"

Shelley smiled modestly. "It was all right," he admitted. "It certainly wasn't in need of any embellishment this time, was it, my darling?" he directed at Mary.

At the way Shelley said the word *darling*, Pan's hand inadvertently shaped itself into a fist. How very strange. He thrust the fist behind his back.

"No," Mary murmured. "It was quite good all on its own."

Jane/Claire got to her feet. "And now, in the spirit of the evening, I should like to perform a small monologue from—"

"Actually, I have a better idea," said Byron. He grabbed a small bloodred book from the mantel and held it up. "I have recently come into the possession of this most thrilling book that's all the rage in Germany. But I was able to get an English translation. You're going to love this!"

Jane/Claire crossed her arms. "What kind of stories? Because I still think it might be nice for me to perf—"

"Ghost stories!" Byron exclaimed. "It's called *Fantasmagoriana! Tales of the Dead!*"

CRACK! went the sky.

Pan felt the hairs on the back of his neck rise. He hadn't even been aware that he had hairs on the back of his neck. He tried not to dwell on it.

"Ooooooh!" said Shelley excitedly. "Ghost stories!"

Then he said *Ooh* several more times in a way that Pan did not understand.

"I know what a story is," Pan said. "But what is a ghost?"

"You're never heard of ghosts?" Shelley scoffed.

"I don't know if I believe in ghosts," said Ada. "I have never seen any solid evidence of their existence."

"I believe in ghosts," Byron said. "But then of course I do."

"A ghost is a spirit," Mary explained.

Pan nodded. "I see. And a spirit is what, exactly?"

Mary frowned, the tiny furrow appearing between her brows again. "It's a bit hard to explain. It's thought, by some, that a spirit is what makes a person . . . alive."

This was getting very interesting. "What makes a person alive!"

"Yes. It's the idea that there is this invisible force inside of each of us, which animates us. Some call it the spirit, and others call it the soul."

"It's all quite vague and theoretical," added Ada sagely. "I don't know if I believe in souls, either. But I do think we each hold a kind of energy inside of us—and we all know that matter can neither be created nor destroyed, so I find this immensely comforting in those times when I imagine the great black void swallowing everything when I die."

Pan had a sense that this was an extremely important bit of information, something that was vital for him, as a human being, to understand. He turned to Mary. "But do you believe it? In the soul?"

"Yes," she murmured. "And the idea is that when a person dies, that soul is left behind, outside of one's body. And some believe that if you are a good person, your soul goes to a good place after you die."

"There are many theories," Ada interjected. "Some more plausible than others."

"I know I'm going straight to hell if there is one," Byron chuckled, and downed his goblet of wine. "But I'd rather stick around here and haunt people, if given the choice."

Pan focused on Mary.

"A ghost is meant to be one of these souls, which lingers on in this world after a person dies," she explained. "And sometimes, people claim to see them."

"Which is terrifying!" exclaimed Jane/Claire. "I had a ghost haunting the back of my closet when I was a child. No, I did! I saw it several times—a shimmering lady wearing all blue. I was in the process of writing to the Society—you know, the Royal Society for the Relocation of Wayward Spirits, the one you can call if you're having ghost problems—but then my mother met Mr. Godwin, and so we moved."

Pan blinked a few times. This was really too much information to take in all at once. But underneath his confusion he became aware of a spark of hope. "Do you think . . . I . . . might have a soul?"

Mary and Ada glanced at each other. Mary put her hand gently on Pan's shoulder. "Well . . ."

"Oh goodness!" Shelley said loudly. "We're all getting so serious all of a sudden! This is supposed to be fun! Let's hear some ghost stories! I do love scary stories! Let's get on with it!"

BOOM! agreed the sky.

And so (even though Pan still had so many questions) Byron opened the book and began to read *Tales of the Dead*. "Imagine," he said in a much lower voice than he normally used, "a dark and stormy night."

They could.

Then Byron recounted, in this spookier voice, a story entitled, "The Death Bride," which was about a young man who wooed a girl and then dumped her to marry another. The first girl died of a broken heart. (The modern method of handling a breakup, aka ice cream, hadn't been invented yet, so death was the only available option.) But when the young man arrived at the church to marry the second girl, there was someone else, her face hidden by a veil, standing between him and his lovely bride.

Shelley was quite caught up in this particular story. And Mary, for some reason, would not look at him. Pan wasn't sure why this tale would affect them so. It seemed to Pan like the young man in the story got what was coming to him.

"Well, that was indeed thrilling," said Jane/Claire as Byron closed the book. "But let's get back to the subject of fae. So far, the only demonstrations of fae abilities I've seen are what Mary has done. The horse, the carriage—things like that. But you, Lord Byron, you must have so much more experience than my sister."

"Yes, it's true. I am most adept at imagining things," Byron said. "For example—" He opened the red book.

It was difficult to see from where he sat, but Pan could have sworn that the text on the page *changed*.

"Oh my!" Shelley took the book from Byron. "Did you just imagine an entirely new story onto the page?"

Byron gave a single, dramatic nod. (This nod was a lie, however. He'd simply transferred a story he'd been working on all month from its place in his notebook upstairs onto the pages of *Tales of the Dead*.)

"Oh, this is brilliant," Shelley said, his eyes skimming over the page. "Will you do us the honor of reading this work of absolute genius?"

"Well," Byron said demurely, "I don't know if *genius* is the right word for it."

"But it is!" Shelley thrust the book back into Byron's hands. "Please, regale us!"

"If you insist." Byron cleared his throat and began to read. "'The Vampyre,'" he intoned.

It wasn't a long story, only a handful of pages, but as Byron read, Pan felt fully immersed in the tragic tale of a young man who lay dying from a mortal wound. As he bled out, he spoke of his past, a young lady he loved, his quest for contentment. He spoke of all that he still wanted to do in life. And then he went still and silent, and was therefore pronounced dead.

But he wasn't dead. He was only *mostly* dead. (But in that time, without monitors or other equipment, people who were mostly dead were often declared all dead. There was even a trend of rigging a rope attached to a bell in graveyards, so if a person found themselves accidentally buried, they could ring for somebody to dig them up.) And as the young man lay there, mostly dead, a beautiful young woman entered the room. She was a great admirer of his, and seeing him lying there seeming dead, she threw herself across his body, weeping. With great effort, the young man opened his eyes. All he could see was the tender length of the young lady's neck. She was so full of life, and here he hardly had any. Without another thought, the young man clasped the girl to him and bit down into her neck, sucking the blood straight out of her veins, every drop pouring life into him. He took and took, heedless of the girl's protests, and by the time he came to his senses, she was decidedly all-the-way dead, but his own wound had healed.

And so, the young man was forced to roam the world, carrying the burden of what he'd done, how he'd taken someone else's life in order to extend his. He was racked with guilt, reminded of her at every turn, but he knew that soon, he too would die, having wasted these stolen years.

"The end." Byron lowered the book. His eyes were dark.

"How beautiful," Shelley said. "How tragic."

"I thought there could have been more character development with the girl," Ada said. "She just showed up and died. But what did she want? What were her hopes and dreams? Perhaps she was meant to be—"

"Who cares?" Shelley said. "She was a supporting character. A plot device. The story wasn't about *her*, but about the young man. What did she do, really? Focus on what's important."

Pan glanced at Mary, thinking about the life she had given him. He didn't want to be a vampire. He didn't want to take and take.

Mary caught him looking at her, and she flashed a reassuring smile.

Byron dropped the book onto a chair. He looked shaken, unsettled by the pages he'd transformed. "Let's do something else. Oh, I have a wonderful idea."

Another idea? Pan held in a sigh. It was late, and perhaps he was not dying, not yet anyway, but his body was tired, and he was weary, too, of Byron and Shelley and all their various dramas.

He wanted a cup of tea, he realized.

And to go to bed.

"I love your ideas!" said Shelley. "What is it now, Byron?"

"You should all tell your own stories!" Byron cried, throwing his hands into the air triumphantly.

Shelley gasped in delight. "Oh, let's!"

Ada groaned.

Jane/Claire made a frustrated noise in the back of her throat.

Fanny said nothing.

"Our own stories?" Pan repeated. "But don't you already know our stories?"

"I mean, my dear mechanical boy, that you should each make up a terrifying tale of your very own. A ghost story." Byron clapped his hands together. "That will be most amusing."

Mary's mouth was open, Pan noticed. "You wish us to each compose a ghost story . . . tonight?" she asked tremulously.

Byron tilted his head to one side. "No, I suppose you must take your time with it. You can think of your idea tonight, and then start writing first thing tomorrow morning."

"But what about Pan?" Ada said.

"He can write a story, too!"

"Surely this isn't the right time to tell stories," Ada persisted.

"It's always the right time to tell stories!" Byron laughed. (And reader, well. We can't really argue with that.) He raised his fist toward the ceiling. "You must all adjourn to your chambers, and write the scariest, darkest, most ominous tale you can imagine. And tomorrow night, we'll come together in this very place and you'll share what you've come up with. And whichever one creates the most terrifying, blood-curdling, bone-chilling tale wins. I, of course, will be the judge, as I have already shared a tale with you."

"Wins what?" Jane/Claire was already looking for a piece of paper.

"He wins . . ." (It is not lost on us that Byron said *he* here. Bleh.) "A wish. Anything I can make with my fae imagination, the winner shall have."

Mary clutched at Pan's arm. "Anything," she said.

Mary
THIRTY-TWO

"Mary?" Shelley asked. "Are you all right, my love?"

Mary sighed. She wished Shelley would stop calling her his love, especially in front of Ada, whose nose always wrinkled ever so slightly when he said it. She'd been walking with Ada and Pan along the lake when Shelley had come jogging down from the house to join them, and now she was feeling guilty that some part of her had inwardly cringed when he'd approached. "Yes, of course," Mary said lightly. "I'm perfectly well."

"You look deep in thought, is all," he said.

She was. There were so many things to contemplate lately, but since last night, all that Mary had been able to think about was this _story_ that they were all supposed to come up with. She knew the contest to be a trivial thing that Byron had suggested on a whim. A distraction. But she found, in spite of her trepidation about writing, that she desperately wanted to win. She *should* be able to win, given her pedigree. She was the progeny of two great writers. She *must* win. *And when I win*, she thought, *I will ask Byron outright to save Pan.*

At breakfast, Ada had once again tried to bring up what could be done for Pan, but Byron had continued to put off this conversation. He was visibly hungover, and he said the sound of all these female voices around him was making his head hurt, so he told his guests that they should go outside, while he retreated into his study and closed the door. Why was he avoiding the subject? Mary had imagined that, upon their arrival at Villa Diodati, this larger-than-life man would solve their problems right away. He was *Lord Byron*, after all. But now she was beginning to doubt that he was even interested in helping them—he seemed far too concerned with helping himself.

Or perhaps (she swallowed nervously) there simply wasn't a way to save Pan.

Not without draining away the life of someone else, like in Byron's story last night.

She shivered at the thought. She would not be capable of such a thing. Even for Pan's sake.

But when she won the contest and asked Byron to help Pan, at least he'd be forced to confront the problem, and perhaps they'd be able to discover something together, using Byron's great experience with the fae magic and their powers combined.

"Mary?" said Shelley again.

"I'm fine." She blinked a few times. Tried to smile. "I'm right as rain."

Shelley's eyebrow arched. "We both know there's nothing right about rain."

They both peered up at the sky, which was, for the moment anyway, clear.

"I estimate that we have about twenty-two minutes before it starts pouring," said Ada, checking her pocket watch.

"Twenty-two minutes exactly?" Pan asked.

Ada patted her notebook. "I've been working on an algorithm concerning the weather."

"As one does," said Mary with a smile.

"Will you take a brief boat ride with me, my love?" asked Shelley. "I would like to speak with you, in private, if you'll allow me that honor."

Ada glanced pointedly away and then launched into an explanation to Pan about how to skip stones on the surface of the water. Pan's silvery eyes held Mary's for a moment, and then he bent obligingly to pick up a stone.

"All right." Mary took Shelley's arm and allowed him to lead her away, to the waiting canoe. She stepped in gingerly, and Shelley rowed them out into the lake.

"What bliss," he said with a sigh. "I find that being out in nature always cleanses the soul, don't you?" He put the oars aside and cast his head back, lifting his face to the rare sunshine.

Mary nodded. The water was smooth as glass today, a bronze

light cutting through the white Alps in the distance, blue and violet clouds bunched against the horizon, rolling in. It smelled like rain. (Reader, it always smelled like rain.)

"So have you thought of a story for Byron's contest tonight?" Shelley asked then.

"Oh. Well. Perhaps," she answered vaguely.

"I hardly slept a wink last night, trying to come up with an idea," Shelley confessed. "It's so much pressure! It can't be just any kind of story or passing fancy of the imagination. It has to be a scary story. Something that will speak to the mysterious fears of human nature and awaken thrilling horror. Something to make the reader dread to look round. Something to curdle the blood and quicken the beatings of the heart."

"Oh dear," said Mary faintly. "Is that all?"

"It needs to be something glorious!" Shelley cried. "But *what*?"

"I'm sure you'll think of something." Mary patted his hand.

"I've tried and tried," said Shelley. "I've racked my brain, but I just feel this . . . blank incapability of invention. Gah!" He squeezed his eyes closed.

Mary knew exactly how he felt.

His eyes popped open again. "But you've had an idea?"

She glanced at her feet. "A small one."

She'd been awake last night, too. She'd gone to the window and stared out into the storm. As she'd watched, lightning had struck a tree on the edge of the lake, a forked silver bolt so bright it lit the entire sky for an instant. And just like that, Mary had experienced *a thought*. Or not so much a thought, but rather, an image, which blasted through Mary's brain like the lightning had traversed the sky. A clear, terrible, blood-curdling, heart-quickening image:

A man bending over a figure upon a table. A pale student of the unhallowed arts kneeling beside the thing that he had put together.

"Tell me," implored Shelley.

"It's not much yet," she said. "There's a man, a scientist."

"Like Aldini," Shelley said.

Well, yes, Mary supposed that the man in her head resembled Aldini, or at least that fervent gleam in his eyes. But in her head, he was younger, more like Shelley himself, actually. Although she didn't say this now.

"Go on," said Shelley.

"And this scientist goes on to build a thing," Mary said. "He assembles the body parts of dead men to craft an entirely new being and then brings it to life."

Shelley was nodding eagerly. "Ah!" he said. "Like you and Miss Byron did with the PAN."

Mary frowned. "Not like with Pan." She and Ada hadn't been trying to build a person. That had just happened automagically. "No, in my story the scientist wishes to create the perfect human, but everything goes terribly awry. He doesn't create a man, but a monster." She rubbed at the back of her neck, under her hair. "It's a beginning, anyway."

"It's perfect." Shelley fumbled in the back pocket of his trousers and withdrew a small leather notebook, which he opened and held out before Mary like an offering. "Put it here."

"What is this?" she asked.

"Just some scribblings. Nothing good." He thrust it toward her again. "So give it to me."

"Give what to you?"

"Your story. Imagine it here, in my notebook, the way Byron did last night."

A breeze picked up and ruffled the pages of the book. Mary stared at it, baffled. "You wish me to magic my monster idea into your book?" (To which your narrators collectively sigh wistfully. If only writing worked that way.)

"In my handwriting, if you can manage it," Shelley said. "Although I don't suppose it really matters. I'll be presenting it to Byron out loud."

"You wish to present my story as your own?"

"Well, we could say it's *our* story," Shelley said. "As we're writing partners."

"But it's not your story. It's mine."

Shelley's forehead rumpled. "Surely you don't intend to enter the contest yourself?"

"Why not?"

"It wouldn't be fair."

"Why wouldn't it?"

"Because you're fae. You have an unfair advantage."

"I don't know how he did that," said Mary. "It doesn't work that way for me. *I* will have to craft a story in the same manner as anyone else. Word by word, as you would. I cannot simply will a novel into existence." (Again, we really, really wish it could happen this way.)

"You could write your story and magic it into my notebook." His expression brightened. "Or you could transpose your idea straight into my mind, and then I could write it."

Mary's mouth opened and then closed again. "Perhaps I could. But why would I?"

"So I could win the contest, naturally," he answered.

"But *I* would like to win the contest," Mary said. "Myself."

Shelley closed the book and shoved it into his pocket, then grasped her hand. "If I win the contest, I shall ask Byron to give me an epic poem. A long one, the kind he writes, exactly as he would write it. Then I could publish it myself, and it would of course be wildly successful, and establish my career, and fortune and fame would be at my fingertips at last." He glanced at her troubled expression. "And then—and then, my love!—I could pull the strings to open the door for your writing career as well. Of course I would."

"But if I won the contest, could I not ask Lord Byron to open the door for my writing career himself?" Mary asked, even though that it not what she intended to do with her Byron wish, should she win. "Or perhaps when I write this story it will be good enough to set my career in motion, all on its own."

Shelley was shaking his head emphatically. "No. That would not do. Not at all."

Mary pulled her hand from his. "And why would it not do?"

"Because Byron will pick a man to win the contest. He said 'he,' did he not, when he described the winner?"

"But then it would not truly be a contest," Mary countered. As Shelley and Pan would be the only competitors, and Mary had a feeling that Byron would pick Shelley over Pan no matter what Pan managed to produce for the contest.

Shelley shrugged. "I don't make the rules."

But it sounded like Shelley was making the rules. He was making them up. On the spot. "But you do not even have an idea," she said.

"I shall have one," he said. "When you give it to me. We're partners, are we not? We work for our mutual benefit. So go on—" He lowered his head as if he were expecting to be struck with something tangible. "Hit me with your best shot. Fire away."

She was tempted to hit him, all right. But with an oar.

"So let me get this straight," she said, trying not to grind her teeth together. "You wish me to give you my story idea, so that you might claim it as your own, so that you might ask Byron to give you another idea, far superior to mine, obviously, so that you will become rich and famous."

"See?" Shelley beamed. "We understand each other."

"No!"

"You don't understand?"

"I'm not going to give you my idea."

"But, my love—"

"Stop calling me that!" she cried. "I am not your love, Shelley.

I did not choose to run away with you, the first time you asked, or the second. I do not belong to you."

"But I love you," he said.

She sat back and looked at him. He was exquisitely dressed, as usual. His bright eyes were hungry, almost predatory, the way one might look at a piece of chocolate cake.

"Perhaps you love the idea of me, Shelley," she said. "But that is not me." She felt enormously foolish for not realizing this sooner. Shelley couldn't love anyone but himself. "And I do not love you, either." Love wasn't kissing and sweaty palms and racing hearts. Love was being able to trust each other. Love was sacrifice.

Shelley stared at her, stunned. "That is not possible. You cannot be seriously breaking it off with me."

"It's not you, it's me," she replied. (It was mostly him.)

He scowled and grabbed at her hand again. "At least give me some of your energy," he demanded. "You owe me that much."

She pulled back, but he did not release her hand. "My energy?"

"Your creative energy," he said. "As a fae. Byron said it was possible to transfer it. I want it. I need it!" His fingers tightened around hers painfully. "Please!"

"No!" She pushed at him, but he only tightened his grip, and she saw so clearly now that Shelley's interest in her had always been about her fae abilities. From the very first moment, he'd been seeking her power. He was a vampire, metaphorically speaking. She could almost tangibly feel the suck of his mind, trying to withdraw her magic.

"No," she said again. She would not let him.

She imagined a distraction—any distraction would do—a fish leaping from the waters of the lake, and at the thought a fish did appear, arching upward toward the boat and then landing in the middle of Shelley's perfect hair.

Shelley shrieked and dropped her hand. Mary placed that hand on the center of his chest and pushed. Out of the boat he went, for a moment causing everything to be silent, just a ripple in the water where a boy had once been.

Mary let out a breath. She was feeling about ninety percent better already. Lighter. Freer. As if Shelley had been a weight dragging her down.

Then Shelley's head appeared above the surface. He sputtered up at her. "But you need me!" he gasped, treading water. "Mark my words! You will never be a writer without me, Mary. No one will ever know the name of Mary Godwin."

"Mr. Shelley," she said coldly, staring down at him, "I no longer wish to be your writing partner. I release you from any obligations that ever existed between us."

Then she picked up the oars and rowed the boat away from him, out of his reach.

THIRTY-THREE
Ada

"What do you think they're talking about?" Jane asked.

"Given that Mary pushed Shelley into the water," Ada said, "I suspect it was an argument."

"What do you think they're arguing about?" Jane amended.

"Possibly about him being a lying, cheating rake who was never good enough for her." Ada gazed out fondly over the water, to the place where Shelley had gone under. Sadly, he resurfaced. He sputtered and started to swim to shore. "He writes the oddest poems, too. 'Ode to a Fish'? 'Ode to Kale'? They're so random. It's like he doesn't have any good ideas so he just writes about whatever is right in front of him at the time. What's next? 'Ode to a Rainstorm'?"

"Perhaps 'Ode to Getting Thrown Overboard,'" Pan said,

and then he skipped another rock across the now-rippled surface of the lake. Eight skips.

"Not bad." Jane handed him another rock. "Now see if you can pop this one into Mary's boat."

Ada leaned back against the large stone where she and Fanny were sitting, watching all the goings-on. Well, Ada was watching. Fanny was embroiled in her embroidery; a thread had gotten tangled and she was struggling, unsuccessfully, to straighten it out.

"What is all this racket?" Lord Byron's voice came from the villa where he had just emerged. Somehow, the bags under his eyes were even darker than they had been earlier, when he'd sent them all outside. He stopped next to Ada and leaned on his cane. "I'm trying to work, and all of you are out here playing in the water and shouting."

"At least we're outside," Jane said. "Imagine if Mary were shoving Shelley into the water inside the house. Wait, no, don't imagine that. You might make it real."

Lord Byron groaned and rubbed at his temples. "I can't do magic when I'm hungover. Drunk? Yes. I can do *so* much magic when I'm drunk. But right now, I can't even imagine that I don't have this headache. My existence is beyond wretched."

"If you don't like feeling like this," Pan asked, "then why do you get so drunk?"

Lord Byron shot Pan an annoyed look. "Because it's the only time I feel good. Perhaps, if you live long enough, you'll understand regret one day. Or not. Perhaps you'll be lucky enough to die first."

Ada gasped. "Father! That was mean. You should apologize."

"Why?" her father asked.

"Because it was mean," Ada repeated. "In fact, you've been cruel for our entire visit. You've ignored Mary, spoken over Jane—"

"That's right!" Jane said.

"You constantly dismiss Pan as an object, rather than a person, and you haven't even said a word to Fanny."

Everyone looked at Fanny, who was now back at work on her embroidery. The image, now that it wasn't obscured by lengths of colorful, tangled thread, showed a startlingly realistic representation of Villa Diodati, the Alps rising in the background, and the entire group standing in front of the house. Everyone was in the positions you'd expect, with Shelley's and Lord Byron's arms thrown over each other's shoulders, Jane clearly performing a dramatic death scene, Ada with numbers around her head, Pan and Mary tending to Ivan, and Fanny herself off in the corner embroidering something.

"That's quite good," Pan said. "But Ivan isn't here. I miss him."

"I know." Fanny patted Pan's arm.

Ada turned back to her father, who was rubbing the bridge of his nose. "All you do is drink wine and talk about poetry with Shelley. Even I, your own daughter, who came all this way, cannot get a moment of your time, an answer to a simple question—"

"I didn't ask you to come," Lord Byron said sharply. "And let's not pretend that you came to see *me*. You came for your PAN because you thought I might know how to save him."

"I came because I thought you might be interested in helping me when I'm in trouble, but clearly *that* was not true. And yes, I thought you might also have an idea for how to help my friend. I thought you might see how important he is to me—how much he deserves to live."

Lord Byron snorted. "None of us *deserve* to live. We are given life, whether we want it or not, and then, when the time comes, that life is taken away. There is no stopping it."

"But there is," Ada pressed. "You did it. In Greece."

"I have tried to tell you," he said. "I cannot help in this matter. I can't help any of you."

Ada looked at him, taking in the sallowness of his skin, the haunted look in his eyes. He had tried to tell them, he said. But . . . "The vampire story," she murmured. "It was autobiographical, like all your work."

Lord Byron perked up. "Have you read all my work? I'm surprised your mother would allow it."

"Oh, no." Ada shook her head quickly, trying not to think too hard about her mother. (Hopefully she was doing all right in Transylvania. . . .) "I haven't actually read any of your tales or poems. That's what someone at the bookstore said—that your work is all autobiographical." Even if it somehow didn't include his daughter.

"You saw my books in the bookstore." He smiled in the way that she was getting used to—the one that meant he was (again) attempting to change the subject. "Tell me, how many copies were left? Which bookstore was it? And you said there were people around?"

"The shelves were absolutely full," Ada said. "Now, your vampire tale."

"Oh, that old thing? That was a story, something I made up to entertain you all."

"No," Ada said, almost gently. She was angry still, but yelling at him would not be useful. "It was a confession. It's how you survived the war. Perhaps you didn't drink literal blood. No, I understand that the blood is a metaphor. But you took life—pure life—from someone, a young woman, probably, and now you are racked with guilt, which is why you can't even talk about her, which is why you change the subject every time I ask for help, which is why the girl in the vampire story last night had no name, no personality, no nothing."

"I worked hard on that story," Lord Byron protested weakly. "She had exactly as much personality as she needed. Which one of us is the famous storyteller?"

"You've been leading us on this whole time." Ada's fingers went tight around her cane. "You let me believe that you knew how to save Pan's life, but you don't. You're no help at all."

"Well now, I've provided a roof, haven't I, and—"

"I shouldn't have come here," Ada said. "I shouldn't have brought my friends here. We have enough problems without you adding to them." Aldini. Various mothers. The distressing lack of spoons. And, oh yeah, saving Pan's *life*.

Lord Byron gazed downward. "I know I'm a failure in your eyes. A failure as a father, as a person. There's only ever been one thing I'm truly good at, and that is writing, which you refuse to enjoy."

Ada narrowed her eyes. "You are the most selfish person I've ever met."

"We are all selfish, and I no more trust myself than others with a good motive." He stabbed his cane into the ground and declared, "All this sunshine is giving me a headache. I'm going inside to work. Don't bother me." He turned and marched back toward the villa.

"That's right," Ada called. "Run away again. Add that to the list of things you're good at."

"Oh dear," Mary said. She had docked her boat and walked up sometime during the fight, but Ada wasn't sure how much she'd heard. "So he really doesn't know how to help us?"

Ada shook her head.

Pan sat on the rock beside Fanny, his head in his hands. This whole thing was, in fact, life and death for him.

Jane crossed her arms over her chest. "He's really nothing like his characters, is he? Here we are, damsels in distress, and he's done nothing for us."

"Never meet your heroes," Mary commented.

"I'm sorry," Ada said to everyone. "I had hoped this would work out."

"I'm the one who suggested finding him," Mary said. "I'm as

much responsible for this as you are."

They both looked at Jane, who'd been the one to start writing Lord Byron letters, but she just dusted her hands off on her skirts and said, "Well, I suppose we won't be staying here much longer, then. Will we at least stay tonight? For the contest?"

Ada exchanged glances with Mary, who suddenly looked as hopeful as Jane. "Yes," Ada said. "We should. We'll need to talk about where to go after this, anyway. Back to Paris, perhaps? Or perhaps Rome. Barcelona? Madrid? We have so many options." She forced a cheerful smile, but it didn't feel real. Would they get *anywhere* before Pan stopped?

"I suppose, then, I should go work on my story." Jane picked up her skirts and started for the villa. "He may be the worst man in the world, but that just means he will have no compunctions about conjuring us up a few dozen spoons when I win. Or perhaps actual cash. That would probably be easier to carry than an entire box of spoons."

"The wind is tangling my thread." Without any other comment, Fanny got up and went after Jane.

And then Ada, Pan, and Mary were alone on the beach.

Pan bent to pick up another rock, inspected it for flatness, smoothness, and other ideal skipping qualities, and then let it fall back to the ground. "It'll be all right," he said. "I'm most eager to see Madrid. Or perhaps a place without quite so much rain."

"It's raining everywhere," Ada said. "There was a volcano."

Pan nodded, but he wasn't his typical enthusiastic self. In fact, he looked ashen, completely exhausted. The hollows under his eyes were darker than they had been earlier, before the fight with Lord Byron.

Mary touched his arm, her brow furrowing in concentration. "We can go wherever you'd like, Pan."

Color rose in Pan's face. His eyes brightened. Even his breaths seemed to come more evenly. But the renewed energy did not come with a smile. Instead, Pan turned to look at Mary, his eyes narrowing. "What was that?" he asked. "Mary, what did you just do?"

THIRTY-FOUR
Pan

She didn't answer right away, but Pan finally understood what was happening. He had been so tired, a wet-blanket sense of fatigue stealing over him as he'd tossed that last stone, but at Mary's touch, that weariness had left him. He felt renewed. He gasped and put his hand to his chest, feeling the zing of energy throughout his body. And then he turned back to Mary, and he saw that her face had gone pale, lavender shadows under her eyes.

"Oh, Mary," he breathed. "Why would you do such a thing? How could you possibly make the decision to further cut short your life?"

"Because I cannot bear the idea of going on without you," she admitted softly.

Pan was caught in a wave of feeling then, joy and terror and anger and tenderness all at once. "This is not acceptable." He caught her hand and pressed it to his face. "Take it back."

Her jaw tightened. She pulled her hand away. "No."

"Yes."

"No."

"Yes," he insisted. What was happening? Was he actually having an argument with Mary? And why? He was right. She was wrong. Surely she must see that.

Ada cleared her throat. "I'll leave the two of you to talk," she said, and began to pick her way carefully over the lake stones toward the house. She checked her watch. "You've got two minutes before the rain." Pan and Mary watched silently as she climbed the grassy slope and disappeared into the villa.

Pan faced Mary. "Take it back." There was a quiver in his voice as he said it, because he was afraid. If Mary took the life back, would he die? Possibly. But then Mary would live. It was most important that Mary live.

Mary shook her head. "I will not do that, Pan, and you cannot force me."

"I would not ever force you to do anything you did not wish to do," he said, confused.

She smiled. "You mustn't die, Pan. That is my wish."

"But it isn't rational," he said.

"No," she admitted. "It isn't."

"And *my* wish is for you to live a long and fruitful life," he countered. "Will you not at least consider my wishes in this?"

423

She glanced down at the water lapping at their feet. She did not answer him.

"It is enough," he said. "Truly."

She looked up. "What is?"

"What you and Ada have given me already." They'd given him such beauty in the time he'd been alive. One month, he calculated. That was all he'd had to take it in. Rainy nights on rooftops and stained glass mornings in cathedrals. The delight that sparked in Ada's eyes when she did math. The light as it spun through Mary's golden hair. The song of the thrush. The taste of chocolate. And now the smell of snow that drifted from the Alps down to the shore of Lake Geneva. "I am grateful," he murmured. "You and Ada have been my family. You've given me laughter. You've offered up your knowledge and your friendship and your comfort. Your . . . love."

"Yes," agreed Mary. "So is it any wonder that we would give most anything—Ada and I both—for you to remain alive and well and with us?"

"You are the kindest of girls," he said. "I have been so fortunate. But I do not wish to do further damage to you. So please believe me when I say, it is enough." He straightened. "I will no longer accept any of your life, Mary. You would not force that upon me, would you?"

"No," she conceded. "I would not force you."

"So we're agreed, then," he said. "If the time comes—when it comes—you must let me go."

Her eyes shone with tears. "I'll never let go, Pan. I'll never let go."

But she was being metaphorical, he thought.

She sniffled and then swayed on her feet. He caught her arm. "Come," he said. "Let's get you back to the house. You should take some rest."

"All right," she said.

"I felt a raindrop." Pan held out his hand and turned his face up. "Ada is a minute behind schedule. We shall have to rework the numbers." He took Mary's hand and began to lead her to the villa, relishing the soft, cool press of her fingers against his. "I've read all about the hydrologic cycle in an attempt to become less concerned about the rain. It's wonderful how efficient the earth is. The sun heating the ocean's water until it evaporates. Then the water vapor cooling into droplets, which become clouds. And then, when the clouds grow heavy enough . . ." A drop pinged into his hand. "Rain. Which runs back into the ocean and begins again. A perfect circle that makes all life possible."

"Yes, I suppose that is wonderful," Mary murmured.

They reached the house just in time—it was starting to pour. The sky overhead quickly darkened, blotting out the sun, and a cold wind picked up. They ran the last few steps into the house.

But the house was dark, too. Empty. Which Pan found odd, considering all the people who'd retreated into the house in the past hour. There was no one in the kitchens, when usually there were at least servants present. There was no one in the front hall, not even a lit candle to illuminate the room. No one in the billiard room or the conservatory or the library. No one in any of the bedrooms. Not even Byron in his study.

"Where is everyone?" Mary asked, her forehead rumpling.

"I do not know." Pan was concerned. Where was Ada? He had a bad feeling now, like when he'd heard the big *THUMP* from downstairs when Aldini had kidnapped Ada. He squeezed Mary's hand. He did not wish to alarm her. "I am sure we will find them," he said.

There was a faint noise, a scraping, from the other side of the house. Mary and Pan both stilled to listen, tilting their heads. More scraping. A muffled male voice.

"They're in the parlor." Mary sounded relieved. "Byron has probably gathered everyone in the parlor for some form of entertainment."

Pan winced. He had not been a fan of the ghost stories last night. "Do you suppose Lord Byron wishes to hold the contest now?"

Mary's nostrils flared slightly. "I hope not. He said after dinner. My story is not ready yet."

"I have been trying to think of a story, too," Pan said. "But I do not believe that I was meant to be a writer. I drew an illustration of a most frightening house earlier—at least I think it's frightening. I was hoping that would suffice."

"I'm sure it will," Mary said.

They stepped toward the parlor but took their time about it, in no particular hurry to be among the other guests. "And you have a story?" he asked her.

Her cheeks colored. "The beginnings of one. It's about a

monster, and . . . well, it's just the start of an idea."

"I'm sure it will be wonderful," he said. "Or rather, terrifying, if that is your goal. I'm afraid I don't fully understand why people should want to be frightened on purpose, but I accept that is something people do. I will try to enjoy it," he promised. "Because it's your creation."

She nodded and seemed about to say something else, but then they'd reached the door of the parlor. Pan pushed it open. Then he frowned. He didn't understand what he was seeing.

The chairs that had been in the parlor last night had been pushed up against the walls, and each chair now held a person, but there was something unusual about the way they were all sitting. They were tied up, he realized. Byron was slumped in a chair, his arms bound behind him, his eyelids closed as if he were asleep. Beside him, Shelley was also clearly being held against his will, still wet from his tumble into the lake, his hair a mess (oh dear, how he must hate that, Pan thought, but he couldn't bring himself to be truly sorry about it) and his eyes alight with fury. Beside Shelley was Jane/Claire, who was not only tied up, but had a strip of cloth drawn across her face, stopping her mouth.

"Mmmm mmmm!" she exclaimed.

Pan and Mary stepped farther into the room. "What's happened?" exclaimed Mary. "What's going on?"

"Isn't it obvious?" came a voice, and a long, horrible shiver made its way down Pan's spine, because he recognized this voice.

The door closed firmly behind them. Pan and Mary swung

around. There, standing with a wicked smile, was Mr. Aldini. He had one long arm wrapped about Ada's shoulders, and the other hand held a small pistol.

"It's a party," Aldini said. "And you are my welcome guests."

This did not seem like a party Pan would ever wish to attend.

"Please sit down," Aldini said sharply.

Pan and Mary didn't move—they still felt frozen in shock—until Aldini shoved the pistol into Ada's side and she whimpered.

"I've encountered you before, haven't I, lad?" Aldini stared intently at Pan. "Who are you?"

"His name is Peter," Mary interjected quickly. "We were in attendance at your show in London not long ago. What is this all about?"

Aldini nodded thoughtfully. "Peter," he said. His eyes flitted to Mary. "And you are?"

"Mary," she answered.

"Ah, the mysterious Mary!" Aldini exclaimed triumphantly. "At last, all the pieces are coming together. Sit down, you two. Let's get this party started."

Mary→
THIRTY-FIVE

Aldini tied up Ada, Mary, and Pan with the quick efficiency of some-one who regularly tied people up. He gagged all of them, except for Lord Byron, who appeared to be unconscious or drugged. Then Aldini threw open the adjacent doors to the dining room and dragged his captive audience (with the air of someone who also regularly dragged heavy bodies from here to there) around to face the long dining room table, upon which was an ominous figure cloaked in a sheet. Mary was getting rather tired of objects covered by sheets. She could only imagine what this was. The image from her story (a man assembled from different body parts) loomed up in her mind, but she forced herself to think of something else. Any-thing else.

This wasn't a time for stories.

"Mmmmm mmmmm!" said Jane. (She wanted to know: "What's under the sheet?")

An excellent question.

Aldini didn't answer her, nor did he remove the sheet. Instead, he positioned Ada's chair facing them near the sideboard, upon which he had set up the Dynamo Disc. He placed the cage hat on her head and strapped it on.

"This again?" she groaned. "I told you—"

"When I interviewed you before, I do not believe that you were properly motivated," he said. "But now I have assembled all your friends and family to support you." He chuckled. "Now you will have to do as I ask."

"Mmmph mmm mmmph!" declared Jane. (What she was saying this time was: "Actually, you haven't captured all of us. Where is Fanny? She was right behind me as I was coming in, but now—poof! She's disappeared." It was a good thing, then, that she wasn't saying this in any way Aldini could understand.)

Mary, however, could understand. She glared at Jane. "Mmmm mmm!" she said. ("Be quiet, Jane! For once in your life, hold your tongue!")

"Mmmm!" retorted Jane. ("I have asked you repeatedly to call me Claire!")

"Silence, silly females!" said Aldini. Then he approached the table, and with as much flair as he would have in front of his normal audience, whipped off the sheet from the shrouded object.

Mary sucked in a shocked breath. There, lying on the table,

was a man-size metal automaton.

Ada's eyes widened. "Pan?" she whispered.

"Have you missed him?" Aldini asked, patting the metal chest, which emitted a hollow sound. "You abandoned him so abruptly that night of the show. It was quite cruel of you, really. And sad that you left him in this dilapidated state, devoid of life and therefore utterly useless. I might have let you go if you'd given him to me as he was before."

"Mmmmm mmmm mmmm mmm!" said Jane (okay, fine, CLAIRE), which meant: "Holy crap, is that your robot? But I thought you made the robot into a boy." Then she glanced over at Pan, confused.

Pan looked pretty confused himself. His silver eyes were wide. Poor Pan looked like he was on the brink of some kind of existential crisis, in fact.

But Mary knew the truth: the metal man on the table wasn't Pan. It was the corpse from Aldini's laboratory. When Mary had made Pan look like a real boy, she had transformed the human likeness of the dead man into Pan, which would mean that the corpse would also transform, to resemble the automaton. Indeed, the more closely that Mary looked at the figure on the table, the easier it was to tell the difference. Pan had been built as a complex, able-bodied machine. This automaton was much cruder in its construction (Mary didn't know that much about robots, after all). In fact, this machine was more of a metal sculpture than a working automaton.

Did Aldini truly believe that this was the same Pan he'd made perform on the stage?

Apparently he did, because he crossed to the window and pulled it open. It was still raining heavily outside. Aldini reached out and withdrew a length of wire attached to one of those metal rods he used in his show.

"While you were all out playing at the lake, I took the opportunity to set up a re-creation of your experiment," he explained. "I have put a lightning rod on the roof, and attached it to this length of wire, which I will now affix to our friend here." He connected the wire to the chest of the corpse/automaton. Then he sighed. "I have tried this myself. One of the wonderful things about this terrible weather is that there is always a thunderstorm handy. It's almost embarrassing how many times I've electrified this fellow, trying to make him live. But this time it will be successful. This time it will be you who does it."

Lightning flashed on the other side of the lake. And then, several moments later, *BOOM*.

"Ah," said Aldini cheerfully. "Right on time. The storm should soon be directly over us, and you will be a good girl and bring your machine back to life."

"I could not," Ada said stiffly. "Even if I wanted to. I told you—" Her eyes met Mary's and then skittered away, afraid to reveal any further connection between them. "It was a fluke. An accident. I'm not even sure how I did it."

Aldini tsked his tongue. "You don't expect me to believe that.

After all, you were also responsible for the frog at Mr. Babbage's party, were you not?" He picked another thing up from the table: a board, upon which was fastened (what else?) a dead frog.

"Mmmmm mmmmm mmmm!" exclaimed Claire from behind her gag. Which translated to: "Would you like me to ascertain whether this frog is truly dead as well?"

"Perhaps you would rather start small," Aldini said, gesturing grandly to the frog.

Ada pressed her eyes closed. "I cannot help you, Mr. Aldini."

"Oh dear," Aldini said with pretend mournfulness. "Will I have to zap you?"

Mary was thinking very hard about what she could do to get them out of this situation. It would be easy enough to acquiesce to Aldini's demand—to give the frog life—but what good would that serve? The only advantage they seemed to have right now was that Aldini didn't know anything about the fae. He still thought Ada had accomplished her miracles with the frog and Pan using science. So while Mary could do a few things to help them—she could turn Aldini's pistol into a noodle or make the pretty floral pattern on the dining room rug become actual flowers and vines that would twine themselves around Aldini's feet—if she did something like that, he would *know* that magic was happening.

And then he would never, ever let them go.

And so Mary, even though it went against every instinct, did nothing. Well, not entirely nothing. She imagined that the ropes binding her wrists behind her back, quite of their own volition, had come undone. The ropes dropped to the floor. And she imagined that Lord Byron would wake up, because surely he would want to put a stop to someone torturing his daughter, no matter how selfish he was, and surely Byron was a more formidable fae to tangle with Aldini than Mary herself was. But Byron stayed stubbornly slumped over in his chair.

"It's simple, Miss Byron," Aldini said. "Make the frog live. This is the last time I will ask nicely."

"Go ahead," murmured Ada wearily. "Zap me. You still won't get what you desire. And if you fry my brain, you certainly won't get anything more from me."

Aldini tapped a finger to his chin. "Perhaps that is true. Perhaps I shall have to zap someone else. Someone whose well-being you value above your own." He walked along the line of chairs holding his captives. "Not you, obviously," he said, passing Claire by.

"Mmmm mmm," said Claire hotly. "Mmm mm mmmmm mm mm mmmmm mmmmmmmm!" (We won't translate that first sentence. But the last one was: "I am going to be a great actress!")

Aldini's cold gaze skimmed quickly over Pan. "I don't even know who you are. And you." He paused at Shelley. "You're a silly man, aren't you? Why are you all wet?"

Shelley glared at Mary, but thankfully he was also gagged.

Then Aldini stopped at Mary. "You're Mary, the lady's maid, correct? You were there during the experiments?"

Mary felt it best to play along. "Yes, sir."

"I think I'd like to leave your brain intact, for now," he said. Then he turned to where Lord Byron was still slumped. "But, ah— Miss Byron, you will surely be concerned about your dear father. Yes." He returned to Ada's side, removed the cage hat, pulled Byron's chair up to rest beside his daughter, and placed the hat over Byron's dark curls.

"Now," he said cheerfully to Ada. "The frog, please."

Ada said nothing. She did look stricken—even if things had not been going well between Byron and Ada, she wouldn't want him to suffer on her behalf, Mary knew. But what could she do?

There was a flash outside the window again. Then, *BOOM*.

"Closer," remarked Aldini. He sighed. "Why must you be so stubborn? Very well, you force my hand." He crossed to the Dynamo Disc and placed his hand upon the crank. "I apologize, my lord, for what I am about to do to you."

Then they were all, well, shocked, when Lord Byron's eyes popped open, even before Aldini turned the crank. "*It's Mary who has the power!*" Ada's father cried. He tried to gesture in Mary's direction with his head. "Not my dear Ada—she's a bright, enterprising girl, but she seems to be a bit of a late bloomer when it comes to the fae abilities. But Mary—she's a natural. It was Mary who brought the PAN to life. And, as I understand it, your frog."

"Father," Ada breathed in dismay.

He shrugged. "It's Mary or you, isn't it, my dear? I choose you."

But really it was himself he'd chosen. (A surprise to no one.)

"Fae?" said Aldini, his nose wrinkling.

"Father, think about what you're doing," Ada said.

Aldini promptly gagged Ada. "What is this fae?" he asked Byron.

"Oh. Bollocks," sighed Byron. "I really shouldn't have told you about that."

But then he went ahead and told Aldini all about the fae. Aldini sat back and listened patiently, but it was clear he did not believe a word Byron was saying.

"You expect me to believe in this . . . magic?" he said after Byron spilled the beans about everything. He said the word *magic* like it was some vulgar thing. "Ha! The lengths you will go, my lord, to avoid the pain you know is coming!"

He moved again toward the Dynamo Disc.

"I can prove it!" Byron shouted. "I am a fae, after all. What would you have me imagine? Wish for anything, sir, and I can make it happen."

"I wish for you to make the automaton come to life," Aldini said simply.

"Er, about that—" Byron grimaced. "Anything but that. Bringing things to life involves giving up some of your own life, and I don't have very much to spare. Ask for something else. Would you like a cup of wine?"

"I am Italian, am I not?" Aldini said.

"True. Yes. One goblet of wine, coming right up," Byron said. "Hold out your hand." He closed his eyes and concentrated as Aldini sighed, still unbelieving, and held out his hand.

Nothing happened.

Aldini scoffed. "You waste my time."

Byron frowned. "I'm still hungover. And you drugged me, didn't you, with chloroform, when I first entered the house."

"I may have," Aldini admitted.

"Well, that's why. I cannot use my magic without a clear head," Byron said.

"How convenient." Aldini stepped toward the Dynamo Disc. "Prepare yourself, sir. This might clear your head a bit."

"But there's Mary!" Byron yelped. "You could get Mary to perform fae magic. She's definitely a fae!"

Aldini sighed. "I tire of games," he said. But instead of zapping Lord Byron, he picked up the pistol again, and pointed it straight at Ada's heart. "Someone had better start making sense. Or Miss Byron here is going to die. Since apparently she is not the scientist I thought she was."

He could have been bluffing—he probably was—but Mary couldn't take that chance. Her heart had turned to ice at the thought of Aldini shooting Ada. She reached up and pulled the gag from between her lips, then called out, "It's true. Everything that Byron said was true. It was me."

"Mmmm mm," said Ada softly. ("Mary, no.")

Aldini's head swung around toward her. "You? A chambermaid?" He smirked. "Prove it."

Mary nodded miserably and turned her gaze to the poor dead frog on the board. *Just a bit*, she thought. *Just a jump or two.*

FLASH! went the sky. *BOOM!*

Aldini made a surprised sound as the frog began to move. No electricity required. Nothing touching it but Mary's focused gaze. It drew its legs up under itself. Gave a soft *ribbit.* And hopped.

Everyone seemed to let out a breath.

Aldini poked at the frog with his index finger. It hopped again. He turned astonished eyes on Mary.

"It's alive," he said.

THIRTY-SIX
Ada

It was dead. And this time, when the frog croaked, the frog croaked for good.

"What happened to it?" Mr. Aldini gave the frog a little shake. "What did you do?"

"I gave it only a moment of life," Mary said. "To prove that I could. I wasn't going to give the frog an entire year or anything. I think of myself as a good person, but I'm not *that* good."

"Mm mm mmm mm," Pan said. (Which translated to, "I think you are.")

"Mmm mm mm!" said Claire. ("I don't think you're all that great, but I suppose no one asked me, so I guess I'll keep my mouth shut. Why am I involved in this, anyway? I haven't been to the theater, brought frogs to life, or done anything that would offend anybody. This is all wildly unfair to me.")

"Quiet, all of you," Mr. Aldini said. "You're making it very difficult to think."

Well, he had asked a question. It seemed to Ada that he'd brought this upon himself.

"Here's what's going to happen," Mr. Aldini said. "Mary, you will bring the automaton to life." The pistol swung around to point at Ada. "As for you—as much as I'd like to be rid of you, you still serve a purpose. The automaton needs a bit of work. You'll do it, and you'll do it quickly. And if either of you refuse, or Mary so much as twitches an eyebrow or seems to be . . . *imagining* anything out of the ordinary, someone will get shot." Now the pistol swung around to Claire.

"Mmm!" Claire protested.

"So, Miss Byron, what do you need to fix the automaton?"

"Mmm mmm," Ada said.

"Ah, yes. You are still tied up, aren't you? How unfortunate. Well, I will remove your gag for now, but I don't want to hear any sass." Without moving the pistol away from Claire, Mr. Aldini quickly untied the gag.

"I'll need a spool of wire, bolt cutters, and a gear from your pocket watch," she said as soon as she could speak. Ada wasn't sure how much time they had before the storm was directly over them, but it certainly wasn't very long. She needed to think, and to think, she needed to tinker.

FLASH! Lightning flared across the lake. *BOOM!* The entire house shuddered.

"From my pocket watch?" Mr. Aldini scowled at Ada. "Why do you want the gear from my pocket watch? You should use your own."

"It's your automaton," Ada said.

"Hmph!" Mr. Aldini walked over to Lord Byron and took *his* pocket watch. "Here, use this one." The watch landed on the table beside the broken automaton.

A moment later, Ada was free of her restraints. She went to the automaton and, without any more urging from Mr. Aldini, began cleaning away the char from the previous times the automaton had been electrified. Then she worked the tiny cogs and rods in their joints, adjusted the gears in the shoulders, and repaired the connections in the knees. While her hands worked, so did her mind.

She needed a plan. A good plan. Mr. Aldini knew all about fae abilities now (thanks, Lord Byron, who shouldn't have told him that), so whatever they did would have to work the first time.

There would be no second chance.

"Hurry," Mr. Aldini said. "You're running out of time."

"I'm working on it," Ada said. But then the work was over. The machine was slightly more functional than it had been before, but it would never be an elegant automaton, not like Pan had been. This poor thing might move and lurch about, but it was fundamentally dysfunctional. It would be a monstrous thing, frightening in every way, if Mary were to bring it to life.

And Mary could absolutely *not* bring it to life. Ada could not allow it.

FLASH! BOOM!

The storm was drawing closer.

"Are you finished?" Mr. Aldini asked.

"Yes. If you insist on hurrying the process, I suppose I'm finished." She stepped back.

"Good." Mr. Aldini looked at Mary. "It's your turn, my dear."

"But first," Ada said, "I need to powder my nose. And so does Mary."

Mr. Aldini scowled. "At a time like this?"

"It's not something that I can help," Ada said.

"My nose is in desperate need of powdering," Mary agreed.

"Mmm mm mm!" Pan said. ("Your nose looks very nice to me.")

Ada cringed. "It isn't really about noses, Pan."

Mary nodded soberly. "It's, well, female problems."

"Oh, for the love of everything!" Mr. Aldini pointed toward the door. "Go deal with your noses. I don't want to know. You're making me quite uncomfortable."

"Mmmm mm mmmm!" Claire said. ("What a shame, the nefarious villain is feeling uncomfortable. I, too, should like to powder my nose, though, so would someone please untie me?")

No one untied Claire.

"You have three minutes." Mr. Aldini pulled out his pocket watch, then he pointed the pistol at Pan. "Do I even have to make the threat?"

"Three minutes," Ada said. Then she and Mary hurried into the bathroom and shut the door.

"I'm sorry about the frog." Mary's voice was soft. "I couldn't let him shoot you."

"I appreciate that," Ada said.

"So, do you—" Mary motioned at the commode.

"No."

"All right. That's good. I assumed you insisted that I needed to powder my nose as well for a good reason, but I was going to step out if you needed to use this."

"Oh, no. I wanted to tell you that you can't bring the corpse automaton to life."

Mary nodded. "We're in absolute agreement."

"If you do what he asks, he'll never stop making demands. There is no way that he just lets everyone go."

"I agree," Mary said. "I wanted to imagine all sorts of bad things happening to him, but I wasn't sure I could do it before he shot someone."

Ada checked her pocket watch. "I have an idea."

THIRTY-SEVEN
Pan

The girls returned from powdering their noses with five seconds to spare. Aldini had spent the entire three minutes talking about how he was so sorry to have to point the gun at Pan, that it really wasn't about Pan at all, but it was such a shame that Mary and Ada were going to save themselves and leave everyone else to die horribly.

But now they were back, and Aldini lowered his gun, almost disappointed. "Well, now that you have, I hope, solved your female problems, perhaps you are ready to solve *my* problem."

They both nodded. "Stand back, everyone," said Mary. She stepped forward and held her hands out toward the automaton on the table.

"This won't be pretty," warned Ada.

They were actually going to do it. Mary was going to bring the automaton to life as she had done with Pan. Which meant that she was going to give away more of her own life.

"I want at least a few years," Aldini said, obviously thinking about the same thing. "Not like the frog. This one has to last." He tilted his head to one side thoughtfully. "And perhaps after this I shall have Miss Byron build me a female automaton, so I have a matching set. We wouldn't want this one to be lonely, would we?"

Pan's throat was tight. He tried to speak, to say something like, "That sounds like a terrible idea," but he was still gagged.

"Mmmm mmm mmm," said Claire, which meant, "I put an order in for a robot boy first! Get in line!"

"One step at a time," Mary said, and turned and lifted her hands again.

No! She mustn't do this! Pan thought about her ashen face when she'd given him some life earlier today. What if she gave too much? What if, after expending herself in this way, *Mary* were to simply stop? The thought was unbearable. So he did the only thing he could really do in this situation.

He panicked.

"MMMM!" he cried. (Which meant, "STOP!") He jerked at the ropes that bound him. His legs kicked. His body lurched to one side, and he crashed over, chair and all, onto the floor, knocking the air from his lungs. The chair came apart, and suddenly, happily, Pan's hands were free.

Ouch. That had hurt.

"Mmmm mmmm!" he wheezed, which meant, "Help! I've fallen and I can't get up!"

Ada and Mary rushed to his side. Mary untangled the ropes

from around him. Ada pulled the strip of cloth from his mouth. "It's going to be all right, Pan," she said.

"No, it won't," he gasped. "I cannot allow this to happen."

"You're not in a position to disallow anything," said Aldini. "Now, girls, get on with it."

FLASH-BOOM! The storm was now almost directly over them.

Pan struggled to his feet. "If you must do this, use my life in place of your own."

"That isn't how it works," Mary said softly.

"Then make me metal again!" He turned toward Aldini. "Mary can turn me back into the automaton, and I will go with you, and pretend that you have brought me to life at every show. I will be your servant if you will agree to let everyone else go."

"Wait—what?" Aldini said.

Mary stared at Pan in horror. "You can't mean it."

He frowned. "I do mean it. I do not say things that I do not mean." He cast a significant look at Aldini. "I am no liar, Mary."

"I know, but . . ." She shook her head. "I couldn't possibly do that to you."

"You could," he said simply. "If you could make me this way, it stands to reason you could turn me back to the way I was."

"You are the automaton?" Comprehension dawned in Aldini's eyes. He stared at the crude metal man on the dining room table. "And this was, what, some kind of decoy?"

"Not a decoy," said Byron oh so helpfully. "Apparently Mary, in order to escape your theater, transformed the automaton into the living, breathing young man you see here, and in doing so also transformed the corpse you had, into a metal man. It's delightfully morbid when you think about it."

"I see," said Aldini. "Well, that does seem like a solution, then."

"But, Pan," Mary protested. "You're not meant to be trapped in a metal body, made to serve the whims of some showman like a circus animal. You're not . . ."

"I'm not sure that I am *meant to be* anything," he contradicted her. "My creation was an accident. You didn't intend to bring me to life. You didn't know what I would become."

Mary clasped his hand in hers. "You were the happiest of accidents. And you are my friend, Pan. You're more than that. You are—" She was suddenly sniffling. "I will not give you over to that monster. I cannot. I will not!"

"Hey," said Mr. Aldini. "I'm standing right here."

"Your friendship means a great deal to me," Pan murmured, "and I would do most anything for you. This is not such a big thing, really. Please let me do this." He met her eyes. "Let me go."

"There now, you see?" Byron beamed. "The boy is willing. I do think that would be for the best, don't you? How very chivalrous."

"Mary," Ada said slowly. "I think it really would be the best *plan*."

"You do?" Although Pan himself *did* think this was the best plan, he hadn't expected Ada to form the same opinion quite so quickly.

Mary took a deep breath. "I suppose you're right."

"What?" Pan blinked a few times.

"Mmm mmm mmm?" Claire said, meaning: "Did they just agree? Well. I did not see that coming."

"All right," Mary said.

All right? But . . . she'd said she would never let him go.

"I'll do it right now," Mary announced.

Pan swallowed. There was a shakiness to his breath, but his silver eyes met hers without fear. He drew himself up to his full height. "Yes," he said. "Right now."

She laid her hand on his chest. There was something warm in her eyes, something that made him feel that everything was going to work out for the best. "Are you ready?"

He nodded. "I'm ready. Change me back."

"I should like to give you something first, Peter Pan," she whispered.

He held out his hand.

She laughed and put her hand over his. "A kiss." Then she leaned in and kissed him.

"Mmm, mmm mmmm!" Shelley said perplexedly. Translation: "Is that a necessary part of this process?"

"Mmmm mmmm mmm!" Claire sighed. "Mary gets all the boys."

"Even I feel a little uncomfortable," admitted Ada.

But Pan heard none of this. For Pan, in this one briefest of instances, it was only Mary he heard, her little sigh as her breath mingled with his. Only Mary he felt and smelled and tasted. The smooth fabric of her dress as his hand touched her waist. Her scent of lake water and soap and, faintly, lily of the valley. The soft, soft press of her lips.

It was enough, he thought. He could die happy.

Mary ↗
THIRTY-EIGHT

Pan tasted sweet, like tea and lemon drops. Mary lost herself in the feel of his warm, crushed-velvet lips. It was quite a different kiss from the ones she had previously shared with Shelley, who'd been intent on seducing her. Pan's kiss was so gentle and earnest and full of tenderness. It was a kiss in which he meant to say goodbye, but what he did not know, what he could not, as he was unaware of Ada's plan, was that this was a distraction. (Mary struggled not to let *herself* get too distracted by this distraction, as she had things that she must see to in order to save them. But kissing Pan was just so *nice*.)

"I say!" Aldini interrupted loudly, jarring them both. "That's quite enough of that."

"It was a rather delicious-looking kiss," said Byron. "Gracious!" Aldini shot him a glare. He cleared his throat. "But yes. Yes. Time to get on with it."

Pan's eyes were still closed. Very slowly, as if he were reluctant to leave the moment, he opened them.

Mary smiled. "Think happy thoughts," she whispered. "Trust me."

Ada gave her a quick, self-satisfied nod.

Then Mary had to concentrate on the change. Her eyebrows furrowed. Her lips set into a determined line, and she began to imagine flesh transforming into hard metal, bones into steel rods, the inner workings of a person becoming a network of clockwork parts. Eyes that were fixed and expressionless. A face that could no longer smile or frown. A heart that no longer beat, but clicked in a series of cogs.

A human being, transforming into a metal one.

From behind them, Aldini suddenly started to scream. And everyone else gasped. (Everyone except Ada, who was busy at the moment. Because plans.)

"What have you done?" Aldini shrieked in an oddly muffled voice.

But it was quite obvious what Mary had done.

She'd turned *Aldini* into the metal man. Instead of Pan.

"What did you do?" came Aldini's muffled cry. "How dare you?"

Pan's eyes were wide. "Does this mean that he will be performing in his own shows from now on?"

"What a possibility!" Mary laughed. "Imagine that presentation: the amazing metal showman."

Aldini made a metallic shrieking noise.

"Fascinating," Byron said. "Please tell me what it feels like to be made of metal. I have a story in mind, you see, an epic poem that describes the futility of—"

"No!" Aldini raised his metal arms, not quite all the way, as Mary still wasn't exactly sure how automatons should work. Also, mystifyingly, there were bolts sticking out the sides of his neck. What use did those have? None, as far as Mary could see. Either way, Aldini was now groaning and lumbering toward her, his arms outstretched, his clothing shredded from the transformation and jerky movements.

"Fix this!" Aldini cried. "Fix me!"

And that's when it happened. Right on time, according to Ada's previous calculations.

FLASHBOOM!

Lightning struck the lightning rod atop the villa, and electricity surged through the copper wiring, which Ada had (while everyone was distracted by the kissing) disconnected from the corpse-turned-automaton. Now the wire was connected to Metal Aldini. Lightning blazed into him. He shrieked again. It was too much energy. Sparks flew from his head.

And then, without any ceremony at all, Metal Aldini fell face-first onto the floor.

For a moment, they were all quiet, just staring at the smoking pile of metal before them. Even the storm seemed to lower its voice, leaving only rain pattering on the roof and muffled rolls of thunder.

Mary, creeped out by the corpse (who was back to resembling a corpse), instantly imagined him in a nice plot of ground behind the house. While she performed that small bit of magic, Pan and Ada worked to untie and un-gag everyone else. There were a few minutes of stretching and moving one's limbs about. But the moment Claire was free, she strode up behind Byron, hefted a large book entitled *Don Juan* in both her hands, and bashed him over the head with it.

Byron crumpled to the floor, clutching his head. "Ow!" he cried. "Why would you do that?"

Claire raised the book again.

Bryon rolled out of her way. "Why? Ja— I mean, Claire, beautiful Claire, why would you do this to me?"

"Because you gave the villain all of our important secrets. You put the life of my dearest sister at risk! And, worst of all, you've been ignoring me all week. You, sir, are a villain yourself!" Claire bashed Byron over the head again. This time, he slumped the rest of the way to the floor as though unconscious, although it was clearly a ruse to avoid getting hit a third time, since afterward he cracked open an eye to see if they had bought the act.

Everyone turned to Shelley.

"Now, Mary," he began nervously.

"Don't," said Mary. "Don't even bother, Shelley. Just go."

Shelley looked as though he would protest further, but then Claire pulled out a slimmer volume—one called *Queen Mab: A Philosophical Poem, With Notes, signed by the author*—and held it up threateningly. Shelley went pale, nodded, and slipped out without another word. (And that, dear reader, is when history truly changed, and no one would ever come to know the name Mary Shelley. But we believe this is for the best. Percy Shelley was the worst. And Mary, for one, was feeling optimistic about her future without him.)

"Good work, Claire," Mary said. "I'm quite proud to call you my sister. Speaking of which, where is Fanny? She still isn't here, is she?"

"Oh, I'd quite forgotten about Fanny," said Claire. (Hadn't we all?)

Fanny was nowhere to be found.

"Well," Pan said cheerily. "I guess we've won. Is this what winning feels like?"

Mary grabbed his hand and grinned up at him. "Yes. This is what—"

A low, metallic groan came from the smoking spot on the carpet where Aldini had shorted out, and everyone turned to look as sparks danced across the metal of his body. One steel palm hit the floor and elbow gears cranked; the automaton pushed himself up, one single jerking movement at a time.

"Uh-oh," said Claire.

"Drat," said Ada. Her chin lifted. "It's probably fine. I'm sure it's just nerves, like a spider's legs still twitching after it's dead."

"Automatons don't have nerves," Mary said. She would know. She hadn't made him any.

Aldini reached his feet and spun to face the group. His eyes glowed an eerie red.

Terror coursed through Mary. He truly was a monster.

Strangely, she felt the sudden urge to write. But now was not the time.

"I may have miscalculated how much energy would be needed to incapacitate him," Ada muttered, getting out her notebook to do the math again. "The lightning should have done it. Let's see. Multiply by seven. Carry the one. Oh dear. Perhaps I've made a horrible mistake."

"It seems that you've made the giant metal monster very angry," Claire said. "So yes, I think that qualifies as a mistake."

"You will be assimilated," announced the creature formerly known as Aldini. "Resistance is futile." The red-eyed monster lunged for them.

Mary had to do something. Imagine something. Make something. But what—

She didn't have time to think, however, before thunder clapped and a torrent of rain poured from the . . . ceiling.

The ceiling?

Everyone looked up, even the creature that was once Aldini.

Dark clouds gathered and grew against the plaster above them, swelling even as they dumped rain directly into the room.

"Oh dear," Pan said. "Where's my umbrella?"

"Whaaaaat haaave youuuuu dooooone?" The evil automaton growled, trying again to cross the workroom to them. But then metal screeched and reddish-brown streaks grew down the monster's chest plate, the arms, and even the head and face. His movement became even more erratic, and finally slowed. Then stopped.

It was rust, Mary realized.

Aldini had rusted solid.

THIRTY-NINE
Ada

The indoor storm only lasted for a moment. Even the outside one was fading now. Evening sunlight poured through the window, shining on the rusted automaton of Mr. Aldini. Water clung to every one of his non-moving parts (that was all his parts now), and the long rays cut through the droplets, scattering tiny rainbows across the room.

"Mary?" Ada said softly. "Did you . . . make that storm?"

Mary shook her head. "No, but it was a good idea. I wish we'd started with that."

"I don't trust rain," Pan said. "It's too unpredictable. And"—he waved toward the rusted Mr. Aldini—"dangerous."

"Claire?"

"Obviously not. I'm not a fae." Claire crossed her arms,

pouting. "Although that was going to be my wish, if I had won the contest."

Ada looked at Byron, but he remained on the floor, pretending to be unconscious. It seemed unlikely he had done it, as Byron had never done anything to help anyone else.

POP. A door appeared atop the dining room table, where the corpse had been.

"Oh no. How did *they* find us?" Ada groaned.

Claire stared at the door, mouth agape. "Now we have to fight evil doors?"

"Worse." Pan shuddered. "Godmothers."

Perched high on the table, the door swung open and Fanny Imlay stepped through. "Hello," she said sweetly.

"Fanny!" Mary cried. "Where have you been? I mean, why are you coming through a godmother door? Are you all right?"

"I'm fine. Thank you for asking. Sorry I had to leave so abruptly before." Fanny smiled and hopped off the table as another figure appeared in the doorway.

Miss Stamp came through and looked about the room with bright, searching eyes. "It's all clear!" she called over her shoulder, then took Fanny's hand to step off the table herself. Then Miss Stamp approached Ada and held out Ada's cane—the aluminum one she'd made. "I believe this is yours, my dear."

"At last!" Ada tossed the inferior cane to the side and took her proper one. "Thank you. Did Mr. Aldini have it? Or—"

"No, he left it at your house the day you ran away."

"Then how—"

A third figure stepped into the doorway, backlit for an instant before she came into the villa, but Ada didn't have to see the details. She knew that tall posture, the silhouette of that fine gown.

"Mother," she whispered. Distantly, she felt Mary's arm link with hers.

Lady Byron entered the room and gazed around at the damp chaos, her eyes catching on Ada (standing with her friends) and Lord Byron (lying on the floor). "What a mess" was all Lady Byron said before she accepted the help off the table.

Then, because this day wasn't terrible enough, several other women (presumably godmothers) entered the room and surrounded the rusted Mr. Aldini.

"I'm half expecting my stepmother next," Mary murmured.

But gladly, Mrs. Godwin did not appear.

Ada stepped forward. "What's going on? How did you find us?"

Miss Stamp smiled. "Fanny brought us here, dear. When she realized that nefarious villain Mr. Aldini had come to the villa, she knew more help was needed. I'm afraid we didn't exactly believe her at first, but we finally came to an agreement. And just in time, it seems." Miss Stamp looked around. "Do any of you own a mop?"

"Wait," Mary said. "*Fanny* is *fae*?"

Fanny nodded.

"Is Fanny a godmother?" Ada asked.

Again, Fanny nodded. "In training."

"Doesn't anyone care that a door appeared in the middle of the table?" Claire cried.

Fanny only blinked at her.

Miss Stamp looked at Mary. "Fanny is one of my most gifted students. You should see the beautiful work she does with fae magic on pillowcases. And she has always created quite responsibly."

Mary looked at the floor. "I know, I know."

Fanny smiled. "You meant well. You always do."

"But why didn't you tell me?" Mary rushed to her sister. "All this time you never said anything."

Fanny bit her lip. "It wasn't my place."

Miss Stamp moved aside as several of her associates hefted up Mr. Aldini and carried him to the doorway, presumably to be taken to the godmothers' headquarters.

Lady Byron was gently kicking Lord Byron. "Get up, you scoundrel."

Lord Byron, perhaps sensing that all the attention had shifted to him, pretended to wake up. "Wow, this is all so interesting and surprising." He climbed to his feet and scrambled away from Lady Byron. "So many things happened while I was unconscious. Oh, my lovely wife. What a pleasure to see you, my dear. Looking as beautiful as ever."

Ada rolled her eyes.

"You rake! You dirty rotten poet! You cad!" Lady Byron shouted. "You put my daughter's life at risk!"

"She's my daughter, too," Lord Byron replied calmly. "And

no matter how much you deny it, my influence shows. She's clearly creative and imaginative—"

Lady Byron grabbed the lapels of Lord Byron's jacket and started to shake him, but Miss Stamp intervened.

"Now, Anne, we talked about this." Miss Stamp drew Lady Byron away.

"You said no lighting him on fire," Lady Byron said. "I've hardly reached that point."

"I meant no violence in general. I brought you here to see that Ada was safe. And, as you can see"—both Miss Stamp and Lady Byron looked at Ada, whose hair stood on end, whose dress was dingy and torn, who had dark circles under her eyes—"she's fine."

"Very well." Lady Byron turned back to Lord Byron. "But I want you out of Ada's life. For good this time."

"She came to me," he protested. "I wasn't going to seek her out, was I? Not knowing how you must have poisoned her against me."

Ada's chest tightened.

"George Gordon Noel Byron," Miss Stamp said, stepping in front of Lady Byron, "this is your official warning from God-mothers, Inc. You have behaved very badly. You have violated the godpeople's rule of confidentially most dreadfully. You have failed to report threats to the fae community. You have used your fae abilities to benefit yourself. And—most inexcusable of all—you have siphoned away another person's life. That is unacceptable behavior."

"But you're not going to punish me?" He smiled hopefully.

"We will detain you. We'll leave the punishment to the godfathers," Miss Stamp said darkly.

"Oh no, please," Lord Byron pleaded. "I didn't mean any harm." He glanced around the room, as though searching for backup. But Claire threw the book at him, and Mary and Pan had edged away from all the action. Fanny shook her head. He didn't even try Lady Byron, who still looked willing to give him a black eye. Finally, Lord Byron's gaze settled on Ada.

"My daughter," he said. "Won't you—"

"No." Ada made her voice firm. "I don't need you. I don't want you in my life." The knot in her chest slowly began to loosen. "I don't care who left first and who left second. The fact is, I am your daughter and yet I couldn't count on you."

"But Ada—"

"No," she said. "You've already shown me who you are."

Lord Byron sighed, looking sad for a moment. Then one of the godmothers bound his hands again behind his back and led him through the fae door.

Miss Stamp glanced around. "And what about this distasteful Mr. Shelley? Where is he? We need to have a word or two with him."

"He won't have gone far," Mary said.

"He's probably on the lakeshore composing an epic poem about how women always misunderstand him," said Ada bitterly. "The rake."

Lady Byron came over to Ada. "Darling. I'm so glad you finally see what I've been trying to show you for all these years. All poets are rakes. And your father is the worst—"

"Stop," Ada said. "I'm tired of you trying to pit me against him. I won't listen anymore."

Lady Byron's mouth dropped open. "My dear, he was a cruel man, a selfish man—"

"I *know*, Mother," Ada said. "But just because he hurt me doesn't mean you are absolved of all the ways you hurt me, too."

"I would never—"

"You have!" Ada cried. "You kept me isolated. You tried to crush all the creative parts of me, not understanding that math and science require as much imagination as poetry. You've locked me in closets. You strapped wooden boards to my back to make me stand up straighter. And now you're rushing to marry me off to Lord King."

Lady Byron's face was turning red.

"You cannot treat me that way anymore," Ada continued. "If you want me to come home, then you need to change."

Lady Byron crossed her arms. "We'll talk about it."

"I will talk," Ada said. "And you will listen. And, while we're at it, you'll give Pell a raise. She deserves it."

"I suppose I don't have much of a choice now, do I?" Lady Byron muttered.

Miss Stamp had the godmothers escort Ada's mother back through the fae door. "That was very well done, my dear," Miss

Stamp said when the door was closed. "It's always best to be straightforward, when you can be."

Ada's chest tightened. "In the spirit of straightforwardness, I feel I should tell you—"

"Yes?" Miss Stamp arched an eyebrow.

"I'm not fae." It felt good to say it out loud. At last. "I never have been. But I'm not upset about it. I'm fine. I just—I just thought you should know."

Miss Stamp looked thoughtful. "I see. I'm glad you told me." Then she glanced around the room. "I suppose there's only one more thing we need to cover. Pan? It's time to talk about what is to be done with you."

Pan was trembling as he stepped forward. Ada took his hand. "I'll protect you," she whispered.

Then Mary was on Pan's other side. She said, "We both will."

FORTY
Pan

"Let's go into the parlor," suggested Miss Stamp. "Where we can all sit down and discuss this predicament. And some tea would be nice."

Pan (still flanked by Ada and Mary) trudged along behind the godmothers—Miss Stamp and apparently Fanny and many other women he'd never seen before, who filed in through the fae door on the dining room table. They all crowded into the parlor.

Pan's only thought then was that they were going to take back the rest of the life Mary had given him. He clutched at Mary's arm. "Do you think I have a soul?" he gasped.

"Yes," she said quickly. "Yes, of course."

That was kind of her, he thought, since he knew there was no rational way for her to truly know, since he'd been told souls were invisible.

"Sit here, Mr. Pan." Miss Stamp gestured to the center of the sofa.

Pan sat. Again, Ada and Mary took places on either side of him as the godmothers crammed in around the room. Somehow, probably through fae magic, there was tea, but it held little comfort for Pan. His cup shook slightly as he lifted it to his lips.

"So," said Miss Stamp.

"So," said Ada with a defiant glint in her eye. "Let's start with the obvious: we must find a way to give Pan more life." She started to list her reasons on her fingers. "First of all, because he is very much a living being, and he is a person. I can prove it. He definitely is able to regulate his internal environment to maintain a constant state. For instance, right now he is sweating."

Pan was. He was sweating buckets.

"I haven't had a chance to look at any bit of him under a microscope," continued Ada, "but I am quite certain that he is composed of cells—organic material." She pinched Pan's arm.

"Ow!" he yelped.

"See? He has nerves. And he eats. A lot. I think I might have accidentally given him a hollow leg," Mary joked weakly. "He loves food."

"Except kale," Pan amended, in the spirit of being totally honest. "I loathe kale. Is that wrong? I can try harder to like it, if it will help."

"The point is, he has a metabolism," said Ada. "And he's been growing. He's at least an inch taller than he was a month ago, I swear."

Pan thought to mention the hairs that had been growing on his chin (and other places) but the girls had told him not to dwell on that before. It was private.

"And he shows a very clear response to stimuli—" Ada leaned toward him, her index finger and thumb extended.

Pan cringed away from her. "Don't pinch me again!"

"And, as you can see, he adapts to his situation," concluded Ada.

"And I am able to think and feel and move about and breathe," Pan said. "But I am having trouble breathing. It is probably a response to stimuli. As I am quite afraid."

"He's a real boy," Mary said. "Please."

Miss Stamp nodded. She exchanged knowing glances with Fanny. "I know. And from what Miss Imlay has told me, he is a remarkably brave and kind and selfless young man."

"Oh. Well, I try," said Pan.

Miss Stamp smiled at him. "We have decided, my dear boy, that you are indeed a person, and as such, you have as much of a right to live as any of us."

Whew. That was a relief.

"But the problem is," Miss Stamp continued, "that the life you possess is not really your own. And there's no way to measure what was given to you before. In our experience, one must carefully and deliberately give a portion of one's life. And you were not being very careful, now were you, Mary?"

Mary gazed penitently at the floor. "I've also been giving him supplementary doses of life," she confessed. "To keep him going."

"Oh dear," sighed Miss Stamp. "This really is a fine kettle of fish."

Pan lowered his head. His throat was strangely tight. His chest was flooded with a feeling similar to what he'd experienced when he lost Ivan. It was good that they'd decided not to destroy him. But he understood what Miss Stamp was saying. Which was: he didn't have much more time.

"What can be done?" asked Mary. "I'll give him more. Deliberately and carefully, like you said."

"And so will I," said Ada again. "If such a thing is possible."

"No," protested Pan. "I won't have you dying young on my account."

"I will, too!" cried Claire, dabbing at her eyes with a handkerchief. "Take a year or two! I want you to live!"

"Claire, who let you in here?" said Fanny indignantly. "This is a secret godmother meeting!"

"But that really is quite nice of you, Claire." Miss Stamp touched the back of Fanny's hand. "Let her stay, dear." She turned her attention again to Pan. "Actually, we've had a similar idea. There are thirty-two godmothers present today."

(Dang. That's a lot. The parlor was super crowded.)

"And each of us," continued Miss Stamp, "has already volunteered to give you one year of our lives."

"But . . . isn't that breaking the rules?" Ada said.

"Who cares?" Mary whispered fervently.

Pan said nothing. He was stunned. "I couldn't accept. It's

much too generous a gift," he murmured.

"Nevertheless, it is ours to give."

"All right," he said at last because he really did want to live. "But only if you're sure."

Miss Stamp gave a brisk nod and suddenly all the godmothers reached out, either to touch Pan himself or the godmother beside or in front of her, like Pan was the center of a wheel.

"On my count," said Miss Stamp.

"Wait," said Pan.

"One. Two. Three," said Miss Stamp.

Ada was very gently slapping his face. He opened his eyes. Ada and Mary were kneeling in front of him on the parlor sofa.

"What happened?" he asked blearily.

"You fainted," Mary informed him.

Oh. What an interesting experience that had been. He crossed "find out what the big deal about fainting is" off his mental to-do list.

"Can you sit up?" Ada asked.

He sat up. "I can."

"Do you feel any . . . different?" Mary touched his cheek. Her hand was cool and soft against his flushed skin.

Pan silently analyzed his various body parts. "Well, I'm hungry," he assessed. "The other thing I feel is probably private."

They didn't have time to properly respond to that little tidbit of inappropriate news, because Fanny came forward, holding out her fist, which was closed around something.

"I understand that this was taken from you," she said. "And we thought you should have it back."

Pan held out his hand. Fanny dropped something into it.

The small silver key.

"Thank you" was all Pan could think to say.

Fanny nodded. "You're welcome. Keep up the embroidery. I expect great things from you."

"Oh, I will," Pan promised.

Fanny turned to Mary. "I'll see you at home. Use the door. The godmothers will take it from there."

Mary's mouth opened and then closed again. "But what about . . . Father? And Stepmother? Surely she won't simply let me come back home when—"

"I've taken care of it," Fanny said mysteriously. "You owe me." She fixed Ada with a no-nonsense stare. "And you."

"Me?" Ada squeaked.

"No more automatons for you. We've had enough problems retrieving Pan and the horse."

Pan sat up straighter. "You found Ivan?"

"He was right where we left him," Fanny said. "But now he's back in his place at the Byron estate. Not alive, mind you. But there."

"Thank you," Pan said again. His favorite thing to learn about so far, he decided, was kindness.

"Don't mention it," said Fanny. "Really. Don't ever mention

it. Ever." She pointed at Ada and Mary both in turn. "No more bringing things to life. CREATE RESPONSIBLY. Understood?"

"Yes, Fanny."

"Good." Mary's sister's stern expression broke into a smile. Then she spun on her heel and disappeared back down the hall toward the dining room and the waiting fae door.

Mary and Ada and Pan found themselves alone.

"Well, that all resolved itself remarkably well," commented Ada. "I would have said the odds were 692 to 1 that we didn't survive this evening." (To which your narrators say: never tell us the odds.)

"I just have one question." Pan smiled up at Mary.

"Oh yes?"

"Before. When you were about to make me a metal man again."

"I was never about to make you a metal man again."

"Yes, but I didn't know that."

"True."

"So right before, when we all thought we might die, why did you kiss me?" Pan asked.

Mary glanced down, her pink lips (which were alluringly close to his, Pan noticed) curving up into a shy smile. "Well. I just . . . I . . . We'll talk about that later."

"Yes," said Ada. "Later. Please. Let's get out of here. I've had enough of Switzerland."

"Perhaps we should have gone to Transylvania," Pan remarked.

(Nope. They shouldn't have. Let's all agree that Transylvania would have been a bad idea.)

"Let's go back to London," said Ada.

"Yes," agreed Mary. "Let's."

The girls both held out their hands and helped Pan to his feet. Ada grinned at him. "You're aliiiiiiiiive!" she said.

"It's true. I am," he said. "Let's go home."

Epilogue

It was a clear and starry night. (We know. We're shocked, too.)

When footsteps sounded in the side parlor at Mr. Babbage's house, Ada turned away from the window to find Mr. Babbage himself entering the room. Through the open door, she could hear the hum of the party: people talking and dancing, music playing, and somewhere, in a far-off corner, a guy with floppy hair reciting a poem. (But it wasn't Percy Shelley. Because we'll be content if we never see that guy again.)

"Ada," Mr. Babbage said, "thank you for coming tonight."

Ada smiled faintly. "I wouldn't miss it."

Mr. Babbage nodded. "I'm still sorry for my part in that terrible Aldini business."

"I'm sure that, to you, he seemed like an intelligent, ambitious man—someone worth knowing," she said graciously. "So please do stop apologizing. I have too many things to do, too many ideas to develop. I don't have time to hold grudges. Especially against those who I consider to be my friends." She wandered over to the table where the silver dancer stood motionless, her bluebird's wings outstretched. "There is one thing I would ask of you in the future, however."

"Yes?"

She turned the key in the silver dancer's back. Music played, and the automaton curtsied and began to spin. "If you use my equations for something, please tell me. Don't hide it."

Color rose in Mr. Babbage's face. "You're right. I used your math for this dancer, and I should have told you before. I shouldn't have pretended she was fully my own. Please forgive me."

Ada's annoyance with him faded away. "You know that I am always interested in your inventions, Mr. Babbage, and that I am happy to help where I can. Why, just last night I was thinking of new applications for your Difference Engine."

"Ah." Mr. Babbage cringed. "I'm afraid there's something I need to tell you about the Difference Engine. That is, I've moved on from it. I have a new engine in mind. A better one, partially inspired by your practical automaton. I'm calling it"—he stretched his hands in the air as if the words would appear there—"the *Analytical Engine*."

Ada blinked a few times. "You—You switched projects."

He nodded.

"Without completing the first one."

He nodded again. "Don't tell the king."

A smile tugged at the corner of Ada's mouth. "Your secret is safe with me, sir."

"Thank you," he said. "You're so generous, as always, dear Ada. And brilliant. That's what I wished to speak to you about tonight. There's actually a question I need to ask you," Mr. Babbage said nervously.

Oh dear. Ada's heart began to beat like a drum. A (gulp) question? From Charles Babbage, of all people. He was the last person Ada would ever expect to . . . He was old enough to be her father. (He was actually older than her father. But his wife had died some years ago, and her mother was always speculating on what woman—an older woman, Ada had assumed—would snatch him up now.)

"Miss Byron," Mr. Babbage said, and cleared his throat.

"That's my, uh, name," she said faintly.

"Ada. Dear Ada. Will you do me the great honor of becoming my . . ." Mr. Babbage took a deep breath. "Science partner?"

That was obviously not what she had expected him to say. "Your what now?"

"I was hoping you might be willing to work with me on the Analytical Engine," he explained. "Not as my student or apprentice, but as my business partner as well. So we'd be equals, in every sense. We'd work on the Analytical Engine together. And share the credit equally. And whatever profits there are to be had from it—which, if it ends up doing what I think it might do, could be quite significant—we would split. Fifty-fifty. I know that's not a traditional role for a woman, and perhaps your mother will object, but—"

"Yes!" Ada blurted out. She beamed at Mr. Babbage. "My answer is yes. I'd be honored to be your science partner." It was certainly better than toiling away on other people's (*cough* men's) inventions in complete obscurity, translating notes and inserting her own thoughts and ideas, only for all her work to be lost for decades until someone randomly picked them up one day.

Mr. Babbage smiled. "Excellent. I'm so pleased you agreed. We're going to do amazing things together."

And Ada knew he was right. Already her mind began to churn with ideas. She could imagine the Analytical Engine and all the ways science and mathematics would shape it—improve it. And all the ways the engine might shape and improve the world.

Also, becoming Mr. Babbage's business partner meant she didn't have to get married. In fact, she would never have to worry about romance at all.

"Oh, look," Mr. Babbage said, "there's Michael Faraday. He's such an interesting young man, isn't he?"

"Um, yes." She turned to look through the door just as Mr. Faraday looked, too. When their eyes met, he gave a little wave. And she waved back.

Suddenly, all she could think about was electromagnetism.

At that very (rather electrifying) moment, Mary was in the

next room over, teaching Pan to waltz, which, like everything else, he picked up on with exceptional quickness and enthusiasm. He clasped her to him carefully as he swept her across the ballroom floor.

"I do have one regret about our adventure together," he said after a time.

She gazed up at him, perplexed. "Regret?"

"You never got to tell your story." He twirled her. "In Lord Byron's frightening story competition."

"Oh," she said. "That. No, I suppose I didn't. But I don't believe Byron would have chosen me to be the winner, in any case."

"Still, I should have liked to have heard it. Perhaps you will tell it to me one day?" He perceived the hesitation on her face and nodded quickly. "I see. It is private. I won't pry, then."

She laughed. "Not private from you, Pan. I do not wish to keep anything private from you." Then she blushed at how her words might be interpreted.

But Pan only smiled. "I am glad."

"So, regarding the story," she said softly. "I have decided to write it into a novel. When I have finished a draft of it, I will gladly let you be the first to read it."

"And is it still about a monster?" he asked.

"It's about a scientist who becomes a monster in his endeavor to gain the power over life and death."

"Hmm," Pan said. "So it is not entirely fictional."

"Not entirely. The story is also about his creation, a kind and gentle soul who only wishes for love and connection, but, as the scientist rejects him, becomes rather monstrous himself. That part is fictional."

"I should hope so. It sounds terrible," Pan said with a shiver. "And wonderful. And spine-tingling."

"I hope it will be." She had been writing it rather obsessively, day and night. "For the first time in my life, I'm not writing with the visage of my famous parents hovering over me. I am writing for myself. And I find that suddenly I have so much to say. Writing has become part of who *I* am."

He drew away from her and glanced up and down her body, again causing her to blush. "Which part?"

She gave another laugh. "You're always so very literal."

"I apologize. I'm afraid figurative language often goes right over my head," he said teasingly.

"I find it charming," she said. "I find everything about you charming, Pan. Literally and figuratively."

His silver eyes danced with amusement. "I am glad. I find everything about you . . ." His brow rumpled. "There doesn't seem to be an adequate word."

She squeezed his shoulder. "I know exactly what you mean." Then she cast her thoughts upward, imagining the ceiling as a reflection of the sky overhead, a deep velvet blue scattered with stars, the moon beaming down on them, making Mary's pale gray dress appear silver and sparkly in its light, and Pan's hair gleam as brightly as real copper. From around the room, there were exclamations of delight, but no one knew who was creating this wonderful illusion. (Except, perhaps, for Ada, who came to the doorway of the ballroom and grinned at the sight of Mary and Pan together. And Claire, who giggled and fanned her eyelashes at a nearby poet. And Fanny, who suddenly threw her head back and heaved a frustrated sigh.)

But being fae was part of who Mary was, too.

Pan looked again at Mary. "You are a wonder."

"We both are," she said. "What do you want to be, Pan, now that you have your entire life before you?"

"I already am what I want to be," he answered simply. "But I've been meaning to tell you that I was recently accepted into the Royal Academy. Mr. Babbage put in a good word for me there. I'm going to study architecture. I want to build big, beautiful buttresses someday."

"That's perfect for you," Mary said, and it was.

"I want to do good things in the world."

"A noble aspiration," she said, and if they weren't standing among so many people, she would have kissed him.

He smiled. He could tell. "Anything seems possible to me now. What do you think will happen next?"

Under the lights, her hazel eyes twinkled. "I can only imagine," she said.

Acknowledgments

As usual, we have a lot of people to thank for imagining this book into something real:

First off, our magic-making team at HarperTeen, starting with our real-life fae god-editors, Erica Sussman and Stephanie Stein. Our amazing cover designer, Julia Feingold. And all the behind-the-scenes people: Alexandra Rakaczki, Louisa Currigan, Sabrina Abballe, Ebony LaDelle, Cindy Hamilton, Jennifer Corcoran, and Anna Bernard.

Secondly: Lauren MacLeod, Katherine Fausset, and Jennifer Laughran, our agents, who absolutely earned their fifteen percent. Also Holly Frederick, our film agent.

To our families: Jeff, Sarah, and Jill; Dan, Will, Madeleine, Rob, Allan, Carol, and Jack; and Carter, Beckham, Sam, Joan, and Michael.

And finally: thank you to the librarians and booksellers who champion our funny little (or not so little) books, and to our readers. We can't imagine doing this without you.

Create responsibly.